BLOOD, WINGS AND WHISKEY

ON THE TRAIL OF A KILLER

A Detective John Morgan Novel
Inspired by TRUE Events

ANDREW JAY GILLESPIE

tellwell

Tellwell Talent
www.tellwell.ca

ISBN
978-1-77302-295-6 (Paperback)
978-1-77302-296-3 (eBook)

FOREWORD

ANDREW JAY SAYS NOT ALL COPS ARE ASSHOLES

Why are cops like they are? Why do some seem to have a stick up their sphincter? Why are some of them just assholes? These questions may be hard to explain. In this age of constant connectivity and social media everyone is a critic of the police. The miniscule percentage of my brethren that have had the misfortune of appearing on the internet in a one-sided negative light regrettably only give the public a tiny snapshot into one particular incident. While some can appreciate the limitations, a large number will grab the nearest giant paint brush and proceed to decorate every cop with a giant pink, puckered asshole where their face should be. One cannot understand, not unless one can walk a mile in their shoes. The answers to the former questions are not on a physical level, but more on a mental, emotional, or psychological level. Sometimes they are not the 'rock', 'the impenetrable fortresses' that they may portray on the exterior. Sometimes their emotional survival on the job is overlooked in lieu of their physical survival. A high rate of alcoholism, depression, divorce, and various levels of post-traumatic stress disorder run rampant in the policing community. It can be hidden behind a façade of toughness, pushed away like a side of lima beans. Is that something the general public would ever stop and think about if Johnny Law acted like Johnny Dick? Doubtful. All they would see is an asshole cop. Police train, train, and train some more for that one traffic stop that goes bad and turns into a fight for their life. They may stop five thousand vehicles, write five thousand traffic tickets – thus perhaps pissing off five thousand people – but on vehicle stop five thousand and one, the shit hits the fan and the fists are flying or worse, the bullets are flying. This is what the hours and hours of training are for, to gain tools to survive the physical attack, lifesaving, for them, and maybe even for someone else. The main goal is to have the police officer go home after their shift to solidify yet another day of physical survival. As a result, police can spend the majority of their career in a constant state of hypervigilance.

Hypervigilance is an elevated state of awareness that is the body's natural reaction to be constantly on the lookout for danger, for potential threats, for death. They go home unable to come down from this state and things begin to happen, things begin to get weird. The metaphoric stick goes up their butt. Then they go back to work and the circle begins again. Same shit, different day. The emotional survival that is overlooked comes from the day-to-day dealings like the domestics, people's inane bullshit and the inability to shake the hypervigilance. Cops can become cynical assholes that view the world differently, view people's behavior differently and use dark humor to cope. Their brains get totally rewired as they drive down the long road that is their career. They go from idealistic rookie to sarcastic veteran. Their health suffers and a once fit police officer becomes the slovenly, fat sloppy one that can barely get out of their cruiser due to a sedentary lifestyle of too much beer and chicken wings. If one could do a survey of retiring police officers asking them if they would do it all over again, to choose their job again, the answer would be a mixed bag of yes and no at best. Their goal should not be to survive to retirement, but live a fulfilled life; unfortunately, many do not. They fall into the abovementioned pit of depression, alcoholism, and sometimes suicide.

Hopefully this helps, maybe even a little, to explain differing attitudes that police have as compared to a regular citizen. Aren't they supposed to be able bury everything inside, swallow it like a bitter pill and stay the course? Not always. Whoa ... stop ... cease ... freeze police ... this makes it sound like they're the victim here.

Victims can come in many forms. One could bet some good money that most people have been a victim of a crime and it would be a pretty safe bet. Being a victim of crime can take on many forms and to varying degrees. For example, a person can be the victim of a break and enter. They come home from work or a trip and find that the front door has been kicked in, barely dangling on its hinges, or maybe a window has been slid open, one they were always meaning to secure, but never did get around to it. After the original panic of '*are they still in the house*' wears off they survey their belongings. They notice a bare rectangle in the dust on the entertainment center where the DVD player once was, which may not have been amply valuable, but was the only one they had. They notice that mason jar of change on the fridge, the vacation fund that has been kept for a year, unceremoniously swiped. That stack of compact discs of various musical genres, all gone. Then the person notices the thieves have been in the bedroom. The perpetrators have rifled through their most personal of items; drawers have been opened, undergarments, bras or frilly lingerie now strewn about. Scanning the room in earnest their eyes zero in on the bureau. The jewelry box is open and various bracelets, necklaces and trinkets stolen, but also of little value. The DVD player, the change, the cheap jewelry, all replaceable, except for one thing.

"Please," they would say silently and rush towards the bureau. "Please, no."

The goosebumps on the skin are now protruding, the pulse quickening, and with a peek inside the jewelry box their heart sinks to its lowest point in their life. It is gone. Dear old grandmother's wedding ring, the only inheritance she had given when she passed on. Its intricate gold and silver design pattern embedded with an immaculate gem stone was one of a kind and can never be duplicated or replaced. This or any item of priceless sentimental value so shamelessly stolen makes anyone feel violated, disgusted, and sick. This person has just become a victim of a break and enter by some uncaring individual quite possibly feeding a drug habit, merely a stereotypical criminal looking for quick cash to buy the next needle to stick in their veins.

There are those out there who have been victims of violent personal crimes, like assault or robbery or even rape. Think of a woman being held down by a gross, fat, stinking man with his purple and red-blistered penis and being violated with his disgusting tool against her will. These types of crime affect us on a wholly different level. Having been a victim of a violent or sexual crime can affect a person for the rest of their life; thoughts of suicide, to jump from a bridge, to slash their own wrists, are common reactions to such a crime. And even further, a person can come face to face with Death. He wields his sharpened scythe and grins with his chattering skeleton teeth, not caring in the least that a person is a helpless victim; they're all the same to Death.

"*Murder,*" he whispers in their ear, his deathly robes blowing in the soft breeze. This is the ultimate madness one person can inflict upon another.

Now consider the family of a murdered person. They lost someone they loved and nothing will bring them back. They gather at the gravesite, all dressed in black suits and somber dresses, blaming God for taking their loved one in such a violent way. They too are affected the rest of their lives and they certainly too, are victims. Feeling hate toward the criminal is natural. Feeling hate toward the police is natural.

When anyone feels they have been a victim of crime, in whatever form it may manifest itself, it is alright to seek help from the police. They really are there to help. Sometimes they can go above and beyond their call of duty, like to help a grieving family by providing extra support in their most desperate hour as not all cops are assholes, few are. But conversely, there can be the uncaring cop who robotically finishes the investigation and is never heard from again. It is alright to ask for help, but it is unfair to assume they can wave a magic wand and all troubles will be gone. They, like everyone on earth, are human, and humans are full of faults. But not Death, he is always the same; he is always waiting and when the time comes, he is there for us all.

BLOOD, WINGS AND WHISKEY
ON THE TRAIL OF A KILLER

PROLOGUE

EVIL INCARNATE

He was ten years old. His younger sister was only eight. These two darling children didn't have a regular childhood that most children have, not ever the glimmer of a chance. Their father, a man in his early thirties with his receding hair line in typical male pattern baldness fashion, was an alcoholic and a monster. It could have been a result of his own deplorable upbringing. The peripatetic childhood he endured at the hands of his own parents, products of a hippie generation that just shot up drugs and did nothing to nurture - or perhaps he was just born evil. Whatever the case, the unprecedented horror the children and their mother bore daily was akin to the profound wretchedness of hell.

Competent recollection of those tear-filled years of constant beatings and thrashings had faded with incontestable permanence. Their little screams that reverberated off the chalky stone walls of the dank basement were indiscernible, save for their mother sitting at the kitchen table with her eyes and ears partially muffled in her encircling arms. The savagery at the hands of their callous patriarch often left the young boy unable to move, let alone function like a normal child.

Some things he can remember are happy memories that every child needs, such as playing board games with his sister. They would sit for hours, rolling dice, moving their figures about the cheap cardboard not worrying about the trivialities of preprinted rules. Any trace of importance a rule book conveyed was to shoo away the occasional rat that came to investigate the child-like fun. The two siblings loved each other and were quite used to playing games in the grim solitude of the basement. Their unshaven, perverted fiend of a father only allowed them to play in the basement, because he had hidden the fact from the entire world, however implausible that may seem, that these two angels even existed. The limited education they possessed, came from their battered mother.

Adorning one of the darkest corners of the basement was an older oil furnace from the nineteen fifties or sixties. The children hated that furnace, they called it the devil. The pipes that extruded from its fiberglass and metal frame resembled the flailing tentacles of some kind of monster from the deepest ocean. The iron grate that opened up on the front would bring to mind an evil mouth and the spaces in the grate its evil teeth salivating for child flesh. This mouth would fill with flames when the furnace fired up, when the devil awoke. Two upper vents were the eyes. Those wicked eyes that saw into their souls were derived from the most vilified fiend of a child's nightmare. When the feeble overhead bulbs were dimmed the flickering of the flames cast sinister shadows that danced around like tiny spectral demons, dancing for their master's amusement.

Then came that night. The night the children could hear the thunder cracking with such force the booming penetrated through the thick block walls of the basement. The demons danced on the walls, laughing, laughing hysterically as the boy clutched his younger sister tightly in his arms. The door to the basement flung open and the children peaked through their tightly closed eyelids and saw their father standing at the threshold, his silhouette outlined by the kitchen light and in his right hand they saw him dragging the belt. The boy had seen this belt before, and he had felt this belt before. His father had fashioned this belt himself out of a thirty-six-inch leather strap. He had bored numerous holes all along the length of the belt and attached razor sharp hooks that he had machined himself and punctured them through the holes so that they dangled freely. The unencumbered hooks could twist and turn three hundred sixty degrees, slashing, gouging and utterly ripping apart anything it sunk into. Each thump of his boots on the stair boards sent shivers up the spines of the children as they trembled in each other's arms. The hooks that protruded from this belt glinted off the luminosity of that damned furnace. It snapped like a bullwhip possessed, piercing the air as his boots clomped his descent. The hooks jingled against each other like the bells on Santa's sleigh as it soared through the crisp air on a cold Christmas night. Sleigh bells they were not, and the cloaked driver of this sleigh gleefully cracked the reins, wielded his scythe, whilst flying behind eight skeletal reindeer. His purpose was not to bring toys to the little boy and girl in the filthy basement, but bring them death.

"Come here baby, time to give daddy some honey."

The young girl did not move but remained huddled tightly with her older brother. Through the flickering light of the furnace fire, almost under the guidance of the immoral devil, the boy could see his father grab his sister by her tiny ankle, tearing her from his embrace and dragging her towards the flaring mouth of the furnace. Their eyes were affixed upon each other, frozen in a moment of mutual mortification. His one handed grip was steadfast on her ankle and the other hand released the hooked belt which fell to the floor with a clink. He turned to the boy, smiled malevolently, and strangely, the furnace appeared to smile right along with the deranged man. A surge of flame erupted partially blinding the boy with the sudden flash. The dancing shadows whipped into a frenzy, seemingly teasing, snickering... beckoning.

The boy removed his slight hands from his surprised eyes, and they were sodden with a crimson red that flowed from deep gashes in his palms. Suddenly, shockingly, he could see body parts strewn about the floor. Two torsos, one large, one small, lay with disembodied arms and legs. Blood was spattered about the basement walls and exuded with voluminous elongated drips downward. Was this a delusion? Was this a dream laced of chaos and imperceptibility? The implacable truth of the carnage before him could not be comprehended due to the imminent failure of his juvenile brain. His father was walking towards him braying with unhinged laughter. The boy's mind went blank, a piece of clean white paper, or fresh undisturbed snow; the next thing he recalled was walking barefoot and alone down the cracked sidewalk of a dimly lit street of a strange rural town. The boy wearily limped his way along the pavement stepping on the occasional pebble or snippet of broken glass until his little feet bled. The tiny bloody footprints left behind finally alerted one of the town folk who found the boy huddled under the warmth of a store front light. His own name was now one of his only few memories as he was whisked away by ambulance to the hospital and eventually he entered foster care.

CHAPTER ONE

DOMESTIC JUSTICE

There was a squashed fly on the wall.

It had been there for several hot and hazy months, glued to the wood by the dried remnants of its own bodily fluids. Three of its thin legs were broken, reaching skyward from the streak of black that used to be its thorax. Insects are curious little creatures, essential for our decaying process. They feed on our corpses, they return us to the earth and make the circle of life complete. Their corpses, however, there's no one to naturally remove their husk and break it into nothingness. They don't just fade away; they must be cleaned, but it had been overlooked by the lazy janitor who could have taken care of the job with a simple disinfectant wipe.

The temperature was a sweltering eighty degrees Fahrenheit in the stuffy courtroom. Beads of sweat dripped down the furrowed brow of convicted offender Jake Gurracci as he sat hunched in the prisoner's box wearing the typical orange jumpsuit with a black stenciled 'Moravian County Jail' plastered across the back. His large hairy hands were chained to his belt. His feet, covered in blue prison slippers, were shackled together. The cold steal of the handcuffs that were tight around his wrists made him unable to wipe the perspiration that dripped into his eyes. He would flip his head to the side every few seconds to futilely attempt to clear the sweat, but only managed to send scattering salty droplets towards the corpse of the fly. He stared blankly at the dead fly, oblivious as the rest of the courtroom choked on the noxious cloud that was his overpowering body odor. Jake Gurracci had long since been desensitized to his own inhuman stench, and therefore felt no need to accept the daily prison showers that had been available to him. The odor had a life of its own and would make most turn and flee, or at least stand upwind for slight nasal relief. He was up for early release having served two years of a five-year sentence from a brutal assault that almost killed his wife. This was his first crack at a parole hearing and the skeptical board sat in a line conferring with each other while seasoned police detective John Morgan looked on from the front pew.

Good behavior my ass, Detective John Morgan thought, his deep frown lines accentuating his feeling of disgust as he sat in court. He too was affected by the courtroom sauna; his own beads of sweat were dripping down his back underneath his blue suit, adhering the fabric to his damp skin. His eyes narrowed. *Good behaviour on the street, good behavior in life, not good behavior in jail.*

As he watched the dull proceedings with expert familiarity he shook his head in wonderment at the fact Jake was even given this chance at freedom. He usually showed up to these hearings even if he needed to rearrange his already busy schedule, especially if he had a hand in landing the guy in jail. Morgan was a dying breed of detective. He was the kind of detective that would go an extra step to see a case through, from the first call on 911, to seeing the sentence completed to the fullest extent the law would allow. For the true victims of crime, Morgan still cared. For those victims whose mindless inane behavior led to their own troubles, he just poked fun at. With his twenty-two years of service he was starting to wish for retirement; the glory days that were filled with adrenaline and excitement had ended in what felt like an eon ago. Over the course of his career he had watched Jake Gurracci progress from a teenage punk involved in petty crime, to a violent abusive adult, and finally the inevitable jail bird that sat stinking away in the prisoner's box. In the same span, Morgan had progressed from enthusiastic rookie cop, to a cynical, weathered, shell of a man who drank so much his face now resembled a leathery ragged catcher's mitt, like the kind seen on nineteen thirties baseball cards.

Gurracci looked away from the fly occasionally to glance at Detective Morgan. The detective could feel the hairs on the back of his neck flutter to attention with each glance from Jake Gurracci. Or perhaps it was because of the fresh wave of pure stink that wafted over the room every time Gurracci as so as twitched. In a brief pause in the proceedings, the courtroom staff's collective breaths echoed, labored and thick in the insufferable heat. Morgan pushed his finger into a bubble the heat had created in the cheap government grade wallpaper.

What the hell is wrong with the air conditioning? Morgan mused, tugging at the collar of his shirt. The mickey of whiskey hidden in the breast pocket of his suit bounced off his chest, reminding him of the smooth treat that awaited him after this kangaroo court was adjourned.

The weary detective wiped sweat away from his forehead with an already saturated and slightly sticky handkerchief. As his hand trailed back down, his finger caught the raised, puckered one-inch scar beside his left eye, a war wound from the job. The scar had been planted there, if you want to call it that, years earlier by the man now sitting chained in the prisoner's box and drowning the courtroom with his almost visible clouds of foul stench.

Gurracci's eyes quickly darted back to Morgan for a fleeting second; Morgan's fingers had been brushing the puckered mark, and he was sure that a ghost of a satisfied smile flashed on the criminal's face. Morgan's mouth twisted, a sharp crunch resonating as his teeth ground together. The scar was a constant reminder for Morgan of the day about six years ago - one of the many days now permanently etched into his mind - when this bastard, this criminal asshole sucker punched him and busted his temple wide open.

Oh, that day was as clear as memories could be, and Morgan recalled it in exquisite detail, each sense captured perfectly. Detective Morgan had been assisting one of the uniformed officers of the Moravian Police Department, attending to yet another call at the residence of Jake and Sheila Gurracci. These calls were quite repetitive in nature and it had become a reluctant chore for the road officers to drag themselves to their dump of house time and time again. This day was different; Detective Morgan sensed that immediately upon pulling up in his unmarked police cruiser. When he stepped out of the vehicle, he noted that the road officer visibly relaxed, tension easing slightly from every locked muscle, once experience had arrived. Morgan remembered that he gazed at the house with tapered eyes, as though a haze of hostility could be seen as a vicious red aura around it. But perhaps that was just a reflection of the setting sun.

There had been a call to 911 dispatch made from the Gurracci residence at 969 Mason Road, however when the operator answered, the caller hung up. Morgan was trained to investigate to a high rigorous standard, but even his less experienced partner was aware a relationship that is volatile can spell disaster for anyone getting in the middle. It's almost astonishing the speed that two people can go from loving each other more than life to hating each other with every fiber of their being, and Morgan knew this from firsthand experience. It's a vicious switch as fast as lightning and just as dangerous so with trepidation the officers tread carefully up the front porch steps.

Morgan went up to the door, maneuvered himself slightly off-center, and knocked with the side of his fist.

"Moravian Police," he called out.

No response, almost an intentional quiet.

"Moravian Police. We received a 911 call, we need to come in and talk to you," he called out as he rapped a second time.

Still no response.

He put his ear to the door and couldn't hear anything but perhaps some cockroaches scurrying at the noise he was making from outside the front door. His eyes flicked towards Jake's rusted out pick-up truck in the gravel driveway of the rural disheveled home. He was confident both Jake and Sheila

Gurracci were indeed inside; he could see the likely situation quite clear in his mind. Jake's sweaty, beefy hand holding her mouth closed cutting off air to her lungs, silencing any shouts to her would-be rescuers, enfolding her thin body in a grasp that her feeble strength could not break. As though the pretense of silence would cause the police to give up and leave, they would be huddled somewhere away from the door, the violence only on pause.

Morgan pounded again, this time so hard his hand began to sting with each thump and the dry flecks of paint on the white front door sprinkled to the floor of the rotting particle board porch.

"We are going to kick your door in if you don't open it!" he shouted, authority pouring into his voice as he switched into hardcore cop-mode.

He heard movement. Then a scrape on the door. Morgan was slightly alarmed that the person that now moved was always standing just in front of the door. Aside from the quick listen, Morgan and the other officer had been wise to stand off to the side when he knocked, something that becomes second nature to a trained cop, to stay out of the line of potential fire. After a few seconds there was the sound of a latch being lifted and the wooden door opened, just a few inches, revealing Jake's ugly mug.

"Yeah?" Jake asked from behind the door, his lips tight and his nostrils flaring.

"Checking out a 911 call, we need to come in to make sure everything is okay." Morgan said simply.

"Everything's fine."

Jakes tone was short and dismissing. Both officers could easily detect deception in Jake Gurracci's American-Italian accent.

"Then we shouldn't be long at all."

"I ain't letting you in without a warrant."

Jake's eyes were red and bloodshot, an indicative sign of mass alcohol consumption that Morgan himself was quite used too, and then Jake started to close the door. Morgan stuck his foot in the door before it could be closed, an old police trick he liked to use, to get the hardened part of his shoe or boot inside quickly to act as a doorstop. The door could be slammed on Morgan's foot over and over and in this position, he wouldn't feel a thing.

Morgan scoffed at the line that he'd heard numerous times throughout his career, barstool lawyers one and all. He has spoken to many a citizen with an ill-advised belief that police always need some kind of warrant or similar judicial authorization to enter a house, a man's castle, to conduct an investigation. Jake had gamboled off into pure speculation on the legal power Morgan possessed to enter his house. An inevitable horrible sequel would be the appalling consequence if they did not get inside to check on Sheila.

"Don't need a warrant Jake," Morgan grunted while pushing back at the door.

Jake shoved back and the front door wedged against Morgan's toe, but the quick thinking detective applied his own middle-aged strength which was no match for Jake burly biceps. The two officers together were able to win the contest, barely, and pushed Jake out of the way. Jake fell back against the wall, unfazed by the impact and stood heaving and shaking in front of the two officers, barring them from attending to the crying they could now clearly hear coming from upstairs. Dubious images flooded Morgan's mind that would never placate until he could come to her rescue so he skirted to the left to gauge Jake's reaction. Jake matched Morgan's movement, that is, until he saw the second officer's supercilious expression, two fingers tapping ever so gingerly on the butt of his service pistol, his reflexes taut, his inner spring coiled to take this creep out with one quick shot. The psychological advantage was his, even though it was a rougher and cruder fashion, but enough to convince Jake to stand aside. Jake Gurracci stared the officer down with squinty bloodshot eyes, but made no move; he knew the officer was ready.

Morgan found Sheila locked in an upstairs bathroom. He delicately tapped on the door and identified himself as Detective Morgan with a softer voice, although doing so seemed redundant as they had met on a few occasions and her recognition of him was soon immediate. When she emerged, she was wearing only an oversized t-shirt stained with blood on the area near her left leg. Morgan did a quick but comprehensive survey of the bathroom floor where Sheila had been sitting. He saw what vaguely resembled a medallion sized piece of steak that had been chewed, then spit out.

"What happened here?" he asked, concern coloring his voice.

Sheila peeled her long T-shirt back with quavering hands. She carefully covered her womanhood, and in minuscule increments revealed to the detective the near private area of her hip where her husband Jake had taken a mouthful of her flesh. Her flesh was red and puckered around the edges of the misshapen bite, and despite what he could tell was her best attempts, she had not been able to properly stop the steady ooze of blood. Morgan shifted his wrinkly features into a grimace and stared with profound sympathy. Under his gaze, she swayed uneasily on her feet, her face pale and sweaty.

Morgan was just able to catch her as she quivered and collapsed into his arms, and for one strangely static second, her pain-filled eyes met with his. It was odd, how long that second was, and the longer it stretched, the more his chest tightened in response to her pain. He wanted to kiss her on her dry cracked lips, hold her, save her, take her away from this madness. The gaze they shared, though only momentary, was retained vividly in his mind, and hers. He assisted her to the bed and while gently rubbing her hunched shoulders, he listened intently as she began to tell her tale.

Her voice trembled as she did, trying to hold off the oncoming torrent of tears as she detached herself from the pain momentarily. Morgan was told Jake had raped her. He had forcefully rammed his penis into her without any prior lubrication. He withdrew from her, held her legs tight and bit as hard as he could into her thigh. He pulled the chunk of flesh off and continued towards her vagina biting hard as he moved, leaving the trail of teeth marks. He focused his teeth on her clitoris and with a low growl he had bit down. She remembered her head spinning and the world tilting. She had clenched her eyelids and fists tight while her entire body stiffened, unable to block out the excruciating pain. He released his vice-like clench and her tender bud did not come off as her extremities returned to lucidness, a wave of relief that made her temporarily forget about the agonizing wound he inflicted. A tiny droplet of blood dribbled from his bottom lip as he rose and looked into her tear filled eyes.

"It's mine. Anytime I want it. It's mine," he had hissed into her ear. Then, like an unremorseful possessed demon, completed what he had started.

When Sheila finished she buried her face into Morgan's chest. The wetness of her tears penetrated his suit jacket and as one single bead ran down his skin, oddly, he felt close to her. Morgan swallowed hard and in turn, swallowed his feelings. With a parting comforting stroke to her matted hair, and a quick call for medical assistance, he got up and returned downstairs, steadfast in his sworn obligation.

Jake Gurracci had moved from the base of the stairs and was now seated at the kitchen table; this was perhaps not the best move for the officer, as this kitchen was no different than anyone else's. Drawers full of knives, forks, meat cleavers and other cooking implements that could be easily turned into tools of murder were nearly at hand. The officer never really thought of it that way, as his skill with his pistol was beyond reproach and he kept his eyes trained closely on Jake Gurracci's every movement, every breath he took, and even every time he blinked.

Morgan entered the kitchen to a single cockroach skittering up the side of the counter and into the sink containing a mountain of unwashed dishes. It seated itself at the top of the dish mountain and stared out at them, as if it knew a human shit show was about to begin.

"You're under arrest, Jake. Stand up and put your hands behind your back," Morgan commanded with an air of conviction, his stance set and his eyes again narrowed at the filth in question.

"Fuck you, pig," Jake growled defiantly, and held his large hands tightly to the kitchen chair.

The proficiency in which Morgan read the telltale signs of Jake's insolence was carefully crafted through years of dealing with disgruntled people. He sighed with an exasperated exhale. He no longer craved this kind of calamitous insolence. Bound by duty, Morgan and his partner each took one of Jake's massive arms and with a wrench and backward twist, tried to wrestle them from his grasp on the chair. A sudden jerky inclination of his right shoulder and Jake pulled an arm free from the other officer. Morgan could only watch with desperate self-pity as Jake's fist, unforgiving and roughly equivalent to kissing a freight train, connected with Morgan's temple.

Morgan was propelled into the counter, then downwardly oozed onto his sorry ass. He first saw stars, bright bursts that clouded his vision, and a dull ringing pierced his ears. As he shook the spots and the errant noise away with sharp jerks of his head, his eye socket began filling with blood, as if all the veins in his face intersected at that one tender spot and had suddenly ruptured. With untrammeled flow the blood gushed out and ran down the side of Morgan's face from the uniform one-inch wide gash. With only one eye operating, he scrambled back to his feet and viewed his partner in one elegant, fluid motion draw his pepper spray and erase Jake's contemptuous expression from his face with the ejecting stream. Red blotches blossomed from the flowing capsicum that soaked into the skin around Jake's cheeks and forehead; his eyelids immediately snapped shut at the burning sensation and he released a rough yell. Both officers took the opportunity to tackle him again and he fell forward like a granite tombstone into the kitchen table, convincingly flipping it ninety degrees onto its side. While the immediate effect of the pepper spray was favorable, the lingering consequence of the hanging vapors made the fight more intense by two-fold. Morgan and his partner wheezed, panted and coughed, each labored breath was like sucking lava through a straw as the cockroach, seemingly enjoying the performance, still looked on. All three combatants were cocooned in fatigue and literally sapped of strength but finally, with the distinct clicking of the handcuffs, Morgan and his partner were the victors.

Morgan's chest heaved as he fumbled with a tacky, striped tea towel that lay beside the dish mountain and put it to his eye. The fabric was stiff and crusty from lack of use, but quickly became sufficiently pliable as it became saturated with blood. Although ringing still permeated throughout his left ear, he could faintly hear Sheila sobbing at the further violence in her household. Though she shouldn't entirely have been surprised; the resonances of crying, screaming and slapping was the soundtrack to her pitiful life.

Jake lay on the kitchen floor partially in a puddle of Morgan's blood and his own snot and spit. Morgan looked down on Jake, his mouth twisting into a thin line.

One swift kick in the side of the head, Morgan thought, partially blinded by blood, pain and anger. His foot twitched and he stepped forward wondering if he should punt a field goal with Jake's head. His partner was looking at him, nodding.

Morgan inwardly scowled at his own conscience, put more pressure on his flowing wound instead and began to read Jake Gurracci his rights. He threw the dish towel at the sink, finally disturbing the single cockroach that had enjoyed its front row seat to watch the idiotic humans perform and it disappeared into the grungy drain. The stripes were now soaked in blood, no longer the colourful tacky design it once was, permanently stained. Morgan and the other officer had to drag Jake by his ankles out the front door and down the steps, and as the crunch of his thick cranium rang off each step, he continued to curse out the cops.

Even that atrocious act was not the reason Jake was in the midst of serving five years. Those eighteen months that he received as a sentence were just blip on the radar. The wound he inflicted was a mere foretaste compared to his next violent outburst taken against his wife that in retrospect, should have killed her.

Sheila Gurracci, another woman among millions reduced to nothing at the hands of her so-called husband. She took a wrong turn in life and ended up in this loop of viciousness from which she could not escape. Her years with Jake had taken their toll on this potential beauty queen. Her once flowing blond hair was now languid and unwashed. The sparkle in her gorgeous blue eyes and the beaming smile that used to stop men dead in their tracks were long since wiped away by her husband's hair-trigger fury. Her wardrobe, which had once consisted of apparel from all the fashion greats, were destroyed in fits of jealousy. They were replaced with the undeniable grubbiness of long t-shirts and frumpy, cotton track pants.

The money situation in her relationship played a big part of the decline. Jake couldn't, or wouldn't, hold a job. He'd occasionally have a job as a roofer or painter but that would never last long. He'd be fired within the first month, if that, for not showing up. It was usually because he was so obsessed with his wife's whereabouts, if she went out and defied his wishes, and if he didn't know where she was at every minute of every day, he would leave his job to make sure she was always home and not fucking around with other men, as was his misguided delusion.

Sheila never worked. He kept her on a tight leash, like a dog that wrapped its rope too many times around the pole, and was now only afforded a few inches of movement. She did however, wish for a baby, badly. She wanted someone to love her unconditionally, which she knew could never could come from Jake, as his love was littered with conditions and limitations. She longed for the kind of unrestricted love that only a baby can give. She wanted that feeling that a mother gets when her baby looks up and smiles and you can see the love in his or her eyes. She wanted that, but it wasn't meant to be. Not with Jake, and as long as he was around, not with any man.

When she would visit Jake it was usually a one-sided conversation, as it was at home. She would enter the visitation area with her matted hair pulled back into a ponytail. She would dutifully approach the glass. Other prisoners milled about talking to their lawyers or significant others in a line behind the glass. Jake would sit with a stone face and accusing eyes, for at least half a minute, before he'd pick up the phone and begin to steer the conversation. And she would sit there, numb, letting it happen.

"What's the count up to?" Jake would say in his usual condemnatory tone.

Jake was always fishing, every visit, to see if Sheila was sleeping with other men while he was incarcerated. She never did, but in his mind she was the town bicycle, ridden by every man while he was locked up.

"Nothing, there's no one, you know that," Sheila assured, in a weak tone.

The conversation was always the same, nearly word-for-word lines being exchanged every time they both sat in front of that glass. And as though he was reading it from the same script each time, he would always spout this:

"I never meant to hurt you. It's just that I love you so much. The thought of you with someone else...well, I love you too much I guess. When I get out, it will be different. We'll be happy. We'll have kids, you know, start a family. I'll get a good job, my roofing job. It will be different, I promise. I promise to God," he said changing his look to one of phony concern, but the feeling never touched his blank eyes.

Jake wasn't smart. His IQ was too ill-proportioned to be measured and any teacher would have to bend down to the floor just to put a tick on the intelligence scale but he could speak the words she needed to hear when it suited him. He was good at manipulating Sheila, and the corners of her mouth would twinge upwards, ever so slightly, upon hearing those lies.

The eighteen months flew by as time always seems to do. Even when he was in jail, she was swept along by the tidal force that was his evil spell. He was released, she agreed for him to return the house, and the circle began anew.

* * *

Back in the sweltering courtroom, Jake thought the fly moved as he spied it in his peripheral vision. It actually didn't, but Jake leaned his ape-like body over a little closer to study the mish-mash of tiny, squashed arms and legs. He blinked, it remained dead, yet still managed to provide a source of amusement for his baser self. The words being used in the courtroom were indecipherable to this mental midget, so he did what he did best as the board assessed his potentialities: he just sat and stunk.

Morgan continued to run his finger along the scar while trying to mentally block out the tremendous odor. To distract himself from it, he thought of those news stories where the station sends an artist to court to capture the moment in drawings and how one could not possibly draw a picture of Jake Gurracci without animating stink lines wafting upwards. He chuckled inwards at the image. But the distraction was only momentary, and his ears picked up the proceedings once more.

"Eighteen months for a violent rape of your wife," Morgan muttered under his breath, not caring about the charge that arose from his scar, but he did care about the devastating consequences that Sheila, a true victim, had to endure.

Sheila sat alone in the back row of the stale courtroom. Morgan didn't turn around to confirm this, but knew she was there and had seen her come in earlier. She wore a pretty tapioca colored floral dress, a stark contrast from the usual T-shirts and gym pants. Her alabaster beauty and hourglass figure had returned to the youthful shape of days gone by and she crossed her legs with dainty precision. Her soft skin, seemingly immune to the heat of the courtroom, shone anew. Jake dared not look at her any more than just to steal a peek when the moment was right. He hadn't seen her in more than a year as miraculously, she eventually did stop going to visit. Seeing her again sparked an internal rage. The inner acrimony that he had suppressed for a long time was rekindled, like starting a fire with a splash of gasoline. He closed his eyes but could only envision Sheila degraded to a slut-like status, surrounded by men with the sounds of ecstasy and fulfilling moans coming from her. He took long deep breaths and forced himself not to look again at her; instead, he returned his fiery gaze to the dead fly to attempt to temporality shake his misguided fantasy of her infidelity.

Without visitors Jake had nothing to do but pace, exercise and eat three square meals a day. This unfortunately only served to pump his arms full of strong, solid muscle and fuel his blind rage. Even though she had stopped visiting him he still kept bombarding her with letters for forgiveness. The letters, sufficiently intimidating and laced with blame but also, in a twisted way, expressing his undying love. In the back of the courtroom she held one of those letters. She had brought it in case the court wanted to see some manner of evidence of his dysfunctional animosity. No one asked, or even acknowledged she was there, a two-minute phone call a week ago was her only input. She unfolded the letter and reviewed the chicken scratch writing, a graphite manifestation of grammatical errors and spelling mistakes from the man with the lowest IQ on the chart.

> **"Derest Sheila**
>
> **You will never relize how much I love you. This hell hole you put me in has only made my love for you stronger. When I get out we will pick up were we left off. I know you have been with so many other men since you ratted to the fuckin' cops and got me busted but I don't fuckin' care because I will take care of them to. I still love you and will be forever and a day and I miss you with all**

my hart and soul. You will be happy to know that I am cured of all drugs and alcohol. I was in agony puking my guts out 24/7 for 9 full days and nights and I didn't eat anything. It wasn't until the 10th day that I ate some potatoes and some ham. I didn't do what you said and it is you that needs help and medicine. No body will help me get out of jail but I hope you come to your senses and come to court to tell them I didn't do nuthing and I was falsely arrested thru your lies and accused of a crime I didn't commit. It is the cops fault my lawyers fault and your fault but I am willing to look past this bullshit for us to be together again.

Love always with my hart and soul

Jake

He even went as far as to get a jailhouse tattoo. It read: 'Jake and Shila Forever.' Her misspelled name was surrounded by a deformed blood-red heart sloppily drawn with cheap ink and a guitar string to substitute a tattoo needle. Drawn with amateur proficiency, its poor artwork was obvious, but he still wore it proudly, a trophy representing her and his stay in jail, for all to see and for her to fear.

Two years served of a five-year sentence and the bastard is about to go free, Morgan thought as he wiped away another bead of sweat. His tongue swirled around in his dry mouth. *Gosh it's hot today.*

After twenty-two years Morgan could predict the outcome of these things. He was prepared for Jake to go free, conceivably why he preloaded a bottle of whiskey in his suit, but more realistically the alcoholic detective was just always ready to sneak a quick swig here and there. Morgan directed his mind back to the event that landed Jake a five-year sentence as the discussions in the courtroom became a buzz in the background.

* * *

It was two years ago, almost to the day. All the promises made during his eighteen-month incarceration were again unfulfilled. The circle of old familiar grievances returned and the relationship foundered in the same mire, like the filthy kitchen, where she now found herself cowering against the wall. Jake, his eyes ablaze, was standing in front of her with his fist gesticulating in exaggerated motions as he again yelled false accusations of infidelity at her. She eyed the phone sitting on a desk near the kitchen window, out of reach as he stood between her, and her only chance at salvation. The man that had told her many times how much he loved her was mentally on edge, his alcohol induced wrath fueling his mental attack on the trembling woman. He teetered on the brink of pure, unadulterated rage as he cursed, spit and punched the air with his flailing clenched hands. A veritable parade of his emotional shortcomings and fragmented logic stood in the path of any resolution of reason. Grabbing her thin arms, he pinned her against the wall with a thud that jarred her insides and snapped the back of her skull off one of the studs. He squeezed so hard Sheila felt her hands start to go numb; she couldn't see them, but they were turning a purplish-blue. He pulled her forward and slammed her back a second time. This time she both heard and felt a cracking in her spine that discharged electric bolts which tingled all the way up to her brain. Finally, he eased his grip and she slumped limply to the floor, much like a rag doll that had been tossed by an angry child. From her position, she warily glanced at that phone again. Gathering what feeble strength she had left, she slinked across the floor to the phone. She picked up the receiver and pressed 911. There was no time to pray that the call had gone through; all hope of a savior now crumbled when Jake tore the phone from the wall.

Saliva projectiles were released from all his yelling and the corners of his mouth were white and pasty with the congealed chunks of spittle. With clumsy deliberation she struggled on her stomach across the dirty floor to the archway that led towards the front door. Her weak attempt to escape, all for naught. He put his hand around her throat and lifted her upwards; her eyes were wide in silent screams, her windpipe totally cut off from air, save for a single squeak that she emitted at the grab. She felt her life slowly, painfully, slipping away, as though it was this tangible, thin string being pulled farther and farther from the center of her being. She lost consciousness before she felt it rip out entirely. He dropped her to the floor, yet again, and like a mindless brute devoid of the semblance of rational thought he held a wooden kitchen chair high above his head and brought it down upon her splayed body. He landed the agonizing blows again and again until the older chair finally split and it lost usefulness as an implement of murder. A trickle of blood ran from the corner of her bruised mouth.

Jake stopped. His hands were shaking and still held the broken pieces of the wooden chair tightly. His wife Sheila lay in absolute stillness at his feet. The silence of the moment was deafening. Jake stared at her motionless body and had thought he had surely killed her.

"Tap, tap, tap..."

Jake shifted his gaze from Sheila to the knocking he heard from the front door. His mind was a fervent storm of fantastic possibilities. He pictured Death tapping with his sharpened scythe, unsympathetically and unapologetically, coming to collect his dead wife.

"RAP, RAP, RAP..."

The rapping was louder a second time and under the power of a steel-toed police boot, two officers burst through the shabby, thin wood of the front door. Jake was already making his hasty getaway through the back door into the blackness of the night, his every breath seeming to echo throughout the woods. He batted at the branches scraping across his face as the trees ostensibly came to life and reached to impede his escape. His run became a stumble and he faltered forward, slamming his shoulder into the forest muck. He looked upward through the spinning trees to the gloomy sky. In his mind's eye, he had killed Sheila and it was indeed the grim reaper he was escaping from - surely it was Death's cloak fluttering on the edges of his peripheral vision? But to break the trance, he heard the barking of a police dog and the beams of numerous flashlights darting about the forest behind him. He scudded along on his belly as the world stopped, everything that was happening seemed to be in slow motion. He felt a searing pain shoot through his leg and this tough man that threw his weight around beating on women, screamed like a pansy under the powerful bone crushing jaws of the police K-9. The tussle with three police officers was short. Tonight's reign of terror was over, and for this incredulous assault, in which Sheila missed Death's frosty hand by and inch, he got five years.

* * *

Morgan stood up and shook his head. His stomach was churning, his blood pressure spiked. He felt like throwing his mickey at the parole board, but he was not one to waste good booze. Jake Gurracci smiled at the fly as he stood up and was released from his shackles. He was a free man, free with only words on a piece of paper to stand between his rage and his wife.

The expression in Sheila's puffy eyes was enough to imprint into anyone's memory as she rushed out of the courtroom. Morgan pushed through the throng of people fleeing the stuffy and stench-ridden court room, trying to catch up to her, hoping to comfort her with false palatial theories that the parole board, full of Mensa scholars (not), must surely have the proficiency to make sound decisions. When he reached the bustling corridor, Sheila and her pretty flowered dress were gone.

"Asshole," an elegantly garbed Judge Neilson silently mouthed towards Morgan as he walked by him.

Morgan's disappointment in the decision exasperated his unrelenting frustration with the system so he thought it best to ignore the judge. The judge did not stop to follow up on his off-color comment to the detective, but Morgan knew why the judge hated him so much and was quite used to his weekly berating. Shrugging it off, he shoved his hands in his pockets and mindlessly followed the crowd to exit the courthouse.

The sun beat down on the Moravian community with a merciless, record-setting vengeance. The paved roads buckled and cracked and the metal street signs seemed to bend over like wilting plants in an attempt to escape the heat. Cars honked here and there in the background of the sweltering day as Morgan trudged up to the crosswalk. His mind was devoid of optimism regarding the decision of the parole board to release Jake Gurracci. Their so-called greater wisdom failed to implant any solace in the knackered detective. Using his hand as a makeshift visor, he held it above his eyes to blot out the rancorous sun and stepped onto the sizzling roadway only to hear the screeching of tires and a loud ten-second blast of a horn.

"You asshole!" the vehicle driver shouted at Morgan, his head thrust out the window and a fist waved with menacing intent in his direction.

Morgan blinked slowly, more than exhausted with the day, and in no mood to deal with any more shit. He shook his head. "I'm an asshole, twice in five minutes," he grumbled to himself, more out of amusement than of a real tally.

Morgan sighed heavily and wished he could sneak a drink from the bottle in his breast pocket. He took another deep breath and the veteran detective raised the middle finger on his right hand and directed it toward the belligerent driver. Upon seeing Morgan's gesture the driver flew into a road rage, jerked into park, and exited his vehicle. Slamming the creaking car door, he clenched his fists, tilted his to the side trying to look convincingly tough and confronted the detective. The driver stood about five inches taller than Morgan as he cranked his neck upwards to look at the man's angry expression.

"Aw fart, this isn't going to be a good day," Morgan commented to the irritated man, as though he was merely talking about something as common and trivial as the weather.

"You got that right, asshole!" the driver barked, not taking in Morgan's cool, calm, but coiled body. He stepped further into Morgan's space, and Morgan was immediately put off by the heat of the man's breath adding to the heat of the day, tickling his forehead.

Morgan considered the man in front of him with a raised eyebrow. "That's three assholes in five minutes, probably about enough for one day, eh?"

With a flash image of Jake invading his mind, Morgan drew back his fist and cold-clocked the driver right on the end of his nose. He punched him so hard that he sent the loudmouthed guy descending to the sidewalk, landing on his rear end and wincing as his hands touched the hot pavement. The man quickly cupped his hands around his nose as the blood ran down his humiliated face.

"You asshole, you broke my nose!" he whimpered as Morgan walked on, uncaring.

"Four assholes, gotta be some kind of a record." Morgan ignored the vulgar shouts of the fallen man behind him, and opted to pull at his damp collar again. "Man its hot today."

He continued across the street and stepped onto the opposite sidewalk. Other rubberneckers had slowed to check out what they thought would be a one-sided fight in favor of the bigger man, but merely drove on when that didn't turn out to be the case. The fallen big mouth picked himself off the pavement, his nose broken and his pride shattered.

Numerous blocks away and well out of sight of the fallen driver, Morgan entered the white marble porticos of the Moravian Police Department. He removed the jacket of his cheap suit and slung it over his shoulder, relishing the cool air that flowed out of the air conditioner, bringing him back down to earth.

"Hey Morgan," the plain front desk clerk beamed as she pushed the entrance buzzer on the front door and it unlocked.

"Just another minute." Morgan closed his eyes and breathed deeply.

"Hot one ain't it?" she laughed. "Everyone's been doing that when they walk in here. Come on in, the air conditioning ain't going nowhere in here."

The door buzzed again and he entered the office with a certain level of chagrin, as he knew he would have to get back to doing real police work. He loosened his tie and walked into the broom closet-sized detective bureau to relax for a few minutes before he got down to business. The armpits of his white shirt were soaked with big oval shaped sweat stains that burned cold under the power of the air conditioning. Morgan casually sniffed his pits in the closed door privacy of his office and was impressed his deodorant was holding its own against the combative heat. At the very least, Morgan was glad he didn't smell like Jake Gurracci. He roughly sunk into his chair, the squeak in his aged chair matching the cracking in his 47-year-old bones. His thick fingers grazed over the surface of the files on his desk, and he made a repulsed face at the stack of red and blue folding envelopes. The incoming far outweighed the outgoing in a disproportionate hodgepodge of sex crime, extortion and even the occasional murder. He was the only detective at the Moravian Police Department; no one seemed to want to do the big messy jobs and even some of the smaller tasks the officers would still leave on his desk for the detective to look after.

Moravian was a fair-sized city with a predominant Irish population. Its surrounding rural residences and once fertile farmlands were now being encroached by the growing city limits, but all that prosperity appeared to fade over the decades and now it just seemed it was the country's capital for crime. Statistically maybe not, but if one asked the over-worked police officers they would tell how they felt about the never ending stream of calls for service. He flipped open the top folder. The inner contents were scribbled with the fruits of misguided maunderings, self-serving statements and half-truths that Morgan would have to wade through to find some kind of workable middle ground.

"Fuck it," Morgan piped, throwing the file back to the crowded desk. It slid precariously close to the edge of the desk, the papers within teasing a trip to the floor.

He wasn't in working mode at the moment, despite the fact that he knew that there was loads to be done. No, his mind was elsewhere. All he could think about was Jake Gurracci and how that ultra-piece of lowly scum was now walking the streets a free man. A room at the dirt bag Moravian Inn, paid for by the welfare office, and hence paid for by the taxpayers of Moravian, was most likely going to be his temporary residence. The Moravian Inn was the city's hotbed of transients, mentally ill and other such down on their luck people; with its paper thin walls and discounted hard mattresses it certainly was a normal citizens sight to behold, and to revile.

He looked at his bottom drawer as he thought of Sheila and what she must be going through mentally after the release of her husband. Morgan reached down and pried the stiff drawer open. He fished under a pile of completed case files and pulled out a bottle of salvation. He hadn't forgotten about the mickey of whiskey in his suit pocket, he just wanted to continue on the bottle that was in his desk drawer that had been opened and already half-finished. He held the partial bottle of whiskey in his right hand and unscrewed the cap. He wafted the aroma around his nose then took a swig, letting the whiskey slide down his throat, savoring the taste as long as he could. Orgasmic would be too strong a word, satisfying would be too shallow. Morgan, like many others, was under a false assumption that he needed it to get through the day. A nip here, a nip there and if he was not careful he could finish off an entire bottle in one shift. He took two more massive gulps and replaced the bottle back to its hiding spot under a stack of the completed file folders. He slid the drawer closed with his foot and returned to an upright seated position.

In the adjacent office police members milled about doing their normal daily routine of typing police reports on the system, fielding phone calls from the public or dealing with the inane antics of upper management. The Moravian Police Department was going through a transition period as all departments do now and then and it seemed the office was full of fresh faces. Every few years a hiring push would take place when some of the older coppers retired. Morgan sometimes couldn't remember who the new faces belonged to, as things were changing so fast.

The new officers were always gung-ho when they first started. Morgan could remember his first year on the job. Pressed shirts, shiny boots, standing straight and tall, walking with a purpose - all bullshit now. Morgan found it hard to believe he actually once acted like the unsure new people in the office. Through his years he's watched many an officer change. He's even marked the individual stages that each one passes through. There is the officer who is fresh on the job, eager to please, full of piss and vinegar and ready to take on the world. A few years pass. The fresh officer now has the confidence to work on his or her own with little help from a supervisor or a seasoned detective like Morgan. A few more years pass. The officer has now seen and done just about everything and the bravado of wearing the uniform is ending as fast as a pre-ejaculating teenager. The will to come in to work is diminishing and sick days are on the rise as the officer tries to find ways to get out his job, yet still collect the paycheck. A few more years pass and the officer is now fed up with spending ninety-five percent of their time dealing with five percent of the population. The same problematic people are arrested at the same row of low income houses for the same reason week in and week out. This level of police officer may find themselves looking the other way at petty crime. They may be crabby and short-tempered with the public, and the public wonders why this police officer is an asshole. Some can exist like this for a long time, but the last category, they are broken, simply just existing. In some sad cases, these broken and battered officers become alcoholics, like John Morgan.

Morgan slouched in his chair and rubbed the temples beside his tired eyes. He ran his finger up and down the scar, his own habit, each time reminding him of the newly freed Jake Gurracci. He generally didn't wish death on another human being, but today he did. He wished Jake Gurracci was dead. Dead, buried and rotting away with the maggots that would feast upon his putrid corpse with impeccable finality.

Problem solved. Morgan clenched his fist in frustration and almost opened his drawer again, but was brought back to reality by a boisterous tone from the next room.

"You have the right to remain stupid. You have the right to contact a potbellied, money grubbing lawyer who will lick your shitty ass and call it ice cream."

Morgan sat up in his chair and started snickering at the young officer in the next room who was obviously making fun of an accused person's Miranda rights, albeit in an offbeat way. He got up and walked to the door and poked his head around the corner. There was young officer Bobby Grant with his usual erudition and flamboyance showing off for the new guy. Bobby Grant, an impressive go-getter full of tenacity and dedication, had been recently assigned with showing the ropes to the recently arrived fresh police meat. His only downfall so far as Morgan knew was that he seemed to have a weak stomach for blood. Bobby Grant, occasionally referred to as 'Pukey', certainly made up for it with enthusiasm. Cliff Henderson, the newest member of the service, was a veteran of only two weeks but Bobby Grant walked around like he had already ascended to Chief of Police.

From what Morgan had heard and knew of Grant's recruit file, Grant had come from a normal suburban up-bringing, strong community ties, stable family life. He was well-educated; mom and dad were always able to provide and above all, he seemed to be fitting in well as a smart young cop. He had the kind of background that police services seem to gravitate towards, possessing the right mix for success. Morgan had been watching Bobby Grant for a while with hopes he would be willing to take over the position of detective in the future.

Henderson, on the other hand, was a farm boy. He didn't always have much but had what was needed to get by. His country up-bringing taught him hard work and responsibility, not to mention he was strong as an ox. The strength he possessed was just a bonus but the rest of his characteristics screamed of life experience and that also seemed to make a good police officer. When Henderson smiled, baby-faced dimples would appear at the corners of his mouth as large as craters of the moon and some of the female officers considered the new guy kind of cute, in contrast to Morgan's middle-aged horrid face. They definitely could have used him to help with big Jake Gurracci, but he just wasn't around yet and if there was a tangle with Jake Gurracci in the inevitable future, Morgan was glad Cliff Henderson was here. Officer Henderson laughed a tolerant laugh and rolled his eyes at Grant's wise-cracking interpretation of a lawyer's sedentary lifestyle.

Morgan walked into the office where the two rookies were seated. Having met Grant on many occasions and attended the odd call for service with him, Morgan was well aware of his impressive abilities so far. Morgan walked up to Henderson with his hand out-stretched to meet this new officer.

"I'm Detective John Morgan," he said, trying to hide the booze on his breath.

"Henderson, sir, nice to meet you."

Fresh out of the academy, Henderson was still in the 'ma'am' and 'sir' mode that the new recruits get brainwashed with during their three-month stint on learning how to walk, talk and eat police work.

"Academy's over, kid. Don't call me sir."

"Sorry. The habit is tough to break. Sometimes I feel like I'm in the army or something."

"We're all just people. I ain't any better than you, stick with this kid," he said referring to Grant, "you'll do fine. My door is always open if you either of you get stuck." He nodded as a way of exiting the conversation, and turned to return to his office.

"Hey, Morgan," Grant called to his retreating form. "Any words of encouragement for us new impressionable cops to get us through our nightshift? Mold us, sculpt us, make us like you."

Morgan stopped, with his back toward the pair.

Like me? Why would you ever want to be like me? he thought, actually stumped for a moment. An alcoholic like him? So sick of the days that he had to deal with the dregs of society, so cynical that everyone was an optimist next to him. He stood frozen like this for only a few seconds, then turned back and faced them. Both stared back at him with bright, new eyes. Morgan almost pitied them for what they would turn into, and decided that he would actually try to impact some real knowledge onto them. "If there is anything you remember from your training, throw it out the window and remember this. Someday you will screw up. Someday you will go too far. It happens to everyone. It happened to me, maybe even today, who knows?"

The wide-eyed two were now transfixed on Morgan, each poised with undivided attention and they were putty in his hand to mold.

"There is a three step process to get you out of trouble when shit you created hits the fan. One, act surprised. Two, show concern and three, deny, deny, deny. The third one is the most important boys, so take that with you."

Henderson's eyebrows were lifted comically in surprise. Grant, conversely, frowned in concern. Morgan was just glad he shut up Grant and stalked away at last, returning to his office to continue staring at the unfinished case files. The door clicked shut behind him.

Henderson and Grant were silent for a moment as they mulled over Morgan's 'advice'.

"What the hell do you think he meant by that?" Henderson said to Grant after a time.

Grant shrugged. "I don't have a friggin' clue, but word around the office is he is an excellent detective and we should strive to be like him, his investigative competence is unmatched around here."

Sgt. Samuels, the platoon watch commander who always seemed to be lurking just around the corner, walked into the room. Samuels was the only one at the Moravian Police Department who had been around longer than Morgan and was the next one scheduled to get the golden handshake and head off into the sunset of retirement. Samuels had the distinction of training Morgan when he was a new officer back in the day. Samuels always reeked of cigar smoke, much like Morgan reeked of booze. If he wasn't just around the corner, all you would have to do is look in the office garage, the only place in the building people were allowed to smoke. He spent countless hours in the garage, sitting amongst the stored tires and replacement janitorial supplies, doing his supervisory chores while munching on a cheap stogie. Samuels would puff away merrily checking the officer's police reports under a dark fog of cigar smoke that resembled his own personal rain cloud. If Morgan's face was a leathery ragged catcher's mitt, Samuels face was the same catcher's mitt, only having been cured in a meat smoker. Samuels interrupted the pondering of the young officers and directed Bobby Grant to speak to a person that had come in the front door to report having been assaulted earlier.

An enthusiastic Grant jumped at the call and darted to the front door where he was met by a man holding a bloody rag over his bleeding nose, mumbling something about a mystery guy in a suit punching his dripping beak. Unaware of what was transpiring, Morgan finished off that bottle and stayed in his office for the rest of the shift.

As he left for the day, Morgan walked by Grant, who was studiously typing the police report for the earlier assault.

"Whatcha got?" Morgan asked.

"Nothing much, just a bit of road rage," Grant said. "Broken nose guy shall be his moniker."

Morgan fought to hide the grin forming on his leathery face. "Well, sounds like the heat is getting to people. See ya later kid, he probably deserved it. If ya need me, I'll be at Gillespie's."

Morgan couldn't help but chuckle dismissively under his breath, with no regrets about flattening the rude driver earlier. Grant may be good, but Morgan felt Grant would be hard pressed to solve that one.

* * *

The setting sun was ablaze with orange and reddish hues as the sweltering day changed to a muggy, humid night. There wasn't much relief from the heat, even as the brilliant sunset eventually relented to the drawing of nature's dark curtain. Clouds had moved in and blocked out the stars; their comforting twinkle was non-existent tonight. There was no rain but flashes of heat lightning and the ominous rumble of thunder could be seen and heard approaching.

Sheila Gurracci sat alone at her kitchen table, her mind burning with speculation on whether she would survive the night or be thrust violently into Death's waiting arms. The kitchen was not the decrepit mess that it once was two years ago. She had long repaired and repainted, attempting to paint away the scars she suffered in kitchen that night, the night Death came knocking, but she was not yet ready to answer. Her pretty dress was in the hamper and she returned to an oversized ratty shirt and gym pants, her garb of choice during her relationship with Jake. There was never a man to look good for, and certainly Jake did not count. The fear Jake had instilled in her through years of mental torture and physical assaults was the catalyst to her broken existence.

A crash of thunder was heard, much closer this time, and it jerked her to seated attention. The wind started to pick up and blew through the window. The white curtains danced like exuberant ghosts under the dim light of the kitchen bulb. These imaginary apparitions of her mind sent shivers down her spine and the tiny hairs stood up on her arms. She swallowed hard, got up and walked toward the open window. The ghostly white curtains blew into her face as she reached out and grabbed for the handle, jerking at the always sticky window. Her trembling hands made the effort to close the window that much more difficult. After a few tries she forced the sliding pane shut with a loud slam. The wind immediately ceased and the curtains returned to their normal hanging position.

The silence of the kitchen was only disturbed briefly by the approaching thunder outside. She sat back down at the table.

Maybe he's changed, she thought trying to reassure herself. *Maybe he learned his lesson in jail.*

Another crack of thunder made her jump again from her chair. It was so close she thought the storm clouds had purposefully stopped atop her rusty metal roof in an obscene gesture of ill will. The thought she just had disappeared from her mind because she knew Jake better than anyone, better than any police officer, better than any prison psychiatrist or better than any judge. She knew he would come and he wouldn't stop until she's dead. Slowly, she walked across the room to the newly cleaned kitchen counter. She opened a drawer and removed one of the biggest knives she could find. Its honed blade with a minutely detailed serrated edge was just right for the job but this job however, was not food preparation and it was not protection.

The phone rang behind her with a shrill squawk and Sheila released a high pitched yelp in response. She stared at the phone, gulping frantically to try to quench her heavy breathing. It rang again. She reached out a shaking hand and put it on the receiver. It rang again and she instinctively snatched her hand back like she was pulling it out of the jaws of a crocodile. With trepidation, with caution, she reached out her hand again and picked up the receiver.

"Hello," she said in a small soft voice.

There was no response.

"Is anyone there?"

Still there was only silence on the line.

She swallowed thickly.

"I'm going to call the police if you don't say something."

It started lightly, and then got heavier. She could now hear the sound of someone breathing on the other end.

"Jake?"

"SLUT!" a male voice spoke out.

Sheila slammed the phone down and began sobbing uncontrollably. She held the kitchen knife tight to her flustering chest, trying to regain her composure. The rumbling thunder epitomized her hopelessness as it continued to mock her from the black sky above. She knew she should call the police and even through this ostentatious ugliness, she thought of Morgan and how on many occasions he had comforted her. She reached out for the phone, hoping he'd answer, but it rang again. She gasped erratically, rational thought stymied by the continuous ringing. She couldn't stop her hand from reaching for the ringing phone. It was if someone else was controlling her actions. She picked it up and put it to her ear. She never spoke. She never had to.

"Tonight, you die," Jake hissed in a low evil tone.

Sheila slammed the receiver down as hard as she could.

The phone rang again. In shear panic she took the knife and wildly chopped at the phone. The recklessness and abandon of her actions came to an ill-fated fruition. One unintentional but well placed swipe severed the cord. Sheila stepped back from the phone and the reality of what she had just done set in and she fell to her knees with her hand still wrapped tightly around the handle of the knife. She descended deeper into the depression she had been in for years. It wrapped tight around her chest, a dark shadow for her to drown in. She felt like driving the stainless steel blade into her broken heart and walk calmly into death with welcoming arms. Her will to live was crushed and she felt only death could set her free. She didn't want to die at the hands of Jake. She wanted death on her own terms. Death was her answer, death was her savior and should Death knock tonight, she was ready to answer by her own hand.

She rose to her feet with the knife still tight in her grasp. Tears flowed freely down her cheeks as she slid the deadbolt into place on the front door and turned out the kitchen light. The blackness of the room was unequaled by the blackness of the thundering night sky. Her labored breathing returned to normal as she wondered to herself what death would be like. Would it hurt? Would it be fast? Who would care?

Sheila was at the lowest point of her life. She ascended the staircase with knife in hand and each step creaked under the pressure as one more roar of thunder penetrated the air outside and a quick bright flash of lightning lit up the vacant kitchen behind her.

Sheila went into the bathroom and turned the water on in the tub. She knew what she was going to do. A nice warm bath, a quick slice of her wrists and soon it would be over. The sound of the water hitting the bath tub reverberated throughout the mostly empty house. The steam from the hot water began to fog the mirror. She slid her track pants down and looked at the wrinkled scar tissue on her hip. That ugly reminder was the reason she had never been with another man in the two years Jake was imprisoned. She felt branded by it, forever marked as a signal to other men to leave his property alone. Pulling them up, she put her dirty blonde hair into a ponytail. Her thoughts now focused on being found. When Death came to collect or whoever it was that found her body, she wanted it to be presentable. She wanted dignity, the dignity she never had. She got the pretty flowered dress back out of the bathroom hamper and slipped it on as the room filled with steam. She put the knife to her wrist and pressed it into her skin. Her hands began to tremble again as the pain of doing it slowly became unbearable and she backed off slightly from her self-imposed penance.

Fast, hard and deep. Fast, hard and deep. Fast, hard and deep, she thought over and over in her troubled mind.

The phone rang again.

Something wasn't right. She only had one phone but could distinctly hear a ringing over the sound of the running bath water. This ring was different. It sounded closer. It also sounded sicker. She walked towards the sound of the ringing. She held the knife in both hands in front of her as the ringing continued. It was coming from her bedroom.

The hallway to her room seemed longer than usual, like she was moving through a dream sequence. Time seemed to be standing still as her heart pounded against her chest with each step she took. Reaching the door, she slid her hand inside and felt around the door frame for the light switch. She flicked on the light and that sickly ring was now insufferable. Sheila froze. There in the center of the bed was a bouquet of dead flowers and a cellular telephone that just rang over and over.

She fell back into the door frame, her head plunged to the brink of insanity. He was already here. He was already in the house and had called her from upstairs.

"No!" she screamed out. "Not like this!"

She tore back down the hall and ran into the bathroom securing the flimsy door behind her. The steamy bathroom air and locked door denoted false feelings of safety. These feelings faltered in a maelstrom of despair when she detected an all too familiar stench. Her body stiffened when she felt something on the back of her head. It started softly caressing her hair at first as Sheila stood solid, too scared to move. The soft gentle feeling turned quickly to extreme pain as Jake grabbed her ponytail in his large meaty hand. He squeezed his fist so tightly that he ripped a handful of strands from her aching scalp. He stood close behind her and wiped his hand across the steamy mirror.

She looked into his eyes which were locked in a gaze of pure evil, pure hatred, despite his former declarations of love.

"I've missed you, baby," he hissed between his teeth.

Jake drew back his fist and punched at his own reflection, shattering the older bathroom mirror and impaling tiny shards into his fist. He held up his bloody fist, considered it for a second, and then wiped his mouth with it. Calmly, Jake took the knife from her hands. She put up no fight, and hoped that her death would be quick. His lips were caked in his own blood, and he swirled his tongue around, smearing it in the dirt and scruff of his face. He spun Sheila around, not releasing his grip on her hair.

"Taste me, whore."

He kissed her deep on her lips. It was so disgusting. She could taste his blood; she could smell his stench. She hated kissing him when she thought she loved him and now this was churning her stomach. Jake pulled her tighter to himself and shoved his tongue down her throat as far as he could, triggering Sheila's gag reflex. Her stomach and throat convulsed of their own free will and finally she vomited. He still did not release her and she ended up vomiting into his mouth. Jake pulled her head away from his and she coughed uncontrollably as she tried to regain her breath. He licked his lips again, tasting the bitterness that was her bile.

"My little whore, how many guys did you fuck? Ten, twenty? Did you swallow them all? Did they all taste your sweet pussy that belongs to me?" he said as small chunks dripped from his chin. "You know you're not allowed to wear that dress; it makes you look like a filthy whore. Time to die my darling, and when you are dead, I will fuck your beautiful corpse and be the last man you ever have."

Jake smashed Sheila's head off the bathroom sink with such force the porcelain chipped and her vision blurred, then things began to go black. She did not see the sink become coated red with the blood that spewed from a gash in her forehead. With his grip on her ponytail still intact he smashed her head onto the porcelain again, but this time, she saw a white light.

Jake picked her up and carried her to the bedroom. The blood from her wounded head dripped onto the breast of her pretty flowered dress as he laid her on the bed. He arranged the dead flowers around her, a sacrifice to his carnal lust and rage. He stood and stared at her unconscious body as if to admire his handiwork, like he had just painted the perfect morbid picture. He pulled up her dress, removed her panties and put them to his nose, inhaling deeply. He spread her limp legs open, exposing her wide for him as he had done many times before in his frequent horrid acts of non-consensual sex. He unbuckled his belt and pulled out his erection. He spit on her exposed vagina and began to position himself at her female entrance.

The phone rang again.

Jake turned his head just in time to catch a glimpse of the axe that sliced off his head.

Jake's flying head struck the wall with a disgusting thwack as the rest of his body dropped to the floor like a stone. The boots of this mysterious figure tromped on the hardwood floor of Sheila's bedroom, stepping over Jake's blood-spewing corpse and went to the bed. The figure pulled her dress down to cover her exposed genitalia in a strangely compassionate move. A gloved hand patted her gently on the side of the face, then bent over and picked up the head of Jake Gurracci by his greasy hair. He placed the decapitated head under Jake's dirty T-shirt and took him by the ankles, pulling him out of the bedroom, down the stairs, and out the front door.

Sheila floated pleasantly along a meandering brook toward the white light. The welcoming atmosphere of the light filled her with feelings of solace, contentment and safety. In the haze of the shimmering light, an angel with a windswept blue gown appeared. The intensity of the light was getting brighter and brighter and soon she had to squeeze her eyes shut as tight as she could. She turned her head to look away but an inextricable force overwhelmed her and she felt her closed eyes being pried open as the brightness became agonizing. It was a losing battle for the wounded and battered Sheila, and she could no longer resist it.

"Easy, ma'am. Easy. You're all right. You're going to be all right. Calm down, you're safe now."

As her eyes adjusted she could make out the unmistakable ice blue of a paramedic uniform, and a young man holding a mini flashlight.

"Who are you?" she gasped jerking to an upright position.

"My name is Andy. I'm a paramedic. You're in an ambulance. You're safe. We're taking you to the hospital. You're going to be just fine."

"How did I get here? Where's Jake?"

"I'm sorry, ma'am. I don't know who Jake is. We were called by the police. Someone called 911, the police came and they found you. That's about all I know."

Andy the paramedic was lying to Sheila. He had just come from her house, and had witnessed the sickening melee first hand.

"What happened to Jake?" She grasped the side of the stretcher in earnest.

"Just relax, ma'am. Lay back and we'll take care of you," his voice cracked a bit as if he was going through puberty; he was not used to lying to the patients, and even an experienced paramedic like Andy could not believe what he had just seen back at her home.

Sheila laid her spinning head back on the stretcher. It hurt like hell and the movement of the ambulance enhanced the dizziness. She couldn't remember what had happened and was confused, but, she felt safe. The dull thunder was now barely audible on the horizon. The twinkling stars came out and helped guide the ambulance as it whizzed down the road on the hot, sultry night.

* * *

The flickering of the TV illuminated the empty whiskey bottle sitting on the floor beside Morgan as he snored away in his easy chair. His phone was ringing, his cell phone was ringing and his pager had gone off but still he continued to snore.

Samuels pulled into the driveway of Morgan's house. He got out of his police cruiser, went to the front door and knocked hard enough to wake the dead but there were no dead inside, just drunk Morgan. The light of the TV was noticeable through the crud-covered window and Samuels was well aware of what he would find inside. He tried the knob and luckily Morgan had left it open as he usually did after drinking.

"Get up you jackass. Drinking at Gillespie's again?" Samuels yelled as he came into the room where Morgan was snoring in his easy chair. Morgan jerked at the sound of Samuels' heavy boots stomping across the threshold.

"Fuck off, geezer," Morgan slurred. He kept his eyes closed and shifted further into the fabric of the chair.

Samuels sighed, shook his head in exasperation and went to the kitchen. Rifling through the cabinets, he found a dusty pitcher and filled it with cold water. He returned and held it over Morgan's head.

"Sorry old buddy, we need your services."

He dumped the water on Morgan's snoring dome. Morgan jumped out of the chair, shocked back to reality.

"Jesus Christ!" he shouted, shaking his soaking head. "What the fuck did you do that for?"

"Well, if you answered your phone, I wouldn't have had to."

"I didn't hear the phone."

"Of course you didn't hear the phone, you were half-passed out."

Morgan threw a dark glare at the sergeant before letting the matter drop, curiosity at his appearance winning out.

"What the hell is going on?" Morgan inquired.

"Jake Gurracci's dead, we need you to go to the crime scene."

Morgan sat back down in the wet chair and rubbed his bloodshot eyes, a smile on his face.

"So what, fucking great news. Don't tell me, overdose?"

"Fucker's missing his head."

Morgan furrowed his wrinkly brow and looked at Samuels with puzzlement.

"You mean he's been murdered?"

"No you geezer, he cut off his own head. Yes, he's been murdered. Now we need a detective at the scene, so if you don't mind..."

Begrudgingly, Morgan stumbled out of the room to get his work clothes. He pulled out a grey suit jacket and slipped it on over his shoulders. While Morgan fumbled in his closet, Samuels surveyed Morgan's living room. It wasn't hard to tell that years of neglect had taken their toll on his home and years of drinking and police work had taken their toll on its owner. The nineteen eighties shaggy living room rug was slowly decaying from lack of care throughout the years. Liters of spilled booze and a cache of chicken wing bones adorned the area around the foot of the chair where they'd tumble to the floor upon Morgan passing out. Morgan still had a thicker ancient tube style TV attached to a just as ancient VCR. An old porno video lay on top of the VCR with the roll stuck somewhere in the middle of the dirty movie. Samuels looked with solemn distress at the weathered and yellowing pictures scattered around the living room. Morgan still kept a picture of his ex-wife on a credenza, the thick dust that adorned the glass and frame was a tribute to the failed love they had once shared.

"Everything all right, old buddy?" Samuels asked in a tone of concern, his eyes flicking from one mess to the other.

"Yeah, everything's fine," Morgan lied as he reentered the room.

Everything was not fine. Chaos reigned in his home life; he had no purpose, and was as empty and transient as the last drop of whiskey or the last swallow of beer.

Samuels nodded, but said nothing about the lie he had clearly been told. He thumped his hand on Morgan's shoulder. "Come on pal, I'll take you there."

"So, where are we going?" Morgan asked as they trudged out of the house and into the cruiser.

"Well, it ain't pretty. His body is just outside his house. Someone took the time to nail him to a fucking tree in the front yard."

"You're fuckin' shitting me. How did you find it?"

"Not entirely sure, I think someone called 911 from a cell phone and said to get over to his house. Our people got there first and no word of a fuckin' lie, there he was up in a tree like Christ on the cross."

"Who called 911?"

"They didn't say but I am sure that will be the first thing you look for."

Morgan was perplexed. He had a thousand questions but had to be patient.

"Crappin' Christmas!" Morgan exclaimed with his eyes aghast as the car pulled up to the scene.

The headlights lit up the most horrific sight Morgan had ever laid his eyes on in his twenty-two years with the Moravian Police. Jake Gurracci was about five feet off the ground and tied to an oak tree with his arms out-stretched in such a way he seemed to be begging heaven for forgiveness. The illusion of divine intervention was short lived when Morgan realized whoever had deftly raised him to this position had also pounded nails through his palms. Morgan cautiously walked up to the oak tree and systematically perused Jake's once muscular flesh that was already turning the blueish-grey that signified blood circulation had come to an end. Jake's left hand appeared to be covered in cuts. His gaze was then attracted to something carved into the bark. The oak tree had not only been violated by the hanging body, but now displayed one word, 'DADDY.' That lone word wasn't really carved, more so chopped, into the old oak at 969 Mason Road.

Morgan followed the trail of blood into the house, up the stairs and into the bedroom where Sheila had slept alone for two years and no man had ever dared to enter. Morgan was careful not to disturb potential evidence but from a quick examination of the interior of the bedroom Morgan could distinctly make out four different sets of footwear impressions in the blood that had spilled from Jake's neck and onto the floor.

For God sakes how many people have tromped in and out of here? Morgan thought, partially frustrated at the extra work it will take to effectively eliminate the shoe prints made by the police and the paramedics.

Still, he found it hard to blame anyone for walking through the blood. Sheila's medical rescue was paramount and trumped the impending investigation. Morgan found his antipathy had not evaporated and he could care less that Jake Gurracci was dead. He was almost glad part of his murder scene was potentially ruined by the many footprints that littered the bedroom floor. Morgan noted one footprint in particular that appeared to be larger than the rest and surmised that Henderson may have been the first police officer on the scene.

From the top of the stairs Morgan looked downward with jocular allusion at the blood trail left by whoever dragged Jake

Gurracci outside. It reminded him of the time he and another officer did the same thing while he still had his noggin'.

He then checked out the bathroom. The tub full of cold water with small red droplets spattered on the metal side sat adjacent to the porcelain sink that was chipped and also had dried blood on it. The mirror, smashed out in a fit of sightless frenzy, turned Morgan's mind back to the cuts that riddled Jake's left hand that he observed at the oak tree and with impressive meticulousness he tabulated his findings in his notebook.

Something was missing.

"Where the hell is his head?" Morgan said returning to just outside the front door.

Grant and Henderson shrugged their shoulders; one looked confused, and the other looked surprised.

"Get forensics in here for pictures and samples, and then cut that fucker down. Tie a yellow police ribbon around the old oak tree and guard this murder scene until forensics finishes up in the morning."

Samuels stood by his car smoking his stogie and chuckled to himself at Morgan's wit.

Samuels had to admit Morgan, a man who had taunted the dangerous and out-foxed the cunning, still knew what he was doing when he turned on his interior switch.

"I need to listen to that 911 call."

"We'll have it for you in the morning. We'll get the body to the hospital for the autopsy. You go get some rest, you smell like you need it. You got a lot of work ahead of you."

Yeah, well, who cares about that prick, Morgan thought to himself rubbing the scar on his temple.

Grant looked pale as the ropes were cut and the corpse plummeted earthward. Gravity cared less about the nails driven into his palms, and they tore effortlessly through flesh and bone and the body hit with an impersonal splat. He ran around the side of the house so he could void his puke alone. He could feel the gag welling up in his stomach then rising up his throat as he wretched once, twice, then vacated his dinner into the dried brown grass. A slight cool breeze blew by which gave a small bit of relief from the heat of the night. It was quite dark at the side of the house, the porch and police cruiser lights did nothing to illuminate this area. Another breeze wisped by.

"Madness."

That word seemed to enter Grant's ear, giving him a chill. The word, faintly and repressively, was intertwined in the blowing breeze. He lit up his flashlight and pierced the darkness with the powerful beam scooting about looking for the source of what he thought he had just heard. There was nothing to be seen except a few garden tools leaning against the house including a shovel, rake, a rusty scythe and a timeworn lawnmower that had long surpassed its usefulness. Grant shone his light on the rusty scythe and it gave him the same chill he had felt just a minute ago.

"Death came here tonight," he said quietly before returning to the action around front.

Morgan got into the car with Samuels and left the scene. Grant and Henderson were assigned to guard it for the rest of the night and as they were directed, tied the yellow ribbon around the old oak tree, then ran it all around the entire property until the scene was encased in the impenetrable force field that is yellow police tape.

"Well, see you in a few hours," Samuels told Morgan as he dropped him off. "You sure you're okay?"

"Yeah, but I'll feel a lot better when that shithead is buried and I piss on his grave."

"I hear you. Get some rest, old friend."

"Thanks, but that's what I was trying to do before you doused me like was on fire or something you old geezer."

Morgan entered his house, threw his keys on the table and plopped back down in his easy chair. He certainly wasn't in any position to criticize Sheila Gurracci for the condition of her house. Morgan lived no differently. He stared at the picture of his ex-wife Julie, as he did daily. Morgan still had a disgruntled preoccupation with the demise of his marriage and every time he looked at the picture he was flooded with mixed emotions. He loved her and he hated her. When they met they were smitten. They fell in love, got married, and thought it would be forever, but doesn't everybody? The years went by and his own unreported domestic skirmishes began, which left each one pointing the finger at the other for their difficulties. Morgan held a grudge towards her for her infidelity. His job, his own inadequacies and his drinking alienated her, right into the arms of another. His spirited belief that he could keep it together with suggestions of counselling fell on deaf ears, and she just continued screwing another guy.

He stared at her picture with continued petulance and remembered a regretful incident while returning home from an office get-together. He probably shouldn't have been, but Morgan was driving, having had his share of drink at the party and she wanted to stop for cigarettes. Despite his distaste of her smoking, he pulled into a convenience store and she went in, coming back after only a minute with cigarettes and a carton of chocolate milk. Nothing for him, never even asked. Morgan pointed out her oversight, or perhaps she didn't care to ask, but this nonsensical trivial bickering continued as he drove up the road. She opened her chocolate milk and tipped it to her lips to take a drink. Morgan hit the gas causing the vehicle to jolt forward. She ended up spilling the chocolate milk all over the front of her white blouse with Morgan breaking out into boisterous laughter at his childish prank. They never spoke for days after.

Julie Morgan, now Julie Neilson, daughter of a judge, had resumed using her maiden name. She was now living on the other side of Moravian with her father and they were not on speaking terms in the least. It is apparent each time Morgan finds himself in court, Judge Neilson has it in for him. It transcends the occasional asshole remark and extends to Judge Neilson tossing Morgan's cases out for any petty excuse, an uncrossed 't', a spelling error and Morgan's favorite – he was probably drunk.

Morgan picked up the picture and drew a mustache on her in the dust, and then tossed it back down, cracking the glass. He sat down, laid his head back and promptly fell asleep. The easy chair had a John Morgan sized dent in the cushions and was his primary sleeping area. The bed remained virtually unused since the divorce, and like Sheila Gurracci's bed, no one had been in it since Julie.

* * *

Morgan was awoken by the irritating beeping of his alarm clock and he jerked upwards, grabbing at his palpating heart. His once beautifully tailored grey suit was now beyond wrinkled from having been slept in yet again. With surprising accuracy, he pitched an empty whiskey bottle across the room and struck the clock knocking it from the stand.

"Fuck me, I hate that alarm clock," he grumbled, rubbing at his aching eyes.

He shook the cobwebs out of his brain and groggily arose, half of him now wishing last night was a dream. The fact Jake Gurracci was dead was of no concern; it was the work that it caused Morgan resented.

Why couldn't he have buried Jake, then told no one? Life sure would be easier, Morgan thought as he looked in the bathroom mirror. His face seemed to have aged twenty years in ten to become the leathery catcher's mitt he had always described to himself. His unphotogenic body was now a far cry from the muscles that once adorned his chest and arms with graceful conformity back in his rookie years. He tried to strike a muscular pose without success, then grabbed a quick shower then headed out the door.

As he locked the door he heard the city garbage truck come rumbling up the street. Morgan had plenty of garbage to put out to the curb, but as usual, he put out none, leaving it to decay and stink another week in his house. Morgan noticed Grant pull into his driveway, having just returned home to his basement apartment from his night's assignment. He jumped out of his car with gusto and scurried about to get his bags to the curb, racing against the approaching truck. Morgan stood at the end of his driveway and watched the entertainment. The truck passed Grant's place and headed up the street, knowing well that Grant was trying to rid his apartment of the week's refuse. Grant, with a bag in each hand, started to chase the truck while yelling for them to stop. The employee at the back of the truck hammered on the side and the driver stepped on the accelerator. A dark puff of exhaust escaped the pipe as the large vehicle sped up slightly. The garbage men brayed with robust laughter, as did Morgan.

"The only thing missing here is comical chase music," he said slapping his knee.

Finally, they took pity on Grant and stopped the truck. Grant tossed his bags into the trash scoop, exchanged a derisive glance with the employee who quickly covered his name tag. Morgan honked his horn and waved as he drove by Grant who could only shrug his shoulders before returning the wave, a little embarrassed that Morgan had seen his performance.

* * *

Despite the events of the previous night, it was still business as usual at the Moravian Police Department. Most just shrugged off the murder and remained immersed in their own world, leaving Morgan with all the leg work and not even an offer of help.

"Get any sleep?" Samuels asked as Morgan entered the office.

"A few hours. I'm living. Got that 911 call for me?"

"Few hours for me too, thanks for asking. Here, just pulled it off the computer dispatch. I had it burned onto CD for you."

"Thanks, geezer. I'll listen to it in my office."

Morgan took the CD into his office and shut the door. He wanted to listen to it alone without the distraction of someone breathing over his shoulder throwing off his concentration, or worse, see him drinking from the bottle he kept in his drawer. He put the CD into his police issued laptop that he lugged around and clicked the play icon on the display. He sat back in his chair almost hiding behind the unfinished files, listening as the recording started.

> "Emergency 911."
>
> *"Yes, I'd like to report a problem at 969 Mason Road."*
>
> "What is the nature of the problem ma'am?"
>
> *"A man was beating up a woman."*
>
> "Is he still beating her up?"
>
> *"No, he's not anymore. No...Not anymore..."*
>
> "What's your name? Are you still there? Ma'am, are you still there?"

The voice of the caller seemed female, or possibly a young male, pre-puberty. Morgan, perplexed, listened closely, but that was the end of the dialogue. There was a squishing noise on the line that sounded like someone was ringing out a wash-cloth, then nothing for about thirty seconds. After the short silence, there was a whack, like something had hit the phone. It was followed by another, then another. Morgan counted thirteen in total before the line went dead.

"Fuck me, that didn't help," Morgan lamented.

He sat in his office, just he and his bottle, and played it over and over intently listening. The more he listened, the more the voice was starting to sound like a young male, not a female. He was fraught with subdued animosity as no plausible theory entered his besieged brain and he snapped his laptop closed in frustration. Two hours had flown by in what seemed an instant and the conundrum that was this mysterious call into the dispatch would have to wait.

* * *

Morgan drove the unmarked police unit to the Moravian General Hospital where he knew the pathologist, Dr. Francis Halpin, would be waiting for him to begin the autopsy. Morgan had met Dr. Francis Halpin on many occasions before, most of them being suicides or regular at home deaths of the sick or elderly. He jokingly called Francis Halpin, 'Dr. Death'. Not just because he was a pathologist, whose main job is to cut up dead people to determine cause of death, but because he really seemed to enjoy his work, almost too much. Halpin was a doctor of many credentials, all good, and Morgan would defer to his expertise on the science of death anytime.

Morgan entered the hospital through the emergency entrance. He knew that somewhere in the hospital Sheila Gurracci was in her bed, forever safe from Jake's unrelenting fury. He wondered if she had any of the answers he sought, and if she did would she tell him?

Morgan walked by the surly people in the emergency waiting room. It was quite hot in the crowded hospital and the overworked staff rushed about trying their best to satiate the irritated patients. Some had been waiting more than four hours and tempers seemed to be pushed to the limits again under the remorseless heat.

"Looks like another hot one," Morgan said to a man sitting with his nose covered in bandages. The man with the bandages virtually ignored him at first, until that is, he sat forward in the chair and squinted his eyes incriminatingly at the detective.

"Oops," Morgan whispered under his breath and sauntered like a penguin towards the elevator. The bandaged man jolted to his feet from the waiting room chair and with an outstretched arm and wagging index finger he shouted - "You're the one that brode my node!"

His smashed nasal pathway and the resulting gibberish gave Morgan a well-earned chuckle as the elevator door opened with perfect timing and he stepped inside. The bandaged man charged for the elevator like a rhinoceros bent on revenge only allowing the detective a few precious seconds to get the door closed.

"Close damn it, close," Morgan said, jamming his finger into the button over and over.

The steel doors of the elevator finally came together and Morgan cringed as he heard a thud on the other side.

"Fuh, my node!" The diatribe of profanity laced with pain dissipated as the elevator descended to the sub-basement.

The doors of the elevator opened to a long corridor stinking of a mix of disinfectant and rotting meat. Morgan felt instant relief from the heat, not from the air conditioning, but from the giant refrigerator where Jake Gurracci was stored in his headless slumber.

"Finally!" Halpin said as he sat chatting with the officer who was assigned to guarding the freezer door.

"I second that, why did I have to sit in front of this stupid fucking door all night?" the officer inquired. "It freaked me out, all these bodies in here."

"Continuity, kid. You never know what a lawyer would come up with if you don't take care of your evidence properly."

"Yeah, someone may come in here and kill him again. If you ask me, this asshole deserved it," the officer said.

"Can't argue with you there."

"Besides," said Halpin with childlike giddiness, "it gives me something to play with. Want to stay and watch the fun? I mean, we're gonna turn this guy into a canoe. First we make a 'Y' shaped incision from breast line to pubic bone, then we pull the skin back like opening fleshy curtains and expose his rib cage. Then comes the bone saw – ka chunk, and the breast plate is removed allowing easy access to the goopy guts inside. Once all his guts are out, he'll look like a canoe and we could paddle down the river in his hollowed out chest cavity."

"No thanks. I've been up all night and I can do without your sick camping trip," the officer said, his face a little pale, before he walked into the hall and pushed the elevator button.

"If you see broken nose guy in the waiting room, you don't know me," Morgan called after him. The officer gave a small wave before the steel doors closed and he ascended to the surface.

"You and me again pal," Halpin said. "Okey dokey then, here we go."

He wrenched the handle on the giant metal refrigerator door that housed the dead and slowed the decaying process to an insignificant crawl. He went inside, his white coat blowing under the breeze of the powerful cooling fan. Morgan had seen the inside of the cooling crypt before but each unnerving time was always like the first. The humming of powerful fan and the instant drop in temperature sent a shiver down his spine and goosebumps sprouting along his arms. Morgan stared hypnotically at the white bags flapping to the breeze of the fan and zoned in on the bloody bag perched atop a gurney, alone, in the center of the icy mausoleum.

"Hey doc, sorry I'm late," came a voice from behind them.

"Fuck!" Morgan cursed, almost having a heart attack.

"Sorry, kind of jumpy eh," the thin man smiled.

"Morgan, this is the new guy here, Ted Boland," Halpin said introducing them both, waving a hand as he maneuvered around the gurney.

"How's it going?" Boland said shaking hands with Morgan.

"He's, ah, an intern. He wants to be a pathologist someday too."

"Another sick one," Morgan joked. "I like."

Boland and Halpin pushed the gurney out of the refrigerator. The white bag had bits of dried blood where Jake's neck stump had brushed against the plastic as he was being sealed up last night and Morgan noted the forensic seal that had been placed across the zipper. The two positioned the gurney beside the tray of sharpened cutting implements, each one with a distinct purpose, to cut, rip, tear and shatter. Whether it be the skull chisel, to separate the cranium and expose the brain or the bone saw and rib cutters, the goal was expose the innards like the contents strewn across the floor of a slaughter house, and Halpin relished them all with absurd affection.

"Okey dokey, lift."

The two lifted Gurracci onto the table and despite being devoid of a head he was still heavy. Morgan broke the seal and noted the time in his case file. Without missing a beat Boland unzipped the bag and moved apart the sides to expose Gurracci's lifeless corpse. Morgan exhaled abruptly and turned his head to the side.

"Alright, give me the Vicks," Morgan said pinching his nose shut.

"Why? It doesn't smell," Halpin said, smiling at the detective.

"Yeah, okay, Dr. Death, maybe not to you, but he still fuckin' reeks of B.O."

"There's some on the shelf over there, wussy."

Morgan reached for the Vicks and spread it under his nose. The soothing vapors were good for more than just a stuffy head as the stench of Jake Gurracci's body odor, which had even transcended death, began to lessen.

"Is all this necessary, I mean, I'm not a pathologist yet, but there's no head here," Boland said as he waved his hand around the empty space where Gurracci's head once was.

"My dear young man, pathology is more than just determining the cause of death. It can also help piece together the few remaining hours of his life. What he was doing, what he was eating, alcohol, drugs. Get the picture?"

Boland nodded his head, Morgan bit his bottom lip, getting ready for what Halpin thought of as the fun part.

"Now for the fun part."

"Now for the fun part," Morgan said in a warped sarcastic tone whilst rolling his eyes.

"Bone saw please."

Boland placed the saw in the portly doctor's hand. Morgan turned his head away again as there was an awfully loud crunch as Gurracci's ribs were removed and a tiny smidgeon of blood splashed upwards onto the doctor's white coat, but he paid it no mind, forever immune to the plundering of corpses, and continued without a care. Halpin began to methodically remove his organs, taking samples, recording their weight and making observations all while humming a tune. He poked the scalpel through a sample of Gurracci's pancreas and held it up to Morgan.

"Wanna taste?"

"Piss off," Morgan said shaking his head, leaning away from the sample in disgust. "Raw meat ain't my thing. I'll stick to chicken wings."

"Yes, your love of chicken wings is legendary around these parts. Look here, I'm noticing some internal trauma to the victim, something was jammed down his throat."

"Let's skip using the word victim on this guy. Asshole, prick, dickstick, any of those will do."

"Okey dokey. Well, let's check what you had to eat, shall we?" Halpin sliced open the stomach and almost immediately straightened up, looking perplexingly at the detective. "There's something in here and it is not food."

He tapped on it with the scalpel in over-deliberate motions while looking at Morgan with solemnity on his confounded face. Halpin reached into the opening, his blue plastic gloves were absolutely coated with blood as he fished around in Gurracci's stomach and pulled out a hard, rectangular object.

"It's a goddamn cellular telephone! Check out this, I think someone rammed this thing right down his throat."

"Holy shit, man," Boland said, stepping back. "There's something just not right about this. I mean, I heard this guy deserved to die, but this is downright crazy."

Morgan rubbed the scar on his temple in thought as he exchanged a dismissive glance at the intern's chosen line of inquiry.

"Does it work?"

Dr. Haplin pushed the power button but nothing happened. Morgan then held out an open paper bag and the phone was placed inside to be processed forensically, then stored as evidence.

"Well, I'll make up an official report for you regarding my findings, Morgan. I doubt the tests will reveal anything spectacular so you can bank on decapitation as the cause of death."

"Any idea with what, doc?"

"The wound is pretty clean and uniform," Halpin said pointing to the neck stump and tapped on the spinal cord with his pen. "I'd say one swipe of an axe would do the trick. It would have to be an axe sharper than any of my tools of damnation here. If it was sawn off, it be all jagged and wrecked, but this wound is smooth as silk."

Morgan looked at the bloody tools and grimaced.

Halpin and Boland put Gurracci's organs into a red biohazard bag and threw them into the hollowed out cavity of his chest. They replaced the flaps of skin to their normal position and Boland started to sew him up with an oversized Hagedorn needle and thread. Morgan looked at the cadaver's bare arm. The 'Jake and Shila Forever' jailhouse tattoo was now faded on his pasty blue skin. His unfeigned sense of entitlement to his wife that took him to the lunatic fringe had now taken him straight to hell.

Forever is over I guess. If I had a cheese grater I'd grind that tattoo down to the bone, Morgan mused inwardly.

He walked back down the empty hall towards the elevator, thinking of the timely intervention that undoubtedly saved her life. What kid had called 911? Who dragged him outside and nailed him to the oak tree? No kid could do that. Who even knew she was in trouble? The whole situation was burgeoning with incomprehensible, implausible coincidences but this train of thought was short lived, interrupted by the clang of the refrigerator echoing off the walls and Halpin's jovial call.

"Hey Morgan, you sure you don't want a taste?" he said holding the scalpel with the bloody piece of pancreas dangling like a doggie treat.

Morgan smirked at the doctor's antics. "As tantalizing as that sounds, still taking a pass on that, thanks anyway weirdo."

The elevator doors open and Morgan stepped in, glad to get away from the unusual sense of humor of the strange pathologist. Chicken wings, not pancreas, were definitely the culinary option tonight and the besotted detective almost began to salivate on the spot. He pushed the button for the top floor where Sheila Gurracci would be recovering from the previous night's attempt on her life. He was hoping Sheila would be up and able to speak.

"Can I help you?" a fat snooty nurse said glaring at Morgan as he stepped off the elevator.

"I'd to see Sheila Gurracci, if that's possible."

"I don't think..." she couldn't finish her attempted diatribe before she was interrupted.

"I'll talk to him, please, I'd really like to talk to him," Sheila said from behind the nurse.

The fat nurse lifted her pompous nose in the air and turned around. Morgan cringed at the sight of her ass, which was big enough to have its own time zone, and as she waddled away Sheila came into view. She was holding the loose fitting hospital gown tight to her chest. Her fine, bony face was covered with sizeable bruises, two black eyes, swollen lips and a bandaged head. Her beautiful features were hopefully only temporarily stifled and perhaps poised to return one day as a budding flower returns each spring. She seemed to be standing at an angle and was definitely favoring one side of her aching body with profound difficulty. Morgan found himself staring at the once beautiful woman, not really knowing how to start. Suddenly he felt like snatching at any procrastinary subject, stall, talk about the weather, but he sucked it up forged ahead with his investigation.

"Can I talk to you alone, please?"

She smiled at him gently, brightening up her injured features.

"I remember you…John Morgan. You came when he had bitten me, you saved me after he raped me, you were there when he was released, and you saved me again."

"I didn't save you, but, I like to think I did all I could over the years," he admitted, slightly humble.

"You did, and more. You don't how much just being there means."

Together they walked to the end of the ward, where the collected patients with wheelchairs and walkers stared impolitely at her multi-colored skin.

Morgan ignored their audience, and forged on with what he came up to do. "What do you remember about last night?"

Sheila turned her head to the side, staring hard at the plain walls. She chewed her lip as she willed the energy forward to immerse herself in the memory again. "I remember being alone, being very alone," she started, slowly. "I felt there was no one left in the world that cared about me anymore. I had accepted that I was to die last night, and I was going to, even if it meant at my own hand."

Sheila suddenly stopped and closed her eyes. Morgan reached out and put his hand on her shoulder, something that he had done many times in his career, and she took a step closer to him. One tear escaped her blackened eye and she looked up.

"What happened to him?" she asked, her voice quivering.

"I'm sorry, he's passed away," Morgan said, trying to sugar coat the situation. The gory details of Jake's demise would definitely be deferred for another meeting.

"How? He had called my phone, tormenting me with cruel mind games, but he was already in the house."

"But you said he called you?"

"He called me from inside the house, on a cell phone, from upstairs."

Morgan tightened his grip on the paper bag that contained the cell phone salvaged from the innards of Jake's stomach. He was not about to bring it out and ask her if it was the same phone, not just yet. He was treading cautiously because of her fragile state.

She continued without further prompting, wishing to get the ordeal over and done with. "I remember the look on his face. I'd never seen that look before. Even with all the other things he had done to me, that look was completely different. It was death. He hit my head off the sink, I don't remember anything after that," she tucked her head back down. "Oh yeah, I saw a white light, it was bright, it wasn't a flashlight, it was something more and in that light... I saw an angel dressed in blue."

This made Morgan smile. He pictured Henderson, the first police officer on the scene, or the first paramedic that came to her aid.

"Yeah," he said softly. "You sure did."

Morgan took his hand off her shoulder and before he could say goodbye, Sheila grabbed him with both hands and hugged him as tight as she could. The tears welled up in Morgan's eyes, but he turned his head so she wouldn't see and returned her embrace, unabashed, even though the crippled audience looked on.

"I'm sorry," he managed to get out.

"Don't be."

She no longer held the loose gown against her chest. She was braless under the gown and her tantalizing breasts jangled freely. Morgan averted his eyes to the window but still tried to peek, straining with his peripheral until his reward was a flash of cleavage. She was smiling, a smile as much as could be mustered through bulbous swollen lips, and puffy dark purple cheeks. Again, he wanted to kiss her but always the supreme gentleman, Morgan took his leave of her and walked by the fat snooty nurse, who never acknowledged his departure.

* * *

Morgan returned to the Moravian Police Department with the cell phone that had been dug out of Jake Gurracci's stomach and began the paperwork for forensic processing. Morgan easily backtracked to the cell company by cross referencing the number that came up on the 911 dispatch computer. It was registered to Jake Jones, fake name, fake address. He only assumed, and most likely was right, Gurracci had bought the throw away phone earlier and only Gurracci was dumb enough to use a simplistic alias like Jake Jones. He sat in his squeaky chair and sipped from his bottle of whiskey, meticulously thinking about his next move, then checked the wall clock.

It was his favorite part of the day. Not just because the work day was done, but because it was time to head to Gillespie's Brew House and Tap, Morgan's hang out, the place where he was treated like family. Some lesser bars have about four taps; Gillespie's had a dozen. One dozen of the coldest, most delicious, mouthwatering draft beers in the entire city were adorning the area behind the bar. Not only was the beer selection top notch, but they had an assortment of the smoothest whiskeys known to the Irish, some being specially ordered directly from the factories of Ireland. Aside from the alcohol, Gillespie's was known for having the biggest, juiciest hot wings in town, and Morgan virtually lived on them. Morgan could eat chicken wings every night of his life and never get tired of them, and the hotter the better. His ex-wife Julie had hated hot wings, she had hated everything about Gillespie's including the bartender and be it right or wrong, an alcoholic man would take his pub over his woman, every time. Like Pavlov just rang the bell, Morgan started salivating like a dog at the thought of a shot of whiskey, a cold glass of beer and a pound of hot wings.

The all too familiar chime rang its happy ding-a-ling as Morgan entered the homey pub. The décor was nothing short of pure Ireland, with the green, white and orange flag, dark hardwood wainscoting, county maps, and all complemented with jaunty Irish tunes playing in the background. The smiling bartender waved at the detective as he bellied up to the bar. Morgan never even had to order and the bartender, young reliable Stephen, was pouring a cold glass of draft beer and filling a shot glass with an ounce of whiskey.

"Hot wings for the big dick," Stephen called to the kitchen before sliding the beer down the bar and into Morgan's greedy hand. Stephen neither meant 'big dick' as an insult nor compliment of Morgan's penial prowess, rather a short form of detective.

"Crazy murder that's been on the news today."

Stephen had been Morgan's bartender for many years and while discussing cases was noticeably unprofessional, Stephen considered Morgan family and Morgan felt at ease spilling his life to the man who fills him full of booze. Stephen was a fixture at Gillespie's. He was always there. His blond hair and blue eyes sparkled along with his award winning smile that made the customers feel welcome, and he extenuated a sense of calmness and peacefulness so much that when Morgan sat and drank, he would forget about work, his divorce and perhaps everything vile with the world.

"Fucker lost his head for a piece of tail," Morgan joked and both broke out into boisterous laughter.

A fresh basket of wings seemed to appear out of thin air as they did each visit. Morgan inhaled the fragrance of the special hot sauce as it rose with the steamy goodness that he longed for each day. It was a sauce unique to Gillespie's Brew House and Tap, and even though they were close, it was the one thing Stephen was absolutely forbidden to reveal. Eleven herbs and spices it was not, it was something made by magical leprechauns brewing it in an enchanted cauldron at the end of a fantastic double rainbow.

Morgan devoured the chicken wings and spilled all the majesty and grandeur of the case in an unsanitized tirade to the engrossed wide eyed bartender. After four large draft beers and four shots of some of Ireland's finest whiskey, the two friends shook hands and he departed for home, driving intoxicated in his police issued unmarked cruiser.

* * *

In a dark musty room, a gloved hand held Jake Gurracci's head by the hair. The eyes were rolled upwards in the sockets, the blood had congealed around the stump and his mouth hung open, still frozen in his final scream of anguish. No one else was present in the room, but if they were, they would hear the tone and inflection of a child's voice.

"You can't hurt her anymore. You can't hurt anyone anymore. You were a mean man. So mean. How does it feel to be dead? Does it hurt you like you hurt her? Do you see blackness, or the flames of hell? Those that are mean, need to be taught a lesson. Did you learn?"

The gloved hand held the head up to a dim light that dangled from the ceiling on a single wire, the person having a remote belief that the head may actually answer. The disembodied head of Jake Gurracci remained silent. A gloved thumb rested on Jake's drooped chin and began to move it up and down in an unflattering act of mimicry.

"Yes I did learn, thank you for showing me the way."

Carefully it was placed into a clear plastic bag and tied shut with a knot. The bag was then placed into a small square box, and the box placed upon a shelf that housed many other small square boxes. The strong stench of moth balls filled the air of this dank dungeon. The gloved hand picked up an axe. This implement of callous destruction was specially crafted and honed to be sharper than a Samurai sword with a unique shape to the blade that would make one feel it was not made for chopping wood; it was made for a single purpose, collecting heads. The axe was place upon two hooks secured to the wall, replaced until it was needed again. The gloved hand pulled a string and the light went out.

CHAPTER TWO

DRUGS ARE BAD, DUH

Nobody shed any tears for Jake Gurracci, least of all his wife Sheila. She had cried a thousand rivers and suffered the white hot stinging pain of his rage and now the tears would flow no more. It is said everyone has a mother and Jake was no different, but he had long estranged himself from anyone that had once cared. His body was placed in a plain pine box, which had been paid for out of the city's already tight budget, and even that seemed undeserved to those that had known him. The graveyard was empty, save for the church minister, Detective John Morgan, and an odd looking little man with a shovel. Morgan had earlier made a vow to see him dead, buried and then piss on his grave. The feeling would forever linger like a germ festering in an open wound until the opportunity for pissing could present itself. But Morgan was a patient man.

In an oddly surreal moment, a light rain began to fall on the city. The rain was inexplicably warm, like a hot morning shower, which seemed fitting for Jake's final journey. On cue, the strange little man popped a lever and the cheap coffin was lowered into the shallow depths of the muddy soil as the minister read.

"Ashes to ashes, and dust to dust, God, please have mercy on this, your child."

He spoke in a monotone that contained both equal parts of boredom and tedium. It was obvious he was just humoring his duties to the clergy and really wished he was somewhere else. Like Morgan, maybe he wanted to go to Gillespie's, but it was doubtful.

Morgan stood at the foot of the grave as the dismal rain fell harder. The water droplets skipped across the top of the coffin in the feather light breeze as it descended into the ground. The funny man with the shovel popped open an umbrella and held it over the minister's head. The rain soaked his bald head and the two or three long scraggly hairs that remained on his wrinkled dome as he smiled a toothless grin towards Morgan. The coffin stopped at the bottom of the pit, which now had turned into a muddy slippery sink hole. Unthinking, Morgan stepped closer to the edge of the grave hoping the minister would continue reading in the same robotic way with his head planted in the pages of the funeral manuscript and not notice Morgan spit. He snorted, then horked up an impressive loogie, however the minister looked back up. Thinking perhaps this was not the time he changed his mind, swallowed the mucus, and turned from the edge. He was too close and he began to slip in his cheap brown loafers that lacked the proper traction to withstand the pouring rain. There was nothing for him to grab as he frantically flailed his arms and he started to fall forward landing on top of the thin coffin lid and crashing through.

Morgan found himself face to face, or rather face to stump, with Jake's headless corpse. It had not been embalmed, just thrown in the coffin and the maggots had already begun their dance of decay on his rotting cadaver. In a great gush of panic, he scrambled to the end, doing a country two step all over the body while brushing the maggots that had stuck to his muddy suit. His foot caved into Jake's empty chest and Morgan lost his shoe into what he thought may have been the pancreas. He met the out-stretched hand of the church minister and he assisted Morgan out of the mud-laden grave with one good heave. As though both frightened with disturbing some delicate equilibrium in the morose atmosphere of the cemetery, with unspoken words, they agreed to never mention it. The man with the shovel had an evil crooked smirk on his face, and laughed in a high pitched manner, as though he had orchestrated the whole thing himself. Morgan had to restrain himself from wiping it off with a blow from his fist, but second guessed himself as it suddenly began to seem funny to him too, notwithstanding the fact Morgan didn't need a second broken nose guy wanting revenge. The coffin lid was shattered, exposing the body to the elements and the rain began to soak the inside.

The minister, who had been interrupted from his readings, decided not to finish. He sighed, closed his book, made a crucifix motion on his chest, then walked through the rain towards the church in sinister silence. The man with the shovel, still smiling at Morgan, began to throw dirt onto the collapsed coffin. Scoop by scoop, Jake Gurracci, his legacy, and Morgan's loafer, disappeared forever. Morgan hobbled through the wet grass of the cemetery, back through the rusty gate that swung freely in the wind and back to his unmarked police car. He could hear the funny little man singing 'Go Tell it on the Mountain' in an irritating shrill cadence as he worked in the rain without a care.

* * *

In the weeks to follow everyone in the office had some kind of opinion on the murder, call it coffee talk or water cooler gossip, everyone had to chime in with their two cents. There was Grant, who thought Sheila and a mystery new boyfriend had killed Jake and gone bowling with his head. Samuels, the old codger, thought it may be an enemy Jake had made while in jail as two years in a correctional facility can drum up other criminals who would just as soon kill a person than have to look at them. Whatever the situation that had led to his murder, there was no mournful grandeur, no redeeming acts of exculpation, and no one was sorry he was gone.

"Missing person, Henderson," Samuels called over the office page system.

Henderson ceased typing at his computer and went to the garage to see Samuels. He was puffing on his trademark cigar in the corner and Henderson held his breath as he wafted away the cloud in search of his commanding officer.

"Need you to take a missing fifteen-year-old being reported from a couple at the front desk," Samuels said, in between a puff of smoke. "They state their daughter hadn't been seen in more than a day. She probably just ran away; you know troubled kids."

"No problem, sir," Henderson said.

Calls like this were routine at the station. The information is gathered from the parents, police check all possible destinations and speak to those that last saw the missing party, then wait. Teenagers with heightened emotions that express themselves most typically with destructive behavior are trodden into the police station in hopes the police can become parent for a day. This scared straight tactic hardly ever works so the teen runs, their perceived world falls in tatters, crashing down around them. They usually always show up after a cooling off period or when they find making it on their own when they are so young is not as easy as they think.

Henderson interviewed the parents of the missing teenaged girl. She was a troubled young woman, having had a few brushes with the law over petty issues like shoplifting and truancy. Jenny McGrath entered her teenage years following the wrong crowd. She was on her way to becoming the next Sheila Gurracci, stuck in a circle that she could not escape, if there was no intervention. She had run away twice before, but had always returned after a day. Henderson completed his questionnaire to her parents and bid them good day.

"Give us a call if you hear from her."

Being new, he kept an open mind to the situation, because you never know, it could be that one time where the child fails to return, ever.

"Where are we off to?" Grant asked as they both got in the police cruiser.

"Got a missing girl, runaway most likely, I have to check out a few possible destinations." Henderson paused, his mouth open, before he started waving his hands in front of his face. "Jesus Christ you fuckin' shit your pants!"

"Jesus Christ never shit his pants, just me."

Grant was laughing at the fart he was holding in just to let it go in the cruiser when they both got in. The enclosed space of the cruiser filled with stink as Grant, with a goofy grin on his face, wafted the air towards the suffocating Henderson. He never even got a chance catch some fresh air, let alone even leave the station parking lot, when he was called upon by the police dispatcher.

"Moravian dispatch to unit with Henderson."

"Go ahead," Henderson answered rolling the windows down and gasping for air.

"Please attend the Chatham Street Bridge, we have a report that a male person is standing on the outside of the side-walk guard threatening to jump. I have ambulance rolling to the area."

"10-4. Officer Grant and myself are on our way."

"I'll head that way as well," Morgan said over his radio. He took a sip of the whiskey bottle and put it into his inner suit pocket and put his car in gear.

With lights blazing and sirens wailing Henderson and Grant sped towards the bridge. Few cars pulled over for the highly visible police cruiser, as is usually the case. Motorists become mesmerized or hypnotized by the colorful flashing of the police car roof lights. They just continue driving, their gaze shifts between the road and the rear view mirror. Their brain just can't seem to process something as simplistic as pulling to the side and letting them by.

The bridge he was standing on overlooked another highway. Vehicles of all types, including the odd tractor trailer unit, were zipping to and fro underneath the bridge on the busy thoroughfare. A group of pizza-faced high school students adorned in their lettermen jackets had congregated on the adjacent side, each held their cell phones at arm's length to record the action. In an insensitive act that lapsed to the brink of criminality, one of the insensitive teens in the crowd jokingly started chanting, and monkey see monkey do, the rest joined in.

"Jump, jump, jump, jump."

The teens quickly shut their vulgar mouths when Henderson and Grant exited their police cruiser leaving the flashing red lights active and blocking off access to the bridge. The jumper had scaled the protective rail and now teetered on a two inch outcropping of cement, keeping his balance with just one hand on the bridge rail.

Henderson cautiously approached the young male. His purposeful dainty tread smacked of inexperience, which led the crowd to surmise this dire situation was better suited to a skilled negotiator, but there was none so Henderson had to think fast to try and calm this desperate man.

"Get the fuck away from me pig!" the jumper screamed at Henderson.

Grant was keeping a growing crowd at bay. The two officers needed help, but the situation was theirs to command for the time being.

"I just want to help. Please come back over, we'll talk about it, whatever it is, we'll get through it," Henderson said with a quivering voice. "What's your name?"

"Curtis, but what do you care?" he said, his speech slightly slurred.

He began to lean outward, swaying in the open air as the traffic below still zoomed in both directions with the occasional driver looking up to see the jumper teetering on the edge. Grant left the crowd to mill about on their own and nimbly leapt over a rail like a svelte gazelle. He started climbing down an embankment overgrown with dry thorny prickles, desperately trying to get to the highway below to stop traffic.

"Hold on, Curtis, hold on. Let's talk, I want to help. Don't do anything drastic, please man, just hold on. My name is Cliff. I hope you can come back over the rail and we'll sit down and talk."

Curtis was crying, his eyes wide and dilated. He looked to Henderson to be about twenty years old, rabbity in appearance, extremely disheveled and it wasn't hard to perceive he was tripping out on drugs.

"What the fuck do you think you can do cop, pay my debts? I'm in so deep you don't make enough money and Skinny will kill me anyway. I smoke the rock every day, I fucking need it. Yeah, I'm a junky, who cares about a fucking junky?"

"I care Curtis, just climb back over and I promise you'll get help."

Curtis looked down towards the road below. The portentous lettermen that had gathered knew it would be a fatal fall should he go over and were hoping Death would arrive and give Curtis just a tiny extra shove, send him to the pavement below, so they could post his fall online. Henderson inched his body closer to the rail while keeping a sharp scrutiny at Curtis' limp hand holding on to keep his balance. Grant frantically climbed downward, charging recklessly through the thorns, until he lost his footing and began an uncontrolled roll for the last twenty-five feet. The barbs slowed his downward momentum saving him from careening out onto the roadway, but drove their painful spikes into his arms and face.

"You don't understand...nobody does."

"Take it man." Henderson held out his large hay slinging hand. "Please...we'll get through this...please, take it."

The hand that was keeping him from dropping began to relax, then went completely flaccid. Henderson lunged towards him but only managed to grab a handful of his shirt. The falling body was too heavy and the flimsy shirt tore as easily as a damp tissue under the weight. The two young officers were now helpless; a helplessness neither had experienced before. The man they had just tried to save plummeted to the highway below just as Grant reached the pavement, unable to stop any traffic. Henderson could not turn away. He never took his eyes off the body as it plunged downward in its final decent to be collected by Death. A few screams emanated from the crowd of onlookers, and suddenly the group of teens, their malicious pleasure stifled, changed their tune and were silent. The body hit the cement hard and Curtis died instantly.

"For God's sake stop!" Grant yelled to an approaching tractor trailer, but the officer dared not step in front of the approaching vehicle for his own safety.

Grant could do nothing but watch the tractor trailer totally destroy Curtis' body, and for just a half of a second, Grant caught the bottomless black eyes of the driver and his smiling skeletal face surrounded by a dark hood as the transport screeched to a halt leaving two long trails of steaming melting rubber and a third long trail of blood and bowels. The driver vaulted out, screaming in shock and burying his face into his black hoodie, forever traumatized at the sight before him.

Henderson closed his eyes and bit his bottom lip, tears glistening in his eyes as the ambulance arrived, shortly followed by Sgt. Samuels and Detective Morgan, all too little, too late.

"Come on pal, let's go sit down," Morgan said putting his hands on Henderson's shoulders.

The emotionally wrecked officer went and sat in his cruiser. When Henderson was alone the imperceptibility of the moment hit hard, and after he made sure no one was looking, he let it all out. Henderson looked through his glassy eyes and saw Samuels speaking to a man and a woman. She was hysterical, her legs wobbled and surrendered to gravity but was just barely caught by the man, who was shouting loudly at the sergeant. It would later be deduced that one of the high school lettermen knew the parents, and summoned them to the scene.

"How many times have you put my son in jail?" Curtis' father shouted at Samuels. "How many times and he still got no help. It's like that all the time with you cops. You arrest him, you beat him up, you charge him for drugs and he's back out on the street."

"Hold on, that's not fair," Samuels said to the irate man.

"My boy is dead and I'm going to fucking sue you assholes...you did nothing."

"We did all we could, sir, our officers..."

"Your officers did shit!"

Henderson heard this as plain as day, and it drove his desolation even lower.

Why the fuck do we bother? He despaired inside his mind as he pondered his career choice. *Maybe this shit isn't for me.*

"Hold on. You just hold it right there!" Samuels said with an air of authority. "Your son was hooked on crack. I'm sorry he's gone but I take exception to the fact you think we beat him up and I definitely take exception to the fact you think my officers did nothing. They tried their damnedest to save his life. He was your son, what did you ever do to help him? And if you talk like that about my boys again I'll paste your ass all over this bridge."

Curtis' father backed down as Samuels puffed his chest like a rooster to make himself fractionally bigger, a dominate male in charge of a flock. Henderson felt a little better having heard that and admired the cigar chomping Samuels in a whole new light. He was no longer the hard assed supervisor he had come to know him as.

"I understand that this is the most difficult thing a parent has to deal with," Samuels said in a lighter tone. "Let us know if there is anything we can do."

Curtis' parents, fraught with sorrow, held each other tight. His father looked angrily towards Samuels and Morgan and with a lopsided grimace, he bit his upper lip.

"You want to know what you can do! I'll tell you what you can do!" his voice crackled. "You can get that bastard that put the drugs in my son's hand! Kill that bastard that gives this city his poison."

Morgan went over to Henderson's cruiser and tapped at the window.

"You okay, kid?" he asked.

"Yeah, I guess."

"You can't save them all. That's just one of the harsh realities of this business. It's hard not to let it drag you down. Sometimes you do all you can and people think you didn't do enough. You can't save them all."

"I could use a drink."

"Now you're talking," Morgan smiled, his breath already smelling of booze.

Grant stood at the bottom of the bridge. All the traffic was now stopped and the highway was coated with black and red. The driver of the transport wailed with his hands covering his pained face as he was being loaded into an ambulance by Andy the paramedic. His shiny ice blue uniform shirt and trousers were still sharply pressed in remarkable show of dedication to his craft. He stared upwardly to the screaming distraught father, then nodded a friendly 'how do ya do' in Grant's direction but it just seemed to bounce off the dazed officer's skull. Grant was fighting a one on one battle with his stomach contents, a losing battle. The true loser ended up being the tractor trailer's back tire as he jettisoned a stream of vomit in a weirdly familiar pattern on the smoking rubber.

"You puked in the shape of the state of Florida. That's freakin' amazing. How about you kid, you okay?" Morgan said startling the zoned out Grant.

Grant looked up to the top of the bridge, and then looked back at the detective.

"How?"

"There's a path on the other side."

Grant held up his arms and looked at the dozens of thorns that impaled his flesh leaving his arms a puffy, reddish, itchy mess.

"Fuck."

"We're going to grab a drink, you coming, pukey?"

"Nah, I don't drink. I think I just need to chill at home."

"Hey, easy on the garbage man," Morgan joked.

Grant smiled and chuckled embarrassingly. "If you put the trash out at seven AM they come at noon. If you wait, they come at seven AM and you're chasing them up the road. How about a little consistency people, and you my good detective, are a sarcastic turd."

"I'll get you a mop and bucket and you can get to work on this guy."

The inappropriate comedy made Grant laugh even harder and Morgan felt better; at least he got him to smile.

* * *

The bell over the bar room door was again music to Morgan's ears. Gillespie's was always a welcoming, hospitable atmosphere. He and Henderson walked in and sat down along the bar. Other patrons were scattered around the attractive Irish pub as the two officers bellied up to the bar. Stephen looked up from wiping down a glass.

"Hey Morgan, what can I get for your friend?" Stephen asked.

He poured a glass of cold beer and a shot of whiskey and sat it in front of the detective.

"Uh, beer, please," Henderson answered.

"My young friend, meet Stephen the bartender, not Stevie, not Stephan and this man knows more about me that anyone, better than I know myself, kind of scary sometimes. If you ever need someone to talk to, Stephen here is your man."

"It's not like I have a choice," Stephen said jokingly. "What's up tonight guys?"

"Another junkie bites the dust."

"Yeah, caught some on the news. Hey, I saw you there," Stephen said looking at Henderson.

Henderson nodded his head and sighed.

"Listen man, don't sweat it. Here, on the house, you earned it."

Stephen slid a large glass of draft in front of Henderson. He picked it up and sucked half of it down. It tasted good, wonderfully good.

"Well, welcome to Moravian kid."

Morgan held up his beer and the two clinked glasses and drank the rest down.

"You know what to do, Stephen."

"You got it, big dick," he said promptly replenishing their empties.

"Two baskets of deep fried heaven Stephen. Kid, Gillespie's has the greatest hot wings on the planet earth. The secret hot sauce is to die for, and when I croak, I want to be buried in a giant take out box filled with Gillespie's wings."

Henderson wasn't really paying too much attention to Morgan's raving hot wing review.

"So what do you think about what he said?" Henderson asked Morgan.

"About what who said?"

"That guy's dad, I'm never going to forget what he said. It still rattling around in my head, you know, that we did shit."

"You heard it from me, you heard it from Stephen, you did all you could. Drink up, move on."

"Yeah, you're right. Fuck it."

"You got it kid."

"But still," Henderson couldn't seem to let it go. "Why don't we get the asshole who's selling all the dope?"

"I'm swamped as it is. I'm trying to find out who butchered Jake Gurracci, remember? If I recall you're hot on the trail of a runaway teenager. You can't do everything. You can't please everyone. If you try, you'll burn out and become, well, like me."

Morgan held up his beer, made a goofy face to make Henderson smile, as he had earlier done to Grant, all the while the toe tapping tune Irish Washerwoman played in the background.

"Hey, from what I've seen so far, I don't think it would be that bad."

Morgan couldn't help but also smile at the young officer's compliment. That was not the first time he'd ever heard anyone say they wouldn't mind turning out like him, but if they only knew the true Morgan that existed behind closed doors, he was sure they'd change their mind.

"Eat 'em and weep," Stephen said placing the baskets of wings on the bar.

"Ah, me favorite. Enjoy, kid," Morgan said, digging into the saucy greatness that was his deep fried dinner with gusto.

Henderson picked up a hot wing and bit in.

"Shit, fuck, what the hell is this!" he said dropping the hot wing back into the basket.

Morgan and Stephen began to laugh as Henderson picked up his beer and chugged in vain to extinguish the fire in his mouth.

"Too hot, too hot. Why would you do this? That ain't cool."

"Hot? It's not hot," Morgan laughed at Henderson whose face was becoming redder, much like the mercury in a thermometer rising to burst out the top.

"My mouth is not the numb, dry, leathery flesh that yours is. This is fucking hot."

"A secret sauce like no other," Stephen bragged, still chortling.

"What's it made of?" Henderson asked, his burning tongue wagging about his chin like a panting dog.

"Sorry, buddy, I am sworn to take it to the grave, Gillespie's secret forever."

They sucked back a few more, and a few more after that as Henderson's mouth returned to normal.

Closing time came too fast. Empty pints lined the bar and it was now one o'clock in the morning. Morgan and Henderson slid off their bar stools and zig-zagged towards the door. Henderson didn't feel much better, his insecurities stymied only briefly by a false sense brought upon by the alcohol.

Morgan was careful not to drive in his condition in front of Henderson as he normally would have after a fancy blue collar evening with beer, wings and whiskey. They staggered out into the warm summer night. The air Henderson breathed was thick with the dejection of the day and the hanging carbon wafting from the noisy muffler of an idling black Monte Carlo just ahead. The dim lights that lined the sidewalk were somewhat blurry to the two newfound drinking buddies. Morgan whistled the Irish Washerwoman that had been playing earlier. The black Monte Carlo parked askew on the corner stunk with criminality, perversion and a hint of marihuana. It was odd he had never noticed it in this area before, but he definitely knew the car, and its occupants. There were two inside the vehicle, and two leaning in the window. It didn't take a rocket scientist to know what was going on and Henderson, being inexperienced, looked as if he was about to open his mouth and spring into cop mode.

"Not now, kid," Morgan whispered. "Just keep walking."

They continued on by the obvious drug deal. Morgan glanced inside as they passed and catching the passenger's eye, there was recognition as the sound of crappy rap music emanated from the dirt bag hot rod. Morgan much preferred the sound of fingernails scratching on a chalk board or a jolly Irish tune to rap music. In the spilt second he looked in, he saw a bag with white powder and cash in the driver's hand. The two leaning in the window, he did not know, perhaps buyers or other addicts like Curtis looking for a fix. They walked on by, not stopping or saying a word. The rap music was just a distant low bass like thump when Henderson finally spoke.

"Man, why didn't we do anything?"

"Number one, I don't have a gun, something I like when busting up a drug deal. Number two, kid, we're drunk. You don't turn on the power when you're drunk. Remember when you asked me back there if we could get the asshole who's selling all the dope, well, there they are. I mean, they don't sell all the dope, but I'd say the heaviest hitters in town. I've just never seen them this far out. They're expanding their territory, which ain't good. The music sucked too."

"Who were they? I mean, just so I know for the future."

Morgan rubbed the side of his temple. He was too drunk for Henderson's questions but humored him anyway.

"The driver was Skinny-boy or Todd Smilie; I hear he's got a twin brother. The passenger was Willie; his full name escapes me. They're the main suppliers to the area and that kid that jumped today, I guarantee he bought his trip from those pecker heads. I'm going to say it to you again kid, let it go. We got a specialized unit that looks after that shit. Don't let it drag you down."

Morgan said those words of wisdom knowing perfectly well what Henderson was feeling inside because he had been there once himself in the early years of his career, before he became cynical and jaded. Even he, as a new police officer, had an urge to stomp out crime every time he saw it but had long since learned to coexist with the bullshit of the world. Henderson was yet to become numb and desensitized like the inside of Morgan's hot wing eating mouth.

"Hey, I had a good time. Thanks for taking me out," Henderson said.

"No problem. Stick with it, you'll be fine."

Henderson hailed a passing a cab, the two shook hands and headed for home. Morgan didn't want a ride and continued his walk through the muggy night to try and clear his soused brain while Moravian slept. He walked for about a half an hour before the street lights were just a haze in the distance. He hadn't taken a wrong turn. His tread had the clumsy deliberation of the very drunk yet the destination was purposeful and soon he could make out the silhouette of a steeple up ahead. He strained his neck upwards towards the bell tower and wondered if there was something more at work here, or was this just a drunk in his nightly stupor. He could see the face of Jesus looking back at him from the massive crucifix displayed on the steeple. The ubiquity of his features was stunning as wherever Morgan stood, Jesus seemed to be looking right at him. Morgan was never one for religion; he usually scoffed at those wasting their Sundays in church, but hardly worse than him wasting his Sundays on hangovers. Morgan sat on the church steps to rest a minute. One couldn't help but reflect on life and death when in this setting and looking at Jesus on the cross brought visions of Jake Gurracci nailed to the tree in the same fashion. He thought of the scar on his temple and he thought of Sheila's smiling face.

"Sorry Jeez, I got a promise to keep."

Morgan walked around to the side of the church using only the light on his phone to guide him. The rusty gate creaked as he pushed it open and entered the graveyard. In the day, the tombstones are gentle reminders of our loved ones, celebrating their existence, but at night, they take on a whole different meaning. The graves cast malevolent shadows in the moonlight as the detective navigated through the dark cemetery. He shortly arrived at the plot where Jake Gurracci was buried. It appeared to be falling into neglect already. Built of the cheapest material, its face had moss sprouting outwards, filling in the crevice that bore the Gurracci name and no passages of loving remembrance to be found anywhere.

"Jake, I hope you're having a good time in hell," Morgan slurred, unbuckling his pants. "Have a drink on me, asshole."

Morgan urinated all over the tombstone with malicious pleasure. Since he had been drinking all night, there was an impressive amount. He tried to write '*Morgan was here*' in piss letters, but it kind of came out '*Marin wos her*' as it was hard to write in perfect cursive with his piss, especially when drunk, but quite convincingly got the job done.

Henderson sat silently in the back of the cab. His mind was a haze of alcohol, which amplified his emotions, and he just stared blankly out the window and dwelled on his day, the drug dealers and the ferocious end to a troubled man.

"Here you go, buddy," the cab driver said as he pulled up to Henderson's place.

Henderson just sat and continued to stare vacantly out the cab window.

"Hey, you okay?"

"Yeah, here you go," Henderson said snapping back to reality and handing the driver a twenty.

He walked up the stairs to his empty apartment which was as empty as he felt inside.

"That asshole should be dead!" he shouted to no one. "Not Curtis." Henderson threw his keys across the room in anger. "I'm going to get that son of a bitch. I'll get the son of a bitch that put that poison in his hand!"

His words echoed the words he had heard today from Curtis' father. He sat down on his couch and put his face in his hands. In the alcohol induced emotional outburst, he pictured Curtis falling, the sound of his body hitting on the hard pavement, and the transport that turned him into an unrecognizable mess. He reached in his pocket and pulled out the torn piece of Curtis' shirt, held it in his hands and then clenched his fist around the material.

"I swear to God, he'll get his."

The tall gangly farm boy had begun the typical stressed cop transformation. He curled up into a ball on his couch and fell asleep, still holding the fragment of cloth.

Morgan had finally made it home, stumbled into his kitchen proud as a drunk peacock that he had kept his promise. He fumbled around his refrigerator looking for something to cure his munchies and picked through various Tupperware containers, most of which contained moldy leftovers from Gillespie's. He grabbed some milk and began to chug it straight from the carton however all that filled his dry mouth was curdled white chunks of milk mucus. He made a retching noise and spit all the slimy grossness into the sink while stumbling sideways into the counter.

Why do I live in this shithole? he thought. *And why didn't I get an order of wings to go?*

He ended up just eating some old dried cereal out of the box, not realizing a mouse had eaten through the bottom of the cardboard and he left a trail of Cheerios across the floor toward his easy chair.

"This is my life, see what you did you old bag!" he said to his ex-wife's picture. "Rotten milk and crappy dry cereal in the box... I'm king of the world!"

Morgan poured one more shot of whiskey and sucked it back with shaky hands. He laid his head onto the soft cushions of his easy chair and fell asleep with an earsplitting snore.

* * *

Forty-eight hours later, Henderson and Grant were both on a day off, yet they found themselves together in Henderson's truck, driving through a poor neighborhood.

"You told me we were grabbing a coffee," Grant stated, glancing around at their surroundings with obvious distaste.

"Just a little detour. There's something I want to check."

The neighborhood housed your typical low income families. The rent controlled townhouses were in a state of major disrepair with non-functional vehicles that were eyesores in most of the driveways, laundry hung from balconies and barely clothed children played in the yards without footwear.

"You wanted to check on the slums did you?" Grant asked.

"Not just that, Morgan and I saw these guys on our way home the other night. He told me they probably supplied that Curtis guy with his drugs."

"So?"

"So, I want to take him down when we go back to work."

"Oh, I get it, I'm on duty right now, and I just don't know it. I was pretty shaken up then, but a good night's sleep and I got a whole new perspective. It's like this...who gives a shit! I mean, look at these people. Half of them don't want to work because their welfare will be reduced, the other half are addicted to drugs. I worked hard and got a good job, why can't they?"

"That's why," Henderson said pointing to the Monte Carlo he saw the other night.

It was parked in a driveway at one of the run down shacks in the neighborhood, far from the million dollar mansions those at the top of the drug chain enjoyed. All the kids seemed to be purposely staying away from the shack. It was obvious they knew who lived there, what went on and it scared most of them. No one in the area would tell the police what or who they saw coming and going from there so the drugs flowed unimpeded. Skinny-Boy had the neighborhood in his grip of fear. His reckless reliance on the threat of violence guaranteed no one would dare stand up against him.

"So they don't have to go far to get their dope. Take that for example. If drug dealers make so much money, why does he live in a shit shack like that?" Grant said. "Can we get that coffee now? There's something about being in this crap hole without a gun that I don't care for."

The two off-duty officers pulled into the local donut shop and sat by the front window. They picked the shadier of the tables as the sun was so hot it melted the glaze off the fresh donuts into a circle of liquid sugar.

"Hot one today," Henderson started. Grant nodded without looking, more intent on fixing his coffee to his liking.

"Been hot for a while, feels like hell's come to town."

"So, what do you think...I mean, how should we go about it?"

"Go about what?"

"The drug dealer's man, ain't you been listening."

Grant sat back in his chair and took a sip on his coffee.

"Come on pal, leave it to those in the know. We're too new to be pulling the kind of shit you're thinking of, anyway, I thought you were working on a missing girl."

"Jenny McGrath, I'll check on her when I go back tomorrow. She was a habitual runaway so she's probably home by now."

"Right. But listen, I'm telling you as a friend, talk to Samuels or Morgan before you try to take down this Skinny what's his name."

Henderson and Grant finished their coffee and parted for the rest of the day. Henderson sat behind the wheel of his truck, parked just up the street from the dealer's house, still haunted. He stared like a possessed man, thinking, planning while he watched people come, stay inside for a short period of time, then leave.

Why isn't anything being done about this? he thought irately.

Henderson thought back to his not so long ago days at the academy and the lectures he attended on the problems of drugs. It was a problem that had a snowball effect in which not only did it turn a person into an addict, they would take the money that put food on the table, paid the rent or put clothes on their kids backs and just buy drugs with it. They'd ultimately lose their jobs, if they had one, and turn to crime to pay for the habit. Henderson scowled behind the wheel of his truck as he eyed the Monte Carlo with Skinny-Boy and Willie back out of the driveway. The muffler on the Monte Carlo was louder than a jet signaling to the neighborhood that the drug dealers were out for business. Some of the kids on the street stopped what they were doing and watched the noisy black car pass. At that time, Henderson developed a simplistic plan for what he would do on his next shift to quench the emotional beast inside his mind.

* * *

The atmosphere was business as usual at the police station. There was a constant ringing of the phones and endless trails of paper were being shuffled from person to person, most hoping if they got passed around enough, they would disappear. It was business as usual in Moravian, except in the mind of young Henderson.

"How you doing, kid?" Morgan asked, slapping his hand on Henderson's shoulders.

"Better, thanks. Mouth still hurts from those damn hot wings."

"Hang in there, champ. The more you eat, the easier it gets."

"Yeah, I suppose, gotta go patrol."

Henderson snagged a set of cruiser keys off the hook headed out alone. He took extra care to drive through the low income housing as often as he could throughout the day. The Monte Carlo remained stationary in the brown soil driveway of the rundown shack. He kept himself in a ready state; he was hyper-vigilant, more this day than any other. He felt like a rattlesnake ready to strike. As soon as that vehicle moved, he'd swoop in and get the bastards. He thought of nothing but the black Monte Carlo. As it happened the previous day, people came to the house, stayed for a few minutes then they left.

One guy in particular, was gone about twice as long as everyone else. When he emerged from the house, he had blood pouring out of his mouth and was hunched in pain as he shuffled up the street. He made eye contact with Henderson as he drove up.

"You all right, buddy?" he said rolling down the cruiser window.

"Fuck off, pig!"

"Have a good day, sir."

He was not worried about him today, usually he would, but right now he was out for the big fish. The area children would immediately stop what they were doing and wave each time he drove by. He couldn't help but wave back and feel a little sorry for these kids and the dismal future that lay ahead for most of them. Notwithstanding the fact that breaking out of the slums was an insurmountable task, perhaps what he was planning may help them, even if it was just one. He went around the block again, wondering if that car would ever move but when he pulled around the corner and back into the view of Skinny-Boy's ramshackle drug house, the Monte Carlo was gone.

"Shit, no!" Henderson cursed. "It was just here."

He peered over his left shoulder with an anguished look on his face. He stepped hard on the accelerator and the cruiser rapidly sped up.

"That shit box didn't pass me, so it has to be in front of me."

Henderson's heart began to race and his hands got sweaty as the Monte Carlo started to come into view. The young officer got an uneasy feeling about this whole thing. The police cruiser was now right behind the Monte Carlo and he could see a skinny silhouette in the driver's seat and another in the passenger's seat. Henderson watched intently, his eyes stringently affixed on the occupants, quick to notice any movements inside.

Henderson activated the police emergency equipment and it flashed away in a brilliant display of red and blue. The Monte Carlo continued for another block when he was sure he saw the driver hand something to the passenger.

"Got you, asshole," he said as the vehicle pulled over.

He nervously tapped the handle of his pistol as he exited the police vehicle. He had never done anything like this before and was hoping he could bullshit his way through it hoping to get the big score. He walked up to the driver's window, and looking down the tall powerful cop could only see his own reflection in the glass of the Monte Carlo. Henderson, peeved, tapped on the window.

The driver's window came down approximately six inches and Todd Smilie looked Henderson in the eyes as if to challenge him to make a move. Henderson swallowed a lump and gathered his composure the best he could.

"Driver's license, registration and proof of insurance, uh, please," his voice fluttered a bit.

Smilie jumped all over that.

"Fucking rookie ass wipe," Smilie chuckled. "It's up my skinny ass if you want to look at it I'll have to bend over and spread, but you'd probably love that, its where your lunch hangs."

Willie began to laugh at Smilie's disobedience towards the rookie but Henderson, though nervous, remained steadfast, massive and gauntly. He asked again with more confidence.

"Driver's license, registration and proof of insurance, sir."

He said the 'sir' a little more forcefully. He could also detect the unmistakable odor of marihuana. Willie sat silently in the passenger's seat saying nothing but he seemed edgy, uneasy. He was hiding something; even a newer cop could see that. The tiny hairs on the back of Henderson's neck stood on end. One could call it a spider sense or cop sense. Something definitely wasn't right here. Smilie fidgeted with his identification and finally handed over his driver's license.

"Registration and proof of insurance sir."

"I ain't got it, go ahead and write me up for it. I don't give a shit, I could use some toilet paper."

Unimpressed by Todd Smilie's rant he remained focused on the job at hand and turned his attention to Willie.

"How about you, sir, may I see your identification?"

"No."

"Sir, I detect the odor of a narcotic and I wish to search your vehicle."

"Fuck you, you ain't searching shit. You can search down my pants and suck on my sweaty ball bag. You ain't got shit on me pig."

Henderson lost it, just on the inside.

"Get out of car, sir, you're under arrest for possession of a narcotic."

"WHAT?" Smilie said, his voice erupting with surprise. "What fucking dope, you see any dope! Go ahead and arrest me and I'll sue the shit out of you, you ain't got fuck all on us."

Smilie, in his shifty lawyer tirade, was right. Henderson was unsure if he could arrest them on the smell of weed alone, but he kept going forward, sticking to his gut feeling.

"I'll ask you again to step out of the car, sir, you're under arrest. You're also under arrest, don't move until I tell you," he said looking at Willie.

"You're finished. I'm suing the fuck out of you."

Smilie jumped out of the driver's seat, he was fuming; his fists were clenched tightly and quaking. He stood face to face with the big farm boy but Henderson, knowing there was no turning back, refused to relent. Smilie was as tall as Henderson but about half his weight. Henderson spun Smilie around with one of his colossal hands and pushed him against the side of the Monte Carlo. Skinny knew he couldn't win a physical fight with Henderson, so he continued to try and play with the officer's mind.

"Fucking rookie pig, my lawyer's going to have your job."

Henderson did a routine side of the road frisk search on Smile – nothing found, and put him in the rear of the police cruiser.

"Step out of the car please," he asked of Willie.

Without any protest Willie exited the car and was also cuffed. He remembered something being passed to Willie and he hoped that it was something, anything, because at this point, he really had nothing solid. He leaned Willie over the hood of the car and kicked his legs apart while Todd Smilie continued to shout expletives at him from the police cruiser cage. He patted down this foolishly doting side kick and found a bag containing homemade rolled marihuana cigarettes in his front pockets. There was approximately ten in the baggie. Henderson was almost ecstatic at this find, he cackled inside with sycophantic laughter, he felt he had the bastards.

"Got nothing on you, eh? Well, let's see what the judge says about your joints. Now, what's your name?"

Willie shook his head and did not reply to Henderson's question.

"Tony No-Telly I guess," Henderson said sarcastically and put Willie in the back with Todd Smilie. He called for a tow truck and had Smilie's Monte Carlo impounded.

"Let's go for a ride, gentlemen."

Henderson took Smilie and Willie back through the low income neighborhood where he was before. The children, again stopped what they were doing and waved. Henderson purposely slowed down, as if to display his fresh catch to those watching. There was a look of recognition in their eyes, but not a comforting one. They immediately stopped waving and stepped back as they realized the neighborhood bad man was in the back of a police car. They didn't want Todd Smilie, Skinny-Boy, thinking they were police supporters, or worse, a rat, and because they knew first-hand what the bad man would do to those that cross him.

The garage door opened as Henderson drove up to the cell area of the police station. The rumbling of the metal garage door was powerfully intimidating for the new criminal but Todd Smilie didn't bat an eyelash. He and Willie sat silently in the back of the car with their hands cuffed behind them. Henderson had put the cuffs on tightly on purpose. The cold unforgiving steel dug itself into their wrists, leaving a deep red ring which cut off the circulation and their hands were slowly turning blue. Henderson pulled the cruiser into the garage where Samuels sat in a chair chomping on his trademark cigar.

"Who the hell you got here, kid?"

"Todd Smilie and Willie 'somebody' for possession of marihuana, sir," Henderson said, slightly proud.

Samuels peered into the back of the car where the two handcuffed individuals stared back.

"You better fucking let me go you old fuck," he shouted at Samuels. "I'm suing the shit out of you too. Stupid fucking rookie, I didn't know this ass clown had anything on him. Tell him!"

"It was mine, he didn't know I had it on me," Willie said, finally breaking his silence.

"So it finally speaks," Henderson said. "Well, I guess you sure are an ass clown if you're going to take the fall for this bozo. Just trying to make yourself look good, eh? Big man in the eyes of the boss. Well someone died because of the drugs you sell and if I had my way..."

"All right, book them in kid," Samuels said cutting him off.

Grant sat typing in front of the stations outdated computers when Henderson walked in.

"They're in the cells!"

"Who's in the cells?" Grant asked.

"Smilie and Willie."

"What for?"

"Possession of marihuana. I searched them and they had a bag with a small amount in it." Henderson held up the plastic sandwich bag.

"Not much, but who cares, they're in jail right? We got them."

Morgan was pouring over the Gurracci file at his desk mulling about his recent trip to the cemetery and how he should have arched his piss more fluidly to get his name spelled right. His mind switched gears and he started listening to Henderson talking to Grant in the next room.

"Dude, you should have asked me for help, or back up or something, I would have come."

"I know, it just happened so fast. What a mouth that Smilie has! Fuck this and fuck that and fuck you rookie pig, blah, blah, blah."

Morgan got up from his chair and went into the other room. "Kid, did I just hear you say you arrested Smilie?"

"Him and Willie in one shot!" he bragged.

"What for?"

"Possession of dope, shit, Samuels acted the same way. I got them off the street."

Morgan made an odd face.

"What?" Henderson asked.

"Hopefully nothing, but…" Morgan trailed off and walked away.

Henderson began to feel uneasy about everything. He'd thought there would be more appreciation for his tenacity and enthusiasm in ridding the city of these two ass clowns. He thought maybe Curtis' dad wouldn't sue when he found out that Smilie had been arrested. Henderson began writing in his police notebook knowing something was up. He worriedly furrowed his brow and looked over at Grant who just shrugged his shoulders as he also didn't have a clue what was going on.

About an hour went by when Samuels called the pacing Henderson into his office. He walked into Samuels's office where he and Morgan sat with Willie.

"What the hell is going on?" Henderson asked with puzzlement.

Willie looked at Henderson with daggers for eyes and a sharp stab of panic permeated through every cell of his massive frame. No one said anything for about a minute and you could cut the tension with a knife. Henderson knew he was about to be lynched, hung, tarred and feathered, if he was lucky. Finally, it was Willie who spoke first.

"Ass clown eh? I'll tell you who's an ass clown...you! You who are too dumb to listen to what you've been told. When you've been told to butt out, you should butt out. You! You ass clown, just ruined six months of undercover work. My hands are still fucking numb from those cuffs!"

Morgan spoke up, having let him vent on Henderson long enough.

"Relax Tom, he's new. He was just doing his job," Morgan said. "Kid, meet Tom Giles, our undercover guy."

Henderson began to shrink and despite his size, he felt two inches tall and wanted to run into the nearest mouse hole. His simplistic plan was too simplistic. His labors that denoted tenacity and smacked of achievement were all for not.

"So, what about the charge?" Henderson asked Morgan.

"Well, we can't really make it stick on Smilie when Giles was holding the dope. You arresting them on smell alone is like putting the cart before the horse. It was just a small amount of weed, you know the technical shit that the lawyers pull. Sorry kid, the charge dies and we have to let Smilie go."

"I was going for the big score," Giles said. "We were working on years behind bars for this turkey and his entire pyramid but, thanks to you we're back to square one."

"Can it, Giles," Samuels said. "Ease up on my boy."

Giles sighed and shook his head as he knew his was ousted from the drug subculture and his undercover days in this city were at an end.

"Well, I suppose we should let the asshole go."

Morgan and Samuels walked back to the cell area were Smilie was still kicking up a fuss.

"Oh yeah, you pigs are so sued. You better let me the fuck out of here," he bellowed shaking the bars.

"Settle down wiener," Samuels said as he slid the key into the lock.

"About fucking time! No phone call, no nothing. Where's my man Willie?"

"Just get out of here, Todd."

Smilie looked at both Morgan and Samuels. You could almost see the wheels in his feeble ruined brain turning and even Smilie was able to put two and two together.

"Shit, he was a fucking pig too!" he said in a high pitched whine that caught Morgan's attention. Smilie clenched his fist and punched the wall while Morgan tried to mentally compare his voice to that on the 911 tape.

"FUCKERS!"

Henderson listened from the next room. The cat was out of the bag and he wondered how far Smilie would go for revenge, an entire community afraid of him and his intimidating practices couldn't be wrong. Henderson sunk deeper into guilt as he feared he had now put Tom Giles into harm's way.

How do you apologize for possibly endangering someone's life, and worse, what can you do about it? he thought.

The Moravian Police Department picked up the tab for Smilie's tow bill and vehicle impoundment. Henderson felt he had tried his best to please Curtis' father and failed, miserably. He took the rest of the day off sick. Grant stayed silent throughout the whole incident and was worried about his friend, who didn't seem to be handling recent events well.

* * *

Todd Smilie was seething with rage as he drove his Monte Carlo back to his drug shack. The neighborhood watched in awe, flabbergasted at his early release. The noisy muffler of the Monte Carlo shook their wafer thin windows as it rumbled up the street and pulled back into the weed ridden driveway. He slammed the door of his car as hard as he could muster. Specks of rust sprinkled downward with each erratic kick of the fender. Some parents took their kids inside as Smilie screamed and swore so loud that they knew he would be out for revenge on some poor bastard tonight.

"Fucking pig must die!" He paced back and forth in his yard yelling in truncated sentences and whacking his fists together. "Fucking pig must die! Fucking pig WILL die!"

Smilie entered the rotted wooden doorway of his house as the evening again turned into a hot, humid night. Most people in his vicinity could not afford air conditioning, yet, they closed their windows tonight, consciously choosing to hear and see no evil, their heads buried in the sand like a line of scared camels.

Smilie sat alone on a dilapidated, threadbare sofa with a single forty-watt bulb burning in a lamp that sat upon an Ikea end table amongst a slew of empty beer bottles. The day's events grating on his mind like nothing he'd ever felt before, he leaned over and sniffed a line of cocaine off the coffee table, careful to only use the good stuff for himself.

"Fucking junkie kills himself and the rookie cop blames me." He sniffed another line of coke. "Willie turns out to be a pig."

He reached in between the cushions of the soiled sofa and pulled out a 9mm handgun. He ejected the clip; it was full, so he rammed it back into the handle and it snapped into place.

Holding the pistol made him feel invincible. He pointed the pistol sideways at the wall, made a gangsta face and despite the ingestion of cocaine, he had a surprisingly clear image of Tom Giles dead, a 9mm bullet through his skull.

"I'm going to ram this down Willie's throat, or whatever the pig's real name was. I'm going to make him piss his pants and beg for his life and then I'll laugh as I blow his fucking brains out all over this fucking room."

He cocked the gun, putting a fresh round in the chamber. He held it vertically then ran his tongue along the length of the barrel as if it was a sexual thing.

"You don't fuck with the number one dealer in the city!" he said through his teeth, then wiped away a small drop of blood from his right nostril.

"RAP, RAP, RAP," resonated off the wooden door and echoed throughout the empty house.

Smilie was brought out of his cocaine induced haze and rose from the stained sofa. He put the fully loaded 9mm pistol in his back pocket and with wobbly steps of trepidation, he walked towards the door. He hadn't been aware, but he had been sitting on the couch for hours snorting coke and feeling sorry for himself. He turned the rusted knob and pulled open the door.

Only the sound of crickets chirping in the warm air of the night was audible through the darkness. He felt along the wall for the switch to activate the outside light. He flicked it up and down repeatedly, but nothing happened, the bulb was gone. Smilie stepped back and pulled the door shut.

"What the fuck?"

He stumbled back against the kitchen table and put his hand into a moldy uneaten half of a sandwich that had been decaying there for days. He pulled his hand out, made a disgruntled face and shook the mold from his hand.

"RAP, RAP, RAP!" Twice as loud as before. Smilie backed away from the door, his heart rate starting to increase.

"Get lost motherfucker! I'm closed tonight." Smilie shouted at the door.

Outside, in the darkness, the shattering of glass could be heard. Smilie pulled the gun from his back pocket and again opened the door. He stepped outside with the pistol punched out at arm's length and his finger itching on the trigger.

"Show yourself, bastard!" he spoke uneasily into the darkness.

No response.

He squinted and looked towards his Monte Carlo. With the help of the streetlights he could make out the windshield had been smashed and seeing his poor man's hotrod damaged, it sent him into a mental frenzy. He stepped toward the car and upon closer inspection he could see something had been scratched into the jet black paint of the hood. Smilie was brimming with anger, his hand clenched tightly around the handle of the gun; so tightly the end of the barrel shook. He read what was etched into the hood, but he did not understand.

"DADDY."

Probably the first time in his life, Smilie had nothing to say. He ran his fingertips across the rough, uneven letters, the other hand steadfast on the gun. He started to slowly walk backwards, the pistol covering the area illuminated by the street lights. A shadow here and there would dart in and out of his peripheral vision and he'd make small grunts as he pointed the pistol around at nothing. He inched up the short wooden steps until he was back inside with the door shut tightly. His hand struggled to hold onto the gun as sweat built up on his palms. He no longer had a sense of security or power from holding the 9mm pistol. He felt something else he had never felt before, he felt terrorized as his breathing became rough gulps, wrestling against the humidity of the night. The forty-watt bulb on the small lamp by the sofa went out. He was now standing in pitch blackness; only the sound of his heavy breathing and chirping crickets could be heard. Smilie was hit on the head, hard, dropping him like a sack of hammers under the blow of a blunt object and he blacked out temporarily.

A gloved hand patted him on the cheek and a child's voice spoke out.

"*Wake up, time to wake up.*"

The hand slapped him harder and Smilie began to come around. Blood spewed forth from a large gash in his forehead and ran down to his chin as he groggily opened his eyes halfway. His vision was blurred, but he could make out another figure. He tried to lift his arms but he was tied to the rusty springs of the sofa.

"Who the fuck are you?" he slurred.

"*I'm madness,*" the child's voice said.

"Wh..what, mad..madness?"

"*You're not going to hurt them anymore. You can't be mean anymore. I'm here to make sure you won't hurt them anymore, daddy.*"

"Fuck, what...daddy?"

"*Where are your drugs?*"

"No...drugs...got no drugs."

Smilie's captor bent slightly and picked up a razor sharp axe that was leaning against the sofa. One gloved hand grabbed a handful of Smilie's frizzy hair and pulled his head back exposing his jugular. The stainless steel of the refined blade touched his Adams apple and pushed in slightly.

"*Where are the drugs?*" The voice evinced a child about to lose his temper and throw a fit. The axe was pressed into Smilie's neck further and blood began to seep onto the cold blade.

"Corner...fake boards... under fake boards. Please... don't hurt me. I'll do anything. Please..."

Smilie begged for his life. The revenge-laden anger he had towards Tom Giles faltered into loathing self-pity and only now did he realize the terror he inflicted on others.

The figure pulled up the boards in the corner and brought up a box that was hidden underneath. It was filled to the top with crack, marihuana, cocaine and various other prescription narcotics. The box was placed at the feet of Smilie.

"*You sell this to them, that is mean. You sell this poison to people and don't care. You are a demon on this earth and you will know their pain. You will eat this. You will eat all of this.*"

The gloved hand pinched Smilie's lips open and stuffed thousands of dollars' worth of the drugs into his mouth. His cheeks puffed out as he slowly chewed up the poison. Smilie tried to spit it out, but it was just rammed back in for him to swallow. Over and over Smilie ingested the drugs that were rammed down his throat. It mattered not if it was prescription Oxy's, morphine, cocaine, bath salts, methamphetamines, crack – he was made to eat it all. His heart pounded so hard against his rib cage, it felt as if it would burst through in an alien-like escape. Smilie continued to eat until his bulbous swollen heart now smashed against his upper body. He tried to grab his chest, but his bonds held snug and his hands were purple due to the tightness of the rope. His mouth began to foam, his entire body convulsed violently in a drug induced seizure that produced in him more pain than he'd ever imagined possible. He regurgitated a mouthful of the drugs and the bile dripped onto his bloody shirt, only to have his captor stuff it back in and with the last ounce of strength he had, with his last breath – he screamed.

"You now know, and you won't hurt anymore."

The axe was lifted and shiny blade glinted slightly against the dim lamp light. One swing, and the blade sliced effortlessly through the neck and spine. Smilie's head flew off his shoulders and bounced onto the filthy threadbare sofa. He urinated and defecated in his pants as his groin muscles relaxed, releasing the inner bowel contents. His stressed heart reflexively pounded a few more times, shooting blood upward from the neck stump. The gloved hand grabbed the head by its curly locks and held it up to the dismal bulb. Like Gurracci, Smilie's face was forever cemented with a look of fear, a fear that he had placed on this community then in turn was made to feel himself.

"Madness, daddy."

The remaining drugs were dumped from the box and Smilie's decapitated head placed inside. The poison that he once pushed around the city of Moravian was piled on his lifeless body which had slumped forward slightly, but remained tied to the couch.

"Like the others, you are now in hell."

The gloved hand flicked a lighter and it was held to the cushions of the sofa. The rubbish Smilie had lived in was easily consumed by the flame. It traveled up the brittle walls and onto the ceiling in a stunning flash of red and orange. The neighborhood, with heads still planted firmly in the sand, didn't see the figure simply walk out the door, hop into an adjoining yard and disappear into the heat of the summer night.

CHAPTER THREE

THE BALLAD OF JENNY

Five days had passed since Jenny McGrath's parents had reported her missing to Henderson. The depressed teen trudged alone along a dark stretch of a secondary highway with only the occasional vehicle headlights temporarily blinding her as they sped by the lonely fifteen-year-old. Her parents, fed up with her petty drug use and misdemeanor crimes, didn't look for her and put their faith in the police to do their job. Henderson had become distracted from this investigation by the incident with Todd Smilie and also hadn't lifted a finger to look for her. Jenny had been hanging around Moravian for days, crying for attention, pleading to be found although the help she longed for with all of her suffering heart had yet to come. Now, under the dark cover of the night she dragged her slackened form beside the gravel shoulder with the twinkling lights of the city fading into the background.

Jenny was an undiagnosed manic depressive person with low self-esteem even though her looks would never suggest such a condition. On a good day her emerald green eyes shone with exuberance and her small, sweet smile dazzled the pimply faced lettermen of her school. Adversely, on bad days such as these, the mental illness consumed her to make her feel as disjointed as a Picasso painting. As a result, her grooming would be cast aside and she would withdraw into her tousled brain. She could not yet be considered a woman, and yet she had already experimented with sex, alcohol, and drugs, which became a deadly combination when mixed with an untreated medical problem.

Step by step she slogged forward, not knowing where she was going or where her next meal would come from. A few more cars passed by before Jenny finally summoned up the nerve to stick out her thumb. Another line of cars passed by, however not one of them noticed the fifteen-year-old female who was hitchhiking alone in the dead of night. She watched them pass by with lackluster eyes, feeling utterly lost inside.

The dim lights of a lone car crested a distant hill. The teen stuck out her thumb again in another pitiful attempt as the headlights approached. She squinted as the intensity of the nearing lights became intolerable, then she turned her head to the side to protect her stinging eyes. She waved her thumb up and down, hoping that the driver would perhaps take some pity on her. However, it was as fruitless as the other attempts, and the vehicle sped by. Her heart sank as a sigh escaped her.

Only a second or two passed before the car screeched to a halt. The startled teen was taken aback by the vehicle's sudden stop, and automatically she was apprehensive about walking towards it. Nonetheless her depression clouded her mind, and so she swallowed with difficulty before padding up to the passenger's side. The car was admirable; a newer Chevrolet Malibu, not the typical dirtbag ride like a Monte Carlo. She opened the door and took a peek inside. The driver was male, older, clean cut, with a nice head of dark, wavy hair and impeccably dressed in a pinstriped business suit.

"What on earth are you doing out here?" the man asked.

"I don't know, heading out of town," Jenny said.

"Heading where?"

"I don't... away from here."

"Well, hop in hon, the world is full of crazies you know, too crazy for a sweet, young girl like you."

Jenny got into the passenger's seat of the Malibu with worried hesitation. She still felt uneasy as this was the farthest she'd ever been away from home and the first time she had tried hitchhiking, let alone accepting a ride. She leaned on the door, trying to create space between her and the stranger as he pulled away. Soon, Moravian had become a speck in the rearview mirror.

"So, what's your name?"

"Uh, Shelley," she lied.

"Okay, Shelley it is," the stranger let out a small chuckle.

He started to hum to an oldies tune playing on the radio. Jenny had no idea what the song was, Tutti Fruity, Ruby Tuesday, it didn't really matter to her as his humming actually made her feel better and a little more at ease. She leaned her head on the door frame and a few hours slipped away before the silence was broken by the pinstripe-suited driver.

"Hungry?"

Hungry was an understatement. Jenny had only eaten a few chocolate bars that she had swiped from convenience stores in the last few days and some berries that were growing along the highway. She was so hungry that a flattened squirrel and the spewing guts of some other mashed roadkill had tempted her earlier.

"I'll bet you're hungry. I hear that pretty, little tummy rumbling. What do you say we stop for a pizza or something?"

Jenny nodded at the man and he pulled the car into the next all night diner that was along the secondary highway. The flashing neon sign that read "McGee's Diner" had a warm, homey feel which quickly dissipated upon entrance. The smell of cooking grease permeated the air, the dingy booths riddled with ripped vinyl were sloppily patched with duct tape and the occasional profanity was scrawled into the table tops.

The man asked her, "So, what will it be, hon?"

"Pizza and a coke… well, it doesn't matter.

"Pizza and a coke it is."

The stranger motioned to the rather large-chested waitress who was working the graveyard shift at the out-of-the-way diner that night. She sauntered over and made eye contact with the well-dressed gentlemen in a half flirtatious way and took the order. The waitress made sure to stick out her gravity-defying chest so he noticed, as was her ritual to garner bigger tips.

Inside the kitchen, the cook took a frozen grocery store pizza out of the freezer and popped it into the microwave. He looked with dismay at the crap he was cooking up which was noticed by the large-chested waitress.

"Don't worry about the pizza," she said. "Pizza is like sex. Even if it's no good… it's still okay."

The cook laughed and watched the bubbling cheesy disc of carbs and fat rotate in the microwave.

After a short wait, Jenny and the stranger were eating their late night meal. It wasn't the best pizza in the world, but it was pretty damn close to Jenny. She got up to go to the bathroom, wanting to use an actual toilet and not squatting in the ditches as she had been doing for the past few days.

A thick hand shot out and grabbed her wrist.

"You're not leaving me already?"

The man squeezed hard as he looked directly into her eyes with an unsettling stare.

"I just have to go to the bathroom."

"Okay, hurry back. There's still a lot of pizza to eat."

He released his grip and his fake smile returned.

Jenny went to the diner's unisex bathroom and locked the door. She turned up her nose at the obvious stench of urine and it was no doubt it had been quite some time since anyone had attempted to clean it. The toilet seat was up and the piss she smelled was sprinkled around the porcelain rim from the last inconsiderate man to use it. She thought then that maybe the ditch wasn't so bad after all. She looked at herself in the mirror and even through the grime she could see the woeful expression fraught with regret and longing; the appearance was nothing short of a child in need. That realization hit her like a ton of bricks and she started to cry. She realized then how much she wanted to go home.

Jenny returned to the table and finished her coke. Her eyes were puffy and red, and the man noticed but didn't comment on her tears. The pair finished what they could of the pizza and returned to the Malibu. Jenny was sure he would understand, but she didn't know how to ask him and felt embarrassed about having him drive her back to Moravian because not only did she not know how far it was, she didn't even know in what direction. It was the middle of the night, and not only was she confused, it had also gotten to the point where she could barely keep her eyes open.

"I… I want to go home," she squeaked out.

"Sweetie..." The man turned and looked at her, his smile faltering so that his face no longer likened that of the nice gentleman that had bought her dinner. "You just got here."

"Please," she fought her drooping eyelids, her tears were flowing freely. "I… I want my mommy."

"I'm your mommy now," he snarled.

Through the slits of her eyelids she could make out the man pull off a hair piece revealing a bald head. He spoke in a levelled manner, but to her, his voice was distorted and malicious to Jenny's drugged mind.

"Did you like the little cocktail I put in your drink? It's an invention of my own. Sleep, sweetheart, sleep your pretty head away."

With her last ounce of strength, she opened her eyes as wide as she could and instinctively reached out her hand towards him. He took hold of it and kissed it, swirling his tongue around her fingertips. Jenny, alone, helpless and totally at his mercy, fell into unconsciousness.

"You don't know how long I've waited for you. You are perfect. You remind me of my own," he murmured while softly stroking her hair.

He turned the car off the highway onto a barely occupied dirt road, then into a farmer's field. He dragged Jenny's limp body from the car into the field, far away from the roadway under the cover of the black sky. He softly stroked her cheek with the back of his hand, looking lovingly at the child.

"I miss you, my love, and I just can't wait any longer." He kissed her tenderly on her motionless lips, her breathing stifled, her life slowly slipping, from his hand around her neck.

An owl hooted as it flew overhead, then swooped down and made a mouse into a tasty late night snack.

* * *

All that was left of Todd Smilie was a headless, charred body sitting atop the melted springs of the threadbare sofa. The bones of his skinny ass, as he had once put it, were fused to the metal of the couch's scorched interior. The heat of the fire burned away one of his hands, both his feet and the goopy innards had just barely begun to spill through the hole created in his midsection. He had been covered with a white sheet now stained with the black and grey of the soot that had wafted upwards from the tromping boots of the careless firefighters as they meandered about the former drug shack. Morgan pulled up to the scene in his unmarked police cruiser where already a crowd had gathered to watch the action from behind the yellow police ribbon.

"For Christ sake, there they go again, friggin' firemen's footprints all over a crime scene," Morgan complained out loud to himself.

A child standing in front of the group asked, "Is the bad man dead?"

Morgan, a little perplexed by the question, simply told the truth.

"As a doornail son." His voice and mannerisms were slightly camp, but the child beamed a smile back regardless.

Morgan surveyed the carnage. Everything was gone. No evidence, no helpful clues, just a headless piece of charcoal, and a black Monte Carlo partially scalded by the heat of the fire with the word "DADDY" carved into the hood. Now, a new murder investigation was about to begin and as before, Morgan didn't care; he just wanted to go to Gillespie's and get himself an order of wings, a shot of smooth Irish whiskey, and wash it all down with many beers. Smilie was as dead as they get and although someone will always step up to the plate to continue supplying drugs, that neighborhood, the one that had to live in fear, was now rejoicing in the streets.

Morgan lifted the sheet and crouched before the blackened husk of Todd Smilie's headless corpse. He examined it with meticulous accuracy and after a backwards glance towards a gawking fireman, Morgan just shrugged his shoulders and went back to his car where he had only a precious few minutes to collect his thoughts, take a quick swig of whiskey, then follow the body to the hospital. He took another swig while on the way and spied the driver of the removal van staring at him in an accusatory fashion through the side mirror. Morgan, caught red-handed could only smile a cheesy grin towards the opinionated driver who turned his head back and chose to ignore the situation. Headless Jake Gurracci nailed to a tree like Jesus Christ, followed by a beheaded Todd Smilie left to roast like a pig on a spit, both semi-deserving of their fate, and Morgan was struggling to care.

"Okay, Dr. Death, let's see what you got for me. Hopefully it isn't more pancreases." He got out of his car and started humming the tune to Irish Washerwoman as the removal crew wheeled Smilie inside.

* * *

Henderson and Grant were together in their police cruiser enjoying the few minutes between calls. Henderson was understandably quiet today.

"Dude," Grant said in his usual sarcastic tone.

"Huh," Henderson was awoken from daydreaming. "What was that?"

"Dude, did you do it?"

"What?"

"Come on man, did you off Smilie?"

"Fuck off."

"Hey, buddy, don't be like that. It's me, your partner. It's kind of strange that after what you did to him yesterday, he ends up dead today."

"I'm not a killer of people. Cows and chickens are my specialty."

"Smilie deserved everything he got, nobody thinks you killed him, I was just fucking with you. That dump of a neighborhood you drove me through the other day, they're sure relieved. I bet you that undercover guy, what's his name, is relieved." Grant leaned his ass towards Henderson and let out a big fart and both officers brayed a hearty laughter to soften the moment. Grant got him to smile, even if only for a second, and then they both rolled down the windows and gasped for fresh air.

"Still," Henderson said, "I don't think this shit is for me. I've been on the job for a few months and I feel like I'm up to my armpits in dead bodies and the problems of the entire world are being dumped on my shoulders. I don't sleep well; I can't handle it."

"I don't know what more I can tell you. I've only got two years on you for experience. It bugs the shit out of me too sometimes. Yesterday, when you were off, some Irish dude was laughing about his old lady smashing him over the head with a frying pan, and I mean hard. Didn't knock him down, he took it like a champ and his head was caked with blood and yeah, it was a serious assault but this short stocky red haired bloke just shook it off and said something like, 'That's me mammy.' He didn't want her arrested and was pissed at his neighbors for calling. All I could think of was friggin' cartoon characters... birds and stars everywhere."

Grant started making cartoonish noises like 'b-jong', 'clang-g-g-g' and 'tweet, tweet, tweet', then pretended he was knocked out.

"I wish I could see it like you man. You're going to go far in this fucked up job, because you're fucked up."

"Well, it's sure hot today," Grant said.

They drove for a few blocks without saying anything else.

* * *

Morgan rocked back and forth on his heels as the hospital elevator descended to the sub-basement. Broken nose guy must have gotten his needed treatment, as Morgan didn't see the poor bastard today. The elevator slowly came to a stop once again where the regular public was forbidden to tread. The door opened to a smiling Dr. Halpin, who was standing with his face right up against the opening door.

"Hey, man!"

A startled Morgan jumped back against the side of the elevator door.

"What's your problem?" he gasped as his heart rate returned to normal.

"I don't get this kind often… it's like a crispy chewy cookie. You've got to come quick, this is so cool."

Morgan went into the autopsy room where Smilie's torso was already laid out by the removal staff on the cold metal table. Boland was standing to the side, ready to hand out the razor sharp implements of the trade to Dr. Halpin's awaiting hand.

"So, pay attention, this is important. Scalpel please."

Boland handed the scalpel to the doctor and he started tapping on Smilie's neck stump. Burnt pieces of skin fell to the table with each tap of the scalpel.

"Crispy."

Halpin cut into the chest and straight down to the pubic region exposing more of the interior organs than had spilled out from the fire. Under the charred exterior, the interior organs were still moist and bloody.

"Chewy... Don't you think that's cool? How can the human body undergo such extreme heat and still be moist inside? Don't you think that's cool?"

"Yeah, I guess it's kind of cool," Morgan replied with a half-smile.

"Don't you think that's cool?" Halpin said to Boland.

"Actually, yeah it is cool. The complexity of human anatomy will never cease to amaze me."

"Alright, you guys are beginning to sound like a cookie commercial with all this crispy chewy shit," Morgan muttered impatiently.

"I don't come to the police station and tell you how to write a parking ticket."

"You guys are weird; I can respect that."

"Okey dokey then, here we go."

He took the scalpel and cut into Smilie's bloated stomach. He began to pull out all the pieces of crack, pills and all the other drugs that lay undigested mixed with flecks of a leafy substance that was marihuana.

"I'd have to say this guy ate a ton of drugs. His heart is scarred and swollen. I can safely guess once we do a toxicology report on the intoxicants in his system, my professional opinion is he died of a drug overdose, then beheaded by the same axe as the last guy we chopped up."

"Vigilante serial killer, don't see those too often," Boland said to Morgan.

"That's just another shit stick that I have to lick."

"Is there any family?"

"Yeah, one of our guys dug up his mother. She's going to take care of burying his sorry ass."

Halpin joked again, "Closed casket I assume. Can you picture this guy in a suit? No head, hands, or feet and just remnants of charcoal arms hanging out the end of the sleeves."

"Never a dull moment here."

"No, not really, it keeps us sane. You know how many bodies I cut up in a month? It's not just what you see, the fridge of damnation is always full."

"Are we done here?" Morgan asked.

"I'll send you my report as soon as the toxicology testing on his blood is done."

"Can't wait. Thanks, doc."

Morgan departed the hospital back into the noon day sun. He couldn't help but feel a little guilty for being grouchy with Halpin and Boland, but one man trying to hunt down a serial killer, who so far, has been doing more or less a great community service, was a daunting task.

As it turned out, Todd Smilie had some semblance of a family that did want to see him buried, and were the only few that cared he was dead. His distraught mother and twin brother, while not accepting of his life choices, were still devastated and inconsolable regarding the callous way in which he was killed. His twin brother Terry Smilie draped himself over his brother's casket overcome with grief at the wake. People would shuffle by, tapping him on the shoulder in a patronizing gesture and then depart. Their attendance was more for Terry Smilie and his mother than for the dead drug dealer.

When all had departed and the funeral parlor was empty, Terry opened the casket to look upon his brother's charred corpse. It was hard losing a twin, even though they had their differences over the years. He took hold of the overcooked upper torso that was merely covered in a blanket and cried profoundly as he hugged his brother one final time. The crispy part of the torso shattered under Terry's weight and the right arm with its one remaining hand separated from the shoulder, sprinkling dark specks of skin about the coffin interior. Terry pulled the arm free from under the blanket, put it under his coat, and left the funeral home with this cadaverous memento, forever a reminder of a misguided life.

* * *

In the dank, dimly lit room, Todd Smilie's head sat upon a moldy work bench. A figure patted the cheek before wrapping the head up in plastic and carefully placing it into a box. It went up onto the shelf beside the other boxes, each labelled with a magic marker in child-like scribble that denoted a salutary reminder of who was who.

"You ate your own poison and now you are dead. The world is glad you are dead. No one cares because the poison you fed to the people is finally over. I killed this one too, daddy, because he was bad. They were all mean to people. I HATE MEAN PEOPLE!"

The figure held up the specially crafted axe and slammed it into the rotted work bench taking out a chunk the size of a wedge of pizza. A whet stone was taken from the table and the figure began to sharpen the axe, scraping the stone back and forth along the blade in a constant motion, getting the axe ready for whoever was next. As the axe was honed back to hair splitting sharpness, the figure started singing a jolly limerick, one that every English-speaking child on the planet knows off by heart.

"Beans beans the musical fruit, the more you eat the more you toot. The more you toot, the better you feel, so eat your beans at every meal."

* * *

A hundred miles away in a farmer's field, wild coyotes were now feasting on the young flesh of Jenny McGrath, playing a seemingly demonic game of tug-of-war with her cold, dead limbs. The hungry feral beasts were not minions of death, he had already come and collected the dead teen. The coyotes dragged a partially severed hand and wrist off into the bush, frightened off by the chugging sound of an approaching tractor churning the soil of the parched field. Farmer Jacob Smalls had been in the farming business for over fifty years, and he was not as quick on the draw as he used to be. It had been an astonishingly hot summer, one of the hottest on record and Smalls was no stranger to poor crops. His tractor dragged eight metal discs behind it, aerating the useless summer soil. He had done this so many times before that he drove around the field almost on autopilot, oblivious to the young female form that lay just meters in front of his tractor. Smalls felt an unusual thump from below his tractor that startled him back to the task at hand. He turned his head to look behind at the tilling discs and was shocked to see them coated with congealed blood. He stopped his tractor and got off, thinking he was about to find an animal carcass which certainly wouldn't have been the first time. Instead, he found Jenny.

Smalls looked with pity upon the partially nude female form and his heart sank as he surveyed the grisly discovery. He felt terrible, sick to his stomach, but the poor farmer was blameless for this accidental indignity. Smalls got back onto his tractor and left, as quickly as his old bones would take him, to summon the authorities.

Franklin Falls was the neighboring police jurisdiction to Moravian. It was a scenic place with a more scattered population that was about to be turned on its ear. Morgan's counterpart in Franklin Falls was Detective Jillian Edders. She didn't have as much experience as Morgan, but nevertheless was quite a capable officer. Edders sat in her unmarked police unit doing an interview with Jacob Smalls', whose farm clothes smelled so strongly of cow manure and diesel fuel that she kept the window down while she was talking to him. It didn't help much, but she maintained her professionalism throughout the conversation. Smalls didn't have much to add to the homicide investigation but, the old codger was visibly moved by the situation. He did not know her, but he felt for her.

"Goddamn it, a young life snuffed out like this. So much living left to do. I'm damn near seventy, I've seen a lot in my time… but nothing like this." He put his head down while his words trailed off. His voice then rose up again, and he said while biting his lip, "Nothing like this."

"Well to be honest with you, it's my first one too and I plan to nail this asshole and see him fry," Edders replied. "I promise you that. I'd love to be there when he gets his."

Unlike the murders that burdened Detective Morgan, everyone cared for this lost child. Everyone remained steadfast in their duties with no inappropriate jokes or comments. Edders was determined to find the killer who so mercilessly sent Jenny to the angels. She made it personal.

As far as Franklin Falls was concerned, the young deceased female was unidentified, a Jane Doe so to speak. There was no missing person report filed for Edders to cross-reference and Jenny carried no identification. She would need to rely on fingerprints or dental records, unless someone could come forward earlier to say who this young, female victim was.

The sun began to fade over the countryside, turning the hot day back into the usual muggy dusk. As it slowly sank over the tree line, the body removal service loaded Jenny onto a stretcher and lovingly placed her in the back of their van where she would begin her ride to the hospital morgue. Franklin Falls, being a smaller jurisdiction than Moravian, didn't have the facilities for a proper autopsy, so Jenny began her trip home, back to the place she thought she wanted to run away from: back to Moravian.

Edders was the detective in charge of this murder investigation and the task fell to her to attend the autopsy. She had been to a few in her eleven years, but never to one where the victim was so young and once so beautiful, and she didn't want to go to it alone. She grabbed her cell phone and dialed the Moravian Police Department. Morgan sat before his files reeking of booze; after all, it was the end of the day and time for some more booze and hot wings. He was just going out the door when the phone rang in his office.

"Aw shit, what now?" he groaned as he reached for the phone. "Yello."

"John Morgan?"

"You got him, what can I do you for?"

"Hey, stud muffin," she joked. "I'm coming into town with a body for an autopsy in the morning, I was kind of hoping you'd be free to meet me."

"Why are you coming with it? Is it ... ?"

"Yes it is," she cut him off.

"I got two dead on my hands here, yes, I'm definitely interested in checking it out. Shit, you'd better believe I'll be there. You got someone to sit on this tonight?"

"Aw crap, I never thought of that. Come on, help me out, studdly, get me one of your fresh faces to sit with the body." She changed her tone of voice to one of a sensuous, sexy female as she emphasized the word *studdly* to butter up Morgan.

"Alright, temptress, I'll see who I can dig up." Morgan actually felt a stir in his groin. Certainly it had been a while since he had sex and his love affair with alcohol didn't count.

"Great, get them to meet me at the hospital, then I'd like to see you before we go in. This is my first homicide and I'd like to pick your brain seeing how you've had two recently. Maybe we can knock heads and see if they are connected."

Morgan knew Edders and he tried to shake off the thoughts all heterosexual, single men have when a woman says she wants to get together with them. He had met her a few times before on some smaller investigations. She was married, but had a shapely round bottom on her; some may refer to it as a bubble butt. Whatever the term, Morgan wanted to squeeze that Charmin.

"Alright, I got just the man for the job. I'll meet you at the hospital then jump you."

"Huh?"

"I'll meet you at the hospital and jump in with you," Morgan said correcting his purposeful blunder.

"Easy does it, muffin," she flirted back. "See you there, ciao, babe."

Morgan went into the officer's change room where Cliff Henderson and Bobby Grant were getting ready to head home for the night.

"Gentlemen, I'm afraid one of you will have to pull some graveyard duty tonight. Franklin Falls is coming in with a body that has to be guarded. Easy work, easy overtime, all you have to do is sit there."

"No thanks," Grant piped up first. "Religious holiday, uh, the Passover of Fu Manchu."

Morgan looked over at Henderson.

"How about you, big guy, you strapping farmers got any holidays? It's not Pig Day or anything is it?"

Henderson smirked a tolerant smirk.

"No, not pig day, but I'd rather not, kind of burnt out tonight."

"It's got to be one of you, we're stuck. Franklin Falls should have brought their own people but, well, shit happens. Do you want to work it out between yourselves or...?"

"No, I'll do it," Henderson sighed.

"I knew I could count on you, kid. I'll buy you a coffee."

"Yeah, no problem, coffee sounds great, I'll probably need it."

"I'll even put a surprise in it if ya want."

A shot of the hard stuff in his coffee was tempting, but young Henderson was still leery about the possible repercussions of drinking on the job. The bosses didn't really look the other way for the newer members.

"Nah, I'm just joshing, I don't really drink on the Passover of Fu Manchu, just Pig Day."

Both Grant and Morgan laughed out loud. They didn't really expect such wit from Henderson, and were secretly hoping he was pulling himself out of the downer he'd been in since the Todd Smilie incident.

Henderson sipped at his piping hot coffee as they pulled into the parking lot near the rear entrance, but Edders and the body of Jenny McGrath had not arrived yet. The two sat in their idling cruiser making small talk just to pass the time.

"So how was the Smilie autopsy?" Henderson asked.

"Like a crispy chewy cookie, to quote an insane doctor. Not really much they can tell us right now. Not really much to go on yet."

"I didn't kill him," Henderson spoke with utmost sincerity.

"Relax, kid, you're no killer. I already checked with your superintendent and he said you were home last night."

Henderson's eyes widened and he barely could believe what he just heard. "Are… Are you shittin' me?"

"Yes, kid, I'm shittin' ya, relax. Holy crap you are on edge. We ought to dub this 'The Beheading Vigilante'; he'll take a slice out of crime."

"You came up with that just now? That's pretty good." Henderson drawled with a mouthful of sarcasm.

"I'm not that quick, kid, that's what I was doing in my office all afternoon while you guys were out doing real work."

The headlights of the body removal van lit up the parking lot as it drove by the officers. It was followed closely by Edders. She pulled up and parked window to window, as cops usually do. It had probably been more than a year since Morgan saw Edders and she still had that certain charm and aura that transcended looks that made her a different kind of sexy. Morgan quickly slapped a stick of gum in his mouth to try and cover up the booze smell that Henderson was ignoring.

"Hey guys!" Edders chirped, smiling at the pair.

"Well, well, we meet again my dear. This is Henderson, one of our best new prospects and he's graciously volunteered to do your security tonight."

"Graciously volunteered, okay," Henderson exhaled, rolling his eyes. "Just tell me where to go."

"Just follow the removal guys down to the hospital basement and they'll take you to the morgue and we'll be in tomorrow morning. Edders here wants me to hold her hand while Dr. Halpin does his magic."

"Magic my fat ass!" she exclaimed. "Anyway, thanks for guarding this little girl tonight, I owe you one."

"No problem," Henderson replied. His heart skipped a beat when he heard Edders refer to the deceased as 'little girl'.

He got out of the car and followed the removal employees, who pushed a gurney with Jenny McGrath's remains into the elevator. Jenny was zipped up tight inside the body bag which well concealed the tragedy inside. The elevator descended to the hospital sub-basement where the large cold storage unit was humming away, waiting for its next customer. The door was opened and she was wheeled inside, being placed alone in a corner to be accessed in the morning. The removal service departed, leaving Henderson alone in the basement. The lights dimmed to half capacity as the hospital went into night-time power saving mode. The long florescent bulbs flickered occasionally, and everything became eerily silent.

* * *

Morgan and Edders entered the bar and gave a wave to Stephen as they headed to a table by themselves, away from the other customers who were sipping their drinks as they tried to forget about their own problems. He checked out the wiggle of her full rear end as he followed her to their private spot. He wanted to grab it, squeeze and kneed it, but held back trying to remain a gentleman in the shell of a starving man. Jillian Edders was far from fat, she just had a few extra curves in the right place and in her business attire she looked hot for a woman in her upper thirties.

"So, how have you been?" she asked as Stephen plopped a couple of drinks in front of them.

"Getting by, day by day, divorced now, you may have already known that. The split with Julie was world renowned. Messy, really fucking messy."

"Yeah, I hear you. I split up too. Two years married, didn't work out, you know the story."

Morgan perked up at this news and a sparkle twinkled out of his widening eyes.

"Don't get any ideas, you're not my type if you know what I mean."

"Pardon me?" Morgan smirked, leaning toward her.

"Alright, let's get this out of the way. I split up with my husband, and now I'm seeing another woman. I'm happy, she's happy, he's not happy… so who cares, right?"

"Well… to each his own, or her own I suppose." Morgan did a toast with his glass of whiskey.

He took a big gulp. Now all he could picture was Edders with her face buried between another woman's thighs. This news just turned him on more as they both took a drink and sat in a minute of awkward quietness.

"You can still be my stud muffin," she said, blinking her eyes and breaking the tension.

"Well," he paused. "I suppose it's better than nothing. Maybe I can watch sometime?"

"Dream on, you pervert, dream on. I see you haven't changed. Mind still living in the gutter." Her reply was followed by a clean laugh.

"So what happened to your girl?"

"Not entirely sure yet. I have my suspicions she was sexually assaulted then murdered. My money's on strangulation or smothering, can't tell yet."

"So she still had her head I gather."

"Yes, she did. It's not like what I've read of your two murders. This one may have been someone else. Some kind of no conscience, no remorse sexual predator. Fucking pervert asshole deserves to die and I'll work on this the rest of my life if I have to. The whole thing was wrong. She was young, fourteen to sixteen I'd say."

"Any idea of her identity?" he asked.

"Nothing. Jane Doe. We've checked all the missing person's files on the computer but nothing recent, nothing that matches her description. Hopefully we'll know more in the morning. She was pretty though."

Morgan waved at Stephen and like a well-trained dog, he fetched two more drinks, but placed them both in front of Morgan.

"Here, you could use this." He slid the fresh drink in front of her. "Go with what your gut tells you. Hope like hell the autopsy turns up some forensic evidence and appeal to the public. I've done it, and so far I'm empty handed. People actually clapped for the charcoal piece of shit I pulled from the rubble. Send out a cross country request for similar murders and see what evidence turns up there. Again, I've done that haven't received any responses yet but to be fair, that can take a while."

"Not too much he says. I really appreciate this."

"No problem, Jill."

"So how's your big friend at the hospital? You said he was pretty new," Edders asked while noticing how fast Morgan was blasting through those drinks.

"Well, we got quite a few fresh faces at the office. Samuels is oldest, then me. There's a new kid, Grant, good head on his shoulder and he acts like he's been around forever. Big

Henderson has just as big a heart, but he seems to be struggling with the job. I'm sure he'll be alright, just a rough start."

Edders and Morgan said their goodnights. Morgan returned home with the usual alcohol on his breath but a higher than usual pent up sexual frustration. He sat in his easy chair and threw in the old VHS porno tape and fast forwarded to a hot lesbian scene and thought of Edders, after all, he was just a man and like any other, he could return to a caveman like status where even scrounging for food would be tossed aside for sex. In a few minutes he was done and threw a squishy balled up tissue into a pile of many others that lay beside the chair. Instead of returning the tape to a drawer in the old credenza where his ex-wife's picture sat with her dusty mustache, he thought he'd just leave it in the VCR for next time.

* * *

Henderson was alone in the sparsely lit basement where the very beats of his heart almost echoed off the cold cement walls. Despite the fact he was in a hospital, it seemed the nearest person was a thousand miles away. He stared at the clock that was mounted above the hallway door, and watched the second hand meander its way around the numbered face. Seconds turned to minutes, minutes to hours, and all the while Henderson struggled to keep his eyes open. The plastic chair they gave him didn't provide much comfort for a snooze, but that didn't seem to matter as his head bobbed forward and backward. Henderson was snapped awake from a thud which came from inside the freezer. He got up from his chair and instinctively put his hand on the butt of his firearm. He looked at the clock over the doorway and it had stopped at

4:05 AM. The light flickered overhead with an electrical surge and suddenly the room appeared dimmer than it already had been. Another sound emanated from behind the large steel door. This time, it sounded like someone scratching on the other side.

"What the fuck?" he muttered.

Henderson took a step towards the door, where the eerie scratching noise was arising from. It was unmistakable now. It was the sound of fingernails on metal, and he could detect something else. It was a whispering so soft that it was barely audible from where he stood.

He dragged his heavy feet as he stepped closer. With each apprehensive step he took, the whispering got louder, until it was no longer a hushed garble and he could make out what was being said.

"*Please...help. It's so cold...so cold. It's so dark...so cold. Why didn't you save me?*" the voice sobbed. "*Help me, please, help me. I'm so cold. I don't want to be dead.*"

Henderson put his ear to the cold steel of the refrigerator door but he couldn't get his mind to comprehend what was happening.

"*Open the door,*" the voice pleaded. "*I don't want to be dead. Open the door.*"

Henderson reached for the handle, but then pulled back his trembling hand. The voice behind the door turned demonic and screamed, "*OPEN THE FUCKING DOOR*!"

His eyes were as wide as saucers, his breathing quickened and he pulled his pistol from the holster. His other hand shaking, he grabbed the handle to the refrigerator door and pulled the hulking piece of metal towards him. Nothing but blackness… and the sound of the cooling fans blowing against a single white plastic body bag.

Henderson stepped inside the cooler with only the dim light outside to help him see his way around. Each breath he took turned to mist against his whitening lips. Below the constant hum of the fans, the ghostly whisper was again barely audible. Henderson stood still and strained to listen, until he was certain it was coming from the direction of the body bag. He stood before the gurney where fifteen-year-old Jenny McGrath lay in her deathly slumber. She was dead, yet she whispered to him from inside her plastic tomb.

"*Open the bag, please… Why did you let me die? It's so cold… please, open the bag.*"

The bag started to move, from the inside. Henderson stepped backward in shock and lost his footing, falling into some empty shelves with a crashing thud. His firearm was lost, and it slid under the gurney. The bag continued to move as if someone was scratching away from the inside.

The voice inside screeched again, "*OPEN THE FUCKING BAG*!"

The body on the gurney sat up and one arm tore through the plastic and reached for Henderson who was cowering on the floor. The arm, riddled with animal bites and deep bloody gashes ripped the plastic away from around its head exposing a mutilated, ghastly face. The eye sockets were nothing but empty black holes that teemed with centipedes which skittered their hair-like legs down her cheeks and crawled up into her matted hair. She opened her mouth and groaned as maggots poured out, raining into the torn plastic bag.

"*SAVE ME*!" she pleaded.

Henderson's voice cracked as he whimpered, "I can't!"

"*YOU FUCKING LET ME DIE*!"

The one-armed deathly apparition climbed off the gurney and began to limp on its scarred bloody legs towards the trembling Henderson. Hissing snakes spilled from her chest cavity and slithered around the upright corpse. She grabbed the side of her face and started pulling at the loose chunks of skin. The skin stretched to its limit, then tore off in a bloody mess, revealing a laughing skull.

"*JOIN ME, JOIN ME*!"

Henderson shot up with a gasp. He was still in the cheap plastic chair, but he was now thoroughly drenched with sweat. He held his hands up to his face. No matter how hard he stared at them, he couldn't get them to stop shaking. He tried to stand, but his quivering knees gave way and he collapsed to the floor.

"Oh God!" he cursed. "Oh God, I'm coming apart!"

Like in his dream, he cowered on the hospital tile. The big farm boy was reduced to a blubbering mess and he prayed to God that it was not her inside the body bag.

"Please God, don't let it be her." He meekly prayed, his hands clasped together with reverence in some foolhardy wish that the Lord will shine a garish light upon him and turn back the hands of time. Henderson looked up at the clock as he started to regain control of his faculties. He still had about two hours to go before he would find out if the dead girl in the cooler was the missing girl that fell through the cracks of the system. He just sat and stared straight ahead at the wall and he dared not sleep for the image of her face would not leave him. Each minute that passed he would put a tic on a piece of paper. Each line he drew brought him closer to the truth, but

Henderson knew in his heart that God would not be answering his prayers this morning.

Finally, he could hear the elevator doors open and the voice of Dr. Halpin and his intern Ted Boland bantering as they walked up the hall.

"Hey, big guy," Halpin greeted the weary Henderson, and he gave him a pat on the back along with a hearty smile. "Jeez man, looks like you've had a rough night."

"You could say that. I just got to stay a bit longer," Henderson replied in a low tone.

"As soon as the other team gets here you can scram," Halpin said. "Speak of the devil."

Morgan and Edders stepped off the elevator and walked down the empty hall towards the anxious Henderson.

"Good morning," Edders said to the waiting doctor.

They exchanged their pleasantries but it was easy to tell Edders was apprehensive about the autopsy.

"Okey dokey, here we go." Halpin pulled open the hulking refrigerator door.

Henderson reached into his notebook and pulled out her picture that he had almost forgotten about since speaking to Jenny McGrath's parents. He rubbed his fingers over her pretty smile that was so eloquently depicted.

Boland guided the gurney out of the cold darkness of the refrigerator. There was a pungent stench that crept from the enclosed body bag, and everyone turned their head except for Henderson. He stared intently at the bag with the overwhelming need to see what lay inside causing his heart to twitch.

Boland removed the forensic seal, grabbed the silver metal zipper and pulled it back. He removed the plastic and exposed her partially chewed face. Her frozen expression was that of sheer pain, cementing the absolute terror that she had felt in the last minutes before being strangled to death. Her half-closed eyes stared back at Henderson and in his mind he relived the nightmare he had just had.

Why didn't you save me? These words played over and over in his head, and she seemed to beckon him through her icy gaze, to join her.

"Okay, Jane Doe, let's get started," Dr. Halpin said.

"You alright, kid?" Morgan had noticed Henderson troubled expression.

He looked down into Henderson's hand and saw his fingers still rubbing the photo of the child's once pretty face. Morgan stepped towards him, slowly slid it from his grip, and he and Edders looked at the photo together.

"Who is she?" Edders asked with her hand on his large shoulder.

"Jen-Jenny McGrath," he managed to peep out. "Why didn't I save her?"

"Go home and get some sleep, kid, we'll talk about that later."

"Yeah, I… guess."

He turned and headed down the hall toward the elevator. His big feet slogged along the floor as he left, totally dejected. Dr. Halpin stroked out Jane Doe on the autopsy report and wrote in Jenny McGrath. He said nothing, and Boland did the same. Halpin picked up the razor sharp scalpel, turned towards the dead child, and began to do his work. He first sliced off her clothing, then sliced into her.

Following the autopsy, Morgan and Edders returned to the Moravian Police Department and sat in Morgan's office trying to make sense of this innocent child killed so brutally.

"Sexually assaulted, strangled, and dumped in a fuckin' field," Edders muttered in an obvious, aggravated tone.

"Fuck it," Morgan sighed as he slid open the drawer in his desk. He took out the bottle and ingested a hearty a mouthful. "That's what I'm talking about."

He then held it out toward Edders.

She accepted it and claimed, "This one's for Jenny."

She pressed her lips together and made a sour look as the whiskey slid down her throat.

She packed her files in advance of her return trip to Franklin Falls. In another room, a woman was heard wailing. Sgt. Samuels had just finished telling Jenny's parents their precious, perhaps misdirected daughter had been found, and all the grizzly details that surrounded her death.

"We reported her missing and your police officer did nothing!" Jenny's father shouted through his tears. "Your police officers never even looked! My daughter's in heaven, but I hope that officer goes to hell!"

* * *

Henderson never slept, he never ate, and he could barely function. He found himself now sitting in his apartment watching T.V., although he didn't know and really didn't care what was on. The show was just on for background ambiance. He kept going over and over in his mind what he could have done, what he should have done, and how it was now all too late.

Henderson's phone rang. He had been expecting it, and he knew who would be on the other end.

"Hey, pal," Sgt. Samuels said.

"Yeah," Henderson murmured.

"I hate to do this."

"You're just doing your job."

"Pending investigation of the Smiley thing and the death of Jenny McGrath, well, I have to notify you not to come to work for a while. You will be suspended with pay though. Think of it as a paid holiday. You'll come through alright. Try not to worry I guess. I don't really know what more to say. I'll be sending someone over to get your pistol and badge. Call me if you need anything, alright?"

"Sure… thanks."

He hung up the phone. He was seated on his couch, still in full uniform and fully armed. He pulled out his service pistol and laid it on the coffee table in front of him. For an unknown reason he was careful to put it on a doily so he wouldn't scratch the lacquered finish. He could have picked up the phone and reached out for help; instead he took out his police notebook and began to write his goodbye.

"I'm sorry for all this and the lives I've ruined. I'm sorry I wasn't strong enough, but I can't live with so many deaths on my conscience, especially Jenny, whose death I am directly responsible for. She asked me to join her, now I will."

He wrote a well-known passage from the bible to give him comfort as he prepared himself mentally for the robed figure that was about to pay him a visit.

"The Lord is my shepherd; I shall not want. He makes me lie down in green pastures, he leads me beside quiet waters, and he restores my soul. He guides me in paths of righteousness for His name's sake. Though I walk through the valley of the shadow of death, I shall fear no evil for thy rod and thy staff, they comfort me. Surely goodness and love will follow me all the days of my life, and I will dwell in the house of the Lord… Goodbye. Mom and dad, I love you."

Henderson left his open notebook so it could easily be found and hopefully explain why he was going to kill himself. He hoped he could be forgiven.

He picked up his pistol and placed it in his mouth. He was careful to point it upwards so as to destroy his brain and make death quick. He could taste the cold hardened steel of the pistol, the oils, and gun cleaner used to keep it in order. He didn't care for the taste, but put it aside because he knew he would be dead in a second. He put his finger on the trigger and pulled it back slightly, cringing at the impending discharge. He then released his grip and laid the gun back on the coffee table. He closed his eyes and took a deep breath. In one quick motion, he grabbed the pistol, jammed it in his mouth and pulled the trigger, blowing his brains out all over the wall behind the couch. Henderson's limp body slumped to the side and quivered in the throes of death while the loaded pistol fell to the floor. No one was home in the surrounding apartments to hear the shot, to hear the rapping at his door as he too was collected.

Samuels sent Grant over the next day and he was quite worried about his friend. Having no response at the door, Grant approached the apartment superintendent, flashed his badge, and got a key to let himself in. He turned the key and opened the door. He was hit by an overwhelming putrid stench; the unique stench of death. He closed the door and took a breath but knew he had to go in. Again Grant turned the knob and opened the door about half way. Careful to breathe through his mouth, he turned his body slightly and slipped inside. Henderson's apartment was littered with empty takeout boxes, a typical bachelor pad. Grant stepped into the living room of the small one-bedroom unit and although he tried to prepare himself for what he knew he would find, he was still human and the sight sent him into shock.

"Aw Christ no!" Grant yelled.

He immediately began to feel sick to his stomach. Henderson was slumped to one side and his skin was cold and an odd color of bluish grey. A fly buzzed out of his agape mouth. The bullet that had pierced his skull had mushroomed and blew out the back of his cranium. Blood and brains were splattered in a uniform pattern resembling a bloody fountain that had sprayed upwards all over the beige patterned wallpaper.

Grant knelt in front of his fallen friend and touched his cold neck. He didn't really know why he did that as it was obvious Henderson was long dead. He quickly forgot about his stomach as he began to sob uncontrollably.

"Why... shit... fuck... why!"

He saw Henderson's notebook on the table and picked it up and read it while wiping his eyes with his forearm. He saw the reason spelled out as his tears dripped onto the pages. He threw it across the room and hugged his friend for the last time.

"*Madness*."

Grant looked around, but could see no one else in the apartment save for his dead friend. Sniffling, he slowly stood up, scanning carefully as he rose. Grant could feel another presence in the apartment and it was freaking him out, so he stood outside the door until he witnessed the body bag roll out guided by the funeral home personnel. Grant peered into the open apartment door where he caught the eye of Detective

Morgan who, as usual, was tasked with cleaning up the mess. When Grant spoke to Morgan about the details, he continued to keep the peculiar incident, the disconcerting premonition to himself for now.

CHAPTER FOUR

FOR YOU MY BLUE BROTHER

They stood row upon row, shoulder to shoulder, in honor of their fallen comrade. Each officer was dressed in a sharp, dark blue tunic, complimented with matching white gloves, and the sea of blue in the church was a staunch reminder of the brother and sisterhood they all shared. The how's and why's didn't matter to the multitude of officers that gathered to pay respect, and most that gathered didn't even know Henderson. They understood and were sympathetic of the rough start he had in such a short career and the caring for each other transcended the physical uniform.

Henderson's casket was wheeled down the center aisle of the church while the crowd stared silently and the organ played a somber tune. The coffin was draped with the city flag, which would later be presented to Henderson's family in appreciation of his service.

Morgan, barely fitting into his dress uniform, sat in the back of the packed church. The years of eating deep fried hot wings, drinking whiskey and beer, had somehow made the uniform shrink since he last put it on. He shifted his butt around uncomfortably in the church pew as he sweat in the tight dress jacket.

Shit it's hot in this fuckin' church, he thought as he surveyed the intricate stained glass windows, each one depicting a different scene from the Bible. There was a Sheppard holding a lamb to which Morgan didn't really know who that was or what it was supposed to represent, and of course there was a window dedicated to the crucifixion of Jesus Christ. The brilliant colors that glistened in the jewel-like window seemed to be strategically placed to catch the morning sun's rays. The minister speaking the pre-written funeral service dialogue became, as he had before, a droning blah, blah in the background as Morgan fixated on the window. The eyes of Christ were looking upwards and the crown of thorns with the droplets of blood on his forehead was exhibited like so many other well-known likenesses in other churches. Morgan superimposed a mental image of Jake Gurracci's headless body hanging from the tree over the picture of Christ on the cross before turning his attention to the funny little grave digger looking through the stained glass window from outside. He stood amidst the tombstones grinning from ear to ear and Morgan wanted to shoo the man away like a naughty dog.

"Salvation may you find in the arms of God," the minister finished.

Morgan clued back in and patted his salvation in a bottle that he had still managed to squeeze into the inner pocket. He looked at the different patches on the shoulders of the women and men. He noticed a couple of shoulder patches from Franklin Falls, which made him think of his friend Jillian Edders, who was in the same boat as him, busy concentrating on her unsolved homicide. A lot of places he hadn't heard of, a lot of faces so young, like Henderson.

Grant stood up and marched to the front of the congregation. As Henderson's closest friend he had been called upon to deliver the eulogy. He was apprehensive about speaking in front of such a large crowd of people on a subject so emotionally close to him, but for his friend he remained strong. He stood at the podium and fiddled nervously with some cue cards in front of him. He took a deep breath and swallowed the lump in his throat.

"Why do we choose this career? Why do we put our life on the line each day to be under appreciated? Cliff Henderson knew why. Because one person can make a difference and whether he realized it or not, he did make a difference. In his short time as an officer he touched our lives. It was nothing but my honor to work alongside of this decent human being. Of us all, he was the most dedicated that I knew. I've seen him put more effort and caring into what he did to the point maybe he cared too much, if that is at all possible. I want to share a memory I have of his caring and his dedication. He was trying to convince a man from jumping off a bridge. The jumper had his issues, and perhaps some of us were there because we were being paid to be there, but Henderson was there because he really cared. His upbringing made him a powerhouse, a giant, but with a heart of gold. This is why we come to work, and this is why we are all here today to celebrate his life… because he cared about others… more than he cared about himself."

With that last line, Grant's voice cracked as he began to break down in front of the crowd of police officers, most of who joined him in his tears. Grant spied Morgan in the back and watched him take a swig.

For you my friend, I and everyone here wish you well on your journey. If there is a heaven, you are there, you are the true angel in blue, Morgan thought.

Everyone was silent, save for a sniffle here and there, as Grant stepped down and took his place beside Henderson's casket. A bagpipe player rang out the traditional Amazing Grace as they carried the casket down the red carpet of the center aisle to the rising congregation. As he helped carry the heavier than normal casket he saw a man sitting in the audience that looked faintly familiar, but Grant could not immediately place him.

The casket was carried out into the noon time sun as the rest of the officers filtered out of the church. They found it cumbersome to breathe in the thick, humid air, yet lined up for a final salute in tribute to their fallen brother. Freshly polished boots clomped the pavement with impressive unison and the crowd stood at attention. Each officer snapped a gloved hand to their temple, then down. The hearse drove away taking Cliff Henderson on his final ride back to the farm where he would be laid to rest on his family's land. The crowd dispersed into general conversation when the hearse disappeared around a bend.

The man that Grant had noticed in the church walked up to him.

"I'm sorry about your friend," he said.

He reached out his hand and Grant shook it, still not placing where the man was from. Without another word, the man turned around and walked back through the crowd towards the church parking lot.

"Nice speech, kid."

"Well that suit barely fits ya," Grant joked and poked Morgan's gut.

"Yeah, well, it seems to have shrunk hanging in the closet. They do that when you get older."

"You know who that guy was?"

"Yes, I do. The guy you spoke of, the one who jumped off the bridge. That was his dad. I heard he did sue, but has since dropped it. Are you going to be okay?"

"I think so. I feel going on and doing the best I can is what Cliff would have wanted."

The two shook hands and parted.

"So, that's it," Morgan said to himself as he drove out the church lot. He pulled his tie off and loosened his collar as he drove. He immediately could feel the heat of his body dissipate, causing a sigh of relief from him. Even more relief was to follow as he pulled in Gillespie's and walked inside. Stephen waved cheerfully, then said "Hey, hey. An emotional day needs whiskey, beer, and good old Stephen's shoulder."

"Stephen, my man, my heart is on my sleeve today, and that is just what I need," Morgan said.

One long gulp and the beer was gone, one quick swallow and the shot also disappeared. Stephen poured another round for the weary detective.

"Really sorry to hear about your fellow fallen officer. I'm sure he was a good guy. It was Gillespie's honor to have burnt his face off with our wings."

"That poor kid took his mistake really hard. I mean really hard. We all make mistakes in this job and his mistake was one he could have recovered from with a slap in the face by management. You take you lumps, learn, and move on. If anyone knows that, it's me." Morgan couldn't believe he just contradicted his earlier deny, deny, deny advice.

A second gulp and the beer was gone. It tasted good, but it felt even better. Morgan was an alcoholic that could feel his booze, a feeling of relief, and a feeling of completeness.

* * *

A week passed and life slowly returned to normal, as much as it could, at the Moravian Police station. Henderson's badge number was retired and a picture was hung in his honor for all to never forget the perils of the job and how it can wreak havoc with the mind.

"Grant, missing person at the front counter," Samuels said to the young Bobby Grant.

Grant attended to the complainant promptly and he was resolute not to screw up this case after having learnt from Henderson's blunder.

Grant sat with Donna Keeling, a worried wife, who relayed to the officer that her husband didn't come home from work last evening. The missing gentleman was Dan Keeling and from speaking to Donna Keeling, Grant got the impression that things weren't well in the marriage and it was vastly likely Dan had walked out. That information aside, Grant was determined to do this right and clear this case and help heal the black eye that was given to the Moravian Police Service over the death of Jenny McGrath. He obtained all the necessary information such as height, weight, tattoos, hair style, and any other unique identifying features from Donna Keeling. One thing that she made a point to say was the fact that when Dan Keeling was a teenager he developed a life threatening tonsil infection that should have killed him. He survived, but it left him with an uncharacteristically high voice for the rest of his life. After making detailed notes of this, Grant then drove to her house to double check that nothing was amiss.

He entered her house and surveyed the rooms diligently in his attempt to leave no stone unturned. Grant noted that Dan Keeling's clothes were all there. Numerous overalls hung in the bedroom closet.

"Where did he work, ma'am?"

"He worked for the Municipality," she replied.

"I hate to ask, but is it possible he left and is staying with anyone else?"

"Well, it is possible. We did separate last year for a while but reconciled. We've been fighting a lot lately and I thought it might come to this. I'm just worried, that's why I reported it."

Grant rubbed his chin. A man wanting to leave his wife was nothing new but that was the same pitfall that Henderson fell into in assuming Jenny McGrath was just another runaway. He really didn't know what else to do but make the usual cross country missing person notification, question fellow employees, and hope Dan Keeling makes contact. Grant checked the entire room but noted nothing else, except a feeling he was not alone. He had felt this nervous feeling twice before now and wondered if it was the legendary sixth sense cops allegedly develop that tells them something is awry. Grant again looked around the room and focused on the one place he hadn't checked.

Under the bed, he thought.

Donna stood at the door to the bedroom perplexed at Grant's burgeoning predilection with her bed.

"Everything okay?" she asked.

He pulled up the bed skirt and saw nothing but dust, one old sock, and the missing remote for the bedroom TV.

"All okay here, ma'am," he replied while handing her the remote.

Grant gave Donna Keeling his business card and left the worried wife. She thought Grant was nice, understanding, and very thorough, even checking under the bed for her missing husband. As he drove back to the police station he felt troubled about this case. Grant knew two people were murdered; their heads removed and yet to be found. Dan Keeling didn't really fit into the known criminal category; he had no record with the police. Grant was at least comfortable thinking he could eliminate foul play. Only time would tell that story however, all he felt he could do was wait to see if Dan Keeling decided to contact his wife.

* * *

Morgan sat in his easy chair, poured a whiskey, and flipped on the TV. He didn't watch the old porno tape that was still in the VCR today despite the fact it was a long time since he had had sex. It had been, sadly, years. He surfed the channels and stopped when he saw a familiar picture on the news. It was Jenny McGrath. A picture of her pretty young face was splashed across the screen, obviously a picture from happier times in her short life, and the same one the family had left with Henderson. His sex-starved mind wandered again when he saw Edders on TV talking to a reporter. Flashing images of her round naked butt, spread legs with pubic hair resembling black coconut matting trimmed to perfection entered his unfocused mind. His hand fumbled not to his crotch, but to a bottle that lay on its side amongst chicken bone filled Gillespie's take out boxes.

Fuck, gotta get me some of that, he thought despite knowing it was never going to be.

He wondered what his ex-wife Julie was doing. Does she sit and obsess about what went wrong like he does? Does she even think of him at all, aside from the times that the spousal support check is due? She's moved on and he thought it was about time he did too. He put back a few more swallows of whiskey before falling asleep in the chair with a resounding snore.

CHAPTER FIVE

FATTY FATTY FAT FAT

The next morning, he walked into the police station to the mundane good mornings from the robotic front desk staff. The exchange of pleasantries was getting to be a resentful chore for Morgan who found his fake smile wavering. It was not the staff, their abstract and generic clerical jobs were only broken by the ringing phone or the occasional unexciting conversation with Sgt. Samuels, so he held his tongue. He just wanted to get to his office, close the door and immerse himself in his work, or just sit there and do nothing, whichever came first. Two unsolved murders were weighing on his mind though, and even a sincere 'good morning' was getting irritating to the detective.

Morgan entered his office and noticed two packages on his desk that had not been there yesterday. The packages were in eight by ten manila envelopes with the names of "Thompson Hill Police", and "Dorrington Police" respectively, police services he had not heard of. He opened his drawer to the clinking of empty liquor bottles and grabbed a letter opener he kept that he found handy to chip off the crystallized sugar from around the caps.

"Better clean out this drawer someday," he commented before slicing into the top of the envelope. He pulled the contents out from it: a pile of papers two inches thick, and he started to flip through them.

He stuck out his foot and kicked the door shut from his squeaky chair. He knew he was going to be here for a while. While Morgan secretly wished he could be reading a pile of 'Letters to Penthouse' starring his friend Jillian Edders, this stack of information proved to be more invaluable as an investigative tool than some dirty stories. This, in fact, was some similar cases that involved parallel circumstances, and perhaps could contain a clue in them to assist Morgan with his two unsolved murders. Morgan took out his pen, slipped on some reading glasses, and started to make some notes as he read.

Case #1: Deceased, Judith Reinhold, 53 years old, beheaded. Status: UNSOLVED

On Friday the 17th of April 1998, Thompson Hill police responded to a report of a missing middle aged female from 234 Sanctine Road in the suburb of Thompson Hill. The missing female was one Judith Reinhold reported missing by her husband Jeff Reinhold. Judith Reinhold was a grade school teacher at the small T.H.

public school, teaching grade four. Judith Reinhold was a large woman and foul play was suspected upon the report of her going missing.

On Monday the 20th of April 1998, Judith Reinhold was discovered deceased in the school basement. She had been decapitated. Her head has yet to be located, most likely had been taken as a trophy by the unknown killer.

Background: Judith Reinhold was 53 years old, 5'4, 245 pounds, a larger woman. Common working theory is that a person would have to possess considerable strength to overpower her or possibly taking her by surprise. She taught grade four as stated, and we have canvassed coworkers, and parents of the students she taught. Unfortunately, Judith Reinhold was not the most popular teacher to say the least. In fact, she was not liked among some of the staff and parents for her treatment of some of the children. They considered her a "mean teacher". She would holler so loudly at the children she could be heard by the other teachers on other floors of the school. Investigators have copied her employment file. It contained, ironically, numerous letters from parents calling for her dismissal in what they felt was an overbearing teaching style.

She had been married to Jeff Reinhold for 20 years. The marriage was rocky, and in his honesty, Jeff Reinhold communicated they had their problems. Judith Reinhold was the dominant one for sure; her ability to yell during their arguments drew the attention of the neighbors on more than one occasion. Jeff Reinhold, a person of interest only, has yet to be completely ruled out. Although he appeared genuinely upset about her death, and the manner thereof, he was instrumental in reporting her missing when she didn't come home from work on the 17th of April, but from what has been seen, didn't really look for her that hard. He stated to investigators in his audio interview, "I was just enjoying the peace and quiet of the weekend without her."

He was quite forthcoming in allowing police consent to search 234 Sanctine Road without warrant where nothing at all was found awry.

Scene: Judith Reinhold was located by the school janitor, Al Coles, in the basement of the school, specifically the boiler room, which is off-limits to the students and most staff. The lock on the door was broken and had been so for more than a year. The boiler room is a 10' by 20' room, noted to be uncharacteristically small

as compared to neighboring schools. As stated, the boiler room door was in the basement of the school, but, interestingly to note, the basement is also where children's lavatories are located. Any child attending the bathroom would have to pass this door and, as reported by Coles, they sometimes would open it out of curiosity to see the boilers. The forensic investigators revealed the boiler room doorknob and door on the outside to be riddled with children's fingerprints. The knob on the inside of the door was covered in smeared blood with no discernable prints to be found.

It is quite thankful she was discovered by Coles rather than a child, as Coles was going to do his once-a-week clean in the room. Unrestricted access to the room by anyone is criticism for the school at best, which has now replaced the doorknob and lock.

Her body was lying face down, she still wore red pants and a red top, but, bizarrely, her panties had been pulled up as far into the crack of her buttocks as one possibly could. Investigator opinion is a final insult to this teacher after she had been murdered, knowing this humiliating way would be the way someone would discover her remains.

Autopsy showed the head had been sawn off by a toothed instrument, possibly a hand saw or similar tool due to the roughness of the neck stump. Cause of death was beheading as no other anomalies were located on the deceased Judith Reinhold.

Follow up and interviews: Numerous interviews conducted including Jeff Reinhold, Al Coles, as well as the entire staff, and the parents who wrote negative letters to the school. Audio interviews on file, but nothing noteworthy gleaned from any of them. This case, awaits new information to move forward. To date, mountains of unsuccessful tips followed up and yet there is nothing.

Morgan put down this first case file. The rest of the stack contained various statements, tips, and photographs he would study later. He had never heard of Judith Reinhold or Thompson Hill at all. Morgan was able to find Thompson Hill on his laptop, but it was over one thousand miles away.

Judith Reinhold, killed and head sawn off, he thought. *Judith Reinhold, killed and not liked by a lot of people. Judith Reinhold, killed and underwear pulled up the crack of her enormous ass.*

He could only pause to guess what Dr. Halpin would have said during the closed door autopsy. Most expectedly something along the lines of yellow blubbery butt chunks, then ask him to taste it. Or perhaps comparing it to a bowl of yellow jello, the flavor everyone hates, just like Judith Reinhold, then asking him to taste it. His mind was wandering from his work and he laughed even louder that Samuels, probing why Morgan was alone in his office and laughing so loud, walked up to the door and knocked.

"What the hell ya doing in there, you old geezer?" he asked as he rapped on the wooden door a few times before opening it.

Morgan just sat in his chair with his hands covering his face and continued to snicker away like a giddy school girl. Samuels picked up the report and stood there for a minute reading it while the detective tried to regain his composure.

"I see, I see, pulled up the crack of her ass. Funny, but, same person, even a detective as astute as you could see that. Any help?"

"Not too much right now. We'll see. Just got to think about it a bit, maybe something will come to me later. There is still a second case file here."

"Okay, I'll leave you to it, but try not to laugh so loud at the next one, geezer."

Samuels turned to leave and shut the door behind him.

"No you're a geezer," Morgan said, almost breaking into the giggles again.

* * *

All those years ago in the town of Thompson Hill, Judith Reinhold stood in front of the class bellowing at the children until her face was as red as a beetroot. Judith Reinhold held the students in dread as most sat trembling in their small single desks, exchanging wide-eyed glances, wondering if it would be them that would become the target of her hard-hearted behavior this day. Behind her back, children would call her fatty-fatty fat fat or loud mouth Reinhold, but in the classroom they put on their best behavior or they would face her wrath. This day, a student found himself quivering, his stomach snaking in a knot of dread as Judith Reinhold admonished the young boy in front of the entire class for what she referred to as "very poor printing".

"I don't want to ever see this garbage again!" she hollered at the boy, who by this time had tears brimming in his eyes.

Judith Reinhold clenched the child's notebook tightly in her fat hand and she was shaking it in his frowning, little face. Finally, she threw it on his desk but it was with such force it skidded across and fell to the floor. He bent over and picked it up; sniffing back the tears and struggling to hold his urine while the entire class watched Judith Reinhold losing her mind over something as simple as a child's poor printing. Day by day, Reinhold would yell, screech and reign the class with uncompromising terror. Some students fear coming to school for the brash behavior of a bully, this class feared Judith Reinhold.

It was the weekend that the kids looked forward to. It was their time to try and return to normal and become a kid again without having to worry about printing, standing in a corner, or even being spanked in front of the class. A Saturday and Sunday would be a welcome weekly break from loud mouth Reinhold, but come Sunday night, every child knew Monday was coming next.

On Friday the 17th of April 1998, 3:35 pm, Judith Reinhold was getting ready to head home for the day. She fumbled about with her outerwear and was akin to a hippopotamus putting on a ladies size small jacket. All had gone and she had believed herself to be alone in the school. The classroom in this older school house had a cloak room where the children would put their outdoor coats and boots before changing into their indoor shoes and filing to their desks to await whatever spaz Judith Reinhold would be having that day. Judith heard a thump from inside the cloak room. Thinking one of the kids was still there, she hollered out to them.

"You little snotrag, get your rump out of there and get home!" Reinhold attempted to censor herself but became infuriated when there was no response. "When I catch you, you little shit, I'm gonna slap your ass so hard you won't sit for a year!"

She dropped her coat and stormed towards the cloak room and threw open the door. The windowless cloak room was in pitch darkness. Judith felt for the light switch along the wall. She could feel the chipped paint, child boogers, and years of neglect from budget shortcomings before her hand came to rest on the switch. She flicked it up and down but the interior light did not activate and the cloak room remained in blackness. The daylight outside did not provide any assistance due to the angle of the dark, smelly cloak room. It had the distinct smell of wet feet and shoe odor that comes along with children and their level of hygiene. This smell that she put up with for years, she could no longer stand and each inhalation of the stench tweaked her anger further. As her eyes adjusted to the dimness she could see the numerous old shirts the children used as paint smocks and piles of mixed up sneakers thrown in a frenzy to escape for the weekend. Nothing moved inside and she began to close the door.

"*Hee hee.*"

"What am I hearing a ghost, or a snot-nosed little bastard?"

She opened the cloak room door and peered again into the darkness, confident to find a child hiding inside. Judith was struck, hard, square in the face with a chalk eraser. The wooden end of the eraser connected with the round bone in the nose where her glasses sat and she stumbled back holding her face in pain. A small figure scooted by, running out of the classroom and down the stairs.

"*Hee hee.*"

She shook her head, her double chin flopping about as she did. She then waddled after the figure, screaming, "You've had it, you little shit!"

The unknown person had a head start by one flight of stairs and she could see them go down the creaking staircase to the basement. Judith knew there was no way out of the basement and she would trap what she was assuming was a student playing games, games that she would put an end to.

"I am gonna wring your skinny little neck!"

Judith descended the final flight into the basement where the hallway leads to the children's washrooms and the place she knew the person would most likely hide: the boiler room. She could see the door to the boiler room slightly ajar and stepped towards it. Her seething anger began to decrease as she huffed and puffed, her gut swelling with each arduous breath. She tired quickly due to being so out of shape and gave a quick thought to her junk food diet which caused her to balloon to such a girth. Like the cloak room a minute earlier, darkness met her in the boiler room. Judith's fury, had now turned to fear as she apprehensively entered the boiler room. The hissing of the steam that escaped from the cracks in the ancient gauges proved to be a distraction as she became confused as to which wall contained the light switch.

The door slammed shut behind her she was trapped in the dim gloominess as another boiler whistled out a discharge of steam. Judith screamed. This was not a scream, or a bellow, or a holler that she used to radiate her control of the children. It was a scream with the intensity and sickness affiliated to those that are denied the luxury of notice of their impending demise. A hammer came down on her skull from behind with a noise that can only be described as crunching steel on bone. She dropped to her knees, then onto her blubbery stomach upon the impact of second blow. One eye was shut tight, the other half open as her brain was scrambled for good after the hammer had smashed downwards a deathly third time. The hammer clinked to the floor, covered in a mish mash of bloody hair and skull fragments. Judith Reinhold's body vibrated and convulsed while a boiler whistled another release of vapor.

Judith Reinhold was still not dead but utterly helpless as blood coagulated into her curly grey locks. The killer took a handful of her hair; the other hand steadied her neck and began to saw through skin, bone, esophagus and the arteries. Blood shot out across the boiler room floor in arterial spray, her fat heart stopped beating, and she died. The tools and Judith's head were placed in a knapsack and as the killer opened the boiler room door and let some light in, it was noticed Judith's undergarments had risen up beyond her beltline due to the position her body was in. The killer put down the knapsack and took two handfuls of her extra-large panties, pulling them upwards towards the neck stump that was still gushing the rest of her blood into a pool in front of her. This post mortem wedgie was the last cruel degradation inflicted upon Judith Reinhold before the killer slung on the backpack, and walked out the back entrance of the school.

CHAPTER SIX

THE KEELING CONNECTION

Morgan's phone rang on the corner of his file-covered desk. He threw the Reinhold case down and leaned forward in his creaky chair, the old spring in it snapping the chair forward with a twang, almost sending Morgan face first into the phone.

"Ah jeez Louise, hello?"

"Hey stud muffin!" Edders chirped on the other end.

Morgan perked up at the sound of her lovely voice and pictured spanking the shapely round bubble butt he secretly longed for.

"Hey, you, good to hear from you."

"Can I come over and pick your brain? I got a tip from the media release. I got a waitress from a diner that saw Jenny McGrath with some older guy and video to boot. Maybe it can help with your cases."

"Great, love to check out your tit! Whoops...tip, tip, meant to say tip, ah, just there."

"Well you can check out my tit tomorrow ya weirdo, over clothes of course, be there in the morning."

Morgan hung up the phone, not embarrassed at all over his purposeful faux pau when there was a knock on his door.

Come on, what now, he thought as he stood up and went to the door. Morgan opened the door and there, standing before him was this slim, blond, fine-looking drink of water of a female form.

"Uh, ah, hey can I help you?" Morgan, enamored at this gorgeous woman, stammered out.

He had just finished thinking bad thoughts about what he'd like to do to Edders, and that made him horny, and now this even more attractive lady was standing at his office door.

"You already did," she said stepping in and closing the door behind her.

Morgan furrowed his brow and thought a second as invisible smoke poured from his ratty brain.

"Sheila Gurracci?"

"No, Sheila Appleton, now."

Morgan hadn't even laid eyes on her in the months it had been since her husband's death. Exuberance and love of life had returned, just like her outward beauty had now covered the wounds she endured. He could see slight scars under her makeup foundation but they were hardly noticeable in comparison to her breathtaking looks. Sheila sat her skirt-covered, curvy bottom on the corner of Morgan's desk. His sex starved eyes could barely look away, and she could easily tell, and certainly loved it.

"You came to court that day. Don't ever think I didn't notice you sitting in the front while I sat in the back. When I was at my lowest, you were there, and just being there is all any victim can ask. You are one that I knew would always go the extra step. I know I told you some of this at the hospital, but I have thought about you every day since then. I'm finally able to move on and put the past in the past and I wouldn't feel right if I didn't thank you again."

Sheila stood up and hugged Morgan, even harder than she had in the hospital when she was covered in bruises.

"You were my angel in blue," she said as she kissed him on his unshaven cheek. These words bequeathed a deep feeling of accomplishment and perhaps made the whole job worthwhile, at least for today.

"I did wear a blue suit that night," he said as she continued her embrace. He actually couldn't recall which suit he wore, grey, black or sandy jute, but he did have a few blue ones.

Morgan's penis stood at attention and he backed his hips off, trying to be a gentleman, the consummate professional. He had never ever found himself in this position before and was trembling slightly. Sheila, sensing this hint of tension, pushed her hips into his and felt his erection through his suit pants. She closed her eyes, savoring the first feel of a man in years. When she opened her pretty blue eyes she was staring right into Morgan's glassy brown ones. The feeling that they shared years ago came roaring back like a wave crashing off a rocky break point. She had not come here for this purpose, but found herself unwittingly becoming lost in the moment, as was Morgan. He kissed her square on the lips. Sheila kissed him back willingly, passionately. Morgan wished he had shaved this morning, but Sheila honestly didn't mind the scruff. She continued to deepen the kiss to Morgan's lips, professionalism now too fragile a barrier against temptation and unbridled lust. If it were to stop here the regret and longing would forever spike; Morgan was not letting this opportunity slip by. The files on the desk were pushed brazenly aside and scattered to the floor, clearing a spot for Sheila to lie down. Not as comfortable as they'd like, but in the heat of the moment no one was complaining. Their lips never parted but for a brief second for Sheila to slip off her panties. She sat on the edge of the desk fumbling with Morgan's suit pants and after managing to get the zipper down, she pulled out his erect penis. This passion was one she never knew before. She was about to have quick and dirty sex with a man for the first time. The first time, that is, that she wanted to have it.

Morgan's hands slipped around to her shoulders and began to rub them in a massaging way. Sheila gave into her lustful hunger as the rubbing relaxed her further. Her pussy was dripping wet with shameless anticipation as she laid back and spread her legs. Morgan positioned himself at her womanly entrance, still not believing this was happening, and he slipped easily inside. He began with slow in and out thrusts as Sheila closed her eyes; she finally enjoyed sex and despite the manner thereof this was better than anything she'd had before. Morgan leaned forward slightly and began to thrust faster as their breathing became in sync with the motion of their bodies. He put his hands on her hips and felt a mess of wrinkled skin that he knew was the location where she had been bitten years earlier. She didn't realize he felt it; she was too far gone into ecstasy to care. Morgan didn't even flinch; he just continued thrusting because this was also his first sex in a long time. With her skirt hiked up exposing her sweet pussy being invaded by Morgan's hard penis, Morgan noticed she had unbuttoned her blouse and exposed her voluptuous round breasts. He instinctively put out his hand and touched one to her soft, moaning approval. Morgan began to feel the pressure welling up in his hardness and knew he was going to come. It definitely wasn't the same as pumping it himself to an old porno tape; this was going to be bigger, better. He pulled Sheila to a sitting position and kissed her deeply to muffle the sounds of both their orgasms. Morgan pulled his penis out of Sheila's wet pussy and finished partially on her leg, partially on the floor of his office. A minute passed of just heavy breathing as the passion dissipated. Both looked at each other in disbelief and with a bit of embarrassment at what they just did. Sheila buttoned her blouse and concealed her flawless breasts from Morgan once more. She dropped her skirt back to its normal resting position as her pretty face was turning red.

"I just wanted to say thank you my angel in blue," she said softly, her face now red as the apple in her name.

"I think you just did. You're welcome," he stuttered and did up his suit trousers.

"You can call me if you want. No pressure, no strings. Friends."

"Um, okay, take care Sheila, glad things are turned around with you, I just may..."

She kissed him once more on the cheek, which really is all she ever intended to do, then walked out the door. Morgan watched her walk by the front counter, by old Samuels.

How did she get in here?

He saw Samuels stare at her shapely form as she left, and then Samuels turned towards Morgan and winked his way.

You old geezer, he thought, shaking his head.

Morgan walked into his office and surveyed the files on the floor, some now suspiciously damp. He just kicked them to the side and sat back in his creaky chair. He spied some white lacey material under his desk and reached down, picking up the panties she had left behind. He opened his drawer and put them inside, on top of the empty bottles he had yet to throw out.

As Morgan walked towards the front door he smiled a half-wry smile towards old Samuels, then gave him a double thumbs up.

He drove through the blistering noonday sun admiring house after house, each growing a lawn of horrid, crispy brown grass that every owner could be proud of. He now had round sweaty pit stains under his suit jacket despite the air conditioning. He looked at his watch; it was 12:34pm and time for his noon day pick-me-up.

After another fifteen minutes of driving, Morgan approached Gillespie's, where wings, whiskey and a beer would be a good addition to an already great day. It was almost as if Stephen lived underneath the bar like a bridge troll, as he was always there ready to pour. Morgan excused himself to the bathroom first and stood in front of a urinal. As the stream of urine exited his penis, it jetted sharply left, hitting the side of the porcelain and almost coating the wall beside it.

Oh yeah, after sex pee, I almost forgot how that worked, he thought, shaking the dew off his proudly used dick.

He capered back into the bar like a man that just took a sex enhancement pill and brimming with pride regarding his recent performance. Only a second man was at the pub, seated alone at the end of the bar. It was silent for a minute as Stephen went about getting the drinking glasses ready and Morgan could clearly hear the man breathing in a high pitched whine.

"Good day so far Stephen, if only the heat would break. I sometimes think the city is becoming a desert, it's been weeks."

"Well just stay with good old Stephen and enjoy the AC," he said, pouring the drinks. "What's up today, how go the cases?"

It is strictly frowned upon, and bordering on illegal, for a cop to sit and discuss murder investigations with a bartender, yet the conversation continued as it had many times in the past.

"Well, funny you ask. My hot cop friend from Franklin Falls is coming by tomorrow to show me a tip she received. I was reading a similar case that happened a thousand miles away and I am hoping to link the two because I am confident they were committed by the same killer."

The guy at the end of the bar asked for his bill in a peculiar nasal voice that drew Morgan's attention. He looked over at this poor bastard that sported a crooked nose, almost as if it had been broken and didn't set right.

Oh shit, broken nose guy. Morgan quickly turned his back to the man.

Broken nose guy paid for his bill with a credit card and left without noticing Morgan, the man whose fist caused his current condition. Stephen took notice of Morgan's hasty turn and 'I didn't do it' look on his face and put it all together without issue.

"I take it you did that to him sometime on the job?" Stephen said after the man left.

"Yeah, you could say that."

"He probably deserved it. So, you were saying..." Stephen said with interest, leaning forward slightly.

"I got this similar case from a place called Thompson Hill where this mean teacher was found in the same way as Todd Smilie and Jake Gurracci."

"You mean no head."

"Quite so, but the common thread so far is that those that were killed, were mean, unpleasant, nasty individuals that most couldn't care were dead. I mean, even this teacher's husband didn't care to look for her after she was reported missing because he was enjoying a quiet weekend for once."

"You serious?"

"Yeah, Stephen. I don't really know what to make of this. I mean I got a couple of fucking clues so far, but nothing to write home about yet."

"Clues?"

Morgan leaned closer to Stephen. "A child's voice on a recording, and the word 'daddy' carved on the hood of a dirt bag Monte Carlo and the trunk of a tree."

Stephen whistled as his eyebrows shot up into his blond hair. "That's crazy man, this is another day I am glad I don't have your job. Maybe that dude that just left did it."

"Well," Morgan paused, considering. "Hmm... interesting. Don't know if it is that nasal of a voice, but give me a copy of that credit card bill just in case. I had better watch my head if it is. I hope Jillian's tip leads her in a better direction than my fucked up cases."

Stephen printed out another copy of the bill and gave it to Morgan.

"Don't ya need a warrant for this?" Stephen jested.

"Shut up and pour, Stephen."

After putting the bill in his pocket, Morgan finished up his drinks and walked back outside into the heat.

"Oops," he said and opened the door and stuck his head back in. "I almost forgot to tell ya. I banged a woman on my desk too."

He shut the door before Stephen could properly react and give him a wise ass comeback, walking speedily toward his car. He could hear the bell on the door ring behind him as Stephen opened it and yelled.

"Rather hear those details over your silly stories of dead people any day!" The bells rang again as he disappeared back into the bar.

* * *

Morgan met Edders the following morning when she pulled into the parking lot, driving her unmarked police unit. Her long, shapely legs and squeezy bottom was a reminder of the spontaneous, yet welcome, tryst Morgan had in his office yesterday, although he dare not speak of it to her at this time. Edders was hard at work, following up leads, conducting interviews, keeping her ear to the ground on her case all the time and what was Morgan doing? Drinking, feeling sorry for himself, not caring about the people that have died and fucking past clients on his desk. He spent the better part of the night sipping whiskey, thinking of Sheila's transformation back into the stunning beauty she once was, quite the contrast from Jake Gurracci decaying away in the ground, and he, of all people, got to be the one to have that sweet lady that Gurracci used to covet as his own.

Edders walked across the lot as Morgan watched her through the front office window. She carried with her an envelope that most likely contained her tip that she wanted to share with him. She must have been proud, perhaps a big break, if she would drive all the way from Franklin Falls to bring it to him and Morgan was impatiently curious. She was a good detective; why would she need him?

"Aw crap, the files are still on the floor."

Edders walked into his office and with an astonished look surveyed the office. "What the hell happened here, a hurricane or something?"

He kicked aside some of the suspiciously stained files from her prying eyes. "Hey hey, Jill. Yeah, hurricane, hurricane Sheila," he said trailing off.

"Well I don't even know what that means but I hope everything is okay with you, studdly?" she said, slightly concerned. He had a faint odor on his breath still and she could detect it, but didn't say anything.

Morgan positioned his body in front of the drawer that contained liquor bottles and a lacey pair of Sheila's worn panties. He had a crooked smile on his middle aged mug and secretly wondered what kind of panties Edders was wearing - thong, full back or possibly bikini. They were most likely the kind he would never see. Edders opened her envelope and pulled out a VHS tape.

"Don't see many of those around anymore," Morgan said gazing at the tape.

"It is what it is, but if I can get it copied it may be a major break in this case. I have an audio statement from a rather large chested waitress from a place called McGee's Diner who remembers Jenny and a well-dressed older guy. She remembers them ordering a pizza, eating and leaving. The diner management was good enough to have a surveillance tape available, but, as usual, it is decades old and I have no player to watch it in so I came here because I know your sexy brain will point the way."

"Yeah, lay the butter on thick, Jill, I'm toast. Our office actually has no VHS player either... but," he paused.

Morgan knew he had an old VHS player at home sitting on his just as old television set. He couldn't recollect at the moment whether he ejected the porno tape or not. All he needed was Jill watch him pop out 'Mature Chicks on the Beach' or 'Moms on the Beach' or whatever it was called.

"I think I can set you up because I have an old VHS player at home. Old like me but still chugging away. I had the utmost confidence that something would break following the news story. It tugged at everyone's heart strings, myself included."

"I have to watch this tape. I know it will break this case," she emphasized.

"I think your best bet will be to convert it to a format that we can work with today. I'll grab the player, bring it in and we'll hook it up to a DVD burner and blast off a copy. That way we can have it enhanced, chopped, or whatever the hell we need to do."

"Sounds like you know what you're doing, I think I came to the right place."

"Sounds like, yes, I know the theory behind copying, enhancing and shit like that but am I the one to do it, no way Jose. We'll grab one of the younger guys."

Morgan and Edders drove to Morgan's house. The side-walk was covered with weeds, prickles poked out in between the cracks in the concrete and the weather worn stairs strained to hold their weight as they entered the back door. Old cereal boxes, milk cartons, bones of half-eaten chicken wings and other various straight out of the package food stuffs were littered around the messy kitchen. His dishes remained undone in the sink, and the odd fly crawled around the rotting food, looking for the perfect place to lay eggs. When she saw at least a dozen empty liquor bottles beside his easy chair Jill slowly began to realize what a downward spiral her friend Morgan was riding. Jill desperately wanted to help him as that was her nature. Moravian already lost one of their own and she feared Morgan may be next if he kept up this destructive behavior.

"Are you okay, John?"

For the first time in a long time, someone called him by his first name. Morgan was stunned a bit but also glad that they had progressed to a first name basis. Generally, everyone was called by their surname as cops lived in a world of badge numbers and name tags. No, he was not okay. He wallowed daily in self-pity, while drinking at noon to numb it all. He was depressed due to his divorce and shitty relationship with his ex, compounded by a haranguing judge that hated him. He was stressed due to his job, he had two homicides he couldn't solve, he and others were still reeling from Henderson's suicide and it was fucking hot out all the time. His run in with Sheila was the only good thing that had happened to him in as long as he could remember.

"John, you live like shit," she said. "You can't keep going like this, you'll die."

She stepped towards him and for the second time in as many days he was hugged by a fine looking female. Morgan hugged her back and the two shared a moment of friendship. He desperately wanted to reach around and take two handfuls of her delicious squeezable butt cheeks but thought a slap in the face would ruin the moment. Morgan fumbled with the VCR behind Jill and pressed the eject button as she started to pull herself away.

"One more hug," he said grabbing the ejecting tape.

'MILF's on the Beach' was the correct name of his porno of choice and Morgan tossed the tape to the side hoping the pile of balled up tissues would cushion the fall and Edders wouldn't notice what he was doing. She wasn't stupid, she just chose not to address that, her concern was still on his consumption of alcohol and deplorable living conditions. Behind Morgan was the picture of his ex-wife Julie; the glass within the frame was still cracked from when he tossed it earlier. Edders pulled away and picked it up.

"Where is she now?"

Morgan turned to see what she was staring at. "The bitch is somewhere on the other side of town collecting half my pay and half my pension."

Edders found herself a little tongue tied. She must have hit a sore spot with the ex-wife because Morgan started rifling through some of the empty bottles hoping for a drop in one. Edders again approached and softly put her hand on his. She was starting to choke up to see her friend in such desperation and Morgan could recognize her true concern. He released his grip on the empty bottle and she took it from him.

"Have you ever thought of help, rehab, or at least talking to someone?" she asked.

"I have… I mean, I do talk to someone?"

"Who?"

"My buddy Stephen," Morgan said in a tone a tad more jovial.

Edders shook her head. "That's not what I meant, you know it ya clown."

Morgan changed the subject because inside, he was not ready for help. Rock bottom was coming and it was inevitable, so he switched gears of the conversation back to Jenny.

"Do you want to watch this or not?"

Morgan took the tape from Edders and put it in the VCR. The old machine buzzed to life and began to show grainy images of the inside of the diner.

"Christ, I can see her jugs even with shitty fuzzy picture they provided," he said referring to the waitress on the screen.

"Enough jack ass, watch the tape for Jenny."

For the next hour the two sat in Morgan's living room not saying anything to each other until finally the tape displayed the door of the diner opening, and a young female and older male coming inside and sitting down."

"There she is!" Edders exclaimed, knowing instantly it was Jenny.

The two studied the stranger she was with and made notes of his description. Jenny and the stranger sat eating pizza for a few minutes and then they observed Jenny get up and disappear into the bathroom. After another minute the screen suddenly went to pure digital snow.

"Shit no!" Morgan said loudly jumping up and pressing the stop button. "Not this time you piece of shit from the stone age. Please, please, please," he said over and over while pressing the eject button and hammering on the metal top.

The VCR made a whiny noise and the sound was one that only those Morgan's age would know, the sound of a VCR eating a VHS tape. Not literally, but the VHS tape became tangled inside and when Morgan pulled it out, a long run of tape went from the plastic casing, through the rectangular slot and entwined around the mechanism inside.

"Fuck!" Edders eyes were wide.

"We can fix it, we can fix it," Morgan said knowing he's untangled 'MILF's on the Beach' on numerous occasions.

With ginger fingers, Morgan tugged the video tape a few times. Since he had done this before he took the screwdriver he kept beside the VCR and removed the bolts from the side. Morgan popped the top of the VCR of and examined the path of the old VHS tape around the heads of the ancient unit. Edders watched with trepidation and had visions of her lead going down the toilet.

"Come on stud, don't let me down," she said hesitantly.

Cautiously, carefully Morgan unwound the old video tape until it was free from the VCR. He turned the plastic spindles of the tape until it was again tight inside. Edders breathed a sigh of relief and took the tape and held it against her forehead.

"Shit, John, we gotta get this copied."

"Okay, plan 'B' then. I know where there is another VCR. First, let's have a drink."

Morgan and Edders walked back to her car and drove to Gillespie's. It was just after 11:30 and the sun was blazing so hot Edders worried that the VHS tape would melt in the car.

"Nice to see ya again, my dear," Stephen said to Edders as they walked in.

"I see. Your best customer, here again, and this is the treatment I get," Morgan joked.

They sat at the bar and Stephen popped a couple of beers in front of them. Edders could see Morgan visibly shaking as he picked up the drink and put it to his mouth. He drank about a quarter of the glass in one swallow with closed eyes and as with most alcoholics, the shaking subsided when the sweetness of the cold beer entered his system. Feeling a little uncomfortable, Edders picked up her beer and just took a sip.

"I'll finish it for you if you want."

"Oh shut up, I'm fine," she said. "Just get me that other VCR."

"Stephen my friend, one VCR please."

Edders laughed at Morgan's request of good old Stephen.

"One VCR coming up," Stephen said.

Stephen poured a shot of vodka, then a glass of cranberry, then a shot of rum and put the 'VCR' in front of Morgan.

"You want one too?" Stephen asked Edders.

Edders face depicted a slightly grudging expression of a woman who is entertained, but quickly coming to the end of her rope. She was so wrapped up in wanting, or even more so, needing to solve Jenny's murder that Morgan's antics were becoming highly inappropriate. Morgan was blatantly drinking on duty, she knew of this before, but today he appeared to be going to extremes.

Morgan chugged the 'VCR' and looked at the disappointed Edders.

"Stephen, get this lady a VCR!"

"I don't want one!" a peeved Edders said crossing her arms and turning away.

"Hey, relax honey," Morgan said. "Stephen can provide."

Stephen reached under the bar and brought up an old VCR, a real one.

"You friggin' assholes," Edders said with a smile returning to her face.

"If you have been coming to this place as long as I have, you also get to know what kind of security system they have, or should I say had."

Edders finished her lunch quickly as she was anxious to get the video copied and hopefully this VCR didn't have a hankering to eat her tape. She excused herself to use the restroom before leaving to go back to the station.

"Stephen, quick shot of whiskey before she comes back," Morgan whispered to Stephen.

Stephen was not Morgan's pa, he was not there to judge, only to please, so he complied with Morgan's request.

The whiskey was gone in a second. Edders returned unknowing but if she did, at this point there would be no surprise.

* * *

Riding in his police unit alone Grant couldn't help but think of his dead friend. The option was open for him to ride with another officer but he preferred to be by himself for the time being. He also thought of the missing man, Dan Keeling. In the time since he had left his wife, there had still been no contact from him and Grant was second guessing himself on what he could have done different.

"Unit with Officer Grant come in," the communication dispatcher squawked over the police radio.

"Oh great, what now?"

"Need you to head over to 247 Simpson Street on a 911 call. Complainant in this matter, a neighbor says a male and a female could be heard arguing and the male voice was heard calling the female a skanky whore. No more information at this time."

"Shitty domestic, gotta be the heat," Grant grumbled before he picked up the mic and acknowledged the call.

He sped up and began to head in the direction of the fight. It just happened the route to the domestic disturbance took him by Gillespie's where Morgan and Edders were getting into her unmarked unit.

"Hey there goes young Grant looking like he's driving with a purpose," Morgan said, tracking the vehicle with his eyes.

He and Edders followed Grant to 247 Simpson Street where a male and female were standing on the front steps of the house screaming at each other.

As with most of these calls, the pair just stopped screaming at each other and started screaming at the police.

"I want him arrested!" the female screamed.

"I want her arrested!" the male screamed.

"Calm down please, calm down," Grant asked, holding up his hands to try to diffuse the tension in the air.

The best rule of domestics is to separate the parties and find out what happened individually, so Morgan spoke to the female and Grant took the male aside to speak to him. Morgan put a mint in his mouth and asked the female, who was still dressed in just a bathrobe, her version.

"We have been arguing for weeks. We are separated but we live in different rooms. I was using my computer to talk to a friend and he got jealous and unplugged it so I picked up my cell phone to call my friend and he ripped that from my hand and threw it out the window. It's still over there on the grass, probably busted, the fucking asshole. He grabbed a bottle of fabric freshener and sprayed me all over calling me a skanky whore. He goes through my emails, always looking over my shoulder when I am on the computer, he is a jealous asshole and I want him charged and taken out of here."

Grant spoke to the male and his version was of course slightly different.

"We are separated so I sleep in the basement. The only computer we have is in the basement and she is on it all the time. I never get to use it so I unplugged it to end whatever she was doing so I could reboot it and get my turn on it. I don't think that is too much to ask but she just tells me to fuck off and die. Then she accuses me of just wanting to use the computer for porn so she pulled open her bathrobe and showed me her floppy tits and said she could have any guy she wants because she has D-cups. Then she went upstairs and came back down with a twelve-inch dildo and swatted me across the face with it saying my dick was too small and she needed that. She then starts to jam this dick shaped dildo in my mouth calling me a faggot and saying I love to suck dick. She's fucking crazy, I want her charged."

Even in his two years Grant knew people usually tell convenient self-serving stories where they would deliberately leave out the stupid things they did.

"Uh, just one second sir, let me confer with my partner," Grant said, fighting to hold a straight face. He darted away just as the smile was cracking his lips.

"So, what do ya got kid?" Morgan asked when he stepped away from the female. "This lady said she was attacked with fabric freshener."

"Dude says he was attacked with a twelve-inch dildo."

"Hmm, which one do you think is the deadlier weapon? Getting fabric freshener in the eye probably would sting, but a twelve-inch dildo is a bit bigger than your regular garden variety dildo, you must be able to drive a truck inside her box. Better book 'em both to be safe," Morgan said to Grant.

Grant's eyes widened at the suggestion by Morgan to haul both the male and female into the station. "Uh, okay boss." Grant turned to the couple. "Well, you're under arrest for fabric freshener assault and you are under arrest for dildo assault…" Grant couldn't believe he was actually doing this.

"Best rule of evidence kid," Morgan reminded Grant.

"Oh yeah, ma'am and sir, I will need to seize the bottle of freshener and the dildo."

The couple hung their heads in extreme embarrassment and went in the house and returned with their implements of assault and handed them to Grant. He had the fabric freshener in one hand and a floppy penis shaped dildo in his other hand while Morgan was busting a gut inside at the look on Grant's face, and that he had no idea what to do with either thing.

"Put them in the trunk and bring the people to the station for the paperwork," Morgan said in a slow pace to coach the dumbfounded Grant.

Edders stood in the background, shaking her head in disbelief at the call she just attended with the two. She was speechless at the absurdity that this couple stooped to, and now was going to the police station to face assault charges. She shook her head again and got in her car.

"Happens all the time," Morgan said, joining Edders in the car.

"Are you serious?"

"No, but it's still fuckin' funny."

They followed Grant back to the police station and watched his police car disappear into the garage. They could hear the couple start to argue again as the door closed to finally silence them.

Morgan and Edders went back in the office with the VCR that good old reliable Stephen had provided. The couple that Grant had just brought in was now being released by Sgt. Samuels and Grant joined the two detectives in Morgan's messy office and pulled out the dildo.

"What do I do with this now?" he asked, dildo flopping back and forth as he held it up.

Edders turned her head in embarrassment because she thought the next thing out of Morgan's yap would be some kind of comment about lesbians still needing a penis inside them or even worse, a question about her own collection. She would die if he did; thankfully he did not, because he was thinking of something else.

"What you need to do is this…" Morgan said grabbing the dildo out of Grant's grip and ran out into the general office area where other officers were doing paperwork.

"Who wants some?"

Morgan started waving the long rubbery shaft in the faces of the other stunned officers, some of who got up and ran down the hall of the police station while Morgan mimicked the theme to the shark movie 'Jaws' as he gave chase.

"Dun dun dun dun dun dun dun dun…you love it… you want it…come on, it was probably only up her bum… EAT IT!"

He cornered an officer who put his hands over his head, cowering from the approaching giant rubber penis. Morgan, still a bit boozy, tormented the other officers for a good few minutes before giving the dildo back to Grant.

"Just return it to her, kid."

"Why did I even bring it?"
"So I could do that," Morgan smirked, giving him a small wink.

Grant did not lose any respect for Detective Morgan. In fact, he gained respect. He wished he could have the joking attitude Morgan presented.

"I want to be like you someday," Grant said. "With all the shit that went on here recently, you still keep it real."

Grant had no idea this behavior was only part of Morgan's downward spiral and the 'great Moravian dildo run' was only alcohol induced.

"Nah, kid, you don't want to be like me, but maybe you can help us here? Edders needs this old VHS copied onto maybe a DVD or computer file or something, you know anything about that techno crap?"

"Dude, that's easy."

Grant hooked the VCR up to the DVD player that sat unused in Morgan's office in about two minutes and it was ready to record. He put the VHS tape in the VCR, pushing record on the DVD player and the surveillance tape began to copy in real time. The three watched the grainy image awaiting the part where Jenny McGrath entered with the stranger.

"May be a few minutes' kid, so go give the dildo back. That woman probably misses it. I bet she named it Leroy or something."

Grant walked to the cell area where Samuels was just finishing the paperwork for the female that he had brought in.

"Uh, here ya go, ma'am," he said handing the dildo back to her while Samuels' look changed into suspicion. Samuels sighed and had a pretty good idea that Morgan was behind the seizing of the dildo. The female snatched the dildo back and snapped at Grant. "Bet you guys had a good laugh over this!"

"Why, no, ma'am," Grant lied before quickly leaving to return to Morgan's office.

When he got back he could see on the monitor that Jenny McGrath and the stranger were now seated at one of the diner's tables.

"Cue Boobs McGee," Morgan said.

Grant watched the large chested waitress appear to take their order and leave for the kitchen. There was no audio, as most video surveillance tapes do not record sound, so Grant focused on the strange male that was with Jenny. He stared, not removing his eyes from the screen and made a weird face. Grant felt he has seen this person before but it was hard to tell because of the degradation of the video. The diner, unfortunately, would just use the same few tapes to record over again and again. Doing this slowly and surely drops the videos quality, but anything to save a dime.

"Some guy in what appears to be a business suit," Edders said, jabbing at the screen. "The diner didn't have anything that covered the parking lot so we still don't know what he was driving."

Edders heart sunk that the tip she received yielded so little information but noticed Grant staring intently at the image.

"Anything, Grant?" Edders asked.

"Pretty crappy video, but, a hunch maybe. I think it might be this Dan Keeling dude."

Morgan and Edders looked at each other.

"Who the hell is Dan Keeling?" Morgan inquired.

"This guy that went missing from his home a bit ago, his wife thinks he left her and ran off with another woman. Of course, I am not one hundred percent sure but I just got one of those crazy feelings that I have seen him before."

"Well kid, crazy feelings, hunches, intuitions are all part of the game and we can certainly check out this Dan Keeling. Really appreciate you getting this copied for us," Morgan said.

"No problem. Thanks for making me seize a gross bum juice covered dildo. Too bad it didn't have audio, maybe we could hear Dan Keeling speaking in his crazy high-pitched voice."

"Are you fucking serious!" Morgan grabbed Grant by his gun belt and stared at him, slightly stunned by that comment.

"Yeah, why?" Grant looked taken aback for a few seconds before he recovered. "He had a tonsil infection that almost killed him when he was young and talks kind of weird his wife said."

"Just something I have to check out, thanks again, kid." Morgan released Grant, giving him a pat on the shoulder as an apology for his brashness.

Grant left the office wondering why Morgan became a bit excited at that tidbit of information.

"Something just click?" Edders asked, eyebrow raised.

"Hard to say, but I think we should go and talk to Dan Keeling's wife as soon as possible."

* * *

Edders and Morgan hopped back in her unmarked police unit and Morgan stuffed his mouth full of more cinnamon gum to cover his lunch time hooch. They pulled up to the Keeling's house that had a brown, dead lawn no different than the rest of the town, but the hedges and flowers were carefully manicured and three trash bins stood along the garage wall perfectly arranged in order of size. Donna Keeling saw the police car pulling in and opened the door as they walked up to the impeccably clean house. Her face was red with heavy crying and Edders put on her best sympathetic hat, and held out her arm and touched Donna on the shoulder.

"He just called me. He's with some floozy on the other side of the country and he said he's never coming back. I don't know where he called from, but damn her for stealing him from me. I still love him … and damn him and his high squeaky voice. He even left his damn car," she said as she broke down even further.

Chewing his gum, Morgan asked Donna if she had a call back number for Dan Keeling but unfortunately she did not, and further, they did not advise her he may have just become a serial murder suspect. Donna, having already provided a photo to Grant, gave Morgan and Edders a second one. The photo was nice and clear, but to compare it to the crappy grainy diner surveillance video was not going to be easy. The hair style seemed right, but with a black and white video, it was far from positive.

"Okay, thank you ma'am, we are grateful for the information but please appreciate we must make contact with him to remove him from the missing person's data base. If he calls again, and I suspect he may if a proper separation or divorce is to occur…" Morgan said as Donna began to sob loudly again. "If he calls again either activate the call trace feature of your phone or try and get a number for him. It is imperative we speak to him."

She sniffed, dabbed her eyes with her sleeve and nodded her affirmation as the two detectives left.

"Could be the guy? What do ya think?" Edders asked.

"If it is Keeling on the video and he did kill Jenny McGrath, and he is the same high pitched motherfucker that was involved in the murders of Gurracci and Smilie, I would be flabbergasted. I can't wrap my booze soaked brain around the differences in the cases. They are night and day, just too different."

Morgan was getting noticeably agitated and Edders could see his hands shaking again. Dan Keeling was the first viable suspect for the detectives to chase down but Edders was unsure where to start so she decided to hang around for another day.

Edders had checked into a hotel in Moravian for a few days, but didn't much feel like drinking again tonight with Morgan. She was becoming uncomfortable with his over-indulgence and downward slide, wanting only to spend a night alone so she could think.

Morgan did his best thinking, or so he thought, at Gillespie's and used the return of the VCR as his excuse. Stephen was still standing behind the bar, ever present, as though he was permanently nailed to that spot.

"Twice in one day, nothing new I guess. How did it go today with the VCR?"

"VCR worked great and tasted even better," Morgan joked back.

"Your hot cop friend didn't seem to care for your dark humor."

Morgan snorted into his drink. "She's pretty bent out of shape, pretty stressed about her case I would imagine. It was still fuckin' funny and you wouldn't believe me if I told ya, we left here and seized a dildo on our way back to the station from this twosome that were fighting like a couple of kids."

"Gross," Stephen said, wrinkling his nose at the image his mind conjured up.

"Ya, if I still had it I'd chase ya around the bar, probably been in her bum."

"AW GROSSER!"

Stephen poured the whiskey and beer for the both of them. Stephen generally joined Morgan for a drink when he was just getting ready to close.

"What next?" Stephen, always the nosey one, inquired.

Morgan tilted the contents of his glass around. "Got a viable suspect, I won't name him just yet but I really doubt it was the broken nose guy. I think the first thing I want to find out, even before I find this guy, is if he ever lived in Thompson Hill which is about a thousand miles from here. That may prove to be quite easy. It would just be a matter of checking school records and see if he was ever a student at one of the public schools in the city, or town, or whatever Thompson Hill is. I haven't even checked that yet. If I can get a confirmation that the suspect went to school there, at the very least, I can put him in both places that the 'who gives a shit' decapitation murders happened," Morgan said, slightly slurring now.

Stephen laughed at the crass reference.

"As a matter a fact," Morgan lifted his drink, "I hereby dub these the 'who gives a shit murders.'"

He and Stephen clinked glasses together as they have done for many years gone by.

"Here's to our fallen friend, farm boy Cliff Henderson."

Another clink of the glasses.

"Here's to young Grant who put me onto this guy and for some reason says he wants to be like me."

A third clink and they both downed the drinks. Stephen slid Morgan a fresh bottle, which Morgan stuffed in his pocket as the liquor store had long closed. With that, Morgan meandered out to his unmarked police cruiser and started the inebriated drive home. He threw in a CD called 'Irish Favorites' and began to whistle along to the tune of Irish Washerwoman as he weaved his cruiser along the road. When the tempo of the song began to pick up and become merrier, he started to sing. But of course, Morgan sang it all wrong.

"I met a young lass and her name was Sheila,
She pulled out her tits and said please to meet ya,
They were big, they were juicy, I'm sure they would float
I put in my face, then made a sound like an old motor boat."

* * *

Edders was in the hotel room alone with a few empty take out packages. She lay on the bed and couldn't help but feel a little guilty. One, for eating take out as it generally goes right to her ass, and two, for saddling Morgan with the stress of her case as well. Lying in bed awake is nothing new for an overworked detective, and that is exactly what Edders was going to do this night. She partially understood why Morgan had a drinking problem. She could see Jenny McGrath's pretty face and Jenny McGrath's mangled face as clearly as she could see her own. She wanted to solve this case as she has promised herself, Jenny's family, Jacob Smalls and definitely for Henderson, who took his own life over his sorrow for Jenny. She thought of Dan Keeling. She knew Morgan was right and that poor quality video was hardly convincing her that Dan Keeling was her man. She didn't want to discount Grant's intuition that he had seen the strange male in the video before.

Edders thought of her girlfriend and missed her. She missed the soft lips of another woman the most. She much preferred it over the rough, stubbly face of a man, with his unrefined mannerism, farts, disgusting bad breath and ugly utilitarian body. She did notice Morgan toss 'MILF'S on the Beach' earlier and kind of wished she could borrow it right now, but instead, she continued to lay on the bed thinking and obsessing about the case.

* * *

The gloved hand held up another head in the dimly lit room and admired the swift hack that removed it with one swipe.

"You were mean. You were a very mean man. Every time you came, it was different, and always for your own sick pleasure," the child's voice said. *"You got what you deserved and I will make sure all the mean people get what they deserve. Especially you daddy! Madness."*

This newest head was wrapped in the plastic; a handful of mothballs to accompany the head were placed inside the plastic as it was sealed shut with tape. The face of the deceased was no different than the others, locked in an icy gaze, staring off to the side in the final scream of sheer terror just before their head was collected. It was placed inside a box, and shelved with the others. The gloved hand pulled the string of the lightbulb and the room returned to blackness.

CHAPTER SEVEN

DUMB JOKES AND NAVY BEANS

The case files were still on the floor of Morgan's office since that day he had pushed them off his desk to have a quick romp with Sheila. Morgan bent over and decided perhaps it was time to do a little house cleaning so when Edders got there he would appear to at least be doing something. He opened the drawer he associated with escape and refuge, and put the newest bottle of whiskey beside the lacy panties he cherished like a sports trophy. He remembered the second case file that came with the Judith Reinhold unsolved homicide. Morgan felt stupid that he became distracted with Sheila's sweet body, her sweet smell, everything about that beautiful woman he got to have that day. After he thought about it that way, he didn't feel stupid anymore and contemplated following up on her earlier offer as he knew he was flogging a dead horse with his lust for Jillian Edders. He cast aside his dirty thoughts and looked at the second envelope with disdain as he knew it was time to work. He put on his glasses and opened the morass of information that was sent from the Dorrington Police.

Case # 2: Deceased Mandy Young, 10 years old, beheaded. Status: UNSOLVED

On Friday the 16th of June 2000 Dorrington Police were made aware that 10-year-old Mandy Young failed to make it to school upon leaving her residence at 44 Grouper Drive in the town of Dorrington. She was thought to have been ill for the day and was not reported missing until she failed to return home after the scholastic day had ended. The immediate search by police did not turn up anything and in the days that followed dozens of volunteers were coordinated to assist with the search. The search concentrated in the wooded areas that surrounded the school.

Background: Mandy Young was a grade four student at Clancy Elementary School and was highly thought of amongst the staff and students. She was popular, well liked and excelled at her school work. She lived with her mother and stepfather at the 44 Grouper Drive address and no issues of behavior or involvement with Child Services are reported. Her natural father

lives just outside of Dorrington and as before, no issues there.

Scene: Following an extensive search Dorrington Police received a tip when a construction worker found what he thought was blood in an empty apartment unit currently under development. The body was eventually located at this construction site that would be on the path that Mandy Young would take when she walked to and from school. It was inside a dumpster that was being used for the scrap that was produced by the construction of a six-unit apartment complex. It was purposely placed under a pile of scrap that the workers innocently continued to pile on top of her body. Removal of the scrap showed that Mandy Young was missing her head. Identification was made via her clothing, umbrella and backpack with her name on it. The head was not located at the scene and remains outstanding. Forensic Identification units that examined the scene noted something extremely odd, and is currently hold back information in this case and not to be released. The area surrounding Mandy Young's neck was covered with... Navy Beans. This piece of evidence is baffling to say the least. It was purposely done by the killer for an as of yet unknown reason. The dumpster had been seized and secured for

further forensic consideration but has not yielded any further clues.

The autopsy revealed death was by beheading in what may have been a saw or other such toothed object. Dorrington Police are not aware of any similar murders in other jurisdictions.

Canvass and interviews: Family members, staff, close friends have been canvassed and so far no useful information has come to light. The murder of Mandy Young has gone cold.

Morgan felt sick and reached in the drawer and took two mouthfuls from the fresh bottle. The nauseating facts of this murder would make anyone drink at nine in the morning. This was a game changer. Why did this child deserve to die in the same manner as the others? Morgan couldn't fathom the fear that an adult would sense, let alone a ten-year-old child.

* * *

It was Friday the 16th day of June 2000 in the town of Dorrington at Clancy Elementary School. The children were out for recess playing jump rope, tag, and other such playground games to burn off the excess energy and the typical child heebee jeebee's so they could concentrate in class. This day however, was overcast and as the raindrops began to fall the school bell rang early signaling for the children to come back inside to their respective classrooms. The disappointed children lined up and were herded inside back to class, but since recess was cut short, some classes played inside games like "Heads Up Seven Up" or a round of "Show and Tell". Show and Tell generally consisted of a child bringing something to school from home, showing the class, and telling all about it. Some would bring smart items like a new media player or the coolest new toy while some would bring senseless items like a boring coloring book or a plastic trinket they got from the Red Lobster treasure chest. Some wouldn't even have anything to show and would just stand in front of the class and say something.

Sometimes, kids just get up there and say something stupid. One young boy in particular decided to stand in front of the class and tell a joke. Either it was the best joke ever told, or the dumbest joke ever told, but the boy made it up on the spot, adlibbing without prior thought. Whatever the joke was, it was beyond the mental grasp of the children and not one person laughed, not a snicker, not a chuckle, not even a groan. He stood, and for a second thought he heard a cricket. The poor lad, not being able to connect with this tough audience, returned to his desk, dejected. The students of Clancy Elementary finished the rest of the indoor recess and got back to their studies and finished the day like any other.

The rainy weather continued into the next day as Mandy Young walked alone down the puddle laden sidewalk jumping playfully into the small pools along her usual route. She held a small, pink umbrella over her head decked out with the usual girly images one could expect on a child's umbrella. Mandy would usually meet up with her girlfriends a few blocks from the school, but as she passed a construction site, she caught something out of the corner of her eye. In the front doorway of the unfinished apartment complex she saw another girl with a similar blue umbrella covering her face. Mandy thought she recognized the other person as one of her friends that may have walked up further than usual to meet her and was seeking shelter from the rain in the doorway of the apartment. As Mandy approached the person disappeared into the empty shell of the incomplete complex.

"Chrissy, that you?" Mandy called out as she entered the doorway.

Her words echoed off the cement walls that were sparsely covered in the odd graffiti from some of the older kids that wrote the occasional slang offensive term like "nigga" or "fuck the police". She saw her friend in a corner, or at least she thought so, with the umbrella still over her face. As the person lowered the umbrella Mandy knew it was not Chrissy at all, and the person held a brick in their right hand.

"What do you want? You don't scare me, and I am going to tell my step dad on you! He is a town councilman and can kick you out of town if he wants to." Mandy appeared to know this person and the threat was made with the mind of a child, who obviously thought her step father had the power to decide who could live in Dorrington and who could not.

The brick hit Mandy flush in the face, sending her to the paved floor of the complex. She was stunned, her nose shattered with blood flowing down her tiny face. She couldn't believe what had just happened and through her tears she looked at the person standing before her. This vile individual now had two plastic baggies of navy beans held up to each ear. The person danced around the fallen Mandy while allowing the navy beans to spill from the baggies, as if to simulate the beans were literally falling out of the ears. The baggies shook from the rocking wave of the attacker's head and the navy beans rained on Mandy's face, mixing with her spewing blood and turning the beans from white to red. The rain outside poured down even harder and a crack of thunder split the air. When the baggies were empty, when the last of the beans had fallen, a cement block thrown with tremendous downward force sealed her fate. The mystery person cleaned up the area, pulled out a saw, then walked towards her lifeless, little body.

* * *

Morgan was sitting in his chair, still taken aback from what he had just read from the second case file. He suddenly felt he knew better of what Edders was going through in her attempts to solve a child's murder. Morgan directed his mind back to Dan Keeling, and if he indeed was Jenny McGrath's killer, it may be possible he was the killer of everyone, because he had shown twice, he could kill a child. Morgan could hear the front door to the office open with that loathsome buzzing sound that he suspiciously did not hear when Sheila had been allowed in, and could detect the clip clop of Edders dress shoes as she approached his door.

"Hey studdly, sorry I didn't come out with ya last night, just wasn't up to it."

Morgan rose from his chair and approached Edders, who was suspicious of what he was about to do and leaned back in a show of apprehensiveness. Morgan put his arms around her and gave her a pleasant friendship embrace. She stood straight for a second, and then returned the embrace to her elder detective friend.

"Okay, muffin, what is that for?"

"Let's just say… I get it."

"Don't follow. You get what?"

Edders could smell booze already; she hoped it was stale and leftover from the night before, but knew it was probably not.

"I know what you're going through and I hope I was not too insensitive yesterday."

"Don't sweat it John. I worry about you, you worry about me, we're like an old married couple… but you unfortunately have a gross, old dick. Not my cup of tea you see."

Morgan tightened his lips and shook his head in agreement as he thought about his gross, old dick inside Sheila the day before yesterday. "Yes I do, yes I do. You don't get any grosser dicks than mine."

Grant had started his shift a few hours prior and was just getting back to the station having finished a few early morning calls for service. He saw Morgan and Edders and decided to snoop into any new information they may have on Dan Keeling.

"Old dude, my mentor, my idol, did you guys find out anything on Dan Keeling?"

"I can tell you this kid: his wife Donna thinks you did a bang up job in looking for him and keeping her up to speed on the missing person investigation. He is still technically missing, but she states he called her yesterday, just prior to our arrival actually and told her he'd run off with some new chick. She cursed him and his womanly voice or something like that. We just now need to make contact with him and ask him a few questions, but, we don't know where he may be."

"Good to hear that he at least put her mind at ease that he wasn't dead. My first thought was he left her because of the background she gave me. Any connection with your case?" he asked of Edders.

"Nothing as of yesterday, but working on it," she answered.

"Well, let me know if you need anything else, still think I've seen that guy before. My money's on Keeling."

"Okay, let's find out if Dan Keeling ever lived in Thompson Hill or a place called Dorrington," Morgan said.

"Dorrington, why that?"

Morgan gave Edders the second case file that had been sent to him and watched her eyes widen as she read the miserable details contained therein. She put her hand over her mouth in shock.

"We have to get this motherfucker."

"We'll put our minds and bodies together and the answers will be there," Morgan said with confidence.

"Our minds are probably going to be enough I think."

Morgan was aware that one cannot call up a school and start asking questions about students and former students as there were confidentiality issues that are in place to protect the children from disgruntled parents or weirdos of the sort. Morgan was not one to do just the bare minimum when he really cared about a case, as he did for Jenny McGrath and the stressed out Jillian Edders. Gurracci and Smilie not so much, but if they get solved as a by-product of this investigative angle, that would be a bonus. Morgan deduced he would need the school's entire student list for the time surrounding the murders in the two distant jurisdictions. He would also send for yearbooks or class pictures from those times as well, because a picture is better than a computer printout or handwritten list every time. Morgan needed to write a search warrant for the school records so he sat down in front of his computer, shook his shoulders, cracked his knuckles, and stopped short of reaching for his desk drawer. If Edders was not standing there, a quick nip would be just what he needed to get the creative warrant writing juices flowing.

It took about three hours, but together they banged out a warrant to send to the jurisdictions of Thompson Hill and Dorrington for those respective police services to execute on Morgan and Edders behalf. They both took turns proof reading it.

"What an absolute load of bullshit." Edders put the warrant onto Morgan's desk.

"Welcome to the world of lawyers and judges… everything has to be bling blang blong… or they toss it in the trash, especially if we draw Judge Neilson on this. I have every confidence it will fly and we should get what we need soon."

"Why didn't we just ask his wife?"

"Double life… sounds like she may be in the dark about his past or what he does in his spare time. It's better this way, especially for evidentiary purposes."

"That's what I like about your mushy brain, always covering your bases. Let's see if we can figure out what Dan Keeling may have been driving since he left behind the only car he had."

"Simple drunken logic will suffice. If he didn't use his own, then he used someone else's. If he didn't borrow one, then he stole one. If he didn't beg, borrow or steal, then he rented one. The borrowing part is a little harder to track down, the stolen and rented is a bit easier because there is a paper trail we can follow, and follow we shall, after we take care of a little ugliness."

Before they left for the courthouse Morgan requested a printout from the front desk staff of all the stolen vehicles from the area in the past few months to get the best range of possible hits. He made sure to have them put a rush on it and get it on his desk by the afternoon. He was never usually that demanding, but at least it put a twist in the usual nondescript day of the front office staff. He and Edders were on a roll and didn't want to ruin the momentum.

Edders stood staunchly before Judge Neilson as he read over the search warrant, scrutinizing every line by running his finger over each word, even checking for spelling. His glasses were perched at the end of his nose and his face seemed to be locked in a permanent scowl.

"This warrant has got John Morgan's stink all over it," he commented.

"Yes, Your Honor, he wrote it," Edders admitted.

"Even the paper smells like whiskey. Tell that asshole to hurry up and get this shit solved," he muttered while signing the warrant with his illegible signature.

Morgan's cell phone rang from his hiding spot up the hall from the judge's chambers and he knew the number on the display belonged to the Moravian Police station.

"Yello."

Samuels was the gruff voice on the other end.

"I have the list you wanted. There are about ten that were stolen and only two have been recovered. One was burnt out so there was not much left to look at. Grant investigated that one and it was just towed to McCauly's compound. It was a rental car from town. From reading the report Grant wrote, he notified the agency, and took the name off the contract. It was fake, and it appears he is still working on it. The second recovered one was returned to the owner, it appears that one was taken by a family member and just a warning was issued. Hope this helps."

"It does, I appreciate you doing this so quickly."

Morgan hung up as Edders approached.

"Well scissor me timbers," Morgan said to Edders who looked at him with her mouth a gape due to his over the top lesbian reference. "We got a car we can check out. It was in fact a rental car that was burnt out. Grant was looking into it and had taken the name from the rental contract. Hopefully the company still has it on file."

"Okay… I'm still back on the scissor me timbers remark but I'll let it slide so we can get to the storage lot."

Morgan and Edders entered McCauly's towing compound and stood before a burnt out shell of a Chevrolet Malibu. There was nothing left of it. No seats, no steering wheel, no airbags, no floorboards, nothing. It was just a hulking, charred metal frame reduced to unglamorous anonymity, beyond being useful for any kind of forensic evidence. The plate of the vehicle's identification number had already been pulled off and smoothed out by Grant so the vehicle could be traced back to the rental company.

Edders put her hand on the scorched mess and had a strong intuition that they were standing before the right vehicle. This may have been the last ride Jenny took. The last person she ever saw may have been Dan Keeling. Fighting her feelings of inextricable hatred to Jenny's killer, she knew the Malibu was useless, and this only served to meld her fury with disappointment. Nonetheless, she had an idea.

"Let's get that contract and see if we can lift a print from it."

Morgan complimented her, "Now you're cooking with gasoline, baby. Who's thinking now?"

The drive to the rental company was done in absolute silence. Morgan could tell Edders was deep in thought over the unfolding events of the day and he let her have at it. They were either getting close to nailing Dan Keeling, or either chasing their tails. One way or the other, they had to try.

"Cops back again, I hope you found out who stole and burned our Malibu. It was one of the last ones we had," the manager said. He didn't really care, he merely had to pretend he cared as it wasn't coming out of his pay check.

"May we see the rental contract for the Malibu?" Edders politely asked.

The manager bent over and picked up a file that was labeled "Malibu Insurance Claim" and began to rifle through the papers. He pulled it out and placed it in front of the detectives.

"Yeah, got some fake name on it, paid for upfront in cash, which is against our credit card policy but the employee that rented it out took pity on the guy because he said he didn't have one and needed to go to a family emergency in Franklin Falls. Guess that serves us right for trying to be Mr. Nice Guy. Bet ya he had a phony licence too."

Morgan and Edders, not touching the contract, read it as it sat flat on the rental counter. George Hollandale was the fake name on the contract.

"We're going to be seizing this and dusting it for fingerprints," Morgan told the manager.

"Be my guest, hope you find the guy."

"Does this reception area have surveillance?"

"Yeah the other younger cop asked that. No, it does not, sorry. I am sure that would have helped."

"Could have, but we'll try the prints and see what we get."

Edders went out to her car and got a paper evidence bag and using the eraser of a pencil she slid the contract into the bag and never did her fingers touch it. Should the contract have any fingerprints on it, it will have anyone who may have touched it from the employee who rented the car, the manager and hopefully Dan Keeling. The unfortunate thing was, since Dan Keeling didn't have a police record, his fingerprints would not be on file to compare with any fingerprints that may get lifted from the contract. They were still in a pickle.

* * *

Grant continued to ride alone in his police cruiser occasionally speaking to the empty seat to help himself feel better when he got down. Grant was having a slow day and didn't mind a break from a relentless onslaught of annoying calls but it was not to last, as his police radio chirped at him and jerked him out of his reverie.

"Need you to go check on an elderly female who hasn't been seen by her neighbors in a month," Samuels said over the radio.

Grant stepped on the accelerator and hustled over to the address. He exchanged complicit glances with the nosy neighbors standing at their fence lines as he pulled into the driveway and got out of his cruiser. Ignoring the occasional oblique inquiry from the peanut gallery, Grant approached the door to the older, two-level house. It had a ramp that ran up to the front door which was flanked by two dirty windows with nineteen-fifties styled velvet curtains that covered the entire window making it impossible to simply peer inside. He clenched his fist, knocked on the door, and thought he could hear some movement. He put his ear to the door and listened intently for about half a minute when he heard it again. Looking down he noted a mail slot in the front door so he bent down and flipped it up hoping to be able to peek inside.

"Ah fuck!" he cursed as he was bowled over by the stench.

Grant had smelled this before at Henderson's apartment, but this was more overpowering, one of the worst stenches he had ever encountered. He held his stomach and nonchalantly walked around the side of the house away from the prowling eyes of the neighbors who had now begun to gather on the sidewalk in front of the house. Grant let his vomit fly behind an untrimmed hedge whose crunchy brown leaves had long left the barren branches and now littered the ground.

"Fertilizer," Grant said looking at his regurgitated lunch and perhaps in a touchingly auspicious way, he hoped the hedge would be better off.

Composing himself, he approached the back door and tried the knob to find it also locked. He sighed and kicked at the back door, which flew open with only two well-placed boots just to the left of the ancient doorknob. Grant plugged his nose like a child does when going underwater in a swimming pool as he entered through the doorway. There was a dead cat just behind the door and he noticed there were tiny scratch marks in the old wood where the poor thing had tried to get out to find some food, but had inevitably starved to death. Grant took a few more steps and observed a second dead cat that was virtually skin, bone, and its carcass had become home to a multitude of maggots. Flies buzzed about the dreadful scene in this house, landing here and there on his face so that he had to continuously brush them away. Grant knew this was soon to become much worse when he saw a third dead cat, a fourth and yet a fifth, so far.

He ascended the derelict staircase, stepping over more dead cats as he went. He stopped halfway up. At the top of the stairs was a skinny, ragged cat, staring down at him. It hunched its back, hissed and looked at him with hostility in its eyes. He took another step, it hissed even louder and bared its claws, daring him to step again.

"Oh for fuck sakes, it's a goddam cat," Grant said pulling out his police baton while skillfully keeping one hand plugging his nose.

He walked up another step and poked at the cat, which begrudgingly backed off and ran down a hallway into the bathroom at the end while continuing its vicious hiss. Other than dead cats, of which he counted more than thirty, he still couldn't find the old lady. He looked around her living room and closed his eyes, waiting for the clairvoyance or psychic ability he had experienced prior. Alas, all that came to him was the continued cadence of a ticking grandfather clock and the irritating buzz of the flies.

A candy dish sat on the coffee table, although it was full of cough drops instead of candy, for the old lady that lived here didn't receive many house guests to entertain. He walked to the end of the hall and found her, dead on the toilet. He knew from his two years' experience that someday we all will die, and unfortunately, a lot of us will kick the bucket while sitting on the toilet. The old lady's pants were down around her ankles and the leg had been chewed by the lone, surviving, and starving cat. Grant found it odd that all of the cats chose death, rather than eat their owner, except for this one. It ate her leg right to the bone, the small teeth marks were quite obvious and more maggots had begun writhing about inside her wound.

The hissing feline jumped onto the bathroom counter and continued to stare down Grant. He cautiously looked into the bathroom mirror. He never played Bloody Mary as a kid and part of him thought the Grim Reaper would be the reflection, but it was just him, and the cat. With one hand, he began to slide open windows while stepping over cat corpses until he eventually exited out the front door. He walked back to his car and finally exhaled through his nose, allowing a wave of relief to overcome him.

"Ah Christ!" some of the onlookers exclaimed before they turned to walk away as the stench inside now became the stench outside.

Serves ya right ya stupid gawkers, Grant thought.

Morgan and Edders pulled up to the house after having had been alerted by Samuels to come and give Grant a hand. Morgan went inside, but Edders chose to remain outside to avoid being subject to Morgan's shenanigans.

"Holy crappin' Christmas, it looks like she hasn't trimmed her bush in years," Morgan whistled after viewing the old woman's exposed, blackened body. He peeked over his shoulder to make sure no one overheard that inappropriate comment. The only one that did hear it was the glaring, flesh-eating cat that still sat on the bathroom counter eyeing up Morgan and maintaining a low growl as if it knew his intent was to move the woman, taking away what had served as its only food source for the past month.

"Sorry, kitty," Morgan said.

He turned to walk away, and it was then that the demonic cat sprang from the counter and launched itself onto his back.

Claws pierced into his neck, hooking into the flesh. Morgan screamed, "FUCK! Goddam, stupid fucking cat!"

Morgan ripped the cat from his back and hurled it. It scrambled across the floor and took off out the open front door before he could deliver it a solid boot. He walked back outside where Edders looked at him having heard his bellow.

"What the hell happened?" she asked.

"A cat-tastrophe."

Grant groaned. "I can't believe you just said that."

Edders could and by now, expected no less.

"Natural causes, looks like she shat out the last of her life essence and croaked on the crapper. Clean up and close it up, my young friend," Morgan said as he and Edders returned to her car, leaving poor Grant alone with the old lady's dead body.

The two detectives returned to the office where Morgan didn't forget to thank the administrative civilian that compiled the list of stolen vehicles for him. Edders held the bag that contained the contract and was quite anxious to get it analyzed as soon as possible so that they could submit it for processing through the normal forensic channels and hope for the best. The warrant they wrote that was signed by the persnickety Judge Neilson was sent off as well to the jurisdictions of Thompson Hill and Dorrington, and like the fingerprints, the waiting was the hardest part.

"Well muffin, I'm going to have to get back to Franklin Falls. You don't know how much you helped me these past few days."

They hugged again. Edders was still worried about him. He was getting more fragile and she was hoping he could keep it together. She considered him more than a fellow detective; she considered him her good friend.

"Think of me if you want to change teams."

"Stop it," she breathed as she hugged him.

Morgan watched Edders shapely bottom shift back and forth as she walked back through the busy office to the front door. She turned and blew him a playful kiss, then departed the station back to Franklin Falls. Morgan didn't want her to leave, but knew the friendship was not worth ruining with any old, stupid pick-up moves he may have in his back pocket. Instead, he turned his mind to the attractive Sheila and his all new, stupid pick-up moves. He looked at her panties again, white, lacy, and wonderful. He admired his trophy, looked at his phone and pondered. He wrapped them around his whiskey bottle and took a sip.

CHAPTER EIGHT

WELL-MEANING BOOBS MCGEE

The waitress that Morgan had dubbed Boobs McGee shook her derrière as she walked down the floor of the diner like she was a runway model showing off her new waitress uniform complete with coffee and ketchup stains from Italian designer Gugliano Fantino. An older bald-headed gentleman entered and sat down at the front counter area. He ordered a cup of coffee and commenced to pour numerous packs of sugar into the black sludge.

"Easy honey, you're sweet enough," Boobs McGee said.

"Mmm hmm," he mumbled, just staring straight ahead and partially ignoring her drivel.

He looked in the opening across the counter that showed the greasy kitchen and the cook with a discoloured apron pouring some fries into a steel basket and dropping them into the deep fryer. The sizzle of the cooking oil mesmerized him as the resulting steam rose to the ceiling, adding to the already brown-stained tiles caked with years of neglect. There was a goldfish bowl sitting by the cash register that was strangely not filled with water or fish. He reached in and pulled out some business cards and started reading the companies and people that were advertising their wares. There were insurance salesmen, vacuum cleaner salesmen, magazine salesmen; anyone who travelled seemed to be in the fishbowl. A crude sign taped to the bowl read "free dinner". The bald man deduced the diner had a gimmick to draw a business card from patrons for the chance of a free dinner in hopes of gaining repeat business. He continued to leaf through the cards and stopped at one in particular.

DETECTIVE JILLIAN EDDERS

FRANKLIN FALLS POLICE SERVICE

"I put that in there so as to give that nice detective a free meal," Boobs McGee explained after noticing the man fixating on her card. "She's gonna catch that guy that killed that little girl. They came in here that night and I remembered her from the TV so I gave her our video we got. She was really nice, so I thought it was the least we could do."

Boobs McGee leaned in closer to the bald-headed man while purposely displaying her cleavage that was barely covered by the uniform and whispered to him with a giggle, "I was gonna pick it on purpose next time we did a draw."

"Well, I guess that was quite thoughtful of you," the man finally said.

He didn't seem too interested in her boobs, which was a first for the waitress who shrugged away the tip she had been hoping for. The bald gentlemen sat sipping his coffee, and he ignored her for the rest of his stay. As he got up to leave, he noticed one more sign taped to the side of the ancient cash register.

DAY COOK NEEDED

* * *

Morgan sat in his favorite stool, strategically placed in front of the dozen beer taps. Gillespie's, unlike some other bars, changed up their beer selection now and then to keep things fresh. Morgan checked to see if there were any new beers to try, but still ended up ordering his old standby. The basket of hot wings appeared again, and Morgan savored the bouquet of the secret sauce as was his ritual.

"I can tell you really like her."

"That obvious, Stephen?"

"Hey, don't worry, it's all good. She has a curvy bod, true beauty, and the brains to go with it. The perfect combination that any mature guy would look for in his gals."

Morgan chuckled, "If she wasn't a lesbot I may have a chance."

"Come on now, don't talk about that pretty lady that way," Stephen scolded Morgan.

"You're right. She is special. Even if she was straight, she'd never be interested in me. I am at least ten years older than her, I am mess, face like an old leather catcher's mitt, and I am a blithering alcoholic."

"Well, you're Gillespie's blithering alcoholic and we take care of our own," Stephen said with a sparkle in his blue eyes.

"Anything less would be a cat-tastrophe."

Stephen paused. "I don't get it."

Morgan sipped the whiskey and gulped the beer as a chaser as he did virtually every night of his doleful life. He shook hands with Stephen, thanked him for the kind words and departed back to his unmarked police cruiser then drove home while tapping the wheel to his Irish tunes.

He was too drunk for "MILF's on the Beach". It was too late to do any chores, so the dishes continued to sit in the sink, the toilet continued to not clean itself, and Morgan sank into his favorite chair, closed his eyes and drifted off to sleep. He had hoped to dream of Sheila Appleton making out with Jillian Edders, with their tongues intertwined in lesbian lust, but alas, it never happened.

* * *

It was an uneventful few days and still no results on any of the inquiries into the prints or school records. As Edders had done many times before, she drove the route from the diner to the farmer's field where Jenny's body had been located. She drove possessed, not maniacally or at a high speed, rather slow and methodical, checking every tree, every bush, every inch of the ditch looking for something, anything. She missed Morgan now that he wasn't around. It was strange how she felt that his antics could be overwhelming as they occurred, but now that she was alone, she missed the chuckle it gave her.

Although alcohol induced for the most part, she had to admit, it was funny. Morgan had a way of making people's inane, stupid problems humorous as a coping mechanism for those true victims, and she loved that about her friend. She reached the field as she did so many times before and stopped the car just before the road turned to the dry, barren area that couldn't grow crops this year. Edders got out into the heat to survey the field owned by old Jacob Smalls, hoping something would come to her. However, as per usual, nothing did. She returned to her car and decided to do the route one more time.

About a half hour later Edders returned to the diner parking lot and as she had done over and over throughout the past few days, she took down the license plates of the few cars that were in the lot. It was not a sure thing, not an exact science, it was more of information gathering with hopes she'd get lucky. One vehicle in particular caught her eye. It was a newer Chev Malibu. With the license plate recorded she got out and peeked inside. She could see a contract from a different rental car agency from Moravian. Edders made note of that and entered the diner. Boobs McGee stood behind the counter smiling at Edders as she walked in and sat at the counter. Behind her, a bald-headed cook stood looking through the opening between the counter and the kitchen with a stare that evinced mistrust and loathing.

"Shut up, I was hoping you'd come back in!" Boobs McGee exclaimed.

She reached into the fishbowl and purposely pulled out Edders business card. Edders was rendered slightly uncomfortable because she had given the card to the manager without authorizing it to be used for free food in the diner's makeshift lottery.

"You get a free dinner honey, congratulations."

"I'll take a polite pass on that," she replied.

"Oh, take a coffee then," the bald-headed cook cut in. He put a fresh pot onto the heat plate of the coffee maker.

Edders said with half a smile, "Well, thanks."

"You look like you got a lot on your mind and it's the least we could do," he answered in a tone that rang with condemnation.

A fresh, steaming cup was placed in front of Detective Edders. She inhaled the fresh Colombian aroma that rose from the ceramic mug and began to sip the hot brew. It wasn't the best coffee in the world, which could be said about all the food and drink at this passé diner. It sure smelled better than it tasted, but she finished the abhorrent beverage not to be rude. She wondered who was driving the Malibu rented from Moravian. She sat watching for about twenty minutes but all those that left did not get into the Malibu. Edders decided to leave and hatched a plan to sit up the road and wait for the Malibu to move so she could eye the driver.

Edders yawned as she left the diner suddenly feeling quite sluggish. She got into her car and pulled out of the diner parking lot and began to head up the road in the direction of Jacob Smalls' field. Just as she thought it would be far enough to watch the parking lot, she saw the Malibu in the rear-view mirror.

Back at the diner, Boobs McGee looked with wonderment at the empty kitchen.

"Doesn't anyone want to work here?" she sighed as she put the "cook wanted" sign back up.

Edders continued on her route and tried to see who was in the driver's seat of the Malibu, but the sky was darkening quickly and the headlights of the Malibu were set on high. She put her hand on the butt of her pistol she wore underneath her shirt. Her heart began to race and her breathing quickened. She blinked hard and fought aggressively to keep her drooping eyes open as she drove. With the Malibu close in her mirror she rummaged in her pocket for her cell phone. With the device now in her shaking hands, she lacked the dexterity to drive and dial 911.

The phone slipped from her grasp and dropped to the floor, separating the battery from the back. Edders head fell onto the steering wheel as she wrestled not to lose consciousness. Her arm strained to collect the pieces, and her fingers had just barely scraped the surfaces when her car swerved. It zipped wildly across the road into the oncoming lane, sailed into the ditch, and smashed into a solitary tree head on.

Edders stirred, flopping back into the seat, fumbling with her hostler clasp until the gun released into her trembling hands. Blood dripped down her forehead into half-closed eyes that were already too blurry to comprehend which direction she was pointing the pistol. She heard her dented car door beside her open, then heard oblivion in the silence that preceded her one shot, before she lost consciousness completely. She felt as if she was floating on a soft cloud or drifting blissfully along a meandering brook that is often the tale of those close to death.

"You are so beautiful, my precious one. You played a good game, but now you will play my game," the bald man said before imparting a painful grunt.

Edders did not hear any of the man's rambling. She was too heavily drugged, and it would be a few hours before the drug would wear off. However, in her slumber she only continued down the peaceful brook, and she could see someone waving at her from the shore. She waved back at Jenny McGrath, who was beaming her pretty smile toward the detective.

No one saw the bald-headed man pull Edders from the back seat under the cover of darkness. There were no neighbors with prying eyes here as he carried her limp body behind a house that was well back from the road and shielded by a dark tree line.

He flicked on the dim light to the basement and descended the staircase. He bound her wrists and placed a hook through the rope. The hook attached to a pulley system which the man cranked with a hand wheel and Edders body was hoisted into the air until just the tips of her toes made contact with the floor. The bald man turned a dial on the wall, and with a loud *foomp* and a flash, the basement furnace came to life with an eerie red flame.

He slapped her face with a medium blow. It was just enough to get her to regain some capacities although she still could not function.

"Wake up Jillian … wake up."

He tapped her cheek some more, but Edders just groaned.

"I said wake up!"

The man struck Edders in the face with a slap twice as hard as the first, and she raised her head up and opened her eyes halfway. Her cheek was red with his handprint and her forehead was still caked with her blood from the accident.

Her vision was still smeared but slowly she tried focus. The only thing she knew at this time was that she was not floating on a heavenly stream, she was in hell. As her sight began to improve and her brain returned to reality, she could see the hell she was in. There were shadow demons dancing on the wall around the bald-headed man. The demons darted to and fro, back and forth, and up and down, with their evil eyes reflecting the hellish red flames of the old furnace. Through the moving shadows that appeared to pirouette about the walls, Edders saw what she thought was a circle of red dots. She was yet unaware if her vision was still spotty and tried to focus on these dots. Edders was sure that these dots were not on her irises, she was sure she was being videotaped.

"You are indeed beautiful. She was once beautiful like you..."

The man caressed her hair and moved in closer and smelled it. Edders attempted to back away but was unable to resist due to her inescapable position and ended up just swinging towards him. He put his arms around her and ground his crotch into hers.

"Who... who are you?" she squeaked out.

"I am madness..."

He unbuttoned the top of her blouse exposing some cleavage and put his face to her breasts as she hung helplessly.

"Please... you don't have to do this."

"You had a chance to play your game. Now you play with me."

He ran his tongue gingerly up her neck as her mind became a bit clearer.

"Please... Dan, stop"

The man stopped and looked at her with his expression changing towards anger. He snarled, "I am not Dan... I am madness!"

"Did you take Jenny here?"

"No, no, someone that pretty could not be resisted. I had to have her immediately. The young, sweet flesh needed me inside her. I was inside her…we were one. We were together again."

"You bastard," she spat with a cracking voice. Her tears were now flowing down her red cheeks as the flames in the furnace kicked higher.

"No. Not bastard… *Madness.* She reminded me of my own."

"Your own daughter?"

"Like you remind me of my wife, once so beautiful."

He moved again towards Edders and undid another button on her blouse and resumed his gentle assault on her breasts.

"Your wife and daughter…where are they?"

"They wouldn't play this game…I fed them to the metal devil."

He stepped back and adjusted the flue on the furnace so the flames died down and the demons on the wall began to disappear. He opened the iron mouth of the furnace and two charred skulls, one big and one small, were sitting on the grill inside amongst a pile of charred bones. He turned the flue and the flames resumed burning at full capacity. The demon shadows returned to the walls and again began their dance of death for their master.

"You killed them too."

"They wouldn't play. Will you play?"

He grabbed Edders and pulled her towards him again. The man turned his head slightly left and kissed her on the lips. She kept her eyes open throughout this disgusting mouth to mouth contact, and on the right side of his neck she now noticed gauze and hospital tape. Edders had been successful in landing the one shot, but it only served to wound him. Luck was not with her as she had come within inches of killing him yet he stood here torturing her. He undid the rest of the buttons on the blouse and began to fondle her breasts through her bra.

"Time to play."

The man freed his tiny member from the confines of his pants and began to stroke it while his other hand was occupied with unsnapping the button on her pants. He slid his hand inside her panties and felt for her opening just as Edders mustered enough strength to lift herself up and plant her foot right into the man's miniscule dick.

"AHHHHH!"

He grabbed at his crotch and dropped to his knees screaming. Edders squirmed on the hanger but could not free herself. The man slowly rose back to his feet, and the flames reflected off his face and his expression was evil incarnate.

"They wouldn't play…you won't play. THIS IS MADNESS!"

He began to furiously slap her face with all of his strength, reopening her gashed forehead as her face roughly moved side to side under the power of his blows. He tore her shirt off as Edders continued to try and kick him away unsuccessfully. He grabbed her pants and pulled them to her ankles, leaving her virtually naked save for her bra and panties. As he did this another business card fell out of her pocket. He was in an uncontrollable rage, he screamed, slammed his fists on the wall, kicked at the furnace, knocking the steel door slightly off its hinges, and then grabbed a belt off the wall. The orange light gleamed off the silver of those hooks attached to leather.

"MADNESS! MADNESS! MADNESS!"

He shouted this over and over as he beat Jillian Edders with this belt of hooks. The specially shaped metal shredded into her tender flesh and tore chunks out. She screamed a blood curdling cry of pain as he beat her like a man possessed. She couldn't breathe, she could only scream. She looked right into the camera and knew she was going to die. Her entire body was covered in blood and she was again, barely conscious. The man released the pulley and she came crashing to the cement floor. Edders looked up at the dancing demons and into the eyes of the furnace that was beckoning for a sacrifice, for her very soul.

"NOW WILL YOU PLAY?" he shouted.

"Fuck you," she squeaked through her bloody lips. "Get him for me, my muffin."

The belt flew back before rushing forward to slash across her face. One of the hooks snagged and her left eye parted from her head. It remained pierced on the belt, and the man turned to the camera to demonstrate his catch.

"This is madness."

He dragged the belt across her exposed neck to gash her jugular. The solid steel hooks tore through her, capturing grotesque bits of flesh and esophagus pulp, leaving her head at an ungodly, lifeless angle. Her blood surged freely from the wound while the card that had fallen from her pocket floated down the stream of her arterial spray. Like the card, Jillian Edders drifted down the heavenly brook as Jenny McGrath waved to her from the shore with the same pretty, beaming smile as before. This time Jenny was not alone. Cliff Henderson stood waving beside her in a pressed, blue tuxedo that shone under a warm sun. She floated over to young Jenny who embraced Edders as her redeemer but in reality, Jillian Edders bled to death on the cold cement floor in the shadow the smiling, evil furnace.

CHAPTER NINE

INSANE IN THE LAME BRAIN

Morgan was unaware that the Franklin Falls police were in a furious investigation to find Edders after her unmarked police car was located crashed into a tree along the highway a few miles from McGee's diner.

The phone rang constantly on Morgan's cluttered desk, but he had already left the office so the call went to voicemail. Morgan, a man condemned with the weight of the entire city, was on his way to the dump. A third headless body had been found. His stress level was at a dangerous high and his hands quavered involuntarily as he grasped the wheel in a tighter grip. In the back of his mind lurked an omen that he would be plummeting to rock bottom before long.

The drive to the dump took him to the outskirts of the city, right by a familiar sight. Morgan slowed a bit as he drove by

Sheila Appleton's house. The tree where Jake Gurracci had been strung up in a headless display of preordained defiance vis-à-vis his cold-hearted lifestyle, now had a swing adorned with plastic daffodils hanging from a large branch. Quite a contrast from the ghastly scene of months ago, and strangely this empty swing evoked a feeling of gladness in Morgan. He pictured himself pushing Sheila playfully back and forth, her blond hair flowing in the breeze as they giggled together in blissful contentment. He wondered about her offer again.

Morgan pulled up to the dump where a uniformed Tom Giles stood at the gate with his scene control register to mark the comings and goings of everyone who may trample all over the area.

"Tommy, long time no see. Hardly recognized you."

"Hey, Morgan, living the dream I see."

"Not in the undercover drugs anymore, back in the uniform?" Morgan asked.

"Whoever chopped up my old buddy Smilie pretty much lost me my job. Not complaining, just saying is all."

"What do we have in the dump?"

"Torso of a John Doe I guess. Some bottle collecting garbage pickers were milling around for some quick change and found it in a pile. Stinks badly, but so does the whole dump."

Morgan pulled away from the newly shaven and shorn Tom Giles and parked up beside the yellow tape that Grant had just finished putting up.

"You again!" Morgan stated with astonishment.

"It always is. Sometimes I think that they send me to these dead ones on purpose, and yes, I already puked."

Morgan took a deep breath inhaling the combined smell of everything rotting in the dump, including the body.

Grant said, "Up there."

Morgan looked up what seemed to be the Mount Everest of garbage. In the endless heat, he started to journey up the stinking pile, stopping to swat flies from his face. Some stuck to his sweat, and some crawled up his sleeve. Morgan's hand pushed through a half-melted plastic bag into a combination of rotten food and bug larvae.

"Fuck," he whined before wiping it on his pants.

He was in awe at the lengths these people that had found this body had gone through in order to get some bottles to cash in for change. He kept climbing, a few feet at a time, swatting at more flies as he went. He came across an old liquor bottle, slightly amused that it was one of his regular brands for it actually may have been his at one time, and because these people had apparently missed in their haste to report the body. Finally, at the top of the heap was a naked male, decapitated, skin black as night yet had the appearance of the living due to the crawling maggots in his chest.

Grant stared at Morgan from his position at the bottom of the mountain. The hairs on his arms tingled and goose bumps appeared on his exposed skin. Grant took a deep breath and almost gagged again while preparing for the feeling that he knew was about to follow. He spun around and only could see bag upon bag of refuse that surrounded him. Tom Giles still stood in the distance at the dump gate, but Grant didn't think it was him causing the uneasiness. Still, Grant found it curious that this feeling did not present itself at the crazy cat lady's house. There were a thousand places for someone to hide, so he took extra care to be vigil.

He looked back up at Morgan where he was perched. At that moment Morgan was examining the body with sharp eyes. He noted that like the old lady on the toilet, this one had baked just as well to become the shriveled mess that someone took great effort to place on the top of this heap. He studied the stump and as before, a clean swipe of an axe, and this unidentified bastard met his maker. No marks, no tattoos, nothing at all this time to give an immediate clue to the identity of the corpse. It may prove to be tougher this time, because of the rancid, putrid shape of this body. If there was no visual way to identify him, then fingerprints and DNA would have to be taken with hopes that they return to a known individual.

"Shit, deglove."

Morgan turned around, slid on his ass down the mountain of garbage, and made it down in half the time it took him to climb it. It was still worth it to get down so fast, but Morgan's ass was now covered in the juice of the garbage of an entire city. When he got down he saw Grant looking peculiar and scanning his eyes around the dump.

"You looking for a garbage monster? If it makes you feel any better, we're going to go over every inch of this dump and see if we can come up with any clues, leads, or if we're lucky, a stash of old, dirty magazines."

Grant laughed, "I don't like the sound of that, but I know you, and I know you are serious."

"Embrace your future. A shower and a drink are in my future," Morgan chuckled as he returned to his car.

Grant and Giles remained at the dump, watching over the scene, Giles was still at the gate, and Grant stood at the bottom of the mountain. Grant and Giles now worked on the same shift but hardly ever spoke. There was still uneasiness about the way Giles had treated Henderson just prior to his suicide. Grant didn't place any blame on Giles. It was just something that was out there and seemed unresolved.

"Hee hee."

Grant heard the sound arise from somewhere in the heap of garbage, toward where the headless body lay. The sun was exceedingly bright and now shone directly on the giant pile of garbage as Grant strained and squinted to see upwards and towards the laughter. The sun was too bright; Grant picked up a rusty piece of metal and tried to block it out but to no avail. Through the slits in his eyes he thought he saw a robed figure atop the mountain of trash. He shut his eyes tight, opened them to see nothing. He heard instead a van pulling in behind him. Grant sighed as the search team arrived and he knew it was time to sift through the dump.

With tapering eyes, Morgan watched Grant from the privacy of his car before putting his head back on the seat. It was overwhelming. He now had three confirmed headless bodies and he was alone in trying to get this solved. He began the drive back to Moravian. Sheila Appleton sat in the homemade swing that Morgan noticed earlier on his way by. He continued by and hoped she didn't notice him, but she did, and she waved with a jovial smile. Morgan returned the wave as any gentleman should do, and if he wasn't so busy, he'd probably call her.

She looked as good as she did before. The marks she endured faded into a shadow of memory, and now her blond hair was flowing playfully in the warm breeze as she swung back and forth in a carefree manner. Morgan continued on to return to town. Here he finally grabbed his shower before he headed to Gillespie's.

"You look like a man that's coming to the end of his patience," Stephen stated when Morgan walked in. A shot and a beer were the order of the day, and Stephen did provide.

"A third headless numpty Stephen. No clue who this may be."

"What's the common theme?"

"Well, let us do the roll call. Jake Gurracci, mean guy and no one cares, Todd Smilie, drug dealer and no one cares, Judith Reinhold, a mean teacher, Mandy Young, and now this poor unknown bastard. So logically, each of these people were mean in general or were directly mean to whoever killed them and kept their heads. Gurracci and Smilie, I understand and still could have been anyone. Reinhold, could have been a deranged parent, a disgruntled fellow employee, a student. Mandy Young, a ten-year-old child, like the cops from Dorrington I am at a loss with that one. That's why I need the school records to see if I can connect my suspect with living in those towns when the murders occurred."

"And if he wasn't?"

"Then I am fucked again. I lick the shit stick. Everyone in this friggin' department is looking to me to get this shit solved. This new unknown guy, I don't know what to say on him right now until I can get an identification on him, which ain't looking too easy right now. I need to deglove him.

"Sounds interesting, what does that mean?"

"It means you cut the guys finger, rehydrate the skin, carefully peel it from his finger, and wrap it around your own, then see if you can press a fingerprint to try and match. The only trouble is, if you are actually successful, and if there are no prints on file, identification will not come easily. We'll have to turn to DNA to see if the match can be made that way."

Morgan drank as Stephen pondered and tried to envision this degloving procedure. After climbing the stinky rubbish pile in the heat, the beer, wings, and whiskey tasted good. The leprechauns were at their best this day.

* * *

After four hours of helping search at the dump, a smelly, uniformed Grant was driving back to the police station to change and if luck was on his side, leave early. Unfortunately, it was not to be because there, on the sidewalk, was a naked man. The man was walking by himself, not a stitch on and to make this sight even stranger, the man had one arm. Grant pulled up behind him and was a little irritated at the brash, ballsy behavior of this older gentleman. He could see the missing arm was totally gone from the shoulder on down.

"What the hell do you think you're doing?" Grant yelled towards the man.

"Just enjoying the heat."

"You can't do it naked, old dude, get in my car."

"Fuck off cop!" the old man babbled before trotting away.

"Shit, I don't need this today."

The old man could not run especially fast. He ambled along in his bare feet and Grant was able to catch up to him after only about thirty seconds of chase before tackling him to the ground. The man rolled over and began to kick at Grant while his little penis jiggled between his skinny little legs. It was no problem for Grant to flip him back over onto his stomach and pin his one arm behind his back. Instinctively Grant slapped one cuff on the man's wrist, but then froze.

"Ah shit. How the hell ya handcuff a one-armed, naked man!" Grant shouted to the sky.

The naked old man who was pinned underneath Grant began to laugh. He jeered, "What ya gonna do cop? What ya gonna do now stupid cop?"

Grant tried to snap the other cuff to his ankle, but it wouldn't reach. "I ought to snap the other end to your dick, but it's too small."

He got the man to his feet and kept his arm locked behind his back and marched him back to the car. Once the old man was in the back, Grant secured the other cuff to a portion of the cruiser cage that was strong enough to do the job.

How do you handcuff a one armed naked man…you can't, Grant thought before asking, "Name please?"

"Ronald McDonald!" the old man proclaimed in a snarky tone. "Smells like garbage in here."

"Shut up old, naked dude or I'll play nick nack on your fucking head. I'm not in the mood. If you're Ronald McDonald, then I must be goddamn Mayor McCheese."

Grant returned to the station and Samuels chucked the old man in the clink for the rest of the day. "See ya met Ronald McDonald, another resident weirdo of the Moravian Inn."

"You shitting me? His name really is Ronald McDonald?"

"Strange as it is, his name really is Ronald McDonald."

Morgan had returned to the office following his afternoon meal and drink. He checked on the status of his request for a forensic analysis on the rental car contract, but nothing had come up yet. Nothing had returned from the other jurisdictions. He drank the last few drops of the bottle in his drawer and noticed a new envelope on his desk. It was a plain white envelope with his name on it, post marked from Franklin Falls. He opened it and pulled out a DVD.

"Hey Morgan, how do you handcuff a one armed naked man?" Grant said standing at Morgan's door.

"What the hell you talking about, kid?"

"Just brought this old dude in and he was totally nude, skinny, and wrinkly. The heat is making people do really weird things."

Morgan thought about it. "I see you met Ronald McDonald. You can't handcuff him when he's naked, which he generally is three quarters of his life. Believe me, I've tried."

"Shit, right as usual."

"You smell like garbage, kid."

Grant smiled and went to the locker room for a quick shower and a change of uniform. He ignored Morgan's liquor smell, even though that would have been an appropriate comeback.

Morgan picked up the DVD and as he did, he noticed he had a new voice mail. Instead of checking it however, he decided to call it a day and go home. He threw the DVD beside the picture of his ex-wife Julie and sank into the easy chair. He knew tomorrow he would have to visit Dr. Halpin and hope for some answers in this new stinker of a cooked corpse.

Morgan popped a fresh bottle and sat sipping the nectar while his mind raced with images of death, missing heads, dead kids, and dead cops. His heart pounded against his chest and his blood pressure rose in signification of his declining health. He deepened his breathing and tried to get his heart rate to return to normal. His stress level was through the roof. He wanted to quit, pack it in, and become something simple. He thought of the funny grave-digging man and could totally understand his love of a simple life. The sipping continued as the hours ticked by and the muted TV flashed away in front of him. He turned on his laptop computer and slid the DVD into the drive. He took another drink as the DVD began to play.

"MADNESS... MADNESS... MADNESS!"

Morgan could see the image of a bald headed man beating a restrained woman with a belt. The woman was screaming a blood curdling scream that had a bone-chilling, echoing effect as it emanated loudly from Morgan's laptop. It was a darkened image, the lighting in the room they were in flickered about casting shadows all around and made it hard to focus on the picture. However, after a minute when the flickering light was just at the right angle, he saw Edders' face. He dropped his bottle and rolled out of the chair as the computer slid from his lap and landed on its side, continuing to play the macabre scene. His entire body began to shake as the screams on the screen went on, unrelenting, like driving a spike through his ear into his brain. Then silence preceded the next statement.

"This is madness," the voice drawled in such a slow manner that it could even be considered as seductive. The man, his face digitally blurred, held up the belt and Morgan saw the eye still attached to one of its bloody hooks.

Morgan snapped, crawled upwards to his knees and yelled, "NO! Not her... not her... not her."

He threw the laptop across the room into the TV. It smashed the screen before tumbling to the floor. Anything else he could get his hands on was hurled. Glasses and plates shattered on the walls in his fit of alcohol-induced fury. He was already infinitely drunk before and had now just watched his best friend, a fellow police officer, and a woman he had strong feelings for, murdered.

Morgan was not coherent and just mumbled through his tears, "Not her... not her."

He took the picture of his ex-wife and smashed it against the desk before overturning the entire credenza. One of the drawers slid out and his service pistol landed before him. He picked it up with trembling hands and put the cold steel of the barrel up to his temple. He paused, ran it up and down the scar, his finger jittery on the hair trigger. He threw the pistol across the room; death was not coming for him tonight. Instead he stumbled out the door and got into his unmarked police car.

The quivering in his grip made it hard to put the key in the ignition, but he persevered in starting the vehicle. He shifted it in reverse and peeled out squealing his tires, sailing right across the street and slamming into a car parked in the adjacent driveway. Disregarding or completely oblivious to the collision, Morgan changed gears and sped forward, swerving from curb to curb as he drove with reckless abandon. Morgan was not thinking like a rational person, but he knew where he was going. He drove clear across town, slamming into street signs, mailboxes, but luckily not striking anyone out walking in the darkness. Morgan activated the emergency dash lights and the small red rotating police beacon came to life. He flew through stop signs and red traffic signals until he pulled up onto his ex-wife's lawn. He pushed the accelerator to the floor and spun around her front yard churning up the sod and sending soil flying in every direction.

"FUCK YOU BITCH!" he screamed out the open window.

His ex-wife Julie could not believe what she was seeing, her father, Judge Neilson appeared beside her at the window. Her ex-husband was tearing up the yard in an unmarked police cruiser. Other neighbors peered out through their curtains to the sight of the cop car doing high speed doughnuts with the red light flashing away and a drunken cop screaming out the window.

911 calls poured into the Moravian police dispatch.

Even in his irrational and insane state Morgan could hear other officers being dispatched over the radio to his location and he knew he should get out of town. The judge stormed out the door and began hollering at Morgan at the top of his lungs, making sure Morgan heard his threats, specifically to end his career and making sure he'll never be able to show his face in his courtroom again. He pushed the gas and did one more doughnut, taking out every lawn ornament, and making sure no blade of grass was left untouched. He covered the screaming judge in flying dirt, and ironically leaving a severed gnomes head at his feet.

Morgan raced away before the other officers converged on the scene. He didn't go home, but he instead sped out of the city, all the while wiping away tears and punching at the ceiling of the vehicle until his fist was chaffed and bleeding. He drove just outside of town, pulled into Sheila Appleton's driveway, and as his headlights lit up the tree, he saw a vision of Jake Gurracci's body sprawled out and nailed to the branches as it had been on the night of the murder. Inside of Morgan, hate and anger were mixed with hopelessness and the mass quantities of drink.

With utter disregard for himself, he stepped on the gas again and slammed his police car into the tree. The cruiser airbag exploded into Morgan's face, snapping his head back and the resulting talcum powder clouded the interior like a miniscule dust storm. He wiped away the blood and the tears, he could see the tree was empty and her new swing fell onto the vehicle's windshield. Morgan groggily opened the door and spilled out onto the grass of Sheila's yard as she ran out her front door in her nightgown up to the fallen detective. She immediately recognized it was Morgan and hugged him gently. He was basically uninjured save for his bloody nose but his mental state was an unquestionable mess.

"Not her, not her," he sobbed in Sheila's arms.

They sat rocking and embracing in the shadow of the dimming headlights for several minutes until he was finally able to stand and come inside. Morgan then whimpered, "Don't call, please don't call... why her, oh God, why her?"

Sheila had no idea who Morgan was talking about but she understood what he meant by don't call. Sheila helped Morgan up to the bed where he collapsed in a disjointed, blubbering, drunken muddle; a shell of a man. Sheila recognized and respected Morgan more than any other man she knew and for him to be in this state, she recognized a man who had hit rock bottom. Sheila went back outside and got into his unmarked police car. It was still running and fluid had spilled out the bottom onto her yard. She put it in reverse and to her surprise the vehicle roughly began to back up with grinding and wailing emitting from the engine. She backed it to the side of her house and parked it beside an old lawnmower and a rusty scythe where it was partially concealed by the darkness.

Sheila returned to the burnt out detective and lay beside him. She still did not know what the serious issue was. She had no idea he watched Jillian Edders murdered on video, but she held him. She looked into his bleary eyes and kissed him on the cheek beside his dry, cracked lips. She wanted to save him, like he had saved her.

Moravian police officers looked for Morgan all night, but they were unable to find him.

CHAPTER TEN

TO GLOVE OR TO DE-GLOVE

Grant looked rather dashing in his blue suit and rouge tie as he descended in the hospital elevator. Despite Morgan's breakdown, business needed to go on. Grant was hand-picked by Samuels for a temporary promotion and to go to the autopsy of the unknown headless corpse, and despite Grant's aversion to those types of chores, he was honored to help out Morgan in this prominent investigative capacity. Grant was aware of everything that transpired the previous night with Morgan and hoped he would be found safe and sound.

"Hey Mor..." Halpin stopped short as the elevator door opened and he saw Grant's young face.

Grant smiled sheepishly. "Sorry, doc, you got me today. We'll have to call Morgan MIA."

"Okay, well, that's no problem," Halpin waved it off. "But here, look at this!" Halpin gestured enthusiastically in the direction of the mush on the table, his eyes wide and bright. "This is so cool…he's almost soup, I'm quite surprised that you guys were able to move him without him disintegrating."

"Yeah, wasn't easy, but we got him into the bag and I am not ashamed to say, I puked."

"We'll have a bucket and a camera waiting because when we cut into this guy I want to be ready. It will be one for the Christmas party. Cop pukes at autopsy!" he joked.

"I specifically skipped breakfast for this, so don't get your hopes up. Some retching may be on the menu, but hopefully we're out of puke."

Grant, eager to impress Halpin, hardened his nerves and entered the morgue where the body had been already laid out on the steel table by intern Ted Bolan.

"Okey dokey, here we go," Halpin said cutting into the gooey flesh.

Grant held his breath as long as he could then took shallow quaffs of air. "Don't puke, don't puke, don't puke," he mumbled to himself.

"Great big globs of greasy grimy goopy guts," Halpin sang as he dissected the body like a crafty artist. "So my young Bobby Grant, what is this guy's story?"

Grant made sure nothing would spew from his mouth before he opened his yap to answer. "I'm just filling in today, but what I gather is we are hoping to get an identity for him out of this autopsy, other than that, don't know much about him."

"Well, this is what…"

"I know, I know…de-glove."

"Ding ding ding," Halpin said mimicking a winner's bell. "Give the man a scalpel."

Boland held out the scalpel with a smirk on his face. Grant took it in his trembling hand, determined to get through it and show Morgan that he is still alright in his books by doing a good job with this assignment. The scalpel sunk into the flesh around midway of the right index finger. Grant worked it back and forth until the blade hit bone. He cut around the bone until it was all that held the finger to the rest of the hand. Boland handed him clippers. Grant held them to the bone, cringed, and in one mighty squeeze the finger fell free. Resuming the scalpel work he sliced the skin up the side of the severed finger and carefully peeled the skin upwards. Halpin and Boland watched the young officer do his work and were quite impressed. Grant didn't realize they were watching because he was so intently concentrating on this task, his eyes never leaving the finger. He put the skin around his own index finger and held it up to the light. He adjusted the skin a bit and could definitely make out the lines that made up the unique print of this corpse. Grant pressed it onto a prepared ink pad and made a perfect fingerprint. And voila, the deglove method.

"We are impressed, young man," Halpin said from over Grant's shoulder, looking down at the inked print. "One tip though...." Boland was snickering behind the table of tools. "I know the method is called de-glove, but that doesn't apply to you. You, my young friend, may absolutely wear gloves." Halpin and Boland, both in unison, held up their hands which were protected with blue surgical gloves. Grant looked at his hands, which were now oozing dead guy juice.

"Ah shit!" he bleated, rushing to soap his hands down.

Halpin clutched his side to control his guffaws. "Relax, kid, you ain't gonna die. Stick 'em in bleach and be done with it." Halpin directed his attention to the corpse on the table. "Well, let's see what you've been eating?" Halpin mused, slicing open the stomach. "Hmm… curious."

"What?" Grant scooted closer, still wiping his hands on paper towel.

Halpin's brow furrowed. "Well, I'd say his last meal was a chocolate bar, but he ate it all, including the wrapper."

"That's weird."

"It is. Generally, we can tell what his last meal was, but usually we can't tell what his last beverage was… this time I can."

"What are you some kind of clairvoyant?" Boland asked.

"Nope, just going by the soda can in his stomach."

"Get out of town!" Grant exclaimed.

"Here is a comb, guess he died while combing his hair," Halpin joked.

Halpin and Boland closed it up while Grant sat making his notes, barely believing the development. After finishing, the corpse was wheeled back into the hulking cooler where the others had been before it. No positive determination of death was available at this point other than the obvious beheading and stomach contents. Halpin and Boland declined a good bye hand shake, just jokingly however, and opted for a fist bump.

Grant sat longer making notes than Morgan would have, as he wanted to be meticulous and make sure nothing was missed. It got eerily quiet after the two jokers left. The buzzing of the electric clock and the noise of the cooling fan was even more noticeable in the immediate silence that draped the officer after the two had left.

"*Hee hee*," emanated from the hallway. Grant's head snapped up at the sound. He got up from his seat and poked his head around the door frame and looked into the hallway towards the elevator. "*Hee hee.*" It seemed to echo off the concrete walls in the empty hallway. Then he heard the voice from behind the door of the cooler. "*Madness… daddy… madness.*"

Grant whirled around, reaching for the handle and pulling open the steel door. The blackened, headless body lay unmoving in the morgue cooler, but behind it, a robed figure stood. The deathly cloak was wafting in the breeze of the overhead cooling fan, and in the figure's hand, an axe.

"*MADNESS*!" a child yelled from inside the cooler.

Grant slammed the door shut and bolted to the elevator, pushing the button over and over while looking over his shoulder back towards the cooler. Nothing more was heard. The door to the elevator opened and Grant slipped inside even before the door had finished opening. He stood panting along the back wall, fingers splayed against the cool metal railing. He began to regain composure as the elevator ascended to the main floor where hospital life was bustling with its usual daily activity. Grant returned to the Moravian police station with his proudly pressed fingerprint and submitted it to the forensic lab, again keeping his bizarre experiences to himself.

* * *

Morgan was still lying in Sheila's bed, slowly coming down from the traumatic excitement of the night before.

"Hey, stud muffin," a female voice said beside him.

Morgan rolled over and came face to face with Edders. Her blood-covered face and missing eye was staring back at a shocked Morgan, who drew back to the edge and fell to the floor. The fall knocked the vision from his head and he wished the night before was a dream but in his heart he knew it had all happened. Despite his level of intoxication, he recalled everything he did, like being on some kind of autopilot. Morgan was quite sure he would be facing charges for his behavior but he didn't care. His friend and colleague Jillian Edders was dead and Morgan didn't belong back at work, he belonged in a mental hospital.

"Hi." Sheila hovered over him then crouched to his side.

"Hi. You been there beside me all night?" he asked. He rose slowly from the floor, his muscles stiff.

"Yes. I may have dozed a bit but other than that I never took my eyes off you." She smiled sweetly at him, her eyes displaying nothing but kindness.

"You certainly didn't see me at my best yesterday. I think you saw me hit bottom."

"I hit bottom once. You helped me, and I'm here today because of that. We all need help at some time in our lives. Anyone that needs help shouldn't be ashamed to ask for it."

Morgan quivered for a moment, a wave of emotions warring in his chest before he felt the storm pull him down again. He couldn't stop the torrent of tears as he broke down yet again into Sheila's arms. "Help… I think I am ready."

Arm in arm, John Morgan and Sheila Appleton walked into the Moravian Police Station and were quickly ushered away from some local reporters who were snapping pictures. Morgan's ex-wife Julie was pretty quick to pick up the phone and call a press hay day to expose the mental breakdown of an overworked cop. Her father, Judge Neilson, joined right in the mudslinging as the whole incident amplified his hatred for

Morgan and will to end his career. They landed yet another jab on Morgan, and hit him hard when he was down. Samuels, to no one's surprise, was the one that had to dish out the ultimatums to Morgan. The Moravian Police Chief himself had cleaned out Morgan's office, collected all the empty whiskey bottles and a mystery pair of panties he kept in his drawer.

Samuels sat across from Morgan and Sheila, who continued to hold Morgan's hand. "We know about Jillian Edders," he said, his deep voice soft and understanding. "Franklin Falls was also sent a copy of the DVD with a note on it that you also were getting a copy. They called hoping to stop you before you saw it. I take it, they were too late."

Morgan remembered his unchecked voice mail and then nodded his head while looking at the floor.

"They've set you up in Pine Grove... I hear the food's good..."

Morgan nodded again. Pine Grove was a mental hospital and everyone was in agreement to put Morgan in, and make finishing treatment a requirement if Morgan wanted to keep his job and get a slap on the wrist for any future charges he may be facing. The thousands of dollars in damage would be taken care of by the department and probably deducted from his paycheck, half of which was already claimed by Julie Neilson.

"We've got a car behind the station ready to take you over. I have assigned Grant to take over your position in the interim. He's a bright cop; we'll see what he can do with this mess while you get sober and back on your feet. This pretty lady at your side can come too."

Sheila squeezed his hand harder. The trio began the trek to the back door to the waiting car. Grant stood in the doorway to Morgan's office in his sharp duds. The sight immediately reminded Morgan of himself when he took over that position years ago.

"I'm gonna make you proud. I'm gonna try to be as good as you," Grant said, smiling towards Morgan.

The reporters out front stood around, unaware that Morgan and Sheila were smuggled out the back, leaving them nothing to do but harass the front desk admin staff hoping for a smidgen of information to print. Pine Grove was an hour drive outside of Moravian and it was used to house all types of people from recovering alcoholics and drug addicts, people with mental illness, to the criminally insane. Most were treated in the minimum security section, but the seriously crazy sociopaths and psychopaths, those that would chop up their own mother into a steaming pot of stew, were locked away in the maximum security wing.

The police car approached the gates. A familiar sight to the guards in the gatehouse, but what was not so familiar was the fact that this time police were dropping off one of their own. The rusty wrought iron gate creaked as it labored to roll open. Morgan stared at the intricate designs crafted into the metal of the front gate, then the building itself. It was a drab grey stone structure that had been around longer than both Morgan and Samuels combined. The asymmetric stone that surrounded the windows attested to the buildings age and the creeping ivy climbing the sides hardly provided any means of escape should Morgan try to make a break for it. Samuels had not made a run to Pine Grove in quite some time and didn't remember it this foreboding.

"Tear this fucking place down and build a bar or something," Morgan said, finally breaking his silence.

Samuels only snorted. "Listen you, old geezer, despite the atmosphere, which I admit feels more like prison, Pine Grove has one of the best rehab programs around. I think you'll do well here."

They walked up the cement steps where other patients sat smoking cigarettes, wallowing in their own mental issues and generally paying no mind as they passed. The trio entered the main sitting area inside. The room was adorned with neutral colors, unthreatening paintings and scattered about were a dozen of the permanent residents. Some of them were in regular street clothes and some of them were dressed in light blue gowns.

"John Morgan," a plump nurse said from behind a counter. Morgan approached the nurse who was smiling a wry smile towards him. "Here's your gown." She handed him a folded, clean version of what he saw adorning the other patients.

"Aw, fuck," Morgan said sheepishly, staring with obvious distaste at the blue cloth.

"Say goodbye to your friends and we'll get you checked in."

He hugged Samuels. "Good luck, John," Samuels muttered, his voice filled with support.

"Thanks, you old geezer," Morgan said, then turned to Sheila. He didn't know what to say to Sheila but she took the reins on that issue. She stood on her toes, kissed him on the scar on his temple, then kissed his lips and embraced him as she has done many times today.

"I love you, my angel in blue."

Morgan took his blue gown and disappeared behind the buzzing door.

* * *

"Hello, Donna Keeling please."

"Speaking."

"Donna, its Detective Grant, we met a while ago regarding the missing person report of your husband Dan."

"Yes, I remember you. If you're looking for Dan my bastard of an ex-husband, I spoke to him again the other day and have written him out of my life. I have gotten a lawyer and have started divorce proceedings but since we need to be separated for a year I guess I wait."

"Do you have any idea where he is calling you from?"

"I still don't, but I really don't care. He just taunts me about his new bitch and he is some place where there is sunshine like fifteen hours a day or something stupid."

"Okay, he traded heat for more heat I guess. Again, thank you ma'am for your time."

They both hung up. Grant thought about it for a few minutes. He shifted his line of thinking away from Dan Keeling as a suspect and thought certainly with Dan Keeling's unique voice, his wife would be able to know who she was speaking to. He decided to stop following that lead unless the school records could show that Keeling had been a resident of the other jurisdictions.

"Here ya go, big dick," Giles said, throwing an envelope in front of Grant. "Results from the forensics lab."

"Thanks, dude."

The tension seemed to be easing between he and Tom Giles and Grant hoped they could eventually ditch the ugliness and get things out in the open. He tore the top off the envelope and read the results from the fingerprint analysis of the rental contract from the burnt out Malibu.

> **'Examination of the rental contract provided by Detective Morgan resulted in the discovery of several latent prints suitable for comparison purposes. Comparison to the national fingerprint database resulted in only one of the prints returning as a positive hit.**
>
> **As a consequence of the comparison analysis, Charles Trundle cannot be ruled out as the individual owner of the positive verified print, and hence cannot be ruled out as having once touched the rental contract paper.'**

Scientists, Grant thought. *Can't they just come out and say it. We just got the best lead for Jenny McGrath, and hopefully Jillian Edders.* Grant immediately forwarded the information to Franklin Falls and wanted to update his mentor and friend on the new lead as soon as possible.

* * *

Morgan sat in his blue gown, his emotional state matching the fabric he picked at absent-mindedly. The swirl of depression stemmed from the loss of his friend, embarrassment aimed at himself for the place was in, and not to mention the embarrassment he placed on his police service. There were all sorts of characters that sat around the common room, each with a different distinctive mental issue that landed them in the dismal rehab center. Morgan, now several hours without a drink, was squeezing a stress ball to help with his shaking hands while he checked out the other fellow crazies. There was a female holding a baby doll; Morgan surmised she had lost her child through tragic circumstances. There was a man sitting in a chair staring at the wall, appearing to be drawing something with his finger. He made invisible circles on the wall, then dipped his finger in some kind of invisible paint and returned to whatever picture he was creating with his mind. Morgan wondered if a pile of shit were to be put in front of him, would he paint with the feces like a monkey? He went back to the female holding the doll. He wondered if the murder of Mandy Young did the same thing to Mandy's mother, or Jenny's mother. Her hair was complete bedlam, and even worse, it appeared as if she ripped bare patches out with her hands. A layer of dirt covered her face hiding what were once good looks and perhaps in her mind, hid her from the problems that she refuses to deal with, like Morgan.

A short, stocky older gentleman with fiery red hair carrying a checker board walked around the room, stopping here and there to see if anyone wanted to play. Some politely declined but most just stared blankly, unresponsive. The ginger gentleman finally circled on to Morgan.

"Care for a game?" he spoke in an obvious Irish accent.

Checkers was a game Morgan had not played in probably a decade, but with its simplistic rules, checkers was also a game one could never forget.

"Why not?" Morgan agreed, shrugging nonchalantly. Anything to distract from the yearning tearing at his insides.

"What's your name, lad? Mine's Allister Gillespie, raging alcoholic and proud of it." He thrust his hand forward in greeting.

Morgan grasped the hand tightly for a quick shake. "Uh, John Morgan, also raging alcoholic, not too proud right now." Morgan backtracked in his mind. "Gillespie did you say?"

"Yes, lad. You wanna be black or red?"

"Black please." Morgan accepted the pieces given to him and started setting up his side of the board. "Any relation to Gillespie's Brew House and Tap?"

That's my baby," Allister nodded, smiling proudly. "Red goes first, I like being red."

Allister moved his checker. Morgan couldn't believe this short stocky man with red hair in front of him was the Gillespie of his second home. Morgan moved his black checker.

"Haven't seen you around the pub, Allister."

"I own it, but I hardly go there, lad. You don't send a wolf into a field of sheep. I'd drink away my profits, ya see. The old wifey sends me here about once a year to dry out, but I just start back up again when I get out. Sometimes she hits me with a rolling pin like I'm some kind of comic strip character. For me, it's not about quitting, but keeping it under control."

Allister moved a red checker and jumped one of Morgan's blacks.

"Under control, eh?" Morgan considered the notion.

"You, lad, look like a man that has seen the devil himself. I can tell that in people. The booze isn't the problem. The booze just makes what is already bad, that much worse. It's all about control. I watched ya come in, lad. That was one sweet lass that was with ya. She your sweetheart?"

"No, I don't really know what she is, friend I guess," Morgan shrugged.

Morgan jumped two of Allister's red checkers.

"Black takes two reds. Ha ha, better than orange against green eh?"

Morgan nodded his head in affirmation but didn't get the reference.

Allister stared at the board, but continued speaking to Morgan. "I know you saw the devil. The devil is real, lad. You may not believe it but I do. I know you saw him. If you want to talk about it, you can talk to Allister. It's way better than talking to a head shrink."

The game ended with Allister the winner. They shook hands and Morgan realized that Stephen was an extension of Allister, someone to talk to and never to judge.

Morgan lay awake in his cot staring at the ceiling, as he has done for the past few days there at Pine Grove. His plain room with its barren beige walls, one pitiful shelf and an ancient clock radio was of little comfort. Every time he closed his eyes he saw her. He missed her so much already. Her smile, and the warmth she provided to him. He couldn't even begin to imagine what her partner was going through. He thought about Sheila and couldn't help but admit to himself he was starting to get feelings for her too. There would be no sleeping again tonight.

Morgan could hear a faint tapping sound. He tried to block it out, thinking it was the old heating system or water pipes, but tonight was the first time he had heard this tapping. He thought of the famous line: "a tap tap tapping, tapping at my chamber door" from the great Edgar Allan Poe. Morgan had his first therapy session shortly after his checker game. He couldn't even remember the doctor's name but knew he'd have to see him many more times to come. If the doctor knew what he was doing, Morgan couldn't perceive it yet but digressed to his expertise. A psychiatrist was like an archeologist that explored the ruins of people's minds. A builder that had to renovate and reshape a traumatized memory, but at this juncture, the doctor did more talking than asking of questions. The tapping continued but was more rhythmic now. Morgan actually recognized the tune, in tap form of course, he sat up in his bed and started to hum along, just to make sure he wasn't dreaming. It was Irish Washerwoman. Morgan beamed a smile and started to sing softly to himself as he went to the door, but of course, Morgan sang it all wrong.

"I'm here at Pine Grove and I fucking hate it,
If I had a drink, I surely would take it,
The people are nuts, they say crazy things
Please give me a basket of saucy hot wings"

Morgan opened the door a crack and peeked out.

"Bout time, lad, open up." Allister slipped inside Morgan's room and he quietly closed the door behind him. "Allister Gillespie is here. Now, let's talk of your devil. It's been five days lad, you need to open up."

Five days. It was already five days. Morgan had been sober for the longest he'd been in years and still didn't feel any better for it.

"Allister, I really appreciate this but, I don't know if this is the time, I mean, I crushed the shit out of my stress ball, I..."

"I told you, lad, control, it's all about control. I bet ya could use a stiff one right now," Allister said, cutting him off.

"I hope you're not going to yank an entire bottle of whiskey out of your ass. I'd probably still drink it though."

"Come on, lad, you don't know me too well yet, but we consider you family, and we take care of our family."

Allister went over to Morgan's window and waved at someone outside. He slid the second floor window open, and since it was the 'minimum' or 'voluntary' side of Pine Grove, it was not sealed shut. He lowered a couple of Morgan's bed sheets down he had quickly tied together.

"Come on, lad, I can't lift him myself."

Morgan looked out the window to the end of the sheet and could hardly believe his eyes as a smiling Stephen looked back up. Together they assisted Stephen to the second floor window ledge and each grabbing an arm, heaved him inside. The sound of clinking bottles and glasses emanated from the pack on Stephen's back.

"Shhhh ... I believe you have met my son Stephen Gillespie."

"Hardly an Irish name," Morgan commented.

"Actually, it is," Stephen said correcting Morgan.

"I told you, lad, been coming here for years, we know what we're doing." Stephen pulled out a bottle, three glasses and a take-out box of hot wings. "Now, it's your life, lad. You can tell us both to fuck off and shove the Blarney stone up our asses and there will be no hard feelings ..."

"Allister?" Morgan interrupted.

"Yes, lad?"

"Shut up and pour."

"That's what I thought, lad."

The three friends sat in a circle on the floor and Allister poured a shot for each.

"Here's to swimmin' with bow legged women."

"I think I saw that in a movie once," Morgan said.

"Well, you give us one lad."

"To Jillian, to Cliff, and to Sheila, who made my dick stiff."

"That's what I am talking about, laddie, let it out."

"Remember, we're not that bitch Julie, we are your family," Stephen added.

Morgan felt better than he had in a long, long time. They sat and drank the bottle, right smack in the middle of the rehab program. Morgan let Stephen and Allister in on everything he had been feeling, his losses, his struggles, and the devil that he saw and the two friends listened intently and provided the support that any family could be proud of. Life became clearer for Morgan over the next week or so. Whether Allister was right about it all being about control remained to be seen, as it sounded like he thought of rehab as a vacation. One thing was clear, both had no intention of quitting.

* * *

The vengeful sun shone bright in the afternoon sky as Grant, with air conditioning cranked, pulled up to the gates of Pine Grove. There was no headway for both Moravian and Franklin Falls. Jillian Edders was still not located and the mystery of Charles Trundle had just begun.

Morgan had been gone for about a month and had participated in the program to save his job. He had also participated in many late night business meetings with the great Allister Gillespie and some smuggled-in beer, wings, and whiskey. Despite the meetings, Morgan had felt better than he had in years. He was refreshed; he overflowed with optimism and renewed energy had flooded back to his overworked body. He was well on his way to completing the program and was learning to let the past go, especially with his ex-wife. He was far from being over the death of his friend Jillian Edders, but his new friend Sheila was coming by regularly, and although this was no conjugal visit institution, her presence in itself was soothing and welcome to Morgan. He was now starting to hope there was some kind of a future that included her.

The rusty gate rolled to the side with a groan, letting Grant into the grounds. He looked at the pathetic figures that roamed about on the lawn in their blue gowns hoping his mentor Morgan was feeling better. After parking in a specially marked police parking space, he began the walk up the cement steps while admiring the ivy that ran up the side of the ancient stone building. One girl in particular sat on the steps holding a child's baby doll.

"'Scuse me sir?" the girl said.

"Yes, ma'am?" Grant said as he bent over to get closer.

"I think, I think I cut myself... I'm bleeding... it won't stop. It keeps coming." She started to cry.

Grant's eyes were ablaze with concern as the girl held up her left hand, which was clearly covered in blood, a deep red color of coagulated blood. "Oh geez, ma'am, are you okay? Where are you cut?"

The girl reached into her panties and pulled out a used maxi pad, ripe with fresh clotted skin and vaginal blood, and smeared the chunky mess in Grant's face. "IT WON'T FUCKING STOP!"

"FUCK ME... GROSS GROSS GROSS GROSS! Grant yelled, furiously wiping his face with his suit sleeve.

"IT WON'T STOP... !"

Morgan found the two of them at this point.

"Calm down Marj, calm down. It'll stop. It just takes a few more days. You remember, every month. It comes every month, right? We just have to be sure to keep our bodily fluids to ourselves ... okay?"

"How does it taste?" Morgan said as he rubbed Marj on her shoulders, bringing her back down to earth.

A wide-eyed Grant was turning shades that were not even on the known color spectrum. He turned away and started puking over the cement stairs with his back to Morgan.

"Can't be any worse than pancreas." Morgan was holding in his laughter as hard as he could, while comforting Marj, and watching Grant wiping a mixture of vomit and rotten smelly vaginal extracts from his shocked expression.

"Well, I am glad you're feeling better. I wasn't expecting that kind of a welcome."

"Marj is harmless. Poor dear had a baby that died in the first few hours. You would think that doesn't happen anymore but, here she is. You okay now, Marj?"

Marj rocked her doll as she usually did, nodded an affirmation towards Morgan and smiled to him, not directly thanking him, but he knew how she communicated.

"Good to see ya, young man."

"You too. First things first," Grant said as they sat on the cement steps together. "How ya doing? I really miss your smartassness and shenanigans and from what I can see, you look great."

"I feel great. Any word on her?"

"Unfortunately, no, Franklin Falls has yet to be able to pinpoint a location where the video was made or identify a suspect, other than this Charles Trundle fingerprint."

"Okay, all news to me. What do ya got?"

"The fingerprint from the rental contract that was on file belonged to someone named Charles Trundle. He was put on the system about fifteen years ago for a petty charge, theft of heating oil, or something like that. Turned out he gave a fake address so we don`t know where to find him. We got a mug shot, but comparing it to the grainy video is next to impossible. I don't really know much more than that because that part is Franklin's baby. I was focusing on the three beheadings and the only update I have is that Dan Keeling is probably not your man. I spoke to his wife who again told me that he called her and taunted her and rubbed it in her face that he is with another woman. With his high pitched voice, I took that at face value it won't be connected. Also, the records and pictures you sent away for came back. I took a good look through them and nope, no Dan Keeling, nothing even close."

"Any leads on an identity for headless, soupy guy?"

"Oh you mean after I cut his skin off him and made a fool of myself doing the whole thing without any surgical glove protection? I thought I was gonna get aids or scurvy or something. No, we still don't know who that is or what he did to deserve to get his head removed. Weird shit in his stomach though. Kind of matches the other two. DNA was sent away but like the fingerprint, there is nothing to compare it to. I feel pretty stupid now for even suggesting Dan Keeling may have been the guy on the video."

"You know how many cases I have done where I chased my own tail? A lot, so don't sweat it. Sounds like you've done a fine job, kid. Cell phones, drugs, trash, beans, wedgies, this guy also like to humiliate."

"Anyway, it's pretty somber around the office without you. That stunt at your ex-wife's was legendary dude. You are the hero for all the divorced men at the office who can only dream of doing something like that."

"Hmm, glad to be of service, I guess. What about the charges I may be facing?"

"As far as I have heard, if you finish your treatment here they are going to cut you some slack and chalk it up to post traumatic stress disorder, which c'mon, is exactly what happened. There is a certain judge calling for your dismissal, but we're pulling for you and so far his rants have fallen on deaf ears. You went through some kind of hell that no one should ever go through. I actually admire you even more. I mean, well, at least you're still with us."

Morgan could read between those lines quite easily. If Henderson would have asked for help instead of shouldering the entire burden of Jenny's death himself, he also would still be here.

"How much longer? We need ya back, man. The office is tanking without you. It's just no fun."

"I don't know, from what I am hearing, you don't need me."

"Shut the front door. I'm just keeping your chair warm."

"Great, when I sit on my chair I am gonna picture your stanky ass farting all over it."

With a hearty chuckle Grant left the records and pictures with Morgan which again, is something that would be frowned upon, leaving evidence with an off duty or injured member at an asylum is much like solving homicides with your bartender. The two officers sat on the stairs in silence for a few minutes while hospital staff passed. One orderly in particular was a tall, skinny, giant of a man that had to be seven feet if he was an inch. He walked by the pair and caught eyes with Grant. Both nodded an unspoken hello, and he went about his business. Morgan's heart sank slightly knowing there was no closure for Edders yet. He missed his friend and wished he could work on this Charles Trundle lead. Morgan had to be again patient and had confidence in Grant who's first order of business was to throw his suit in the garbage.

"Hee hee," Marj squeaked with her dirty hand over her mouth.

An indistinct "*hee hee,*" echoed. Grant stopped and looked at Marj, wondering if she, a little witch, could somehow be responsible, then quickly walked away for fear of another pad in the face.

Morgan opened the envelope left by Grant and looked at the pictures from Thompson Hill and Dorrington. There were eight years from both schools to go through, which amounted to hundreds of names, none of which he already knew was Dan Keeling, so he didn't really feel like looking through them. He also had an appointment with the doctor so he tucked the package under his arm and begrudgingly went to see the shrink.

The psyche room was silent except for the ticking of a German cuckoo clock in the corner. "So how do you feel today, John?" Dr. Chalmers, the resident psychiatrist of Pine Grove, asked in his Scandinavian accent.

Morgan's face was painted with an expression of disinterest that betokens a person bored out of their skull. "Feeling okay today, I guess. Not as good as yesterday because I just received news of no progress in my friend's murder. This guy is a slippery bastard and it's hurting me to be in here and unable to help."

"So you have a feeling of helplessness?"

"Uh, yeah, I'm raring to get back. I want to be finished this treatment. I want my life back."

"And you want to be clean and sober."

"Mmm hmm, clean and sober. I don't even feel like a drink having been through this," Morgan lied.

They continued talking to each other but Morgan was not in the room mentally. He knew Dr. Chalmers could probably read that and would most likely extend his stay for non-cooperation, but getting out to work on the case was all he knew and wanted, even more than another nighttime meeting with Allister. He also liked talking to Allister more than this doctor; he felt at ease with Allister and Stephen and was able to open up more to them. It was as if Morgan was getting double therapy sessions. Morgan went through the motions until the meeting was over, as he did with each session these past weeks. He just told Dr. Chalmers what he wanted to hear, no more drinking, dealing with his ex-wife's bullshit, Jillian Edders death, and no more drinking, if that needed to be mentioned again to hammer home Morgan's desire to get the hell out of Pine Grove.

* * *

As Grant drove back to Moravian, he hoped his friend Morgan would make a speedy recovery and rejoin the ranks back at the station. Everyone, especially Grant, was missing his dark humor, snide comments and interoffice shenanigans. He turned on the radio to lighten his mood. Grant was breaching the outskirts of town when he noticed a rundown Monte Carlo in front of him. It appeared to be weaving back and forth within the lane and Grant became suspicious of the car.

"Fucking drunk driver, better safe than sorry," he said turning on the emergency lights mounted on the dashboard.

The vehicle travelled another block before pulling over and Grant's intuition peaked. The Monte Carlo reminded Grant of the one that had been used by Todd Smilie for his career of drug dealings and extortions. He remained cautious, his hand on the butt of his pistol as he approached the driver's window. He noticed the word DADDY still carved into the paint, however the tires had been replaced with four cheap used ones. When Grant saw the driver, he thought he was indeed looking at Todd Smilie, but quickly determined it was his twin brother Terry. Twin brothers are often alike, in more ways than looks, so Grant surveyed the inside of the vehicle carefully as he felt out the attitude of Terry Smile, and noticed a gym bag on the passenger's seat.

"What's in the bag?"

"Nothing, empty," Terry's voice quivered, betraying the statement as an obvious lie.

"Go ahead and show me please."

"No, I don't think you can do that," he said, feeling an overt violation of his rights.

Grant looked down at his suit, and the red swash on his lapel graciously put there by crazy Marj, and became irritated. "I think I'll look in the bag… NOW!"

Terry, who was originally a tad defiant, now started to sniffle and put his head to his chest. Where Todd Smilie was a complete asshole, Terry Smilie just didn't have it in him to be like that, so he handed the bag to Grant. Grant shook the bag and the contents could be heard thumping around. He looked at Terry Smilie, looked at the gym bag, then unzipped the top thinking he was about to find a load of drugs.

"FUCK!" Grant yelled throwing the gym bag onto the ground and pulling out his pistol.

It was not drugs inside the bag. It was Todd Smilie's disembodied, charred arm that Terry had detached at his wake in a fit of emotion. Terry Smilie cried hysterically and immediately put up his hands in surrender.

"I miss... I miss... my brother so much. Please, don't take me away, please understand, I needed him with me. I know he was bad, I know he was mean, but he was my twin brother and I don't think anyone deserves to die like that. I still loved him."

Terry Smilie put his head on the steering wheel and sobbed. Grant knew without a doubt this was indeed Todd Smilie's arm, and no malice was intended by his brother Terry. It was an unfortunate, decidedly poor decision by Terry Smilie to drive around with the arm inside the gym bag. Grant picked up the bag, walked it over to his trunk and placed the bag inside and locked it up. He wasn't exactly sure what to do now. Let Terry go, bring Terry in? He thought of what Morgan would do, but could only come up with some smart ass comments. He decided to let Terry go because logically, if Morgan would just make shady jokes, then perhaps it was just a poor judgement of Terry's, and nothing more. Grant peeled away from the sobbing Terry Smilie with gym bag in tow and returned to the police station.

"And that's the end of that suit," Grant said as he threw it in the office dumpster and walked back through the parking lot in his underwear. He had a pair of street clothes in his locker back in the change room but proudly streaked nearly naked because he couldn't stand to be in that suit another second.

"Didn't like the color of your suit?" Samuels asked when Grant walked in.

"Something like that," Grant sighed. "It turned a crappy shade of red."

Grant sat in his street clothes in Morgan's office which was temporarily his office. Grant was also quickly becoming frustrated with lack of progress and snail's pace the investigation was proceeding. He understood Morgan's position a lot clearer than before and the obstacles an investigator faces with these detailed cases. Grant himself was feeling the pressure big time and to make matters worse, he felt he was losing his marbles with these odd incidents and premonitions.

* * *

Morgan lay awake in his bed, flipping through the pictures that Grant left him. Faces upon faces of children lined up in a row posing with eyes crossed, cheesy smiles and some with missing teeth stared back at him. Morgan had been studying these pictures for the better part of three hours and stopped short when he saw something written in small letters under one of the grade six class pictures from Thompson Hill. If Morgan wasn't examining each picture slowly and carefully he would have missed it, and could understand why Grant had. The tiny letters read: Not pictured – Jeremy Trundle. Morgan flipped to the grade five picture of the previous year. Not pictured – Jeremy Trundle. The grade three picture seemed complete with no Jeremy Trundle mentioned. The grade four picture, however, was the same as grade five and six. From grade six on, nothing. Jeremy Trundle seemed to have left that school and the printed record reflected that as well. Morgan put those photos aside and pulled out the Dorrington Elementary pictures. Meticulously he spent another hour searching for the name Trundle, and he was rewarded for his effort. Jeremy Trundle also attended only one year in

Dorrington, grade seven and then he left mysteriously again with no photo logged. Morgan cross referenced with the dates of the Judith Reinhold and Mandy Young murders, and they matched the time frames. If there was a connection between Charles Trundle and the Trundle child, and if in fact Charles Trundle lived in Thompson Hill and Dorrington, Morgan may have finally connected all the dots and linked seven known homicides. He lay awake and continued to try and piece this all together when he heard the familiar tap at the door.

"Still awake, lad?"

"Yeah, come on in, Allister."

"We're just about done, lad, you and I. I snuck a peak at your file, you're done. Me too for that matter. I'll be back though. Good vacation from the old bat I say."

"Done? That's awesome, when?"

"No date was on it, just recommended you for release, or program complete I should say, you're not a prisoner. Shall we celebrate?"

"We shall, Allister, we shall."

Allister went over to the window and let Stephen inside as he had done at least once a week since Morgan was admitted.

"Ah, come in me boy, a bit of the nectar of the Irish gods ye got with ya."

"You know it pops."

"Stephen she named ya, you'll always be Patty to me boy. What do ya got for us tonight lad?" Allister said, meaning Morgan's files, not the booze Stephen brought.

"I think I made a breakthrough. We have to somehow catch up to these Trundle people. All we got is names right now, but if I can get my mitts on any of them I think we can blow this thing wide open."

"Trundles you say. Can't really help ya there, lad, you'll be out of here soon and free beer and hot wings when you get this whole thing solved, so let us get back to celebrating."

"Allister?"

"Yes, lad?"

"Shut up and pour."

"That's what I thought, lad."

CHAPTER ELEVEN

THE HOMECOMING

Back in his bed, Grant was having trouble sleeping as well. His mind was not only on the cases but on his friend in the asylum, getting hit in the face with a soggy used pad and the premonitions he had been getting. Grant, like a child, now checked under the bed and in the closet, but was yet unsure what he was looking for, the boogieman, the apparition of death or the source of the voice. Grant was not one to believe in the paranormal and continued to rely on his logical, well-educated suburban upbringing to try and make sense of this weirdness, but slowly his rationality was being tested and his eyelids became heavy. There was no clear moment of moving from consciousness to sleep...

Grant awoke to find himself in a darkened patient's room of a hospital. He lay in a hospital bed, his body covered in thick gauze and bandages. Every muscle ached as if he has been beaten like an abused dog. Grant touched one of the pieces of gauze and winced in pain. He decided to carefully peel back one of the bandages and revealed a deep cut, the rest of his afflicted body was no different. There didn't seem to be a soul anywhere on the floor he was on, save for a janitor pushing a mop bucket by his open hospital room door, pausing briefly to look inside. The squeaky wheels of the metal mop bucket pierced the silent air as the janitor continued to push it down the empty hall. The janitor removed the mop from the bucket and slapped the soggy, stringy end into a mess on the floor. The mess on the floor was a large pool of blood. The somber janitor pushed the mop into the blood and smeared the pool around the floor, making the mess even larger. He didn't seem to care the mess wasn't going away, and pushed it around his feet until his boots seemed to be sinking in it. The janitor was now up to his ankles in the blood as he continued to mop away at the ever growing pool. Grant watched this event from the doorway of his hospital room and as he stepped further out into the hall, he could see a headless corpse behind the sinking janitor. A cascade of blood, unrelenting in nature, poured from the neck stump, the severed head lay a few feet to the side. Cautiously, Grant approached the janitor, who was now up to his knees in the pouring blood. The head of his mop had also disappeared under the surface of the blood and he mopped back and forth, back and forth, as if not realizing he was sinking.

"Hey, you okay?" he said to the janitor, who had his back to him. As Grant approached the janitor, he sank even faster and was now waist deep in the dark red flowing blood. "Man, are you okay? Do you need help?" The janitor said nothing and continued to mop. "Are you okay?"

The janitor sank up to his neck and Grant reached out quickly to try and grab him when the head spun 180 degrees and looked at Grant with widened black eyes.

"You can't run away from yourself."

Grant fell back as he saw the head of the janitor, was his own, save for the dark circles, and the vast emptiness that replaced his eyes. The eyes... deep, black, nothingness. Grant watched his head sink under the blood and then reappear. The ghostly form of himself, covered from head to toe in thick, red blood, rose from the pool. Grant stared back at his own crimson covered face, arms, body and legs again standing on the surface of the pool, with an evil look.

"This is madness. You can't run from yourself."

Grant crashed into the mop bucket, stumbling further back from the apparition of himself as it raised a bloody arm and reached out for him while groaning woefully. He scrambled to his feet and turned to run. His feet became heavy; the dream heavy, where running is slow, cumbersome and next to impossible. He staggered down the hallway with legs seemingly burdened with lead as the hospital lights flickered on and off, illuminating a single room at the end. He staggered in and shut the door. He could hear the constant beep of a flat line and saw a body covered in a sheet with a blood stain on the head area. His breathing was heavy and fast as he nervously reached out for the sheet and pulled it back exposing the horror underneath. Henderson sat up with his brain half sticking out the back head and blood caked around his mouth.

"You can't run from yourself. You can't run from madness."

He turned, and his way out was blocked by Edders. Her empty eye socket was as dark as her killer's heart, her gaping throat laceration spewed streams of blood and she gargled as she spoke.

"Madness…YOU ARE MADNESS."

"What do you want from me!" he screamed. "I'm trying! I'm trying to give you peace. Leave me alone!"

Then they were gone.

Grant woke up sweating. He flipped his pillow over to put the damp side down on the mattress. Until he knew what was going on, he wasn't about to tell anyone about this, and all the other similar dreams he had. "Why can't I dream I go to work naked or something like that?" he mourned as he laid his head back down. He looked over at the clock, and then decided to just stay up.

* * *

Morgan lay on the cold leather couch in Dr. Chalmers office. He thought it to be cold and uncomfortable so clients wouldn't get too contented and fall asleep as the boring shrink rambled and flipped through his files.

"So how do you feel today, John?"

"I feel great. I want to work; I want to get back to my life."

"Your sober life?"

"Yes I do," he lied again.

"Well, here's the thing, John. I have been in this business for thirty-two years and there are a few things I have learned. One, to spot liars and two, to spot good people. John, you are liar, but you are a good person. John, you help people, that's what you do and from what I have seen and heard, you do it well. In making my decisions I don't just talk to you, John, I talk to everyone, your family, your friends, your peers." Chalmers pulled a few pieces of paper out of the file in which Morgan could see handwritten scribble on them. "Samuels says 'John Morgan has been my friend for over 20 years. John Morgan is the best at what he does and we are in dire need of his return. John Morgan can get a handle on his alcoholism, I am confident of that.'"

"The old geezer."

"Grant says 'John Morgan is my mentor and my friend. I have learned so much from him and grown as a young police officer with just a few years on the job. John Morgan has taught me that you need to inject humor into what you do. John Morgan hit bottom and can only go up from there and I am keeping his chair warm for his return. I will personally make it my mission to help him control his drinking. I know it will be tough for him, but I think he can keep it in check. I want to be a police officer as good as he.'"

"Hmm, nice words from the young, pukey kid. Why he has to talk about his ass on my chair I'll never know."

"Sheila Appleton says 'John Morgan saved my life on more than one occasion. I don't know why, but I feel a connection with him that goes beyond a cop helping a battered woman in need. Moravian needs John Morgan and I need John Morgan. He has a shining, loving soul inside him whether he knows it or not. He will always have a place in my heart. He is my angel in blue.'"

Morgan stayed silent. There was still some confusion and apprehensiveness regarding Sheila. He couldn't deny he had feelings for Sheila. A cop starting a relationship with someone met during an investigation is actually nothing new, but Morgan was treading carefully and taking it slow.

Dr. Chalmers leaned forward and tilted his glasses down. "The drinking, you have it inside you to control it. You have a circle of friends that love you. You have an ex-wife that hates you but John, and I'm not even going to tell you what she said because I discount it as tainted evidence of your true character. You and I both know that is a common tale in today's world. You see it all the time. Divorce is never easy and always leads to hurt feelings, resentment, pain, and all this you can rise above. John, get out of my office and go home, and keep helping people. Good luck. I hope you don't mind, but I called a friend to pick you up."

Chalmers motioned to his window which overlooked the drive up to the asylum. Sheila stood outside her car smiling a beautiful, beaming smile that Morgan could see even through the dirty, unwashed glass of the office. She was dressed in the sexiest black skirt and boots with her hair done up in highlights that seemed to extenuate her gorgeous face. Morgan waved and smiled back to this hot goddess of a woman and still found it hard to figure out what she saw in him. Morgan was ecstatic as he left Chalmers office and pranced back through the common area. He saw Marj holding her doll and immediately walked up and hugged her.

"Marj, I gotta go but it was nice meeting you. You keep the fluids to yourself honey," he said, and then kissed her on top of her greasy unwashed head.

"Hee hee," Marj giggled.

"Air painting guy, I hope you make DaVinci jealous with your invisible art. Keep painting good sir."

Morgan traded the silly blue gown for his street clothes and virtually bolted out the door into the heat of the day, and into Sheila's arms.

"I missed you my angel. Welcome back." She stood on her toes and planted a kiss on his lips. Morgan kissed her back. He still couldn't put a finger on his feelings for her, but it was beginning to feel right.

The squeaking of the rusty gate was music to his ears as it rolled open. As they drove through, Morgan turned for what he hoped would be his last look at the asylum. He could clearly see the division of the property that housed the criminally insane. The chain link fence with barbed wire at the top was the clear indicator that he ended up on the good side as the dull screams in the distance one could hear from the truly crazy were quite unsettling. The maximum side was an impenetrable fortress that none had ever escaped from, and those that go in, will only come out feet first, or tits up as the old saying goes. None have escaped in its hundred-year history. The front gate and outer fence on the voluntary side were quite easily traversed and probably the reason Stephen could get inside. For the time being, Morgan would keep that to himself for fear of disappointing his friends that banded together to say good things about him. Morgan was glad that his friend Allister was kicked loose as well, even if it was to return to his cartoon life of drinking and being beaten by his wife with a rolling pin.

Morgan admired the skid marks he produced reversing with a vengeance out of his driveway that night many weeks ago as they pulled up to his place. There was no hiding the stench of garbage and stale air that escaped his kitchen as they opened the back door. Morgan was slightly red because this beautiful lady smelled this appalling odor that had been produced by Morgan's pitiful lifestyle.

"Sweetheart, we're here to clean, throw out, and start fresh. I used to live the same way, remember."

The two entered the kitchen and opened every window to get rid of the smell. The circulation of the air reactivated the fruit flies that evolved in the slowly decaying garbage, and they buzzed about the wretched mess. The whole place was still in the state of ruin Morgan had left it in following his mental breakdown. Bag after bag they filled with half eaten boxes of cereal, sandwiches, Gillespie's famous hot wing take out cartons and empty bottles of booze. The dust on his ex-wife's broken picture had resettled, covering her mustache as he picked it up off the floor. He made no depreciating remark, and just tossed it into the trash bag. When Sheila had her back turned Morgan snuck MILF's on the Beach into a drawer; he was still a man, and not one to throw away good porno.

"Feels good to let go, I deserved it and so do you, sweetie."

The two spent the day cleaning every inch of the house. Sheila would touch Morgan's face and steal a peck here and there in an overtly flirtatious manor. Morgan didn't mind, but he didn't know if that meant they were boyfriend and girlfriend and was kind of unsure how to broach that subject, so he let it be for now. But still, seeing her bend over in that hot black skirt and the way she smiled at him made him feel good inside, and out.

A pile of about eight or nine bags was placed outside for the garbage men the next morning. He was glad he was let out the day before garbage pick-up so he wouldn't have to sit on this crap for another week. At the end of the day, the two tired friends decided to call the cleaning spree a resounding success. The garbage was outside, the flies had disappeared as mysteriously as they had appeared and the house smelled better than it had in years.

"Let me buy you dinner," he said to Sheila.

"I think I can be talked into that. Where do you want to go?"

"I think I know a place."

"I'll bet you do. I'm not your mother, my angel. Any place you want is fine with me, even there."

"Well, hard to stay away from my family," Morgan shrugged. There was only one place that he would go to anyway.

The two sat at a table instead of the bar top and opened the menus Stephen had placed before them. Morgan knew the menu off by heart and Sheila was hardly surprised by the pub grub that Morgan called food was about the limit of Gillespie's culinary prowess. The two shared a basket of onion rings for an appetizer, then Sheila changed gears and went for a grilled chicken salad in contrast to Morgan's chicken wings. Since it was only his first day as a free man, Morgan ordered a glass of cola to complement his favorite food and was immediately disgusted by the combination. He and Sheila raised their glasses of soda pop and clinked them in celebration of Morgan's new found freedom. Behind his raised glass, Morgan caught Stephen's eye and the two men could read each other's thoughts. It was one of life's mysteries that only a man and his bartender know.

It had been quite a long day for the two. She pulled back into Morgan's driveway, barely making it beside the pile of bags that represented renewal and will hopefully would be gone before the many maggots begin their amorous orgy. He kissed her goodnight and was slightly proud of himself, being that was the first he had entered and left Gillespie's Brew House and Tap without a beer or a whiskey, or even a made up drink like a VCR. By very nature of the establishment, one was meant to drink there. Sheila left and as she drove home she actually found herself disappointed that Morgan didn't try and do more with her. She couldn't deny she had strong feelings for him, and if he had wanted to make love to her tonight, she wouldn't have been saying no.

Morgan entered his spotless house, the cleanest it had ever been. He sank into his easy chair, which smelled like the clean linen freshener Sheila had used on it. He inhaled deeply. "Ah…this is how that dildo chick smelled just before she smacked him in the face with that twelve-inch rubber dick." Morgan fell asleep quickly in his faithful old chair and slept a profoundly restful sleep, like he had not slept in years.

In the morning he stretched his arms outwards and groaned. His creaky body slowly came to life with the noise of the lumbering garbage truck rolling up the street. Curiosity got the better of him and he wanted to see the look on their faces when they saw the pile of bags he left for them. Morgan laughed as he watched through his spot free window and fresh smelling curtains at the peevish look the garbage man aimed towards Morgan's house. He started throwing the bags into the back and then flipped the middle finger in Morgan's direction.

"Hey, that was uncalled for," Morgan said. "New guy… haven't seen him before and it seems he's already forgotten, he's a garbage man not the freaking president."

Thunderous applause awaited the refreshed detective as he walked into the station. His office, which had been temporarily occupied by Grant, was filled with streamers and a giant 'Merry Christmas' balloon to illustrate stupid cop humor.

"They must have been out of the 'sorry you went crazy' balloons," Morgan said, poking fun at himself.

"Good to have you back, you old geezer. Now get those damn cases solved," Samuels said, throwing him some keys to his new but slightly used car.

"Good to see you too, you older geezer. We'll see what we can do."

After a ton of hugs, handshakes, coffee and cake, all dispersed back to the routine ringing phones and mundane yackity yack that was their daily life. Grant stood in the doorway wearing his freshly pressed police uniform.

"Back to the grind I see," Morgan said.

"It was fun while it lasted."

"Hell of a job, kid. Let me show you what I found while lying in a lumpy old cot feeling sorry for myself." Morgan pulled out the school pictures that he had labeled 'Of Interest'. "You said Franklin Falls got a print from the rental contract that came back to a Charles Trundle. Well, check this out. In Thompson Hill from grade three to grade six the words 'not pictured – Jeremy Trundle'. If I flip to Dorrington, there was a Jeremy Trundle also not pictured for grade seven. This is what I make of that: Charles Trundle, a print, old mugshot of limited use, no driver's license picture, nothing. A Trundle kid, not pictured. They are going out of their way not to be part of mainstream society. If I take the time frames for the murders in Thompson Hill and Dorrington, they fit with the appearance and then disappearance of Jeremy Trundle and to top it off, Jeremy was in Judith Reinhold's grade four class."

Grant stood quiet, not believing he missed that. "That's fucking outstanding. That's why I want to be like you. Even in rehab you are piecing together this fucked up puzzle. You are God dude."

"Well, not quite, but thanks. Both Thompson Hill and Dorrington missed this, don't feel bad."

"What now?"

"Gotta think. Flash forward to now I guess the kid would be in his twenties and if there is indeed a relationship, especially a familial one, we gotta track them down. The one unidentified body we pulled from the dump, still at a loss what to do there. Ever watch those movies where a car load of young people breaks down on an old unused roadway and then have to walk for help? They walk even further into the boonies and eventually come across a house full of murdering hillbillies. I don't like to think about it, but what I saw in the video wasn't pretty and conjures up thoughts of a torturous inbred family with rotten teeth and shit like that." Morgan swallowed his lump as he thought of Edders.

"Yeah. I never saw it, thank God. I think the Chief put it under seal in the vault, along with the envelope it came in. Dude, don't watch it again."

"We'll put that on the back burner. Charles Trundle may be my suspect as well. We shan't discount that, laddie.

"Laddie? Sounds like a dog."

"Just quoting a new friend I met on the inside."

CHAPTER TWELVE

NOT SEX, A SAMPLER

Samuels stepped out of his nook and interrupted the two. "Young Mr. Grant, seeing how you are back in the patrol saddle again, I need you to head over to the Moravian Christian High School and see the principal. There are two younger girls crying rape or something by an older, bald scumbag. I'm sure you'll find out when you get there. You may want to go too, geezer."

Grant looked at Morgan who was looking back at him, just as surprised at the weird coincidence that just came over the phone.

"Let's jump in my car and head over to the high school, kid. I won't feel comfortable unless I hear firsthand what these girls have to say."

Morgan and Grant teamed up and boogied over to the high school principal's office. The two girls, both fifteen-years-old, sat in shameful silence with their heads down. Moravian Christian High School was the typical religious school where the pupils spent half the day praying and learning about the bible. The female students wore uniforms of plaid skirts and the males grey dress pants, both with white button up shirts to compliment the style. The two embarrassed girls looked no different and were hardly the disheveled appearance that Grant had pictured on the way over.

"Thank you for coming detective. Thank you for coming officer," the principal said shaking hands.

"I had to pull these two out of class because the rumor mill is churning like crazy that these girls were raped over the weekend over at the Moravian Inn."

"Raped? Okay," Morgan said, his interest now peaked.

"These young ladies are Natalie West and Nancy Morris. I'm sure you'll have many questions for them. I first wanted to make sure they were safe and removed them from the classroom environment. It kind of broke over the internet when Nancy posted that they were raped together by the same man."

"I wasn't raped. I never even had sex with him! Nancy did," Natalie spoke up, assertive.

"Okay Natalie. I'll talk to Nancy and my partner Officer Grant will speak to you. We'll get this sorted out the best we can okay?"

In the privacy of the principal's office, Morgan pulled out his notebook and began to interview Nancy while Grant went to the vice-principal's office to try and make sense of Natalie's tale.

"Okay Nancy, tell me about what happened. Let's start with how did you meet this guy and end up at the Moravian Inn?"

Nancy kept her head down. She was bursting with embarrassment about the story she was about to give to Morgan.

"This guy came up to us after school on Friday. We were walking home together, Natalie and me. He told us we both looked pretty. He told us he was a millionaire and would pay us for sex with him."

"Did he look like a millionaire?"

"I don't know. Guess not."

"Did he say how much?"

"25,000 dollars."

Morgan's eyes widened. He would have sex with this guy for 25,000 dollars.

"Okay, go on Nancy..."

"He told us to meet him at the Moravian Inn, room twelve if we were interested in being rich. Natalie and I didn't go, but we talked about it all night. All the things we could buy with 25,000 dollars. Clothes, shoes, bags. We even talked about going on a trip to Europe. It's stupid, I know."

"I can understand being really attracted to 25,000 dollars, who wouldn't?" Morgan said, trying to sooth the teen.

"We decided to go to the motel and make him give us the money first. We went to room twelve and he was there. He was just an ugly fat bald guy who tricked us. I can't believe he tricked us!" Nancy started sobbing in labored gulps.

Morgan was at a loss at how he tricked her into thinking she got 25,000 dollars. It was almost preposterous, and he didn't even want to guess but as Nancy calmed down she continued.

"He transferred the money into my account through telephone banking. I gave him the number on the front of my bank card. He let me listen to the recording and it said it was transferred. I thought I had 25,000 in my bank account, and I let him have sex with me. I let that asshole have sex with me and when I went to the bank machine I had nothing."

"Just you, and not Natalie?"

"No, Natalie never had sex with him. She wouldn't let him. He only got a sampler."

"A what?" Morgan asked.

"A sampler."

"Nancy, hon, you will have to excuse my denseness, but what is a sampler?"

"He put it in her."

"He put what in her?"

"His dink."

"He put his dink where?"

"He put it in her vagina," Nancy stressed, now becoming frustrated at Morgan.

"They did have sex."

"No, just a sampler."

Morgan was still not reading this teen. He blinked in confusion.

"He put his dink in Natalie's vagina?" he asked.

"Yes!"

"Then they had sex."

"No! She only let him pump about ten times and that was it. It was a sampler."

"Okay, I think I read you. He didn't finish, so in your estimation, that was not sex," Morgan said, finally getting her flawed logic.

"Yes."

"But you, honey?"

"He put his dink in me and I let him pump me until he finished, so we had sex," Nancy resumed crying.

Morgan now understood this young teen's interpretation of what sex is and what was not. It was certainly misguided, but in her defense she was young, naïve and not too swift.

"I didn't have sex with him!" Natalie stressed again to Grant in the vice principal's office. "He only got a sampler! Nancy was the slut and had sex with him before she knew if he put the money in her account and I was afraid she wouldn't share it with me if I didn't do something with this jerk."

"So, a sampler it was?" Grant questioned.

"Yes, I thought the sampler would be at least worth a thousand dollars a pump and I could get 10,000 for that. When it turned out there was no money, we knew that Nancy had gotten raped. I don't know why she didn't give him a sampler too, and then see if the money was there. Instead she got raped."

Grant, like Morgan, was trying to wrap his head around this sampler story, let alone how this unknown scumbag managed to trick these teens. The girls were steadfast in their version and Morgan and Grant agreed that if it helped the girls cope, they'd just leave the sampler part alone and focus on the investigation that they both were raped by whomever was living in room twelve of the Moravian Inn.

Both Morgan and Grant knew the Moravian Inn. It was a flop house, a rent by the hour kind of joint that hardly housed millionaires.

"What do you make of this transferring of the 25,000 by telephone banking?" Grant asked.

"I don't know but Nancy claims to have heard a recording that 25,000 was indeed transferred and it was at hearing that she made the foolhardy decision to go through with the sex after Natalie just gave the sampler."

"Any connection sticking out for ya?"

"Nothing. May as well go ahead and bust this pervert for the underage rape and all the jazz that goes along with it."

Morgan and Grant pulled up to the Moravian Inn and walked up to the front counter and spoke to the hotel clerk. The paint was peeling, the lobby stunk and the tiles were cracked and uncared for, as was the rest of the motel and all the Moravian Police were quite familiar with this.

"Who was in room twelve this weekend?" Morgan asked the clerk.

The grubby clerk scratched his armpit under his dirty wife beater and turned the register around so the officers could read it. Morgan read the weekend's guest as Grant watched the clerk smell his fingers.

"He's still in there," the clerk said. "Been here for a month."

"Anything weird about him… Peter Barnes I see he checked in as," Morgan said reading the scribble on the ledger.

"I don't know. Everyone here is weird. You know that. One armed guy in room five keeps walking around here naked." The clerk scratched his other armpit and then promptly smelled his hand. "Bald guy in twelve must be some kind of ladies' man because I seen some girls going in there, quite a few young ones."

Morgan and Grant approached room twelve. Morgan knocked on the door while Grant instinctively put his hand on the butt of his gun and prepared for whatever may wait behind the door. A distinct shuffling could be heard behind the door. Morgan put his finger over the peephole, blocking the outward view of whoever was inside. He could tell there was someone directly on the other side rubbing against the door attempting to use the peephole. Frustrated, the male voice called out.

"Who's there?"

Morgan raised his voice to a falsetto and replied. "It's Nancy again."

"That was an absolutely terrible impression of a teenage girl," Grant whispered.

"Like to see you do better."

"It's Natalie. I want to give you more than a sampler this time, you big hairy stud." Grant's attempt was pitch perfect.

"Impressive, ya show off."

The latch on the other side was released in what seemed like an excited pace and the door was opened wide and the fat, bald middle-aged gentlemen that the teens had described had a perverted crooked smile on his fat face.

"Hello, Peter. You can pay me 25,000 dollars not to fuck you up the ass with this officer's flashlight."

Peter's expression changed from bliss, as he thought he was about to get laid again, to disenchantment, as he knew he was about to get busted. "They were willing. I didn't rape anyone!" Peter Barnes blurted out. "They said I could. They said it was okay."

"Oh, I have no doubt they did. Show me how."

Peter picked up the phone and dialed the telephone banking number. When he got to the automated menu he chose a little used option that was the telephone banking tutorial. The tutorial took you through the steps one would need to transfer funds. Peter merely feigned in front of the girls he was speaking to someone and would ask for monies to be transferred then using the keypad, typed 25,000, and then the account number. The end of the tutorial was an automated message saying the funds had been transferred and that was the part he would let the teens listen to. Morgan and Grant were floored, dumbfounded, and virtually speechless. It was freaking ingenious and neither could believe this sorry sack of crap thought that up by himself. Peter came willingly but unknowing to both officers, the scene was observed through the curtains, by a second eavesdropping bald man from room thirteen.

It was well past noon when the two finally finished booking Peter Barnes. Morgan was confident Grant could tie up the loose ends on that. It would be no doubt the teens would require some kind of therapy after that experience, not Pine Grove level therapy, perhaps something a little more local.

"Nice work gentlemen," Samuels commented. "Heading for lunch?"

"I think I deserve a quick bite."

Morgan departed alone to grab some lunch. The morning call was wrapped up swiftly and it was probably just a matter of time before more young girls he tricked came forward. Morgan felt a little guilty, but he pulled into Gillespie's anyway fully intending to have wings, whiskey and beer. Morgan shut off the engine when his cell phone rang. He could see on the display it was Samuels.

"Checking up already?" he joked to Samuels.

"Um, kind of, I'm right behind you."

Morgan looked in his mirror and watched Samuels pull into the parking space behind him. He ended the call. He knew exactly what was going on. He was being followed.

"So this is what it's become?" Morgan said getting out of his car to confront Samuels.

"Stop it. I have been ordered by the Chief to keep an eye on you. In his defense, we are facing a lawsuit from your ex-wife who has a pretty powerful judge on her side and while I think this is a little extreme, I have to agree about the liability that comes from having you around. You do have some bridges to rebuild."

"John Morgan, liability."

"No, John Morgan, crackerjack detective that doesn't drink on duty anymore. How about that?"

Morgan shrugged his shoulders and sighed. "You're here, you may as well join me for lunch. I can still come here right?"

"Free country, as long as you don't have a noon pick me up."

"Not even a sampler?" Morgan joked.

"A what?"

"A sampler?"

"Ah Jesus, I'm getting too old for your goofiness."

"Then let us eat, you old geezer."

The bell rang and the pair of old friends sat down at a table. Morgan ate hot wings and drank water, and again, was disgusted, like it was the hardest thing he ever had to do. Hot wings with water was an absolute sin. The conversation continued with the awkwardness put behind them.

"How's Sheila?" Samuels asked.

"Good, good. She's yeah, good."

"That's all ya got."

"She's more than good. She calls me her angel in blue, kind of gets me when she says that. I still remember when she first said it to me at the hospital after Jake Gurracci nearly killed her." Morgan suddenly stopped.

"And?" Samuels prodded.

"Sorry, had a weird thought, my blue suit or something. Anyway, I can't deny she is smoking hot, a lot younger than me but that's not an issue. She's just…great. She's been a rock for me throughout this past month and a bit. She's visited me many times and I think it is going somewhere. I just need to get over the hurdle in my head."

"The fact that she was a client."

"Pretty much. Feels a little off knowing her past, her husband was brutally murdered and stuff. It's up to me to solve it, but now I might start dating one of my clients, as you say. That's the mental hurdle."

"Hey, I get it. Take it slow, see where it goes. No problems there."

"That the one you banged on your desk?" Stephen said out loud to the empty bar.

"Stephen!" Morgan laughed, almost doing a spit take with his water. "Don't you dare ever, ever, ever, ever, ever and did I say ever, tell her you know that."

"Hey, it's me. Good ole Stephen Gillespie. It will be locked in the vault forever more." Stephen put his finger to his cheek and made a locking noise as if to simulate his head was some kind of virtual information safe, then pretended to throw the invisible key away over his shoulder.

"See, I've forgotten it already."

"He's Gillespie?" Samuels asked.

"Yeah, kind of."

"What kind of Irish name is Stephen?"

* * *

A notably distraught and embarrassed Natalie West finished out the school day in a vain attempt to preserve her dignity. The contemptuous stares from other girls who would bury their heads in into their phones and tablets to tweet about her stupidity cut deep. The lettermen lined the lockers performing extravagant gestures that simulated blow jobs or doggy fucking and as maliciously intended only hammered another spike into her fragile existence. The plausibility of a continuous daily berating drove her to a hopeless passion to which there was only one escape. Natalie went home and turned on her computer to read the comments posted all over social media. She could see that Nancy was online as well, also reading the comments, and also having the same self-destructive thoughts. Both girls were already outcasts as far as the popular crowd was concerned. They were emotionally delicate, profoundly distressed and the cyber bullying was like a virtual hand reaching though the screen and squeezing the will to live from them.

"Those dumb bitches, I got a quarter, can I at least get some head?"

"Hey Natalie, you wanna sample some of me?"

"If I was you, I would kill myself for being so stupid."

"Just get it over with you weird losers."

There were other comments that continued to degrade the girls but the last one really hit home. Natalie typed a message to Nancy.

"Nancy, you wanna get that bastard?"

"Yeah. He should die. My mom said the cops picked him up but he was let out already."

"How u wanna do it?"

"I dunno. Stab him right in the dink?"

"That'd be great. Probly will survive. Gotta stab him in the heart so he dies fast."

"Ok. What should we use?"

"Big kitchen knife, I got one here. If we kill him, they'll know it was us. We'll go to jail forever."

"...then we should..."

"Do ourselves after?"

"Yeah."

"When we take care of that asshole...how should we do it?"

"I dunno. I don't wannit to hurt. Pills I guess."

"Let's do it. We will be redeemed, then die together."

Natalie grabbed a bottle of unlabeled pills from her mother's medicine cabinet and the biggest knife she could find from the kitchen. She didn't know what kind of pills she swiped or even if they would be able to end their lives with them. All sense of reason was cast aside in her quest for redemption, and with blind naivety, put the bottle of laxatives into her pocket.

Both girls with a tearful embrace made a pact to kill Peter Barnes, then to kill themselves after, like the powerful online comment directed. It was just after midnight when the teens, butcher knife in hand walked towards the darkened Moravian Inn, determined to end the life of the manipulating, simple-minded rapist. There was no light on inside room number twelve and that side of the inn was in darkness save for the distant streetlights. The young teens had no real plan of action other than to kill that dirty old man with the kitchen knife and now they stood before the door looking at each other not really knowing what to do from here. Nancy reached over and tried the doorknob and to both girl's surprise, it turned. The ratty old wooden door of room twelve opened with a creak and Natalie holding the knife with both hands around the handle and straight out in front of her, entered first. The girl's eyes adjusted to the dimness of the room and using the paltry light of the outside, tiptoed towards the fat silhouette of Peter Barnes asleep in an arm chair.

"Fuck you!" Natalie yelled and drove the knife as hard as she could into his child raping heart but he made no sound and he did not move.

Natalie pulled the knife from his chest and stabbed him again but he still made no sounds of pain, no grunts, no groans, he just sat there in the shadows. The only sound was the knife hitting his sternum and Natalie became frustrated that killing someone was harder than she thought.

"Bastard!" She abandoned her attempt at his chest and drove the knife into his crotch piercing his penis and scrotum.

The door to room twelve slammed shut encasing the teens in utter darkness. Natalie and Nancy froze and from behind; each of their faces were smothered with a rag. The teens never even had a chance to fight but somehow in the darkness their widened eyes met in ultimate terror as both inhaled the toxic fumes and lost consciousness. A bald-headed man flicked on the light, looked at the decapitated corpse of Peter Barnes, tilted his head, shrugged his shoulders then one at time, he carried the unconscious teens into his waiting Malibu.

"Two for the price of one, how could I get so lucky to have two princesses like you to play with? This is perfect madness, Trina, perfect madness."

He started to masturbate himself through his pants as he drove, thinking about their young bodies and turned to see them out cold in the back seat. The seatbelt rubbed on an irritated wound as he turned and with a grunt he adjusted the belt away from the abrasion on his neck. The stitches on his makeshift patch job were loose and didn't really close the hole the bullet made when it grazed his neck. The bald-headed man drove to his terror cell where Natalie and Nancy would now know fear. The ruse perpetrated by Peter Barnes was nothing compared to the madness that was this sadistic killer. He stripped them both and hung them together on the same hook that he had used on Edders, and nameless more. He turned on the furnace to invoke the psychological dread that comes with the resulting shadows that frolicked about as the girls screamed and cried for their mothers. The fire reflected off his baldness, his maniacal face accentuated the evil in his heart. There was no sampler here; he had his way with them, over and over all the while the belt hung on the wall beside the smiling furnace.

* * *

Morgan sat at his desk. The files were all in order for the first time in his detective career. He was thinking clearly for the first time in his detective career. He drew a timeline on a chart and tacked it to the wall. He put the names of Charles Trundle and Jeremy Trundle in bold letters on the timeline that encompassed the Judith Reinhold and Mandy Young murders. He put the photos in order of time of death and focused his attention on the unidentified corpse found at the garbage dump. He felt he was getting close and he had a hunch. He didn't feel comfortable about doing it, because Grant had discounted it, but Morgan drove over to Donna Keeling's house. She was surprised to see Morgan because she was used to dealing with Grant but invited him in nonetheless.

"Donna, I apologize for the intrusion but as Dan is still listed as a missing person on the national database I just want to do some more follow up on that. Anymore messages from your ex-husband?"

"Nothing in a while and I am glad for that. My lawyer is going ahead with a judgment in his absence and he is gonna pay through the nose. That cheating bastard."

"Donna, can you tell me again what Dan did for a living?"

"He was an employee of the city of Moravian."

"I know you already showed my cohort Officer Grant, but can you take me to the bedroom."

She showed Morgan the bed where they slept and the one side that had been unused for quite some time, to which Morgan could sympathize. Morgan looked around the room where it appeared his things were relatively untouched. He wondered if Donna Keeling may in fact be still hopeful of his return as his clothing still hung in the closet, his toiletries still remained on his dresser. Morgan swiped a bottle of cologne and put it inside his suit jacket, strategically just touching the top with a tissue from his pocket. Morgan eyed the coveralls still hanging in the closet a second time and pressed his lips together before turning back to Donna.

"Donna, I again apologize and I hope things eventually get better," Morgan lied as he departed.

"Well, cheaters have to pay don't they?"

Morgan nodded affirmation and waved goodbye to her. "Somehow, I don't think this time," he mumbled silently. Morgan submitted the cologne bottle to the forensic lab and asked for a rush on it. Before they laughed him out of the room, he explained why.

Grant rolled about the city in his patrol car while listening to some classic rock and trying to make sense of his visions. He knew he'd be next for Pine Grove, a strait jacket instead of a blue gown would be his penance if he didn't get it figured out soon. He was glad Morgan was back, still he couldn't help but be a little disappointed that he was back to answering regular calls for service. A few more years perhaps and he could join his mentor as his partner, and that would be the ultimate cool for Grant, but until then he would remain a street cop and continue to do his best. Grant ironically drove by Madame French's Psychic Readings and Voodoo Emporium and against his better judgement, pulled into the gravel lot of the store front. A chubby black lady garbed in a colorful flowing moo moo stood in the window looking perplexed at the police cruiser in front of her shop. Grant caught eyes with her.

"Officer Grant call dispatch," his radio crackled.

"Go ahead dispatch."

"Please attend 249 Rotham Road for a trouble with youth complaint. Caller states there is a girl screaming on her front yard. Caller does not know who she is."

"10-4," Grant acknowledged. "Maybe next time Madame French."

He waved nonchalantly at Madame French, then Grant set his police GPS for 249 Rotham Road which took him just outside of town. About ten minutes later he pulled into the driveway where he saw a partially clothed girl wrapped in a blanket and sitting on the step with an older woman seated beside. Grant looked at this young girl, and immediately recognized her.

"Natalie?"

Grant was right, it was indeed Natalie West and she looked like she had just been through hell. Her face, arms and bare legs were covered in bruises and she had a blank stare on her face.

"Natalie, what happened?"

Natalie could not answer. She remained mute.

"She was screaming when she came to my door but after she calmed down she's just not talking," the female homeowner stated.

Grant summoned an ambulance for the disheveled teenager who was obviously in an overt state of shock. The missing teens were thought to be runaways due to the public humiliation they had both experienced at the hands of the bullying internet comments. Grant knew that this was something more and tried again to get her to talk.

"Natalie, where is Nancy?" he asked in a softer tone.

Natalie just squeaked something inaudible that neither Grant nor the lady could understand.

"Natalie, where is Nancy?"

Natalie started shaking and began to scream uncontrollably. Grant tried to console her but thought she may be close to answering so he pushed again.

"Where is Nancy?"

"DEAD!" Natalie screamed at Grant.

In her mother's consoling arms, Natalie now found herself with her feet in the hospital stirrups, her legs spread wide as the sexual assault specialist poked inside her vagina and anus taking swipes and samples in an attempt to collect evidence for the ongoing investigation. Natalie was given sedatives to bring her down from the life-altering experience and she babbled away with incomprehensible jibber while Morgan waited outside in the hospital hallway with Grant.

"This is not what we needed right now kid. I just can't keep up."

"She told me Nancy is dead."

"Aw fuck," Morgan said at the news. "I guess nothing yet on that?"

"Not yet."

"I'm getting close. I can feel it. Now this."

Morgan and Grant sat in silence for about a half hour before they were allowed to see Natalie in the hospital room. She was much calmer now but remained in a groggy state. She had been cleaned up, had her bruises treated but still looked rough. Natalie turned her muzzy head to the side to acknowledge the officers as they entered the room.

"Hey again," Grant said.

"Hi," Natalie said hoarsely. She recognized Morgan from the meeting at the high school.

"Natalie, do you remember what happened?" Morgan said turning on a recorder.

"I got away from him."

"You got away from whom?"

"The bald guy?"

"Okay, go on... what else can you remember?"

"He kept saying that he was madness."

Morgan and Grant glanced wordlessly at each other and immediately theorized that a big break was on the tip of her slurring tongue. They listened intently as Morgan continued his questions.

"Natalie, the best you can, do you know where he took you?"

"No. He drugged us when we went to the hotel. We woke up somewhere; I don't know where I was."

"Okay Natalie, lets slow it down. How about we start from the day after school when I last saw you and take it from there."

Morgan had the sinking feeling that Natalie and Nancy had gone back to the Moravian Inn, he wasn't sure why though. In her recollection, Natalie couldn't be sure she had actually seen what she thought, so she skipped the part about stabbing Peter Barnes. For all she knew right now, she and Nancy had killed him, and was deathly afraid of letting Morgan know what they had done. In the way that young people retell events, Natalie continued with the story, but the experienced Morgan could read between the lines as she spoke.

"We went back to the hotel because we were mad at that man that raped Nancy. I don't know why we went there but there was another man there instead and he drugged us and kidnapped us. A thinner bald one. I don't remember how we got there, but we woke up in a dark place. It was so dark, until he lit a fire. Yeah, he lit a fire in a furnace, one of those old ones. It made the whole room flicker with ghosts. He put his dink in us, over and over and kept calling us Trina. Nancy tried to fight him off. She was tired of being raped. He beat Nancy with a belt and she ended up covered in blood because the belt was covered in hooks. He beat her and Nancy screamed. She screamed for him to stop but he just yelled the word madness as he hit her. I was able to slip out of the rope he had me tied with and I ran up the stairs. I just ran out the door and kept going but I could still hear Nancy screaming. I left her behind to die. I know he killed her. She was bleeding so bad. Every time he hit her there was more blood. So much blood, it was...madness." Natalie started to trail off as the sedatives did their work and she became catatonic.

"So what do you say?" Grant asked.

"We'll get a team to start going door to door from where Natalie was found and circle outwards. Where ever she was has to be within running distance. You and I are going back to the Moravian Shithole Inn. Something tells me, Peter Barnes may not be all there."

"May not be all there?"

"I can't see them going back there to try and collect their 25,000 dollars. Call it another hunch."

"I'll put more faith in your hunches that most people's facts dude."

Morgan stopped into the hospital bathroom. His outward appearance as before, a façade. He didn't want to disappoint Grant, let alone get caught by the Chief and lose his job. He reached into his suit pocket and pulled out a bottle of whiskey and took a couple of swigs.

"Control. Do it for Allister," he tried to reassure himself. "Things moving pretty fast, just a couple of swallows."

Morgan and Grant got a key from the armpit smelling clerk, which in turn was redundant as they opened the unlocked door to room number twelve. Both gazed upon Peter Barnes headless body still seated in the chair with a butcher knife sticking out of his penis.

Grant stepped back outside the room door and as if on cue, puked on the step in front of room thirteen. He turned to make sure no one saw him vomit, and again, felt like someone was watching. He quickly scanned around but saw nothing except for Morgan inside the room.

"*Hee hee,*" came from behind the door of room thirteen.

Grant tried the knob but found it locked. He attempted to peer through the dirty, rectangular window beside the door but the curtain was drawn.

"Okay pukey, get a list of everyone that stayed here for the past few months."

He took another swig when Grant left. Morgan saw what he was looking for pretty quickly, which was some kind of evidence that the girls had been here. It was quite evident that the butcher knife that was protruding from his moldy, green, pus-laden penis was the work of the teens. This fit of rage against the sexual organ that caused their whole decent into hopelessness was clearly not done by the serial killer with the axe. Making note of other anomalies, Morgan saw something that he had seen before. 'DADDY' was carved into the table beside Peter Barnes.

"I'm closing in on you, Trundle," Morgan thought taking a drink.

"Ahem," Grant said behind Morgan.

"What do ya got?"

"No familiar names on the list. The guy that was in room thirteen gave a name of Vance Palmer, left without notice about a week ago and no one has been in it since. Stinky pits at the front said he was a thinner, bald dude."

"Fuck ya! Dust it!" Morgan said with enthusiasm.

"What the hell happened to his dick?"

"That my young friend is the work of Natalie and Nancy, I am quite confident of that."

"They stabbed his dick?"

"Yes they did. I picked up that deception when Natalie was talking about her and Nancy coming back here. Look, regular kitchen knife in his nut sack. Beheaded by some kind of super sharp implement that can take people's noggins off with one thwack. Two different attacks on the body, one professional, one amateur."

"That's why you the man. That's why I want to be just like you."

"You'll have to stop puking kid."

"I know."

The examination of rooms took the better part of two days and the forensic team pulled numerous fingerprints from the room. It would not surprise Morgan, Grant or anyone for that matter if the prints returned to a multitude of different criminals. It was the shot that one of them would be Charles Trundle and Morgan was hoping to score with that. The door-to-door team was forging ahead with slow but methodical checks of each house working backwards as Morgan directed from the point Natalie was found. As each house was struck from the list, it was one step closer to a brutal serial killer.

* * *

"How's the pa, Stephen?" Morgan asked as he and Sheila took a seat at the bar.

"Me dear old dad is just fine. Ma conked him with the frying pan again but the tough old bastard just shakes it off and says that's me mammy. How goes the cases?"

"I'm close, Stephen, I am so close I hope that asshole feels me breathing down his neck."

"I see you again brought this lovely young lady," Stephen said, placing a beer in front of Morgan.

"Always a pleasure to see you, ma'am."

Sheila remained silent about the beer that Morgan was no longer trying to hide. She was still too fresh in the relationship to call herself his girlfriend, and didn't think it was her place to nag him just yet. Morgan chugged half the beer in a few gulps and looked across to Sheila's pretty face.

"I need it for the hot wings. Real men don't drink pop or water with hot wings. I can't believe I actually did it the other day."

She smiled back and shrugged. "Keep it under control is all anyone is asking. No one hates you for being you."

"Sheila, there is something that has been really eating at me regarding us being together." He took a deep breath and a swallow of beer.

"I think I know."

"Yeah, sooner or later, and I hope sooner than later, you may to have to reopen your wounds that have appeared to have healed rather well. All the horror that you were put through may be open to the court, and then the world if I catch this Charles Trundle. That won't be the only thing open to the world, we will be too."

"Do you care about that?" she asked.

Morgan never expected her to throw the ball back into his court. "Well, I would be lying if I said I was not concerned, but you stood by me. I certainly know a spiteful judge that would care."

"And you stood by me. You saved me my angel in blue and I am not afraid to tell that to the world."

I think I wore a grey suit that night, he thought.

Morgan had one more beer and cut it off at the two, and was impressed with himself for his small show of control. They drove back to his house through the muggy evening both thinking the same thing, and they could see it in each other's eyes. As soon as they pulled into Morgan's driveway, they were all over each other. Finally, the drought that had encompassed Morgan's bedroom for years, came to a bed breaking, mountain moving, earth shattering end.

* * *

Morgan sat in his office chair feeling like a champion of the bedroom, a high-priced porn star. He had a little bounce in his step when he entered the office and Samuels could see it.

"Here, you old geezer. Fresh from the lab." Samuels handed Morgan a thin envelope which Morgan tore at like a kid on Christmas.

> **'Examination of the cologne bottle provided by Detective Morgan and the degloved latent fingerprint provided by Acting Detective Grant was conducted. Successful latent prints were lifted that were suitable for comparison purposes. Comparison tests were conducted resulting in a positive match.**
>
> **As a consequence of the comparison test, the unidentified John Doe cannot be ruled out as to having once touched the cologne bottle.'**

"Scientists," Morgan grieved. "Why can't they just come out and say it?"

Dan Keeling, was the unidentified John Doe from the garbage dump.

"Get over here kid," Morgan called to Grant. "Got a surprise for ya." He handed the envelope to Grant, whose eyes started to widen as he read the paragraph.

"How... what the fuck? She said he called her. She said she knew his voice. Fuck, I didn't know... I never even thought...."

"I know, kid. I thought it too and it begs even more questions. What the hell did he do to get himself whacked? I hardly think she is lying about the phone calls so, another shit stick to lick, gotta find out who made them. May have to go for her phone records."

Grant was still reeling from the news that Dan Keeling, the missing person that he had taken some time ago was no longer missing, and had become another victim. Samuels popped his head back into Morgan's office.

"Morgue on the phone, you heading down there?" "Yeah, shit, Barnes, gotta go kid. Go poke around down at the door to door canvassing see if ya can help out," Morgan suggested. "There's gotta be a few hundred houses to check yet."

"Sure thing, boss."

* * *

"'Bout time, your majesty," Halpin said to Morgan as he stepped off the elevator. "What is this fat assholes story?"

"Yes Peter Barnes, he liked to trick little girls into thinking they can get rich quick by having sex with him."

"Any closer to catching this axe wielding maniac, the collector of heads?"

"Doc, I am so close it's driving me back to the bottle. I guarantee you, this will be the last, not that I am sick of seeing you, but I am sick of seeing you. I will catch this guy before he kills again and it looks like he did kill another little girl. Gotta step this up. We're so close."

"What do you think will be the prize in this guy's stomach?" Boland asked.

"Pretty sure I can already tell you. I'll put my money on something sex related," Morgan said.

"Okey dokey, let's open the Cracker Jack box and find the prize," Halpin said holding the scalpel over the exposed stomach.

Condoms. Peter Barnes had an entire box of condoms jammed down his throat into his stomach.

"Well Barnes, I hope the sampler was worth it," Morgan said taking down the exposed neck like it was a microphone.

Halpin chuckled as he stood before the table on which sat all of Peter Barnes' guts.

"If you're in the mood for some pancreas, got some right here."

"Deep fried with hot sauce perhaps, but until you get a fryer installed in here I'll have to pass," Morgan joked.

Morgan finished his business with Dr. Halpin and took the elevator upwards from the dungeon to the floor where Natalie West was staying. He entered the room to find her packing her things as physically she seemed to be okay, but mentally she was going to need a lot of work. Her parents were in the room and were helping her pack up for her trip home.

"Hey honey, they let you out already?" Morgan asked.

Natalie looked at him. "Yeah," she softly mumbled.

"I know this is tough, but it is an important part of the investigation and we still have to find Nancy, so I was wondering if we could take Natalie for a drive to see if she could look at some houses and maybe one would jog her memory."

"Natalie, do you feel up for that?" her dad asked.

Natalie's long hair was matted, half covering her face and still quite a mess, but through it she nodded her head wanting to help as much as she could for Nancy. Morgan, Natalie and her parents left the hospital and drove to the house that Natalie had ran to in the previous days. Another police car was parked in the area and Morgan waved at Grant as he continued knocking on doors, taking names in hopes someone saw something. Natalie stared out the window blankly as Morgan started to drive around the road in a pattern. Her mother hugged her and gently rubbed her back in a soothing gesture to her newly tattered reality. An hour they drove around the roads until Natalie's eyes widen, she started to shake, her breathing was uncontrolled and she finally screamed.

"THAT'S THE HOUSE! THAT'S THE HOUSE! THAT'S THE HOUSE!"

Her parents tried to calm her as she flew into a fit of crying and convulsing. Morgan had well expected this reaction if he was lucky enough for her to find the house, and it looked like he was.

"Fuck ya," Morgan said under his breath.

Hallmark Road was short and finished at a dead end with only a handful of houses on it. There was a thick line of trees that hid many of the houses from sight but this one, 65 Hallmark, could be seen quite clearly and in the driveway was a Chevrolet Malibu.

"I remember running down this road. I remember the silver car in the driveway... Nancy..." Natalie moaned in sadness.

"Natalie honey, are you sure?"

She was pale, like she had seen a ghost, and nodded. She was sure this was the place, the house of evil where the demon furnace used to inflict the mental torture was contained. Morgan pulled up alongside of young Grant who was walking back to his vehicle.

"Got a possible, few roads over... see if you can do a drive by and get the plate off that Malibu parked at 65 Hallmark."

"No problem. Hi Natalie." Natalie just nodded through her tears.

Grant wasted no time in pulling the number off the plate and calling it in. The Malibu at 65 Hallmark, was also a rental and it had been rented out of Franklin Falls.

* * *

One by one the specialized swat unit that had been called in painted black and green on their faces like a football team readying for the championship. They put on their camouflage fatigues, slammed the fully loaded magazines into their high powered rifles and packed up their door breaching battering rams. Morgan gave a quick briefing to the team who were almost salivating to smash in the door and catch a potential serial murderer.

"Research on the target residence shows a male by the name of Larry Cartwright as the homeowner. He has no criminal history. It was pointed out by the surviving victim and the vehicle in the driveway was a rented Malibu that the victim also described. Background on that is it was rented by

Larry Cartwright about a month ago. From what we know of the suspect is he travels back and forth from here to Franklin Falls as he has rented vehicles from both areas. We have no information as to weapons or any type of armament in this residence. Good luck gentlemen."

The team filed into their black vans and headed out. Morgan played Irish Washerwoman while the team played Ride of the Valkyries to get their dynamic entry juices flowing. He followed the line of vans to 65 Hallmark Road where the Malibu remained in the driveway.

Under the cover of darkness, the team surrounded the house. The night was still hot and muggy and under their heavy equipment the team members were sweating profusely yet still forged ahead with their duty. They checked their watches. The countdown was on. As they had done many times before, as the second hand reached the top of the hour, the team simultaneously emerged from hiding and stormed the house. In a well-planned, almost picture perfect attack, the back and front door were smashed in, the rams dropped to the floor, flash bombs exploded and the team began to clear the house room by room with the red eye laser scopes piercing the darkness. Door after door of the house was kicked in, thousands in damage was done. After only one minute, the house was cleared, it was empty. There was no one home and even worse, there was a plain gas furnace in the basement.

As the team marched out and back into their black vans Morgan's heart sunk. He felt he was so close and now, dejected, he felt he was back to square one. He walked around the house knowing full well that Natalie was wrong. Morgan opened the kitchen fridge and helped himself to one of Larry Cartwright's beers and sat alone at the kitchen table, estimating the damage that the police will have to come good for. Morgan cared not what flavor of beer it was, it was beer and that's all that mattered. Out the kitchen window he could see the Malibu in the driveway as he guzzled the beer. Something still didn't sit right about it. Morgan found it strange that a man would have a rental car in his driveway, yet not be home. Morgan took a look at the answering machine beside the kitchen phone. He pressed the play button on the machine.

"Hi you've reached Larry Cartwright; I'll be away on business for the next month or so. Please leave a message after the tone. Take care."

"Why would someone rent a car, leave for a month and just leave the car in the driveway?"

More questions that he had no answers for, so he popped the cap and chugged another one of Larry's beers.

CHAPTER THIRTEEN

DON'T GO IN THE BASEMENT

The Police Chief, firm and inelastic in his opinions, was none too happy with the failure of the previous night. He still did not trust Morgan and it was with palpable difficulty he allowed Morgan back on the case. Morgan decided to steer clear of the office for the time being and help with the door to door.

Grant continued on Hallmark Road and pulled over at the base of the driveway at number 70. As there was a limited amount of houses on this dead end road Grant decided to check the rest and clear this road from the canvass list. It wasn't a long driveway, but long enough that the house was partially hidden from the road by a tree line. Grant felt uneasy as he trudged up the driveway looking up at the older house with cracked wooden stairs leading to the heavily weathered porch. Admiring the dirt covered windows, he wondered to himself if he should call for backup. He gathered some courage and continued walking.

"*Hee hee,*" the ghostly child's laugh echoed from the trees.

"Who's there?" No answer returned, but a slight breeze blew through his hair, making the follicles on his arms stand up.

"I've heard you. I'll be going to find out who lives here and if your parents are home, you're going to be in trouble."

"*Hee hee,*" echoed the child again. Another breeze blew by his ear, then… "*Madness,*" a soft disembodied voice said and a flash of black robe disappeared behind a tree.

Grant quickened his pace to the end of the driveway and up the front steps of the house at 70 Hallmark Road. He knocked at the door, all the while keeping one eye on the tree line. There was no immediate answer so Grant knocked again, harder. He thumped at the door a third time and finally could hear shuffling behind the door. It was opened a crack by a middle-aged man.

"Yeah?" he asked.

"Um, hi sir, we are canvassing the area looking for information on a serious case of abduction and I was wondering if I could come in and ask a few questions?"

"Can you come back?"

"Well sir, it will only take a minute and I will be out of your hair…" Grant scrutinized this gentleman's hair. It appeared shaggy, unkempt and the hair was tilted to the side and an unusual angle. The man opened the door further and let Grant just inside the door.

"What's this about?" he asked. "Make it quick. I was just on my way out."

"*Hee hee,*" came from behind a closed door. Grant stared at the door for about ten seconds, a deep feeling of understandable mistrust over took him.

"I ain't got all day."

"Mind if I take a look around?" Grant asked.

"I do mind."

"What's behind that door?"

"Basement, nothing down there but junk."

"*In here,*" Grant heard the voice say from behind the door.

He looked at the man, who obviously wasn't hearing the same voice as Grant, and just stood there staring at the officer with focusing eyes. Grant dropped his guard and approached the door cautiously reaching for the knob and rotating it slightly.

"*Don't turn your back on him!*"

Grant spun around and the man was standing right behind him and covered his mouth and nose with a rag. Instinctively Grant pushed him back but only after having taken a deep breath of the chloroform that laced the cloth, Grant stumbled back against the basement door and his vision went immediately blurry, but still Grant was able to land a punch to the man's face. He was stunned from Grant's blow and it bought him a second to draw his firearm and he squeezed off a shot. It was a miss, the bullet slammed into the stucco wall with an explosion of white dust. The man ran out the front door and down the steps.

"*DADDY!*" the child's voice called out from behind the basement door.

With his vision fuzzy, Grant gave chase out the front door where he slipped on something at the top of the porch steps and went crashing down. He lost his grip on his gun as he fell and it landed barrel first in the dirt. Achingly he rose. A shaggy wig lay midway on the rotting steps. He recovered the gun and looked to the end of the driveway. The now bald man was looking back, and then continued to run off. With an injured leg Grant limped after him. Each step Grant took shot pain up every nerve ending to the base of his spine. His face grimaced as he continued, determined not to give up.

"Don't let him get away."

Grant looked into the trees trying to shake the blurriness out of his head. The voice was following him. When Grant got to the end of the driveway he could see the bald-headed man further up the road and heading into the house at number 65. It was only a second, then the Malibu that was parked there sped out of the driveway. Grant fumbled with his cruiser door and let out a howl of pain as he sat down behind the wheel.

"Pursuit, pursuit!" Grant screamed into the radio. "North on Hallmark. The Malibu from last night! I think it's the guy from the diner video, the one that killed Jenny McGrath!"

Morgan, who had just taken a mouthful of whiskey, spit it out all over the inside of the windshield as he heard Grant's panicked words come across the air. Morgan stepped on the gas and drove possessed, jettisoning concerns of his own safety. He rounded a corner near Grant's location and he could see the Malibu coming towards him. A surge of adrenalin exploded through his boozy veins and with bottle still in hand, he took a swig and threw it to the side. He blocked the road with his unmarked cruiser yet the Malibu still sped towards him. Morgan tromped on the accelerator and turned up the Irish tunes that were playing on his speakers.

"This is for Jillian."

The two vehicles were on a deadly collision course. At the last spilt second, Morgan pulled to the shoulder arced his vehicle into the rear corner of the Malibu. It was a tough, risky maneuver to try and perform, let alone after a few drinks, but it worked. This collision put the Malibu into a spin and the bald headed man lost control, went up onto someone's lawn, taking out their bird bath and struck a tree. Morgan went into a spin as well, but regained control and drove his cruiser into the door of the Malibu, stunning the bald headed driver. He sat behind the wheel bleeding from his temple, and from a reopened wound on his neck. Morgan approached, looked at the hole in this man's neck, then jammed his finger deep into the wound. The bald man screamed in pain from Morgan's sickening act but he only pushed his finger in deeper.

"If I didn't know any better, I would say this is a bullet wound," he said, twisting his finger in the cavity created by Edders final shot. Morgan withdrew his bloody finger and wiped it clean on the man's shirt.

"Charles mother-fuckin' Trundle I presume," Morgan said as Grant limped up beside him.

The man looked at Grant, smiled, and then he held out his hands to be yanked out the window and thrown to the ground.

A murderer was captured.

"You gotta be fuckin' kidding me," he snarled while looking at Grant from his prone position.

"What the fuck are you talking about?" a visibly angry Grant barked at the bald man.

"Don't bother arguing with him here, kid. We'll get our chance. We have to lock down that house. Did you see anything inside?"

"There is something in the basement. Before he tried to gas me, I heard something in the basement. I think it might be Nancy..."

"Get him back to the office. I'll check out the house."

"Hey, you sure?" Grant asked, concerned that Morgan may find the dead body of Jillian Edders.

"Yeah, thanks kid. I gotta do it."

Morgan drove the short distance to 70 Hallmark Road. He ran his hand along the dent he put in the front of the cruiser and hoped it will redeem himself in the Chief's eyes. He looked down, thinking there was a dead rat on the stairs, and saw the wig. Morgan knew in his heart of hearts; he was at the right place. He looked at the tree line and knew it was a perfect wooden row to block any nosy neighbors. Morgan entered the still open front door and called out.

"Is there anyone in here?"

No response. Looking up the hall he saw what one could assume was a door to the basement. He went to the door and turned the knob. The door creaked a long moan as it opened and he saw nothing but darkness, and could smell a rotten stench.

"Is there anyone down there?" His call echoed into the darkness.

Looking down he could see the steps disappear into blackness. Morgan stepped onto the first step and like the door, another long creak. He put his weight on the second and paused.

"For Jillian," he reassured himself a second time. He pulled out the whiskey and swallowed two enormous mouthfuls.

Morgan felt along the wall for a light switch but couldn't find one. He had no flashlight and had left his phone in the car. He relied on his bravery and wits as he continued down the stairs feeling along the wall. Finally, he felt it. Morgan put his hand on what he thought must be the basement light and tried to turn it but it only moved a short distance because of its rusted spring. He put more effort into it and eventually it turned all the way to the right. There was a giant hiss across the basement and two demonic eyes opened before him and seemingly stared directly into his soul. A fiery mouth opened and screeched a beckoning call to the surprised detective as it filled with flames.

"Jesus fuckin' Christ!"

Morgan fell back into the stairs staring in disbelief at the demon before him. The walls suddenly lit up with a hundred more tiny demons dancing for their master. A chain hung from the ceiling to the floor, the hooked end lying in a large pool of blood. The sight was surreal. Morgan thought he had walked down the flight of stairs that ended at the gates of hell. He finally caught his breath and what he had thought was a light switch was the gas flue for the furnace. He turned it back until the flames lessened and the tiny demons danced at half their usual cadence. There was no one alive and there were no bodies that he could see, but the smell, the rancid smell of burning flesh was prevalent in the air. Morgan approached the demon furnace, opened the steel grate and peered inside. There was a set of burning legs on the interior gas tubes. Morgan could still make out the foot and partial big toe attached to a charred ankle, shin and finally ending at a kneecap. It was thinner; Morgan believed it was most likely Nancy. He saw pieces of skull fragments and thought of all the decapitated heads that must be in there, sacrificed to this monster. Morgan recognized this basement from the disc he had been sent and could see a camera set on a tripod in one corner and the implement of his madness...the hook filled belt.

"We got him, Jill. You kept your promise to Jenny. I couldn't have done this without you," he said, choking up a bit knowing that one of the burning skulls would be hers.

Morgan turned the flue off and walked up the stairs. Outside he could hear other police cars pulling up the driveway. Morgan walked out onto the front steps as the arriving officers filed out of their cruisers.

"No one else inside?"

"Its empty boys... we got him."

The officers at the bottom of the front steps erupted into an exhilarated applause.

* * *

Samuels tossed Trundle's ass into the slammer and helped Grant outside to get his head clear of the fumes he ingested.

"I'm good. I'm good now. He was trying to talk head games with me. That was one fuckin' creepy house. Anyone hear from Morgan?"

"Yeah. There was no one else in the house. A lot of death... too much death, and why is it still so friggin' hot out?" Samuels said while lighting a stogie.

"Okay. Could have sworn I heard someone in the basement. Guess it was best to check. It is hot, you're right."

Samuels and Grant could hear the clanking of an engine coming up the road towards the police station. Morgan pulled into the lot showing off the newly smashed in front end of his unmarked cruiser.

"Gives it character," Samuels joked as Morgan exited his vehicle.

He and Grant shook hands then hugged in victory. "Great work kid, but still a mountain of work to do yet, a million questions to answer. It's not over yet."

Charles Trundle sat alone on a plain, four-legged chair in the interrogation room. John Morgan sat across from him; his chair was equipped with wheels, a psychological advantage as Morgan was free to roll about the room, while Charles remained stationary, his hands still cuffed. Grant stood in an adjacent room, watching the proceedings through a two-way mirror.

"State your name for the camera please," Morgan asked.

"Charles Trundle."

"Charles, you are indeed a man of mystery and you have been arrested for multiple murders and I would like to talk to you about these."

"I didn't do nothing," Charles said giving the typical answer while folding his arms the best he could with his hands secured.

Morgan held up his hand in the widely known 'talk to the hand' gesture.

"Charles, there is a mountain of evidence against you and you can only help yourself by talking to me. Charles, you know who I am. You sent the DVD to me. Even in the few words you have said I can already tell it is the same voice… tell me what happened. Tell me why. Tell me of your madness…"

Charles Trundles look changed from a dull motionless expression much like a face carved into stone, to one of wonder and curiosity. His eyes widened and Morgan knew he had hit upon something by using his own words against him.

He now had a mentally unstable look in his eyes but Morgan was undaunted in his task to squeeze a confession from Charles' wicked mind.

"The world is full of madness. You are full of madness. Help me understand your madness."

Charles Trundle lowered his head and looked at the floor. He smiled an evil looking smile while continuing to stare at the blue carpet of the interview room. Morgan remained patient and let the silence continue for at least five minutes.

"Madness," Charles finally said. "All I ever wanted was to play. Why wouldn't they play?"

"What was your game?" Morgan asked.

"They reminded me of my own. I miss them so much. They were beautiful like my little girl. She was beautiful like my wife. I needed to replace them because I lost them so long ago."

Morgan was quick to put this statement into a logical perspective. "You lost your wife and daughter long ago. You wanted to replace them with others so you would kidnap young girls to remind yourself of your own daughter you lost. Jillian Edders reminded you of your wife that you lost, so you kidnapped her to fulfill that empty part of you. It's not easy losing someone. We have all lost someone in our lives and I completely understand the need to replace them. If I was in your position, I may do the same thing." Morgan was obviously lying to Trundle, but the tactic was working. "Your daughter was a beautiful child and losing her must have been the hardest thing a father could go through. Tell me about your efforts to replace that beautiful angel; anyone listening would understand your pain. Any judge that is worth a pound of salt would be able to see that the madness is born from your pain...tell me about Jenny, the girl from the diner. You were so kind to buy her pizza. She certainly would understand your pain."

Trundle continued to smile and look at the floor as he began to recount the story. "She was sweet, young and beautiful like my little Trina. Walking along the road by herself was like she was a gift to me. A present waiting for me to unwrap and take. I couldn't wait and I needed her right then and there."

Trundle took a deep breath, like the memory of killing Jenny McGrath instilled a sexual response. This response was a clear cue to Morgan that Trundle had most likely been a sexual abuser of Trina and in turn would sexually abuse and rape the young girls he captured to bring back the original sexual high, like a heavy user always chasing the pink elephant, the unprecedented sensation of their first drug trip.

"I put my hands around her throat while I took her. I squeezed her little neck until she stopped breathing. It was beautiful, it was madness."

Morgan put out his hand in a gesture to shake with this murderer. To his surprise, Trundle took his hand and shook it. Morgan was slightly disgusted but continued the good cop tactic to keep Trundle talking. He fully intended to wait for him to die in jail and then piss on his grave too.

"Tell me about the man from the tree," he said moving on to Jake Gurracci.

Trundle seemed to snap out of his catatonic state and sat up straight.

"What?"

Morgan took this as another cue that he was about to enter the deny, deny, deny stage that was the beginning of the interrogation. Quickly he changed to Jillian Edders as he suspected if he continued to question about Jake Gurracci he may lose this momentum.

"Sorry, back to your beautiful wife and daughter, the angels of your life. I too lost a daughter," Morgan lied again. "I'm sorry for your pain, for the void in your life it created."

Charles Trundle looked back and the floor and the smile returned.

"Tell me about the lady. You needed a replacement for the special wife you lost and even after I watched the DVD, I could tell you were in pain and what you did may not be so different than anyone else in your position."

"She was lovely. Like my lost wife. I needed her but I also needed you to know that this madness could not be stopped and will go on, even after me. She fought valiantly and as you pointed out, was responsible for this wound that won't go away. She wouldn't play, they all wouldn't play. She needed the belt. She needed to be punished like them."

Morgan held it all in. With every fiber of his being he swore he would keep Trundle talking, get the confession and complete this case right. Following his reaction to the Jake Gurracci question, Morgan was concerned he would shut down.

"She should have played. Things would have been easier. It was her fault, so what did you do?" Morgan just dragged his friend through the mud and didn't feel good about that but if anyone would understand why he said such a hurtful thing, it would be Edders, and it was just a necessary approach to keep Charles Trundle talking.

"She should have played. I took the belt and made her learn about madness. I hit her with it until she learned. When she stopped moving, when I ripped her eye out… I knew she had learned."

The two shook hands again and again Morgan was disgusted by it.

"Tell me about the two girls."

"I knew they would come. I went to that hotel because I knew the pervert in the next room was being visited by young girls. I knew more would come. I got two sweet ones in one shot."

"Two sweet ones like your daughter."

Trundle nodded in agreement and again breathed deeply. "I lost one and the other wouldn't play. I used the belt on her too. I hit her and kept hitting until she stopped moving, sweet madness." He inhaled like he had another mental orgasm.

"She too should have played," Morgan said.

"You understand me."

"I understand you. All anyone has to do is listen, and I am here to listen. What did you do with them? The ones who needed to learn."

"I put them in the furnace."

"Is that where the heads are?" Morgan asked taking another gamble.

Trundle snapped up again with an angry look on his face. "I did no such thing."

He crossed his arms, his bonds still holding firm, and turned his head away in defiance. It was body language Morgan knew well and it generally signaled the interview was coming to an end, although he felt best to give it one more shot.

"Charles, all those people deserved what they got. You did the world a favor by giving them their punishment, they were all mean people."

"I did no such thing."

Morgan again put his hand out and Trundle shook it holding Morgan's hand tight and leaned forward.

"But I know who did..."

It was a revelation that Morgan had suspected was coming. Morgan didn't want it to be true, but in this case, he believed Trundle. There was a second killer.

"How do you know?"

"I watched it. I watched him wield his homemade axe. Blade so sharp it takes a head off like a hot knife through butter."

The deranged Trundle was changing his tune now and becoming even more insolent.

"And that, you asshole cop, you will never get out of me. You think I am madness...you think he is done..."

Charles Trundle had confessed and Morgan knew he had extracted with considerable ease most of what he needed to put him away for good.

"Okay Grant, camera off, interview is done."

Grant tapped on the glass to signal the camera was off.

"And since it may be a while before I can piss on your grave, I guess this will have to tide me over." Morgan jammed his finger in Trundle's wound again and reveled in the wincing that followed.

"Ahh! Fuck you!"

"No. Fuck you!" Morgan said to Trundle.

Grant came in and escorted Trundle back to the jail cell, where he would shortly be transported to another facility to be housed until trial. He shot Morgan a quick thumbs up before exiting the room.

"You deserve it," Morgan said to himself.

He took a swig out of the whiskey bottle that was in his inner pocket. He covered his hands in sanitizer after having shaken hands with that awful scum Charles Trundle. He had to shift gears because he had another person waiting to be spoken to. Donna Keeling awaited Morgan in another interview room. By this time Donna Keeling had been advised that her husband Dan Keeling had not run off and the ghastly mess of a body found in the garbage dump was in fact, Dan.

Donna Keeling sat in a smart looking dress on the considerably comfier couch than the chair that had been given to Charles Trundle. She was well into her grieving process and mentally prepared herself to speak to police.

"Good morning, Donna, thank you for coming. I am very sorry to have to bring you here today but there are some questions about the phone calls you said to have been receiving from Dan."

"He was calling after he disappeared. I was sure it was him. Like I said, he had an issue with his voice."

The crafty Morgan, again prepared, opened a laptop computer and clicked opened a file.

"Donna, just looking for a comment after I play this," Morgan said.

> "Emergency 911."
>
> *"Yes, I'd like to report a problem at 969 Mason Rd."*
>
> "What is the nature of the problem ma'am?"
>
> *"A man was beating up a woman."*
>
> "Is he still beating her up?"

> *"No, he's not anymore. No...not anymore."*
>
> "What's your name? Are you still there? Ma'am, are you still there?"

Donna Keeling was visibly shaken upon hearing that. She started sobbing heavily at the short clip Morgan just played.

"That's the voice... that's the voice... that is who was calling."

"Do you recognize the voice, now that you know it was not Dan?"

"No. I am so stupid. I can hear it so clearly now."

"Don't beat yourself up over it. Is there anyone else you can think of that would want to hurt Dan?"

"No."

"Is there anything that he may have been doing in his life that you may not have been aware of? For example, would he disappear on occasion, say he is going to work and not show up... anything?"

"No," Donna said shaking her head through her tears.

Morgan bid Donna farewell and showed her to the front door again thanking her for coming in. He put on his best sympathy hat for the distraught widow, she made the list of a true victim and someone Morgan would check in with, from time to time, to see how she is healing. Another question was answered.

* * *

Grant was proceeding to the city detention center with Charles Trundle in the back of his cruiser. Even Grant was holding back the urge to pull over and beat the living shit out of the murdering pervert. The air conditioning in the car was at maximum and despite the beads of moisture caking on the interior windshield, Grant was still sweating. Charles Trundle sat in the back, a continuing smug smirk on his ugly face.

"I almost had you. It would have been just like old times."

"Shut the fuck up, asshole!"

Charles Trundle put his face up to the metal screen that separated the back seat from the front and began to speak in a low tone laced with the malevolence that he inflicted on so many others. His voice entered Grant's ear, meandering its way into his mind and struck a nerve that felt as if his brain was going through shock therapy.

"Oh no…the madness…I know who you are. I was there…in the hotel…in the room. I like your work, a chip off the old block."

"Shut up!" Grant said putting his fingers to his temple in a vain attempt to stop what seemed like a migraine bubbling up from hell. Inside his head, the millions of nerve endings jolted, the left lobe, the right lobe, the frontal lobe, all seemed to be fighting one another in a battle for individual supremacy. With bloodshot eyes he looked at his reflection in the rear-view mirror but only saw a grinning child looking back.

"It's been a long time…boy. Come on, where is my Jeremy," Charles taunted.

"Shut up!"

"Jeremy…Jeremy…let me see my Jeremy…DON'T MAKE ME HAVE TO GET THE BELT OUT AGAIN!"

"*SHUT UP DADDY*!" a child's voice screamed out.

CHAPTER FOURTEEN

JEREMY, WHERE IS MY JEREMY?

Morgan sat in his chair, his head back with his eyes closed, deep in thought. *Where is the connection, where is the connection? Why Dan Keeling? What happened to Jeremy Trundle?* His train of thought was interrupted when Samuels came into his office.

"We can't get Grant on the radio or on the cell phone," Samuels told Morgan, his voice full of worry. "He never showed up to the detention center with Charles Trundle. We got units out looking and are hoping it's just communication issues." Morgan didn't open his eyes to respond, merely giving a simple nod as confirmation that he had heard. Samuel's heavy boots thumped back into the hall, presumably heading to ask the front desk to try to ramp up their efforts to reach Grant.

Morgan leaned further back, tempting the limits of the chair as he continued to meander through his mind. He rocked back again, but his luck ran out, and he fell off his chair, into the box that contained the case files. He gave a disgruntled growl to the chair itself before he started to pick himself up. But he paused halfway, and stared at the box his ass had crushed. His face drained of color, and he looked like he'd seen a ghost. "Oh my fucking God!" he whispered, his eyes bugging out. It flashed into his mind ... all at once.

'It's Natalie. I want to give you more than a sampler this time you big hairy stud' - his pitch perfect falsetto voice was the same as the 911 call from Sheila's ... Dan Keeling was the garbage man that made Grant chase him up the road ... My angel in blue – HIS BLUE POLICE UNIFORM. Morgan could see it so clearly.

"No, no, no this isn't happening," Morgan muttered, returning to his chair and flipping open his laptop. Furiously hammering on the keys, he proceeded to do an internet search on Bobby Grant. The first thing that popped up was a newspaper article:

HEROIC DETECTIVE BOBBY GRANT KILLED IN TRAGIC COLLISION: One Survivor

In a tragic accident police officer Detective Bobby Grant was killed when his police cruiser was struck by a pick-up truck. The detective of 18 years with the Dorrington Police Service was transporting a young child who survived the collision. Bobby Grant died shortly after as a result of the

impact while the two were being taken to hospital.

'Click for photo'

The article was dated over ten years ago. Morgan hovered his mouse over the clickable option knowing full well what he was about to discover and with trepidation, he opened it. The photo depicted a mangled, unmarked police cruiser and a paramedic carrying a young boy up to the awaiting ambulance. Morgan studied the photo and the child in the arms of the paramedic was all too familiar to him, and the caption read: Jeremy Trundle, lone survivor.

Moravian's Bobby Grant, was actually a grown Jeremy Trundle.

"Shit, fuck, shit, fuck, shit, fuck...." Morgan chanted, fumbling desperately for the bottle in his inner suit pocket. He took more than a generous swig.

All the available police units were out looking for Grant, and unwisely, even the cops that were protecting 70 Hallmark Road left their post out of worry for their brother. Morgan darted out the back door to his newly dented cruiser, leaving his cell phone on the desk.

"Come on old girl, don't fail me," he said, turning the key. The engine sputtered, rolled over a few times, but didn't start. "Come on you piece of shit, start!" He turned the key again and the engine rolled over, and finally came to life. "Fuck ya!" he said throwing it into gear and peeling out of the parking lot. The cruiser had no air conditioning and handled like a shopping cart with one bad wheel. He drove his wobbling cruiser over to the house Grant rented and pulled into the empty driveway. Strapping his gun to his belt and concealing it under his suit jacket, he walked around to the back of the house and turned the knob on the back door, only to find it locked. He kicked it and fell back on his ass when it remained locked tight.

"Ow, fuck!" he muttered, face twisting in pain.

He pulled his gun from the holster and smashed out a window with it. He cleared the glass from around the frame and hoisted his body through the opening, rolling into the kitchen, over the counter and landing on the floor. Save for the glass he had just strewn about the kitchen, it was extremely clean. Meticulously so. He hastily cleared the upper floor and after finding no one inside he located the door to the lower level.

Morgan opened the door to the basement.

"Aw crap, not again," he said, feeling blindly for the light switch.

Morgan was successful in locating the switch and after turning on the light, he descended the staircase. It was a smaller lower level, with just a laundry room and a door beside the washing machine. The smell of mothballs was overwhelming as Morgan cautiously walked closer to the door. He tried the door and the knob graciously responded. As he slowly opened the door the, stench of mothballs wafted out of the room like a punch in the face, even stronger than before. Using the light from the laundry room, he could see a lone bulb in the middle of the small room, with a string hanging from the wire. Morgan pulled the string and the room lit up with an eerie dimness. There was an old work bench, a grinding stone and boxes upon boxes lining the walls of the room, placed on tiers of shelves. The detective knew full well what each of the boxes contained. The boxes were labeled in black marker in what one would think was a child's handwriting. He scanned the room reading some of the labels. Some he expected, some he didn't know.

'Mean Mandy Young…Mean Judith Reinhold…Mean Lisa Patteric…Mean Jake Gurracci…Mean Todd Smilie… Mean Dan Keeling…Mean Peter Barnes…'

This list continued and Morgan could see about fifteen boxes. He took the one marked 'Mean Jake Gurracci' off the shelf and opened the top. His mouth was set in a grim line as he examined the plastic airtight bag the head was sealed in, along with the multitude of mothballs inside the box. He gingerly lifted the bag from the box, staring into the eye sockets of Jake Gurracci's rotting skull. Its putrid face had dissolved into a blackened mess, absolutely unrecognizable. He replaced the box and noted an empty one on the shelf as well. This empty box had a label written in the child's writing… 'Mean Daddy.'

He saw two hooks for hanging tools on the wall and a faint outline of a large axe in the dust on the bricks. He could tell it had been recently removed from its resting place and taken to fill the empty box. He knew where he had to go next.

* * *

Charles Trundle, his hands still cuffed tight, was led down the basement stairs by Grant at 70 Hallmark Road. The Grant that the Moravian Police knew had disappeared and he had regressed in his mind to ten-year-old Jeremy Trundle, his true identity. Jeremy turned the flue and the furnace erupted into its fiery demon guise. He hooked his father's cuffs to the hanger, the same one used to restrain others before him, the same one that was once used to restrain him and his sister. The smaller demons that danced on the wall gave Jeremy the chills and beckoned his mind to remember what happened that final night over ten years ago...

* * *

Jeremy huddled in the corner with his sister Trina, both kids with their eyes closed tight, waiting anxiously for the demons to disappear. On this final night, the demons continued their traditional dance on the walls laughing, laughing as hysterically as one would find in a child's terror-filled imagination.

The door to the basement opened and Charles was standing at the top, his silhouette outlined by the kitchen light and the occasional flash of lightning.

"Jeremy...Jeremy...Jeremy," Charles drawled slowly. Jeremy cringed further into the corner.

His foot thumped heavily onto the first step; Jeremy could see him dragging that God-awful belt. One by one, he descended the stairwell. Jeremy's mind raced with scenarios of escape, each one more desperate than the last, to save his mother and sister from this bastard from hell. His alcohol-laced breath was evidence of the daily habits; he was nothing but the dregs of society, wasting the days drinking and abusing his family. Jeremy's mother's only wish was that by allowing Charles to abuse her, it would somehow spare the children from the unhinged horror that was about to be inflicted on their tiny figures. The hooks glinted off the fire of that damned monster, it tentacles flayed about in the charged atmosphere of Jeremy's mind. Charles approached the kids with hooked belt in hand, his gaze fixated on Trina.

"Come on, baby, time to give daddy some honey."

"Get up, boy. Get up you little fuck!" Charles said, grabbing Trina by her skinny arm and wrenching her from the arms of her brother. She quickly scrambled away from her father, trembling against the cold basement wall. He directed his gaze back to Jeremy.

"Get in the corner, boy. Watch what a man can do. Watch what you can do when your pansy little cock finally grows up."

Jeremy shook his head in defiance, but only for a second. His father held the belt up, each of the hooks was salivating for the soft flesh of children. Jeremy cowered into the corner, not wanting to feel the belt again. Charles grinned maliciously at his son's figure.

"Yes, you little shit," he barked. "Get in the fucking corner and stay there. Watch. Watch me." Charles stepped closer to Trina, extending his hand. "C'mere my angel."

"No," Trina said softly, her head buried in her knees as she sat against the wall.

"Yes, baby, c'mere and give daddy what he wants. You like it too. C'mere sweetie."

"It hurts."

"I know baby... but I hurt too. C'mere and help daddy with his pain, the honey helps my pain goes away."

Trina did not move.

"GET OVER HERE AND PLAY WITH DADDY!"

Charles grabbed his daughter Trina by her tiny ankle and pulled her to the middle of the floor. He jerked her nightgown over her head, exposing her little panties. As he pulled down his pants, he placed the belt beside him on the floor.

"Watch, boy...watch what a man can do."

"NO DADDY. NO MORE. PLEASE NO MORE! THIS IS MADNESS!"

Jeremy ran from the corner and grabbed the belt. Holding it up, he brought it down as hard as he could on his father's disgusting pock-marked ass. The hooks tore into Charles' ass cheeks, ripping the bulbous bottom flesh just before he could again violate tiny Trina. Jeremy lifted the belt, attempting to bring it down a second time, but it was caught before it could find its mark.

Charles' red face loomed above Jeremy, twisted in rage. "You want madness… I'll give you madness…"

Charles tore the belt from Jeremy's weak grasp and pushed him to the floor.

"MADNESS… HERE IS MADNESS."

Charles brought the belt down onto little Jeremy. The hooks that were salivating for the young flesh were now satiated as they dug into his tissue and his blood began to flow. Jeremy put his hands up to protect himself, but the unforgiving hooks just dug into his fingers and palms as well, nullifying his weak defense. Jeremy scrambled back to the corner, leaving a trail of blood across the floor behind him. The furnace let out another groan as the flames licked the top of its mouth as its smaller servants continued to dart to and fro. Anger radiated off of Charles, thicker than it had ever been before. Fully pulling up his pants, Charles stormed up the stairs to where his wife was sitting, crying in fear, as she knew full well what he was doing to Trina in the basement.

"Get downstairs, bitch!" he roared, pulling her from the chair by her long hair.

Jeremy's mother came tumbling down the stairs, smashing her face off the rock-hard cement of the basement floor. She blearily lifted her head and looked towards Jeremy. Her eyes filled with tears she reached in vain for her children.

Charles brought the belt down over and over onto Jeremy's mother and sister. Blood and flesh sailed freely through the air, splattering the walls to the delight of the surreal, tiny demons. His mother's and sister's blood spattered onto Jeremy's terrified face, dripping downward as he continued to lay helpless in the corner.

"Look at what you've done, boy," Charles growled, towering menacingly over his bloodied family. "Here is madness. This is your madness…this is your doing. YOU ARE MADNESS!"

His mother and sister finally stopped their labored breathing, succumbing to their deep wounds. Arteries had been severed and their midsections had been torn open, ending their lives in a pointless, vicious, savage attack. Charles stopped his attack when the two became silent, quieting himself, and looked upon the results of his rage, of his madness. He remained soundless, staring down Jeremy as he walked to the wall to grab a hand saw. Calmly, he took the arm of his wife, Jeremy's beautiful mother, and began to saw. Blood, so much blood, coated the floor with dark crimson pools that drowned the bodies of his mother and sister. Each of her limbs were sawn off and fed to the demon furnace. The skin sizzled and stunk as it was tantalizingly consumed by the flame. Charles positioned the saw at Jeremy's mother's neck. He looked into her open dead eyes, but his hand stilled, unable bring himself to saw her head off. He instead turned to Trina's lifeless body, and as he had just done, sawed her apart as well.

Jeremy watched the entire macabre scene from the corner, his own wounds aching profusely. Charles fed the torsos into the furnace, bit by bit, all the while continuing to stare down Jeremy with his evil gaze, daring him to move. Finally, they had been consumed almost fully, save for their charred skulls, one big, one small, on the grate inside the furnace.

He didn't take their heads... Jeremy's mind went blank. It became a clean slate and his brain did a total emergency reboot, leaving him remembering almost nothing.

The evil Charles Trundle drove Jeremy a thousand miles away to Thompson Hill and threw him out of the car to fend for himself, a sick game to make his son a man. A near catatonic Jeremy spent days on the street starving before finally being noticed by someone who called police and in turn, child services.

Jeremy bounced around for the next few years, entering foster homes in both Dorrington and Thompson Hill. Jeremy barely knew his own name, let alone any memory of his family and Charles Trundle was successful in leaving no tracks for police to follow. No one knew where he came from and all the best psychiatrists couldn't penetrate his damaged psyche. As he grew he began to excel in school, but not with a few bumps along the way. In Dorrington Jeremy found himself in trouble with the law for something small; he couldn't remember what, but he remembered being scolded by the wise Detective Bobby Grant. Jeremy looked up to the detective, even in this one and only meeting, because he was impressed by his brilliant, blue suit and snazzy red tie. His intelligent reasoning and fine mannerisms made Jeremy reconsider his life destiny. Bobby Grant was driving Jeremy back to the foster home when Jeremy made verbal revelation to the detective.

"When I grow up, I want to be a policeman just like you."

That was the last thing Bobby Grant heard before being t-boned in the driver's door by a speeding pick-up truck that blew a stop sign. As Jeremy grew, he became obsessed with becoming a police officer and wanted even more so to break into detective work. He honed his skills to be the best he could and somewhere in the next ten years, Jeremy took up residence in his subconscious and his brain took on the identity of Bobby Grant. A high-functioning psychopath, so high-functioning that he was able to fool the police recruiters and fake his way into the Moravian Police. Yet, Jeremy was still inside. The visions, the voices, all Jeremy's doing. And Jeremy would take his revenge on mean people, and he was always the one in control.

* * *

"Morgan to dispatch ... come in?"

There was no response from the dispatcher. He beat his mic on the dashboard as if it would help somehow bring it to life, but it remained nonfunctional. The impact with the Malibu had knocked the thin wiring from the battery and the radio, the lifeline of any police officer, was now in unwelcome silence.

"Aw, shit," Morgan cursed, fumbling with his suit pockets.

His cell phone was still at the office. He continued to 70 Hallmark Road, where there were no police standing by, and he knew he'd be on his own. Just him, his pistol, his bottle of liquor, and whatever may await him.

Jeremy Trundle hoisted his father Charles upwards on the hook, leaving him in the same helpless hanging position as Charles had done to Jillian Edders. As Charles hung from the ceiling by his cuffs, Jeremy went to the police car trunk, dumped off his duty belt and vest, and returned with the axe. Jeremy stood at the top of the stairs with the axe in hand, just as his father had done with the belt years ago. As did the belt, its shiny blade was glinting off the flames of the furnace as Jeremy shut the door and descended the stairs.

Charles Trundle remained defiant, his face held as high as he could manage, albeit helpless in his current position. It was father killer and son killer reunited after so many years apart, and strangely, both paths lead back to the feet of the demon furnace. Charles smiled at his son.

"So, this is what you made of your life, boy."

"This is what you made of my life, daddy."

Charles smiled, darkness glinting in his eyes. "Then I can't help but say I'm very disappointed in you, boy. You killed them. You didn't fuck 'em. What good are ya? Where's the fun in that? Still nothing but a pansy ass pussy too chicken to do it right. Now you gonna kill your old man eh? If ya got the guts, go ahead boy, come on you lunatic cut my fuckin' head off. I'm just going to spend the rest of my life in jail, so do it. KILL ME!"

Jeremy tightened his grip on the axe, face twisting in confusion at his father's act of defiance. All of his other victims had never done this, and he wasn't sure how to handle the situation. He felt the control slip away slightly. But he focused on that corner in which he hid, and he drew on the rage that grew from that day.

"You were mean to mom and Trina! You were mean to so many people!" Jeremy yelled, raising the axe to neck height.

Charles still smiled his sick smile and tilted his head back, purposely exposing his jugular. He had no firm promise of an afterlife but in his cold heart he believed there would be something more, another plain in which he could continue his nefarious work. He knew the day would come and was anxious for the rapping of the scythe, but first he resumed his fast talk and intimidation of his son.

"Jeremy…Jeremy…Jeremy…" he taunted, mimicking the tone the regressed adult Jeremy was speaking in.

Jeremy brought the axe back and was just about to swing when he heard something at the top of the stairs. He looked up, the vision of death standing before him, nodding his skeletal head.

"Grant, stop!" Morgan yelled as he threw open the door with pistol in hand.

Jeremy looked at Morgan with an expression of confusion and did not recognize his former mentor.

"Jeremy, stop!" Morgan said, correcting himself.

His pistol was trained on the axe-wielding Jeremy as he stepped down another of the basement steps. Morgan looked about the room as the flickering fire continued to give the tiny demons the illusion of life.

"*Get back, I have to finish this. Daddy is mean,*" Jeremy said, putting the blade right up to Charles throat.

"Put it down, kid…don't make me have to shoot."

"*He killed my mom and sister. He killed so many others. He deserves to die.*"

"What about the people you killed Jeremy? Jake Gurracci, Todd Smilie," Morgan said, trying to stall. "What about Mandy Young, a child, like you, did she deserve to die?"

"*THAT LITTLE BITCH MADE FUN OF MY JOKE... SHE WAS SO MEAN*!"

Morgan's hand was shaking as the pistol began to get heavier. "Life and death for mean people is not up to us to decide. Put down the axe."

"What about you, cop?" Charles said. "You got the guts to shoot me? C'mon... shoot. You know I ain't never gonna get out again. Shoot me and say it was my pussy of a son. I killed your girlfriend. The chick cop, I killed her and burned her corpse in the furnace. She was a feisty one. A few whacks with the belt and she bled out like a stuck pig...SHOOT ME!"

Morgan wanted to. He wanted to see this motherfucker die, but instead, lowered his pistol.

"If I have my way, no one else is going to die today. Jeremy, put down the axe."

Morgan stepped down two more steps towards the smiling furnace. Jeremy fixed his gaze on its mouth, still flourishing with flame, and it now bore little resemblance to a heating unit and fully returned to the monster Jeremy feared as a child.

"You are pathetic, boy. You don't know madness," Charles said quietly to his son.

"*I AM MADNESS*!" Jeremy said swinging the axe and beheaded his own father. With infinite finality, Charles' and his reign of unbridled terror came to a bloody, deserved end.

Charles Trundle's head flew across the basement, twirling in the air, leaving a circular spray pattern of blood on the floor as it traveled across the room. The head hit the furnace and fell before the metal demon's feet, and rolled back a short distance. Morgan didn't hesitate, and fired off a shot, which hit its mark. Jeremy yelled in pain, his hand flying to his shoulder to staunch the blood.

"*That was mean*!" Jeremy said, still in that childlike voice. The muscles of the arm holding the axe flexed and Morgan knew exactly what he was going to do, but didn't have enough time to properly respond.

Jeremy threw the axe before Morgan could squeeze off another shot. The razor sharp blade spun through the air and struck Morgan in the chest. The detective was knocked off his feet, falling the rest of the way down the stairs to collide with the steel grate door of the furnace. The force of the fall knocked the ancient rusty door from its hinges, exposing a now wide-open, fiery mouth. The pistol skidded across the bloody basement floor.

"*You hurt me. I can't believe you hurt me. I'm only ten*!" Jeremy walked to the axe and picked it back up as Morgan shimmied on his butt back to the stairs.

"YOU GODDAM LITTLE CUNT. YOU CAN'T DO ANYTHING RIGHT!"

Morgan did not hear these words. Only Jeremy could hear them, and they were coming from the furnace. Morgan held his chest; he could feel the wetness of the blood beginning to flow from his wound.

"I HATED YOU! A DISAPPOINTMENT SINCE THE DAY YOU WERE BORN!"

Jeremy put his empty hand up to his temple and bent over trying to block out the voice.

"KILL HIM. DO IT RIGHT FOR ONCE. SACRIFICE HIM AND FEED HIM TO ME."

"*SHUT UP, DADDY... SHUT UP*!" Jeremy yelled at the furnace.

Morgan managed to return to his feet as Jeremy argued with the ethereal voice that emanated from the furnace.

Morgan charged Jeremy, shoving his weight into Jeremy's wounded shoulder. Jeremy stepped back, his left foot landing on the decapitated head of his father, causing him to lose his balance and fall, face first, into the open mouth of the furnace.

"*AHHHHHH*!" The shriek pierced Morgan's eardrums as the flames tore at Jeremy's face.

The skin sizzled, crackled and melted from his skull like a bubbling pot of liquefied cheese. He put his hands up to the fiery mouth trying to push himself out, but they too just melted and adhered to the metal sides. Morgan grabbed his legs and pulled him back, tearing the flesh from his hands in the process. Jeremy rolled around the basement floor, writhing in utter pain, curling in on himself as much as he could manage. Morgan could not hear it, but the furnace continued to laugh and the tiny demons laughed right along with their master, laughing at the intense melee, laughing at the bloody madness that was exhibited before them. Jeremy stopped screaming, lost consciousness and lay silently at the base of the flaming mouth of the furnace.

Morgan went to the stairs and sat down, nursing his chest wound. He was trying to catch his breath as he prayed he wouldn't be yet another soul to bleed to death in the hellish basement. He looked at his hand, expecting it to be coated with blood, but, there was none. His chest and hand were wet. No blood. Morgan smelled his hand, and it stunk of whiskey.

"Booze, is there anything it can't do?" he said, picking out the broken glass from his suit.

Morgan turned the flue down and the demons that had danced for so many victims finally disappeared back into hell. He ascended the stairs and walked onto the porch. The heat that had been torturing the town finally broke and he inhaled a lung full of fresh mild air, drinking in the purity that hadn't been felt in Moravian for months.

* * *

Hundreds of police officers descended on the town of Franklin Falls for the funeral of Jillian Edders. Her picture was placed lovingly on the top of her empty coffin. It depicted Jillian Edders sharply dressed in the Franklin Falls police uniform that she wore so proudly. No physical body had ever been recovered, as Morgan had totally expected. He stood in his tightly fitting dress uniform flanked by his girlfriend Sheila. He had come clean with her about his feelings he had developed for Jillian Edders in the time he spent working with her. She was smart, pretty, and dedicated in her profession. Sheila was undaunted, not the least bit jealous and continued to stand by Morgan, a man who treated her like gold. At the front of the crowd were Edders' parents, more unknown family members, and her female partner. Edders' partner was not the stereotypical looking lesbian that Morgan had expected. She was not dressed in plaid lumberjack clothing with a big ass and loose jeans. She was a shapely, tall, dark-haired lady that wore a gorgeous black dress. Her eyes were puffy and red. It had been a rough go for her, not knowing where Jillian Edders was, but today she could finally have closure, perhaps, but Morgan doubted she would ever have peace. Morgan looked around the Franklin Falls church that the service was being conducted in. The stained glass mirrored the church in Moravian where Cliff Henderson's funeral was held. The silent mourners exchanged pained awkward smiles as each stood up and shuffled by the empty coffin and touched Jillian's picture as they passed. Morgan stopped as tears welled up in his eyes. He picked up the picture and kiss his friend goodbye for the final time.

Morgan was somewhat of a celebrity in the parking lot of the church. A hundred officers lined up to shake his hand and thank him for catching Charles Trundle. Even well-meaning Boobs McGee squashed her giant jugs into Morgan's tummy as she hugged him and offered a free dinner. Morgan tried to give some credit to the former officer Grant, but none would have it. Morgan and Sheila departed Franklin Falls for the one hundred mile drive back to Moravian.

* * *

A month passed. Morgan had fallen back into his old ways and snuck the occasional hooch while he worked and the others were back into their old ways of ignoring it. Two killers in a day, not too bad, perhaps he deserved it. That, and a dump truck load of hot wings. Morgan was in the elevator of the hospital as it rose to the top floor where Jeremy had been housed under guard for the past month. He was cuffed to the hospital bed and his entire head was still covered in bandages. The bullet lesion was well on its way to healing over, leaving no hole for Morgan to stick his finger in. Morgan sat beside his bed as he had done many times. Through the bandages Morgan could see into Jeremy's eyes. He could tell, it wasn't hard, that Bobby Grant was gone and his eyes were replaced with dolls eyes, motionless, unblinking and dark. Endless nothingness. Bobby Grant never really existed, at least in Moravian, and Morgan would only be dealing with Jeremy from here on.

"How are you today, kid?"

Jeremy had been silent an entire month but Morgan's persistence would finally win over and for the first time, he turned his bandaged head towards Morgan. The eyes... the eyes were so different it creeped Morgan out, sending a shiver down his spine. Two round, blank discs. It was as though they were not looking at him, but through him. Jeremy finally spoke and the voice remained the same, the grown man continued to speak as a ten-year-old child.

"*Is the demon dead*?"

Morgan was surprised to receive an answer, but continued speaking. "Yeah, kid, the demon is finally dead."

"*It was mean.*"

"Yeah, it sure was."

Morgan turned on his recorder and started the interview from the beginning, the real beginning, over twenty years ago.

"What's your name?"

"*Jeremy Trundle.*"

"How old are you Jeremy?"

"*Ten.*"

"Do you know where you were born?"

"*Moravian.*"

"Where did you live?"

"*We lived at 70 Hallmark Road.*"

"Who did you live with, Jeremy?"

"*Mommy, my sister Trina, and Daddy.*"

He emphasized the word daddy, as the memory still brought upon anger in the soul of the psychopath.

"Do you know where they are now?"

"*Daddy's dead. I killed him. He was mean and needed to die. He killed my mom and sister. He chopped them up and burned them. I remember, he didn't chop off their heads. I don't know why he didn't kill me too. He took me away and dropped me in a place called Thompson Hill where I lived with foster families. I went to school there. I moved to Dorrington and lived with foster families there. I went to school there too."*

"Did you know Mandy Young?"

"I went to school with her. She was in my class. She was mean."

"What did she do that made her so mean?"

"She made fun of me. She made fun of my joke."

Morgan's curiosity surrounding this joke had peaked. "Jeremy, we're having a good conversation here. Let's lighten the mood a bit, tell me this joke."

Through the bandages Jeremy let out a muffled '*hee hee*', like the laugh that he had been hearing in his head all along. *"Well… there was this guy who invented the telephone. He picked up the phone and said 'Hello'… AND BEANS FELL OUT OF HIS EARS!"*

Morgan couldn't help it. Oh, he tried to hold it in, to seem professional, but it was a losing battle. Morgan fell off his chair and started laughing his ass off all the while the recorder continued to roll. The joke was absurdly stupid. It made no sense whatsoever, yet Morgan was busting his guts at the base of his chair over this asinine witticism and Jeremy was pleased he finally found an audience for what he felt was an awesome joke.

"Excuse me, Jeremy," Morgan said through his tears, and scuttled out of the room into the hall where the guard was standing.

"Bwahahahaha!" Morgan just let it all out with the guard throwing him a peculiar look. Here he was supposed to be interviewing a killer, yet he could not contain his laughter.

"Beans out of his ears," he said to the dumbfounded guard.

"I don't get it," the guard said.

"This guy invented the telephone..." Morgan said in broken snickers. "He picked up the phone and said 'Hello'... and beans fell out of his ears!"

"I don't get it."

"Okay, okay. I got this. I got this. We good," Morgan said, finally collecting himself enough to return to the room.

The question of the navy beans that were found with Mandy's body had been answered. Morgan was slightly embarrassed at his reaction that was now saved forevermore on his recorder. Despite the recording that the whole world may hear one day, he agreed the joke was pure genius.

"Jeremy, I'd be lying if I said I didn't like it but did Mandy truly deserve to die for making fun of it?"

"*Yes, she did. I smashed her face in with a brick and sawed off her head and put it in my mean people boxes. Why should mean people be allowed to be mean? Why don't jerks know they're jerks?*"

"Why don't jerks know they're jerks? Jeremy, that is an interesting question that I don't have an answer for." He bit his lip as he thought about the joke again. "Okay, let's move on, Jeremy. Tell me about Judith Reinhold, the teacher."

"*She was a fatty fatty fat fat. She was a mean teacher and one time she put red across my reader and 'very poor printing' in big red letters and yelled at me in front of the whole class. I hated her. Everyone hated her. She would have these big, fat panties that would stick up out of her pants when she would bend over and I thought I would give the biggest butt in the world the biggest wedgie in the world. Hee hee.*" Jeremy continued to face Morgan with his empty, wide eyes as he recounted the story. "*The fat mean teacher chased me to the basement where she finally learned how mean she was. I took her head for my mean people boxes too."*

"Tell me about Bobby Grant."

"He was nice policeman but he died. We were driving and we had an accident and he died."

"Why did you become him?"

"What?"

"You were Bobby Grant, an excellent, young policeman. Do you remember that?"

"What?"

Morgan shut down that line of questioning and decided to leave it to Doctor Chalmers or someone with a wall full of degrees. He knew that's what it may take to break through Jeremy's damaged mind, unaware that many had already tried.

"Tell me about Dan Keeling?"

"Who's that?"

"The garbage man, do you remember the garbage man?"

"He was mean. He made people chase the garbage truck while he'd bang on the side and tell the driver to speed up so people had to run after him to get rid of the garbage. That's not very nice."

"So what happened to him?" Morgan asked.

"I followed him to the dump. He was alone with his truck and dumping garbage and I took his head for my mean people boxes. I parked the truck and hid his body in the garbage, like the garbage he was."

"Why were there things in their stomachs?"

"They have to taste their meanness. They need to learn their meanness. They need to learn meanness… through madness," he trailed off and looked away from Morgan. *"I remember you were mean. I remember you shot me. You survived my axe… how did it not cut you? It took everyone so easily, but not you."*

Morgan smirked, thinking of the mickey of whiskey that had saved his life. "Jeremy, I guess us old dogs just sometimes refuse to die."

"Something is telling me to like you. I like you. I wish I could be a policeman like you when I get better and grow up."

That statement also chilled Morgan's skin and he again shivered like someone walked over his grave. It was something Grant would say and now Morgan was listening to this man-child say the same thing and that was unsettling, deeply unsettling.

"And Peter Barnes, the mean man from the hotel?"

"He was mean to those two other little girls. He made them have sex with him. He tricked them. He deserved to be punished. I knocked on his door and he opened it thinking I was another little girl. I took his head for my mean people boxes. This time, daddy was watching. He saw me do it but I didn't know he was there. Daddy was the meanest of them all but now, he will never hurt again."

Morgan shut off the recorder when the attending doctor interrupted. He came in and began to unwrap Jeremy's bandages to put on fresh dressings. His hands looked like two clubs of burnt sausages and his face was a melted mess of hanging skin. He had no eyebrows, eye lashes, and barely had eyelids to blink over his dead eyes. His lips were peeled back, making him unable to close his mouth properly and he drooled freely. Any resemblance to Bobby Grant the young Moravian police officer was gone and Morgan could accurately guess years of reconstructive surgery were in his future.

Morgan walked back into the hall where the guard was still standing to the left of the doorway.

"I still don't get it," he said as Morgan passed.

Of course all this did was remind Morgan of the funniest joke he's ever heard in his life and it caused him to start chuckling lightly at first, but the more it rattled around in his alcoholic brain the louder he laughed as he walked towards the elevator. The guard could hear Morgan laughing so loud that even the descending elevator did little to mute it.

Fuckin' beans. Why fuckin' beans? Only the mind of a child could come up with unadulterated innocent humor like that, he thought, stepping off the elevator.

Back at the police station, Morgan entered through the front door, still laughing. Samuels caught the delightful chuckles of the grizzled detective and needed to inquire what was up.

"Yeah, I know you are proud of yourself for simultaneously catching two serial killers, but we're taking it on the chin in the media for hiring one of them." Samuels caught Morgan's arm. "But come on, you have to tell me. What the hell is so funny?"

Morgan held his laughter in behind a smirk. "Humor is last defence we have from insanity. Jeremy, also known as Bobby Grant, just told me the funniest joke I ever heard in my life."

"Okay, you got me, lay it on me."

Morgan put his hand on Samuel's desk and squeezed his eyes shut, trying to contain himself.

"Okay, here we go. There was this guy that invented the telephone. He picked up the phone and said 'Hello'... and beans fell out of his ears!" Morgan lost it again, still unable to contain himself.

Samuels stared blankly at him, trying to wait for the punch line to actually make sense. And when it did it, Samuels shook his head. "That is the most fucking ridiculous thing I have ever heard," he stated, an eyebrow lifted at Morgan's antic. "It has no humor, it makes no sense, and what makes even less sense, is you laughing at it."

"Eh, that's what I thought, you old geezer," Morgan said, walking away.

"You drinking again?" Samuels called after him.

"Ah, nope. No siree, bob." Morgan turned the corner and disappeared from sight.

"Old geezer is drinking again. Everyone knows that joke was stolen from an old dumb ditty from the sixties," Samuels rambled to himself. "It got banned in some places because some stupid kids really did put beans in their ears. Jesus."

* * *

"I can't believe that fuckin' squashed fly is still there," Morgan said, viewing the empty prisoner's box.

He took his spot in the courtroom rows amongst all the reporters that had flocked to the city to cover what was shaping up to be the story of the year. The packed courtroom stood when His Honor Judge Neilson took the bench. No one said a word when they led Jeremy Trundle into the prisoner's box. He sat down and stared at the fly, his face and hands still wrapped tightly, his eyes still wide and blank.

An hour of arguments passed and in the end, the decision was easy for Judge Neilson. Jeremy Trundle was not fit to stand trial and furthermore he would be housed in the maximum security wing at Pine Grove. Morgan was neither surprised nor disappointed. He himself was treated at Pine Grove and perhaps was better for the experience.

The judge stared down at the bandaged mess that was once a fine police officer. "Anything you wish to say to the court before you leave to start your lifetime of treatment?" Jeremy stood up, as if he knew where he was, and knew the rules of the court.

"*The madness,*" Jeremy paused for a few seconds after saying those words in the child's voice. "*Is not over.*"

"It is for you!" Judge Neilson said with authority.

"BECAUSE YOU'RE NOTHING BUT A LOSER, A WASTE OF SKIN, A WIMPY LITTLE FAGGOT AND YOU'RE GONNA DIE IN THAT ASYLUM!"

Jeremy turned his head towards the voice and saw his father sitting in the front row, his severed head in his lap.

"*SHUT UP, DADDY*!" Jeremy yelled at the reporter who actually occupied that seat.

"Officer, take him away please," the judge ordered.

Jeremy took one last look at the fly and wondered what mean person could have killed such a helpless creature. Just as he was about to leave the courtroom, he stopped dead in front of the escorting officer. Jeremy cranked his head around and with his dead eyes, took one last look at Morgan. Morgan got the same haunting feeling he did back in the hospital room. The courtroom rose to their feet once again as the Judge got up to leave. Judge Neilson stopped and called to Morgan.

"Detective Morgan ... excellent job."

Most likely the best Morgan could hope from his ex-father in law. At least it wasn't asshole. Morgan knew what melee would soon follow in the hallway. He exited the courtroom into the sea of reporters and flashing cameras.

"Detective Morgan, how did you crack this case?" a reporter asked, shoving a microphone in his face.

"Old fashioned police work. I wasn't the one who found Charles Trundle. That honor goes to another officer, a good officer."

"Detective Morgan, how do you feel that one of the serial killers turned out to be one of your own?"

"How do I feel? I feel like having a drink...excuse me, please direct all questions to the Chief," Morgan said, pushing through the crowd.

He quickly trotted down the cement steps of the courthouse to escape the reporters and the flickering storm of camera flashes on the back of his head. In his haste he stepped out into the street right in front of a car that came to a screeching halt and the driver laid on the horn for about five seconds. Morgan turned and looked at the driver and was about to apologize when they each had an immediate recognition of each other.

"Oh, shit!" Morgan said in earnest.

"YOU! YOU BROKE MY NOSE!"

The driver got out of his car and stormed towards Morgan, standing before the detective with his now healed nostrils flaring.

"Listen friend, the heats broken, killers are off the streets, how about we let bygones be bygones, what do ya say?"

Broken nose guy tilted his head and repeated his tough expression, grimacing, his fists clenched ready to deliver a revenge blow. A bevy of reporters looked on from the courthouse steps with cameras ready to catch the impending action.

"Hey, calm down man," Morgan implored, "Did you hear the one about the guy that invented the telephone? He picked up the phone and said 'Hello'... and beans fell out of his ears."

Morgan puckered his lips snickering, but if he was about to get punched, he intended to let it happen.

Broken nose guy looked at him for a few seconds. His hands relaxed. His eyes brightened and it was obvious he was fighting back a smile. He couldn't hold it. Broken nose guy fell back into his open car door – doubled over with laughter.

"There ya go, he gets it. Humor heals again. I really am sorry, guy."

Broken nose guy waved at Morgan but couldn't form words. He just laughed and laughed as Morgan continued across the street. Another wound healed. Another loose end tied up.

Morgan stood in his sharply-pressed blue suit and trousers at the door, looking up at the sign that was Gillespie's Brew House and Tap. Stephen immediately poured a large glass of draft and slid it down the bar into Morgan's hand like the professional he was. The nectar of beer was a welcome treat to the weary detective.

"Haven't seen much of you this past month, how's the man of the year?" Stephen said, fluffing his hand through his blond hair.

"The boyfriend of the year, my true angel in blue," Sheila said as she entered the bar.

Sheila sat on the stool beside Morgan. The two hugged and she planted one right on his beer-moistened lips.

"Been a rough road," he said, staring into the eyes of his gorgeous girlfriend. "But, definitely looking up."

Stephen poured Sheila a beer and the two made a toast.

"New beginnings," Sheila said.

"I'll drink to that," Morgan replied.

"New beginnings," Stephen exclaimed from behind the bar.

"New beginnings," Allister declared as he emerged from the back of the bar with a steaming order of hot wings.

"Allister my friend, how's the noggin?"

"Just fine lad, just fine. It'll take more than a frying pan or rolling pin to knock down Allister Gillespie, let alone make him stay down, but, that's me mammy."

Morgan chugged his beer and Allister placed the hot wings in front of Morgan. The basket of delicious, saucy hot wings with its secret sauce was a joy to behold and despite Morgan's insistence, they would be taking the secret of the sauce to the grave.

"Another beer, lad?"

"Allister, my friend."

"Yes, lad?"

"Shut up and pour."

"That's what I thought, lad."

Allister put the empty glass to the draft tap and as the sweet hoppy fluid of life was pouring, Allister started to sing to the Irish Washerwoman playing on the bar speakers. Morgan joined in, then Stephen. All four friends held a delicious frothy beer high and sung their hearts out. Morgan led the charge, but of course, sang it all wrong.

"Here at Gillespie's the beers always cold
They treat you like family, they treat you like gold
You drink and you drink to forget all your fears
But don't drink too much or beans will fall out of your ears"
With that, Morgan fell off his stool, laughing.

* * *

At the Moravian Inn, Ronald McDonald was using his only functional arm to open a package that had arrived by mail. The old codger was sitting naked in his room and struggled to hold the package down with his chin while undoing the tape on the box. It was a tussle, but he finally won out and opened the box. He peered inside and noticed a large-sized bag from a popular fast food restaurant. Thinking it was free food, he excitedly pulled the bag from the box and dumped the contents. Todd Smilie's charred, severed arm fell onto the table in front of the old man. Ronald McDonald collapsed and rang his cranium off the table, all the while grabbing at his chest with his one good hand. The disembodied arm rolled off the wobbly table and hit Ronald McDonald square in his shrivelled scrotum sack while a handwritten note fluttered to the floor.

Thought you could use this you mean old naked bastard. – Jeremy

EPILOGUE

THREE YEARS LATER - WEEKEND AT PINE GROVE

"Let me die!" an unknown lunatic from the Pine Grove mental asylum screamed from behind his locked cell door. Jeremy Trundle remained sealed up tight in his room, only allowed out for daily exercise and therapy sessions. The room, only ten-foot square with plain block walls, a single bed, an aluminum toilet with no seat, and a Plexiglas window ordained with thick metal bars had been his home since that day in court. An exceedingly tall orderly, who was seven feet if he was an inch, pushed along the dinner trays as he did every day in his pressed, blue uniform. A contrast from the blue gowns the inmates wore. His daily chore to feed the madcaps of the asylum was something he relished. He loved to insult and he loved to torture the inmates of Pine Grove as it gave him an outlet for his small man's syndrome, despite him being so tall. As he had done every day for the past three years, he stopped in front of Jeremy's room.

"Hey. Hey crazy kid," he whispered into the room. "I made it special for you."

The tall orderly picked up the soup and began to work up some saliva. He put the gob of saliva in Jeremy's soup and slid it through metal opening.

"Here's your dessert."

The tall orderly picked up a small bowl of pudding, then pulled out his penis. He stirred the vanilla pudding with his dick while Jeremy watched through the Plexiglas window.

"Mmmm, eat my dick, lunatic. Hey, I'm a poet and I didn't know it," he said laughing. "Hope you like your new face, paid for by us tax payers."

Jeremy's face had healed and had been reconstructed with operation after operation until the doctors determined it was as good as it was going to get. Line upon line of scalpel marks and needle sewing adorned the wrinkled skin that was Jeremy's new face. It was tolerable, but would never resemble the original features. Forever he would look outwardly different, but inside, inside he remained irreversibly psychotic.

Jeremy sat down and ate the tainted meal. He was used to it. If the tall orderly wasn't spitting or rubbing his dick on his food, he would put other surprises in it. One particular meal, the tall orderly served Jeremy a piece of shit in between two slices of bread. Jeremy took a bite before realizing he just ate a mouthful of human excrement. None of the inmates complained. A few had lashed out and taken their shots at him, but that usually just ended up in being shocked with a

Taser. 50,000 volts was their punishment for standing up to his tyranny.

As Jeremy finished his dick pudding he tore another strip off from his bed sheet. It was so slight, barely an inch that it would not be noticed, and when fresh sheets came in, he would take another strip. This he had done for months.

After he tore the bed sheet, he pulled out the small metal lunch tray he managed to stick up his gown and had stored inside his mattress. This tray he managed to swipe while being escorted from a therapy session. Jeremy had purposely goaded the tall orderly into pushing him into a dinner cart and in the painful crash that sent everything to the floor, he stuffed the lunch tray into his gown as the orderly bent over in ecstatic laughter. He rubbed the side of the tray back and forth along the cement block wall behind his bed's headboard, but just a few times, so he would not be heard. This he had done for months.

He returned the tray back inside his mattress beside the numerous rolls of scotch tape he would also swipe when he was in therapy. The good Doctor Chalmers would tilt his head back and rub his eyes in frustration at his inability to penetrate Jeremy's damage psyche, and in a split second, the tape was down Jeremy's underpants. This he had done for months.

After the items were secure in the mattress, he crawled into bed and pulled the covers up to his nose like the child he still was. It was now they would come. Over the moans and wailing of his fellow crazies, each night after the lights when out, the apparitions would return and taunt Jeremy, like they did when they were still alive.

"That was the stupidest joke I ever heard," Mandy Young said. Her headless, ghostly form stood at the base of his bed.

She held her head by her long, blond hair and it spoke to Jeremy as he cowered in his bed. "Who ever heard of beans falling out of anyone's ears? You gotta be the dumbest one in our class."

She vanished.

"Listen you little snot. I don't ever want to see this garbage again!" Judith Reinhold placed her head on the base of Jeremy's bed and shook the notebook that contained Jeremy's crappy handwriting. "Very poor printing. Very poor printing. Very poor printing, THIS PRINTING FUCKING SUCKS!" the severed head repeated over and over.

She vanished.

"Come on, chase the truck, let's play chase the truck… it's the only fun we garbage men get. Pick up your stinky, smelly bags and run after me. I especially like it when the bag breaks and your rotten food spills all over the road. I just drive away. Put it out at seven and I come at noon. Wait till noon and I come at seven. We do that on purpose you know," Dan Keeling's head smiled at Jeremy.

He vanished.

"How about some cocaine, kid, then you can kiss my skinny, burnt ass," Todd Smilie said, appearing where Dan Keeling just stood. He put a handful of white blow up to the nose of his severed head, and the grinning head snorted it right up. His crispy, chewy corpse vanished just as quickly as it had appeared.

"We thought you were the future," Edders and Henderson said.

"You'll always be a failure to me. You'll never impress your old man. You are not madness."

"Shut up daddy," Jeremy said, pulling the covers up over his head.

The light from the barred window made a dancing shadow on the cell's block wall. He couldn't stop them from coming. He relived the sins of his past every night. He had to escape them. He had to get out of Pine Grove to make them leave him alone.

As the days drifted by each one the same as the other, Jeremy found himself staring at the wall in another non-productive session with Doctor Chalmers. The room was silent as it was every session save for the tick tock of the German Cuckoo clock that ordained the wall of degrees, that in Jeremy's case, were quite useless. Jeremy eyed up the roll of scotch tape but decided not to take it. Sometimes it was too much of a risk. To get caught would mean a room search and he felt he didn't need another roll anyway. The tall orderly entered the office and pulled Jeremy up by the arm, manhandling him out to the hall and back to his room.

"See ya at dinner, lunatic. I think spit soup and glasses of piss are on the menu tonight."

He shut the cell door.

A few hours passed and Jeremy decided that since soup was on the menu tonight, it was time. He pulled out the strips he had so carefully collected and braided them together, like Trina had taught him one sad day in the dungeon like basement of their old house. He wrapped the strips around his neck and tied them off to the bars on the window. It was time for his escape. This would be his escape from the spectres that haunted his mind. The escape from his madness. He breathed deeply, and closed his eyes and prepared himself.

The tall orderly rolled the cart down the hall towards Jeremy's door. The occasional howl was commonplace in this hallway as yet another crazy inmate screamed out. The tall orderly was not kidding earlier and snickered as he actually brought Jeremy a glass of lemonade that he had tersely pissed in.

"Here ya go, Jeremy, enjoy," he said as he slid the soup and urine drink through the opening. He heard nothing, so he pressed his face to the Plexiglas. Inside the room, Jeremy hung from the bars, the braided sheets wrapped around his neck and his head tilted almost ninety degrees to the side.

"Shit, you fuckin' did it you crazy asshole." He put the key into the lock and opened the door, slowly approaching the hanging Jeremy. "Ah, who gives a fuck, another one bites the dust. At least the room will be free for me to serve someone else a pile of shit on toast."

He pulled his walkie talkie from his belt and was about to radio for a supervisor when Jeremy opened his eyes, pulled out the sharpened lunch tray from under his shirt, and slit the throat of tall orderly. He tilted his neck back, exposing the deep gash and the blood shot upwards in a uniform spray pattern with such force, it painted the ceiling red. He could not scream, his vocal chords were severed and he dropped to the floor as the blood continued to spew forth from the soon to be fatal wound. Jeremy released himself from the braided strips of bed sheets and closed the door. The tall orderly, still alive but unable to defend himself, gasped for breath, but only a wheezing sound escaped his esophagus and wind pipe. Jeremy knelt over his head, he was alive, but the look on his face was of utter disbelief. Jeremy began to saw away with the lunch tray. It was tough going through the spinal column and it was now that Jeremy most missed his homemade axe. Back and forth he sawed away until his labors were finally rewarded with the eventual removal of the orderly's head.

Jeremy bent over and did his best to adjust the look of horror on the decapitated head to a wide eyed, goofy half-smile that looked quite stupid, but would have to do. Time was now of the essence as Jeremy took the strips, scotch tape and roll after roll attached the orderlies head to the inverted soup bowl and placed it on top of his own head, much like a hat. He put on the orderly's blue jacket, and fixed it so it covered soup bowl and wrapped more scotch tape around the collar to hold it up so it would appear to be just the tall orderly making his rounds. Jeremy shut the door and stepped back out into the hall, peering through the button holes of the jacket. He continued the orderly's duties and pushed the cart up the hall, stopping and delivering soup and juice to each room. He grabbed a few bowls of soup and poured them down the front of the blue uniform all the while keeping the head balanced on the soup bowl. Too much jerking around and the scotch tape wouldn't hold. Jeremy pushed the empty cart up to the exit door at the end of the corridor and stepped back from the view of the guard on the other side. He pulled out the walkie-talkie and tapped on the glass with it. Seeing an institution issued walkie-talkie, the complacent guard on the other side opened the door as if on autopilot. In his tall orderly disguise Jeremy walked passed the guard, before he looked up and spoke.

"Hey, hold on," he said.

Jeremy stopped but didn't turn around.

"I see those assholes threw more soup at ya," he chuckled.

"*Mmm hmm,*" Jeremy said in a muffled tone nodding slightly back and forth. The head on the soup bowl slid forward slightly, almost comically, but the scotch tape under the collar held.

"Have a good one," the guard at the door said, pressing the buzzer to allow the uniquely disguised Jeremy to walk out of maximum security.

"*Mmm hmm,*" Jeremy said again and walked out.

Bed check was not for a few hours and Jeremy stood in the darkness of a broom closet until just before the staff shift change, a time when most of the staff would be gabbing with one another, catching up on the events of the shift before.

Having been let out of the maximum security side, Jeremy sauntered easily into the voluntary patient side. The lady at the front desk chatted with another employee and paid no attention to the tall orderly, whom they were quite used to seeing daily. Jeremy checked out the common room; only a few were there. Invisible painter was still there, creating as of yet another unknown work of art. Jeremy walked up the hall, walkie talkie in hand, peeking through the buttons and looking through the glass on the doors as he went. He stopped, opened a door and slipped into one of the rooms.

Marj looked up at the tall orderly she had seen so many times before. She went back to brushing the dolls hair that sat in her lap. She was so occupied on making her improvised baby so pretty she didn't see Jeremy pull out the lunch tray and swipe her across the throat. She leaned forward as the blood ran down her neck and she squeezed the doll so tight in her deathly grasp, its head popped off. He swiped her again on the back of her exposed neck with such force that her head rolled to the floor and came to a rest beside the plastic head of the doll and the two pair of eyes met, mother, and child.

"Hello, Marj," Jeremy said quietly. *"Keep your fluids to yourself, you mean bitch."*

Jeremy exited the room, meandered by the front desk and with a friendly wave walked out the front door.

"What are you so happy about?" When she received no answer, she continued on. "See ya tomorrow," the lady behind the counter said before resuming her conversation.

"Mmm hmm," Jeremy mumbled through the buttons as the orderly's head continued to smile the unchanging ridiculous smile.

As Jeremy walked down the stone steps towards the parking lot some of the scotch tape gave way and the head on top of the soup bowl tilted to the left, as if he was now walking with a broken neck. He looked at the key fob to the vehicle that the tall orderly had in his pocket and pressed the unlock button. A large truck flashed its lights in response to the fob signal, quite an obvious choice for a seven-foot person. Jeremy got in the truck and drove up to the gate slowly and cautiously, still peering in between the buttons of the shirt. Again, the guard was quite used to seeing this vehicle blindly pressed the open button, causing the gate to creak, moan and roll open to complete Jeremy's brilliant escape.

"See ya tomorrow." He noted the odd position of the head. "Got a crick in your neck, I see."

"Mmm hmm," Jeremy mumbled waving at the complacent guard.

Jeremy tossed the orderly's head to the floor as he drove the truck into the darkening countryside, taking one last look in the rear view mirror at the closing gates. As the gates rumbled shut under the darkening sky, he saw a robed figure standing with a smiling skeletal face, nodding approval for his current and all future collections. The gate slammed shut and the figure was gone. An hour later, the wailing alarm blasts could be heard all over Pine Grove asylum.

* * *

A thousand miles away a police recruiter sat before an impressive new applicant.

"Your credentials are above reproach. You have passed every step of the recruitment process with flying colors and your references gave you glowing reviews. I understand the disfiguring fire and reconstructive surgery you underwent as a child was quite a traumatic thing for a ten-year-old to endure. The fact that you came through that and made something of yourself says more than words can about you, your personality and suitability for police work."

"Thank you for the kind words," Jeremy said to the recruiter in a deep adult voice.

The ten-year-old was vanishing again, back into the subconscious mind of the highly functioning psychopath that was Jeremy Trundle. The recruiter stood up and with an enthusiastic outstretched hand stated: "It is my pleasure to welcome you to the Thompson Hill Police Service. Congratulations, police recruit John Morgan!"

THE END

DEDICATIONS AND ACKNOWLEDGEMENTS

For Dearly Departed Officers K. Robinson,
J. Chapelle, C. Campbell, and R. Jean.

Special Thanks to Officers S. Owen,
M. Loranger, L. Arnone

Very Special Thanks for the Editing
Services of Erica Brant.

CPSIA information can be obtained
at www.ICGtesting.com
Printed in the USA
LVOW08s0725130217
524093LV00001B/1/P

9 781773 022956